OTHO'S REGRET

The Four Emperors Series

Book I: Palatine
Book II: Galba's Men
Book III: Otho's Regret
Book IV: Vitellius' Feast

OTHO'S REGRET
Book III of the Four Emperors Series

L. J. Trafford

The epigraphs from *The Annals of Imperial Rome* by Tacitus, translated with introduction by Michael Grant (Penguin Classics, 1956, sixth revised edition, 1989). Copyright © Michael Grant Publications Ltd, 1956, 1959, 1971, 1973, 1975, 1977, 1989. Harmondsworth: Penguin. Reproduced by kind permission of Penguin Books Ltd.

First published in 2017 by Karnac Books.

This edition published in 2018 by Sphinx, an imprint of
Aeon Books
12 New College Parade
Finchley Road
London
NW3 5EP

Copyright © 2018 L. J. Trafford

The right of L. J. Trafford to be identified as the author of this work has been asserted in accordance with §§ 77 and 78 of the Copyright Design and Patents Act 1988.

All rights reserved. No part of this publication may be reproduced, stored in a retrieval system, or transmitted, in any form or by any means, electronic, mechanical, photocopying, recording, or otherwise, without the prior written permission of the publisher.

British Library Cataloguing in Publication Data

A C.I.P. for this book is available from the British Library

ISBN-13: 978-1-91257-327-1

Typeset by Medlar Publishing Solutions Pvt Ltd, India

Printed in Great Britain

www.sphinxbooks.co.uk

For Babs and Maxine

CHARACTERS

Rome—Palatine Hill
Marcus Salvius Otho—the emperor*
Salvius—the emperor's nephew*
Tiberius Claudius Epaphroditus—the emperor's secretary*
Onomastus—the emperor's dwarf*
Marcus Celsus—a valuable military advisor*
Servius Sulpicius Lysander—the emperor's announcer
Statilia Messalina—professional empress*

Sporus—empress-in-waiting*
Artemina (Mina)—the empress' bodyguard
Cassandra—the empress' secretary

Brutus—a star gladiator
Honoratus*, Proculus, Lucullus, Paulus—a collection of Praetorians

Rome—Elsewhere
Flavius Sabinus—city prefect*
Titus Flavius Domitian—Flavius' nephew*
Antonia Caenis—a former imperial secretary*

Tiberius Claudius Philo—an imperial freedman
Teretia—his wife
Pompeia Minor—his mother-in-law
Verenia—Teretia's cousin

Claudia Aphrodite—Epaphroditus' estranged wife
Nymphidia Sabina—a grieving mother*

Elsewhere in the Empire
Aulus Vitellius—the other emperor*
Fabius Valens—the other emperor's commander (the cruel one)*
Caecina Alienus—the other emperor's other commander (the handsome one)*
Asiaticus—the other emperor's freedman*
Gwencalon—a wise woman
Salonina—Caecina's paramour*

* Historical personages

PART I

NEGOTATIONS

"The Vitellians dismissed their opponents as a flabby and idle crew of circus fans and theatregoers"
—Tacitus, *The Histories*

ONE

Cologne, Germania, 1st January AD 69

Vitellius picked up a snail and gave it a bite. His teeth squelched through the meat. There lay before him on a low round marble table, a platter of the creatures coated in butter and smeared with Garum sauce. Beside them sat the boiled quail's eggs, the roasted dormice, the crispy lampreys, and the steamed turbot that constituted Vitellius' breakfast. This was the first course. There were another eight to come.

Fabius Valens, stood by the doorway with his younger colleague, Caecina, marvelled at the governor's capacity for food. Valens himself suffered from a sensitive stomach which accounted for his lean appearance. Though to be fair anyone next to Vitellius appeared lean. Even the wild boar roaming the forests of Germania looked distinctly svelte next to Vitellius. The governor was a man of gargantuan proportions.

This was not necessarily a failing for a governor of a Roman province. It certainly gave him presence. The troops of Germania were unlikely to forget Vitellius in a hurry. He made a large, sturdy presence at their parades. They revelled in his excesses, creating elaborately disrespectful ditties to sing as they marched. Valens knew these to be mere approximations of the governor's habits, which had to be witnessed to be believed.

"Are you sure about this, Valens?" Caecina asked.

"Absolutely."

"Only," began his younger colleague. "Emperor? Vitellius as emperor?" His tone was one of scorn.

They watched as Vitellius crunched on a snail. The butter escaped his lips, trickling down his fat chin, disappearing into the folds of his neck before the wiping slave could reach it.

"It's just he doesn't seem very imperial."

"Nonsense. He's highly born and he's held all the proper positions. What more does he need?" said Valens.

Fabius Valens was a grey man. It was the first thing you noticed about him. His face lacked colour, as if he had been kept indoors for most of his life and had never experienced the sun. His lips were similarly bloodless; tight and thin they rarely smiled. Even his hair, which had once been a deep brown, was distinctly grey now. Cut short on top with long sideburns framing his face. A sheen of sweat was a permanent feature on his long forehead and his cheeks were marked from the effects of a childhood pox. He looked distinctly unwell. He wasn't.

Fabius Valens was a man in the prime of his life. He was about to embark on a plan of such audacity that men would puzzle over it for centuries afterwards. However, to pull this off successfully, he needed Caecina's help.

"Galba is sitting in purple on Nero's throne and he did that with one legion. A Spanish legion." His upper lip curled. "He thinks that gives him authority. Legitimacy. Did we get asked if we wanted Galba as emperor? No, we did not. We, the German legions, the best soldiers in all the empire had this old man forced upon us without a say!"

Caecina did not reply.

"Our man will be a fine emperor," Valens assured him. "Emperors are figureheads, that's all. Someone to keep the sculptors busy producing statues that eastern types can worship."

Eyeing up Vitellius' bulk, Valens reasoned the sculptors were going to be kept very busy.

"It's the advisors in the court who hold the real power. Who do the real work. Who reap the real rewards," continued Valens, looking at Caecina pointedly.

Caecina smiled. It encompassed a row of perfectly even white teeth which gleamed in the gloomily lit room. In comparison to Valens, Caecina was a man of staggering good looks. It was a rare person who passed Caecina without taking a second look, be they male or female. At over six feet in height he was truly striking. Particularly as he insisted, despite his thorough Italian blood, in dressing German-style in plaid tunic and trousers.

To Valens, Caecina said, "Let's do this."

Valens attempted his own smile. It lacked charm, warmth, or anything remotely human.

"Galba is doomed," he said. "Long live Emperor Vitellius."

It would be some weeks before they learned it wasn't Galba they would face. Instead, a very different man was now calling himself emperor.

TWO

Rome, February 69 AD

Epaphroditus awoke with an, "Urgh," and then an, "Ow." He held an arm to his pulsating head and dared to open an eye. It looked up at a domed ceiling with a circular opening from which fell a fat raindrop. This landed with a powerful plop right onto the centre of his forehead, an action that spurred him into a sitting position.

He gazed around in some wonder at his surroundings. He was not in his own bed. Or his own room. Rather, he was sat on the floor of the octagonal dining room that featured as the set set piece of Nero's Golden House. Nero was now dead, so it was just any old house spread over 300 acres with a lake so impressive in scale that it followed its own tidal pattern.

This dining room was the finest room of all the rooms in all the palaces. The floor was clad with coloured marble from all ends of the empire, arranged into circles and swirling patterns with dazzling effect. The walls too were marble. The dome of the room decorated with the signs of the zodiac. The roof rotated in time to the sun; or so Nero had imagined. In fact, there was a slave whose only job was to stand behind one of the alcoves with a pole and discreetly push it round.

On one side, a waterfall gushed down, reflecting the bright colours and keeping the room cool. Which was a bonus in the stifling Roman summers but not much of an advantage in February.

Epaphroditus looked down: he was naked. A thin sheet lay tossed to one side and beside him lay a girl, also naked. She gave him a smile. A "wasn't it wonderful last night, darling," smile. Epaphroditus furrowed his brow and asked, "And you are?"

"Erotica, sir."

"Of course," he replied. Although in truth, he had no memory of ever having met her.

He was puzzling out his curious circumstances when there entered the absolute last thing a man with a thumping hangover could ever wish to encounter: a trio of trumpeters. They were dressed in imperial white, their instruments curling over their shoulders. Pursed lips were placed against mouthpieces. Epaphroditus' sluggish reactions were too late to halt them from giving a quick blast of a ditty that was employed whenever the emperor was about to make a grand entrance.

Epaphroditus, hands over his ears, thought his head might explode. Erotica on the other hand shot to her feet and stood, eyes down, awaiting her master. A stance that allowed Epaphroditus the chance to savour what he had apparently tasted the night before: medium height, heavy-hipped, large-breasted, with a tawny skin and long dark straight hair. Not Epaphroditus' usual type at all. He must have been drunk. Tying the sheet around his lower half, he stood up.

There was a brief lull after the trumpeters. Then five Praetorian guards marched in and positioned themselves along the wall. Next in slid an announcer, who declared in as high a volume as the musicians, "Imperator Otho Caesar Augustus!"

The emperor shuffled round the announcer telling Epaphroditus, "Didn't want to take you unawares," inclining his head towards Erotica.

Emperor Otho was not an imposing figure even surrounded by the usual bodyguards, attendants, and his own freedman, the dwarf wonder Onomastus. He was of no more than average height with bandy legs, splayed feet, and a developing gut.

However, his permanently ruddy cheeks, sparkling cornflower blue eyes, and generous personality were peculiarly magnetic.

Even Epaphroditus, who had always viewed friendship as purely a means to an end, counted him as a pal. Otho was a hard man to dislike. Which was just as well since two weeks before he'd been pushed into a choice between death at the hands of his many creditors or death at the hands of Galba, who believed him to be plotting to overthrow him.

Otho had not been plotting then, but faced with imminent execution it seemed like a jolly good plan. He'd enacted a coup of such speed, such impact, that they were still washing the blood off the streets and burying the bodies two weeks later.

Therefore, Otho had a great deal of apologising to do. A lot of charming. And much handing out of coins to the newly widowed plebs of the city. He'd done all this while projecting an image of being exactly the sort of emperor the people needed in their time of distress. A role he inhabited so successfully that many forgot it was Otho who had caused them the distress in the first place.

For Epaphroditus, this was a familiar sensation. He too possessed that strange Otho amnesia. It had led him to completely disregard all the trouble his friend had got him into in the past and throw his lot into making him emperor. Alongside the catastrophe that was Otho's coup, there had also been a catastrophe in Epaphroditus' private life. His wife Aphrodite, who maintained she was the only person who saw through Otho, had slung him out and was talking divorce. Hence Epaphroditus' sudden, and out of character, love for fermented grape juice.

Otho plonked himself on a nearby couch, smoothing out his toga. Onomastus positioned himself beside him, his little muscular arms crossed. Beside the dwarf was a youth of about twenty who was trying very hard not to look at the naked Erotica, his cheeks flushing all the way down his neck.

One of the emperor's attendants dashed forward and helpfully retrieved the couple's discarded clothes which had somehow made it to separate ends of the large room. Epaphroditus slipped his tunic over his head and attempted to regain some dignity.

"Have you met my nephew, Salvius?" asked Otho, indicating the blushing youth.

Looking at him, Epaphroditus could see the family resemblance. He too had Otho's blue eyes and ruddy cheeks. However, Salvius was taller, slimmer, and his thatch of dark hair was all his own, which Otho's definitely was not.

Erotica, fully clothed, had not eased the boy's embarrassment. Her gown was of that oddly voluminous cloth that covers very little while seemingly taking up yards of material. He tried very hard to avert his gaze but his eyes kept straying back. Erotica, aware of his interest, gave him a wink and a smile. His whole face turned a bright red.

Otho, seeing Salvius' pain, waved the girl away. "Thank you for your services. I am sure he enjoyed it immensely." Then, turning to Epaphroditus, "Didn't you?"

Epaphroditus gave a small shrug. Probably he had. He generally did but he couldn't remember a thing about it.

When she had departed, Otho sat regally upright. Garland balanced on his hair. Toga in place. A team of young boys armed with note tablets and styli ready to note down his every whim and request.

The emperor got down to business. "Sooooo," he began. "Last night …" He drawled out that final word while beaming at Epaphroditus stood before him.

"I am sure it was a joy for all concerned. The agenda for today, Caesar."

Otho was not to be distracted so easily. "How are you feeling this morning?"

"I have felt better. The agenda, Caesar."

"You need to train up to such levels of drinking. You can't just jump in with no practice. Very dangerous, very dangerous indeed. But then you were insistent, very insistent."

"I quite fancied some of that vintage," piped in Onomastus, glaring at Epaphroditus.

Otho patted his dwarf on the arm, commenting, "I know, so did I. Being emperor and all, I was hoping for a good sample. But you wouldn't give up that amphora, no matter how much we pleaded."

Epaphroditus groaned under his breath.

"So we let you keep hold of it. It seemed to keep you happy; momentarily. At least until you got through the first third, then you got a little sad."

"You cried," interjected Onomastus. "All over the place."

Epaphroditus winced.

"Yes, it was quite embarrassing," confirmed Otho.

"Very embarrassing," added Onomastus. "It was all Dite this, Dite that. What a wonderful woman Dite is. How you can't live without her. How you want Dite back so desperately."

Dite was Epaphroditus' secret pet name for his wife. Not quite so secret now, apparently.

Otho picked up the story. "Then you made us state that Aphrodite was the most beautiful woman ever created by the gods. Which we did because you were most forceful in your request. But when we complied, you accused us of having designs on your Dite. Which of course we do not."

Epaphroditus wanted to crawl into a hole and hide for at least a month. Or until a better stream of gossip was created. But he managed to hold onto a neutral expression as his innards cringed.

"Anyhow," smiled Otho, clapping his hands. "We're all friends again today, aren't we?"

Onomastus, arms folded, gave the secretary a hard glare.

"I apologise humbly for any discomfiture I may have caused, Caesar." Epaphroditus lowered his head.

"Excellent, excellent. I am so pleased. Talos, you had better scratch that treason charge note I composed last night."

Epaphroditus' head shot up. His friend beamed. "Just my little joke."

A scribe rushed forward with a scroll, handed it to Otho, head bowed, before scuttling backwards. Otho didn't bother to look at it. He handed it straight to Epaphroditus. It was what he employed him for.

"Celsus has the latest dispatches from Germania," Epaphroditus informed the emperor.

"Well we can't hear them here. Not the place at all. This is a place of jollity." He threw an amused look at Epaphroditus. "Most of the time, anyhow."

Otho stood as his attendants fussed about ensuring His Imperial Majesty was draped correctly. A small slave boy took the opportunity to crawl across the floor and polish his sandal strap for him.

"Most kind of you," Otho smiled down at him.

The emperor threw an arm around his nephew declaring, "Come now, Salvius, this is just the type of imperial business your father wanted me to instruct you in. It is most thrilling!"

THREE

After a quick wash, shave, and downing of what his chamberlain swore was the ultimate hangover cure (it wasn't), Epaphroditus joined Otho in a small office situated in the old palace.

"Aha," cried Otho. "Come and meet the chaps."

There were three additional chaps to Otho's usual appendage of Onomastus.

"Flavius Sabinus, I think you know." Epaphroditus nodded at the solid city prefect.

"And this is Marcus Celsus."

Celsus, a tall man with bristly ginger hair, nodded.

"And my nephew, of course, who you met earlier. Salvius is incredibly keen to learn all about the imperial life, aren't you?"

Salvius flushed slightly and looked away.

"Bit shy though," Otho confided. "But we'll hammer that out of you, won't we?"

"You'll grow out of it, Salvius," Flavius Sabinus commented kindly. "Why, I was quite the shy one at your age. Didn't dare speak hardly at all. Terribly, terribly anxious I was. During my coming-of-age ceremony, I shook like a slave awaiting a thrashing. My father thought I was suffering from the falling sickness." He gave a laugh.

Knowing Flavius' tendency for long-winded anecdotes, Epaphroditus cut in quickly, "What news?"

"It is as we heard," said Celsus, grim of face. "Vitellius has definitely been declared emperor."

"By whom?" queried Epaphroditus.

"The German legions, of course."

The secretary waved this away. "No, I mean who came up with this scheme? From what I remember about Vitellius he's never been a leader. He's a follower. A skilled one, I give him that. Nobody lives through as many emperors as he has, unscathed, without the ability to flatter unconditionally and convincingly. But there is not a chance he put himself forward as emperor."

Celsus grinned. "Sources suggest that his two generals, Fabius Valens and Caecina Alienus, are predominant in his administration."

Epaphroditus chewed at the inside of his cheek. Caecina meant nothing to him. Fabius Valens, however, was a different matter. Why was that name familiar? He searched his memory.

"I doubt Vitellius even knows Galba is dead," continued Celsus. "It's a good three week ride to Germania."

Flavius humphed, "That gives us something to work with, doesn't it. Epaphroditus? Epaphroditus?"

He clicked back to attention, leaving the mystery of Fabius Valens to one side. "It certainly does. Vitellius was a favourite of Nero's. If he's pretending to avenge his patron, we have the perfect get-out clause for him. Caesar, I suggest you pen a letter to him explaining the situation. The hated Galba is no more and you are now emperor. Stress that you have no issues with him and then request politely that he stand down his men and relinquish his claim."

"With no harm to himself," added in Celsus dryly, sharing a wry smile with Epaphroditus.

"That will work?" Otho questioned.

"He can step down with his honour intact. From what I know of Vitellius, he'll take the easy way out," Epaphroditus said.

Celsus nodded his agreement. "He's a lazy bugger alright. I'm surprised he's mustered the energy to get this far with the scheme."

"Do it then," said Otho. Turning to his nephew, "Did you see that, Salvius? That was an imperial order given. That is how it's done."

Salvius cleared his throat. "Uncle Marcus, will Vitellius stand down?"

"Bound to. I can't imagine Vitellius wanting to undertake a military campaign in winter. He is far too used to his home comforts. I heard he took eighteen of his own chefs to Germania. Didn't take his wife though, which says a lot about the man."

"He doesn't like his wife?" asked Salvius.

"Likes his food more," supplied Flavius Sabinus.

"And how!" laughed Otho, bulging out his cheeks in imitation of the German governor. "Come, favourite nephew, it is time for me to introduce you to my empress-to-be, the wonderful Statilia Messalina." Turning to Epaphroditus before he departed, he said, "You will pen this letter to Vitellius?"

"Of course, Caesar."

Otho rubbed his hands together. "Excellent."

FOUR

The old soldier leaned forward, balancing a palm on his walking stick. "There were bones as far as the eye could see. A whole forest of bones. Three legions' worth of men were lost there. Cut down and butchered in that evil place. We saw bodies hammered into trees, hung there as sacrifices to their evil gods!"

It was a statement that clearly demanded comment. Philo, sat in front of the old man, note tablet balanced on knees, stylus in hand, thought for a moment: "Gosh." Before scribbling down an approximation of the soldier's words.

"It were Varus' legions, you see, son. Varus who was slaughtered in that forest by the treacherous Arminius way back in old Emperor Augustus' time. They say Augustus used to wander through the palace crying, 'Varus, Varus give me back my legions. 'Course you'd know more about that than I."

Julianus paused, waiting for Philo to finish his frantic scribbling. Once he had, he told the old man, "Bit before my time, I'm afraid."

Philo was an ex-imperial slave now scratching a living as a scribe for hire. Gaius Julianus was his first assignment. The old man had served with the legions in Germania under the renowned General Germanicus sixty-odd years before. Philo's job was to transcribe his army memoirs for publication.

To Philo, a former slave ineligible for service in the army, it was fascinating. His golden transcription rule to note only the most important features had been abandoned. He found it all interesting. All of it intriguing. From the correct method to building a stopover fort, to the number of turns a ballista had to be wound for maximum trajectory, to stumbling across the remains of three legions massacred by German tribesman as Julianus was recounting now. Philo had seven full note tablets of information to pore over. And this was only his third visit.

Julianus had to be, Philo mentally calculated, at least eighty. You would never know it from his solid, powerfully built frame. Or from his fluid speech and keen mind. He walked with a stick but this was his only concession to age.

They were sat in the former centurion's ground-floor apartment situated on Rome's Viminal Hill. The apartment itself consisted of this single room: a bedroom-cum-dining-room-cum-lounge. Julianus had furnished it cosily with two extremely comfy chairs and a round wooden table, on which sat two beakers.

Though he had no stove, Julianus was not short of food. The Viminal street on which he resided was awash with take-away stalls selling tasty offerings such as spiced sausages and slices of pie. There was even a stall selling sweetmeats from the East, set up by an enterprising young Parthian named Volognes. The food was a bit exotic for Viminal tastes. But Volognes was such a charming and nice-looking lad that the Viminal women could not resist stopping at his booth during their shopping expeditions. Resting their elbows on upturned barrels, they regarded the proprietor with dreamy-eyed desire. A state Volognes was keen to exploit for purely business reasons.

Philo had heard that the Parthian was engaged in a long-term liaison with a married woman from Ostia. Which certainly explained his frequent trips for "supplies".

"And Germanicus stood there in that field amid this carnage and he wept. Real tears. Manly tears. There was nothing of the girl about Germanicus. Make sure you make that clear, Philo."

Philo dutifully did. In the shorthand he had devised when a pupil at the imperial training school.

"Germanicus wiped away his tears, and he turns to his tribune and he says …"

But the words of the great Germanicus were cut short by a sharp tap on the door and a cry of, "Can I come in?"

Julianus sat back and took a sip from his beaker. "That'll be your missus, Philo. Our time must be up for the day."

Teretia stuck her head round the door. "Are you all done?" she asked.

Noting Philo's pale complexion, she rushed in and felt his forehead with her hand.

"You've exhausted him. He's all hot!" she chided Julianus.

"I'm fine," Philo assured her, breaking into a yawn.

"Julianus, you've worked him far too hard. He's not to be worked so hard. He's not well enough yet."

Julianus grinned under her soft scolding. "That's told me."

"No, it's my fault, Teretia," insisted Philo. "We were at a most fascinating part and I wanted to keep going."

He broke off into another yawn. Teretia pulled his cloak around him and helped him to his feet. Philo held a hand to his head and staggered slightly. Julianus leapt to his feet and grabbed hold of his elbow with a firm grip. "You alright there, son?"

"I think so. Just a little dizzy."

"Let's get you home," Teretia insisted, escorting him to the door.

"I'll be back tomorrow, Julianus," he said. "I want to hear what Germanicus said."

"Right you are, son," smiled the old soldier, waving him out.

* * *

They walked past the food stalls, bakeries and butchers that made up the Viminal Hill commerce, Teretia's arm linked in Philo's.

"You should have said to Julianus if you were tiring. Once he gets started he can't half go on. I did tell him only one hour today. I knew I shouldn't have stopped at the grocers. I should have picked you up sooner."

"I think I might draw some maps," said Philo, suddenly. "For the book. Some maps of the key locations. So the reader can picture the action more readily."

Teretia detected a hint of joy in his voice. The first she'd heard since the day Philo had arrived at work to find the Praetorian prefect Laco waiting for him. The charge was that Philo had been colluding with Otho to depose Emperor Galba.

Having done no such thing, he'd faced a barrage of questions that he had no answer to. Laco refused to believe in his innocence, no matter how much he pleaded. Frustrated by what he saw as a lack of cooperation, the prefect had ordered two of his guards to give the suspect a thorough beating. Philo had woken some days later at Epaphroditus' house with no idea of how he had got there. It had seemed at the time better not to know.

That had occurred a month ago and Teretia had been pleased by his recovery since. Though Philo possessed a couple of cracked ribs that smarted, a great many tender spots that caused a sharp intake of breath and a wince if knocked, and a jaw that was still yellowy green from a particularly well-aimed punch, he was at least on his feet again. Even if he did tire extremely easily and struggled to walk any great distance.

They dodged through the busy Viminal streets, stepping over rubbish and avoiding the strange slick of liquid that always ran down the side of the road. Teretia called out greetings to the people they knew. Tadius the butcher, stood outside his shop, bloody cleaver in hand, informed her, "I have some thrushes in today. Cook up lovely, Teretia, if you fancy a treat."

Teretia shook her head. "Oh no, not today, Tadius."

"Another day then. And good to see you up and about, Philo," he smiled.

His slave boy was leant on a broom, slack-jawed, openly gawping. Tadius whacked him round the head and yelled, "GET TO IT!"

The boy began to move the broom slowly, keeping his eye on Teretia's departing bottom. Who could blame him for gawping at Teretia? She was quite a vision. Possessed of shining golden hair that today was plaited across her head, large blue eyes, and a curvaceously plump figure, she was a sweetly beautiful woman. A fact that was accentuated by her increasingly tight gowns. For Teretia was pregnant. Not very pregnant. In fact, only a tiny bit pregnant. But she was excessively keen to show off her new status and imagined bump. Hence, she had taken to belting her dresses to display the fact.

Where Teretia was pale, her husband was dark-skinned. Black hair that tended to curl if left untamed, and soft brown eyes. A slight man, Philo was barely taller than his rather short wife. Side by side, they made a very cute couple. Skipping over a rotten cabbage, Teretia informed her husband, "Lysander called round to see you again."

Philo did not reply.

"He's been round every day so far. You should really go and see him," she persisted.

Lysander was Philo's old roommate from the palace. He resided a few streets away from them in a flashy apartment.

"I mean, you are much better now," she continued. "Before when he came to visit, you were not well at all and I could see that you were not ready for visitors. But now you are so much better and quite fit for a few special visitors. He is your friend," she concluded, looking at Philo with concern.

They had reached the door of the home they shared with Teretia's mother Pompeia. Philo pushed it open and said, "Can you help me up the stairs?" Closing down the subject of Lysander.

Teretia assisted him up the stairs. Holding onto his elbow as he painfully manoeuvred his way upwards. One hand clasping onto the banister, the other supporting his sore ribs. At the top of the stairs, they walked through to the kitchen where a strange girl was sat at the long wooden table that took up most of the room. At the sight of Teretia, the girl jumped to her feet and embraced her. Kissing Teretia on both cheeks, she declared, "My dear cousin."

Teretia politely pushed her away and said a little coldly, "Hello Verenia."

Seeing them together, Philo noted the family resemblance. Both had golden hair and blue eyes. However, Verenia was the taller of the two and rather slimmer in figure than Teretia.

"Is this your husband?" she asked Teretia. "Aunt Pompeia said you'd married."

"This is Philo," confirmed Teretia, linking onto his arm proudly.

"Aunt Pompeia wrote to father and I when we were in Alexandria mentioning her plans to take a lodger. Then I come back and here you are, the husband. Quite a transformation." She gave a tinkly laugh. "So convenient. Some parents have to search high and low for a suitable match for their daughter."

Philo could hear Teretia huffing beside him. Luckily Pompeia flurried in. "We're looking for another lodger should you hear of anyone, Verenia. Was it a good session with Julianus, Philo?"

"Oh yes. It was fascinating."

"I got the cabbages, mother."

Teretia placed her basket on the table and began unpacking the shopping.

"Now then Verenia, here's this shawl." Pompeia handed over the pink garment.

"That's mine!" protested Teretia.

"I think, Teretia, that Verenia is more in need of it than you. She's returned from Alexandria and she hasn't any winter clothes at all. It's very warm in Alexandria this time of year, isn't that right, Verenia?"

"Yes, Aunt Pompeia, it was lovely and hot. Rome is quite a shock. Such a chill."

"Verenia has been telling me all about Egypt. It sounds terribly exotic. You should tell Teretia about the camel ride," said Pompeia. "And the market. They have lovely markets in Alexandria."

"Philo's been to Greece!" burst out Teretia.

"Have you, Philo?" queried Pompeia. "I didn't know that."

"Did you go to Delphi? Father and I went to Delphi. And Delos and Crete and Athens. Athens was my favourite. Such history, such style."

Teretia interrupted with a shrill, "Philo went to the Olympics. With the emperor."

Then she stood back, arms crossed, to see if Verenia dared to beat that. She didn't. She merely smiled and commented, "How fascinating. You must tell me all about it, Philo. We should get to know each other now that we are family."

She patted at a space on the bench beside her as an invitation. Teretia held onto her husband tight.

"He can't now. It's time for his nap. Isn't it, darling?"

Philo, flushing slightly at being addressed so in front of a stranger, gave a small nod.

"You do look a little pale," said Pompeia.

"Does he?" said Verenia staring at Philo. "It's rather difficult to tell with that dark skin. Even the Egyptians aren't that black. You do look tired though, Philo. Married life must be most exhausting."

Teretia grabbed hold of her husband's hand and pulled him out the door before he could offer a polite farewell to Verenia. She shut the door of their bedroom firmly.

* * *

Philo, sat on the bed, innocently said, "She seemed nice, Verenia."

Which was the catalyst for Teretia. She let loose a torrent of complaints about her cousin as she assisted him in undressing.

"She is very sly. Didn't you hear her? All that stuff about you being the lodger and us getting married. It was a dig. A dig at me. She thinks she is so much better than me. She always has. Just because her father is a trader and takes her along on his trips, which I'm sure are not half as exciting as she pretends. I bet she didn't see anything at Delphi anyway. I bet she just sat on Uncle Verenius' boat."

Philo felt compelled to point out that Delphi wasn't on the coast. But with Teretia in full flow, there wasn't much opportunity to insert corrections.

"And she's *divorced*," Teretia continued. As if this were highly scandalous rather than an everyday event in Rome. "She married Uncle Verenius' assistant manager, Lucanus. They weren't even married a year when she ran away from their home and refused to go back. Uncle Verenius was devastated. Absolutely devastated. He was ill from it. Isn't that awful?"

She paused, waiting for Philo to agree with her. Though he had little idea of the family ramifications. Though he wondered what the assistant manager could have done to make his wife flee in such a manner. Philo nevertheless gave a nod and agreed with Teretia that it was truly terrible.

This seemed to please her. She kissed him on the forehead lightly before tucking him into bed.

"I shall sit beside you until you are asleep," she said. "That way I can be sure that you are fully resting. Because it's terrifically important that you rest, Philo. Even though you are feeling much better than you were. Because I wouldn't want you to get poorly again. Not like that."

Philo rolled onto his side and closed his eyes. He was drifting off into the muffled, soft world of sleep when he heard the door of their room quietly close. Through the wall much louder, he heard Teretia saying, "*My* husband is asleep." The stress firmly on the "my". Presumably for Verenia's benefit.

FIVE

Mina narrowed her eyes and concentrated on the object: a singular jug that stood on a waist-high tripod table. She judged the distance to be about three feet from where she stood. A quick scan to the left and then the right of the table. She took half a step backwards. Her hand went to her hip. She unclipped the coiled whip from her belt, feeling the length of the leather through her fingers. Narrowing her eyes once more, she readied herself—

"And then what happened?" interrupted a shrill voice.

Her eyes widened. "Sporus! Shut up, won't you. I'm trying to concentrate."

Her companion, a eunuch of indeterminate duties, lain on the couch beside the tripod table said, "If you are that keen on breaking that jug, I can kick the table over from here."

He reached out a slender brown leg and placed his strappy sandalled foot against a table leg.

"Don't you dare," she warned, bringing her whip arm back. "I don't want it to break. I want it to …"

She brought the arm back and thrust it forward. The leather tongue shot across the room, licking at the table top. It coiled around the jug handle and tugged it backwards. There was a smash as the jug hit the floor.

"Hera's girdle! I meant to catch that," cursed Mina, pushing at the fragments with her toes. "I need to try again," she decided. "Chuck me your wine goblet."

Sporus pressed his lips against the glass rim. "Not a chance," he told her before taking sip. "Sit down for Jupiter's sake. For my sake. I need to know what happened."

Mina flopped onto the other end of the couch, her feet touching Sporus'.

"Nothing happened," she told him. "The emperor said to the empress, 'This is my nephew Salvius.' And she said, 'Hello. Nice to meet you. Don't you look like your uncle?' And all that sort of stuff. The nephew went all red. He shuffled his feet. Said it was nice to know her. All that sort of stuff."

"And then…?" pressed her companion.

"And then? And then nothing. The emperor left. Salvius left. And the empress spent the rest of the morning reading some b-o-r-i-n-g book. Most dull."

"Kisses?"

"Only the kind patrician types do as a hello."

Sporus leaned back onto fluffy pillows and expelled a contented, "Ha!" Followed by a smug, "Knew it!"

They were holed up together in Mina's new quarters. She'd recently been promoted from Statilia Messalina's towel holder to her personal bodyguard. Technically, the Praetorian Guard were responsible for the empress' security. However, since their prefect Nymphidius Sabinus had gone bonkers back in the summer and made an unscheduled and disturbing visit to Statilia prior to being killed by his own men, the empress had declared she didn't trust them. Instead, she had looked to her own staff for protection.

Mina, though a girl of slight proportions, had been taught the skills of whip cracking by the slave overseer Straton. The usefulness of which she demonstrated daily by felling random Praetorians much to the delight of the empress. Statilia had dressed her in a chiton-pleated dress and a Greek-style helmet that had Mina greatly resembling the goddess Minerva. As a bodyguard, it was essential she be close by should the empress face sudden danger. Thus, she'd been moved from her small room in the slave complex to this much more agreeable chamber adjoining Statilia's suite of rooms.

Not only did Mina now have a proper bed, no more bed roll on the floor for her, her room also contained a couch, a tripod table, and a wardrobe for her spare uniforms.

Unfortunately, she was forced to share this fantastic space with the empress' secretary, Cassandra, which pleased neither of them. For Cassandra being twenty-nine years old was to Mina's eyes hideously old. And Mina, in Cassandra's view, was but a silly girl. Neither was prepared to change her viewpoint.

"Pass me a date," demanded Sporus.

Yet another perk to Mina's new role was her access to the empress' kitchen. No more thin refectory soup and gruesome porridge for her! Luckily the empress allowed her one exercise hour a day. Otherwise Mina feared her trim shape would have been impossible to maintain.

She tossed a honeyed date in Sporus' direction. Anyone else would have opened their mouths or at least used a hand to catch it. The eunuch merely squealed as the date became airborne. It landed on top of his head. And due to its honeyed state, stuck there.

Sporus' well manicured hands flew up. "My hair! My hair!"

"Your hair? Your hair?" retorted Mina.

Sporus removed the red ringletted wig to inspect the damage, revealing his own dark curly hair. The wig had been a commission of the late Emperor Nero so that Sporus would further resemble his dead wife, Poppaea. A unique role that Sporus had excelled in so much that Nero began to believe that the eunuch truly was Poppaea, going so far as to marry him in Greece.

He stared down at the red wig sitting in his lap. "My darling husband. How thrilled he was the first time he saw me in this!

Speechless he was. Speechless! And he said to me, 'Poppaea, Poppaea, my great love.'"

"So not entirely speechless then," murmured Mina.

"Since my darling passed away, all has been dark. So lacking in light and love. A Sporus unloved is a Sporus no more!" he declared.

In fact, Sporus' grief at Nero's demise had proved not as all-encompassing as he frequently proclaimed. He was now eyeing up husband number two in the shape of Otho. He'd been married to an emperor. He couldn't trade down, could he?

That, as a slave, he was ineligible to marry a patrician, let alone an emperor. That he'd been male (once). That Otho was engaged to Statilia Messalina. These, to Sporus, were no impediments at all. After all, he held the ultimate bonus card: Poppaea's first husband had been Otho. Everyone knew he'd never recovered from her death. Sporus was at the ready to bring her back to life for him.

The door swung open and there entered a short woman with dry mousy-coloured hair held tightly bound in a bun. This was Cassandra.

"Sporus," she said. Failing to hide the disappointment in her voice.

"Cassie," he smiled back. A smile that widened when he saw her tense at his shortened version of her name.

"Are you intending to stay long?" she enquired.

There had been words on Sporus' frequent presence in their room. Privately Mina might agree that the eunuch was indeed a distractingly shrill presence. That he certainly shouldn't turn up in the middle of the night undergoing a mascara trauma and insist Mina help him. And that he really shouldn't be allowed to spy on his rival Statilia through their door whenever he fancied it. Publically, however, Mina defended her friend vigorously.

"He's my friend. He can say as long as he likes." Glaring at her roommate.

Infuriatingly for Mina, who loved a good fight, Cassandra refused to rise to this. She replied with a (highly irritating) smile, "Naturally. But it has been a long day for all of us. I understand you took four baths today, Sporus."

"Five," yawned the eunuch. "It was ex-haust-ing."

"I can imagine," said Cassandra politely. "And all those dress changes."

"Eight," confirmed Sporus. "I have to change every hour. Otherwise the Sporus creases." He smoothed down his skirt.

"Quite a day," Cassandra continued. "I heard the hour slave call as I reached the door."

Sporus sat up. "Did he? Then I need to change. Mina, I need to change. I got my dresser to lay out that red number of mine. Red is soooo my colour. And should my darling Otho call for me, well, I must look my best. It's my duty as a Sporus. Farewell dear Mina, dear Cassie."

And with that he departed.

Seeing Cassandra's slight smile, Mina felt the anger rise up inside her. She pressed it back down again. During their forced cohabitation of this room, Mina had gathered that Cassandra did not like her. Which was fine because she felt exactly the same way. Mina loved creating enmity: all the backbiting, recruitment of others to take your side, and fantastic war of words. However, Cassandra infuriatingly refused to take part in any glorious argument. Instead, she maintained an air of calm condescension towards Mina, which wound her up more than open warfare ever could.

Sitting on her bed, Mina glared at the reclining figure of Cassandra, a scroll unfurled on her lap. There she spent half an hour in a gleeful daydream: the crack of her whip, the scroll flying through the air, her triumphant catch. Culminating in her deliberately holding it over one of the lamps until Cassandra begged her to stop.

SIX

There lay in front of Epaphroditus an open tablet. On the left side he'd indented the word Caecina in the wax; on the right, Fabius Valens. He'd intended to list below each name the known facts. However, Talos returning from his mission to collate them had provided next to nothing.

Valens, as far as his generally underperforming assistant could attest, was from a standard equestrian family of neither note nor infamy. He'd held the usual succession of positions without doing anything memorable. Now in his mid-forties, he should be angling for senatorial rank. Raising an army and marching them 300 miles to overthrow the emperor seemed a rather peculiar way of obtaining this. Particularly since Valens' superior officer, Vitellius, possessed the necessary imperial favour, clout, and cash to do just this. Odd, mused Epaphroditus. Very odd.

But no less odd than Caecina. He was younger, being in his mid-twenties. A decade younger than he ought to have been to hold his current post. A quick scan of his career revealed why. His last position had been in Spain as an aid to Servius Sulpicius Galba. It was the now-deceased emperor who'd promoted Caecina to Germania. Three months later, Caecina turned on his mentor, the man who'd promoted him so highly, and proclaimed Vitellius emperor.

Even odder.

Despite a great deal of mental effort, he still could not place Fabius Valens. Perhaps this was the result of his advancing age. Perhaps the beginning of a decline in his mental faculties. In the old days, he'd have been able to recite Valens' life from memory. He'd have known every virtue and vice of Fabius Valens. Every facet to his character. Every strength. Every weakness.

Actually, that was rubbish. In the old days, he'd have stuck his head out of his office into the adjoining antechamber and asked Philo. Philo always had the necessary facts at his fingertips. A talent Epaphroditus missed. Talos, his new assistant, was adequate but he was no Philo. Talos lacked initiative and intelligence. He was merely an adequate scribe filling in until Epaphroditus found his new protégé. Though the secretary held little hope as to when that might be.

Felix, the head of slave placements, had given him the full low-down of the stock situation post-Otho's coup. He'd filled the vacancies as best he could. But the new stock were unable to speak Latin yet, let alone Greek and the other languages required to deal with a full correspondence from all ends of the empire. Perhaps one of them would show promise. But Epaphroditus really could not wait while the imperial slave babies were raised up to standard in the training school.

He stared down at his blank tablet. Hopeless. His mind began to wander onto other subjects: Aphrodite. She was a permanent ache in his heart. He missed her so much. Not necessarily the sex, though Jupiter knew none of the slave girls he'd used recently could match her. He missed the cheery chats about the children over breakfast. That last cuddle at night. Waking up to her bleary-eyed, rumpled state, where he found her at her most desirable.

Though Aphrodite was adamant that she wanted a divorce, Epaphroditus still held hopes of talking her round. He had done so numerous times in the past. Mostly when she'd discovered his latest liaison with a slave girl bearing more than a slight resemblance to her. Well, he'd knocked that on the head. He'd always viewed these encounters as merely warm-ups for the real thing with his gorgeous, sexy wife. Without that joy, he found the Aphrodite clones depressing. A reminder of what he had lost. No, not what he had lost, he reminded himself. Merely what he had misplaced for a short while. She would calm down eventually.

His crime this time, unusually, had nothing to do with sex. It had everything to do with Otho. Aphrodite despised him for reasons of her own, and Epaphroditus had been instrumental in making Otho emperor. Worse still, whilst he'd been with Otho, she and the children were cowering alone in their home, listening to anarchy outside, in terror for their lives.

Even worse, Martinus, the husband of his eldest daughter Silvia, had unsuspectingly wandered down to the forum and lost his life amid the mayhem caused by Otho's ascension. This to Aphrodite was the most heinous of actions: that he had known what was going to happen that day and had not warned her or his daughter and son-in-law. He had made his choice in Aphrodite's mind: Otho over his family.

He rubbed a hand across his face. This would not do. He needed to write this entreaty to Vitellius. The sentiment had to be correct, proper, reasoned. He did not feel reasonable at that moment. He sucked the air through his teeth, then he placed down his stylus carefully onto his desk.

He'd go see Philo. There was no reason why he shouldn't. In fact, he should go check on his assistant's well-being. It was the sort of thing a good person would do. Philo was bound to know the reason why the name Fabius Valens was gnawing at his brain like some hideous maggot.

* * *

He took the flashiest litter he owned. The one with the floaty, silvery curtains which neatly matched the tight shorts of its four bearers. Accompanying them, he'd thrown in one of Lysander's trainee announcers, a bulky, brutal-looking bodyguard, a messenger boy, a toga draper (even though he wasn't wearing a toga), and a meat carver complete with the sharpened tools of his trade.

He didn't usually travel with such an entourage. In fact, he actively avoided such overt posturing. Epaphroditus had grown up in the imperial palace. He'd seen what happened to those freedmen who gathered fortunes. They were easy pickings for a skint emperor. But today he had a very particular need to show off.

Philo resided in what the locals classed as a respectable street. Epaphroditus, who'd been raised in a palace and followed that with a substantial Esquiline mansion, classed it as a slum. It was a narrow piece of land with five-storey tenement buildings that blocked out the sun. Their ground floors taken over by a variety of shops.

Outside these shops, the residents of the Viminal Hill, bustling about, stopped to gawp at Epaphroditus' litter. He'd left the curtains open so they could see him laid back on the pillows, flicking through some paperwork to demonstrate he was both literate and important. Such was the plan.

There raged on the Viminal Hill a fierce competition between families on a variety of subjects: whose daughter had made the most illustrious match, whose window sills were the best polished, and who it was who got a foot run over by a chariot driven by the captain of the Green team. Underlining Philo's imperial connections would have them gossiping for months and lend a gleam to Pompeia and Teretia in their neighbourhood.

Word had certainly reached Philo in advance. Epaphroditus saw his ex-assistant's face pop out of a first floor window.

He gave him a cheerful wave as the bearers lowered him down.

"Sir, I'll come down."

"You stay there," Epaphroditus called back. "I'll come up."

He instructed his bearers to take a rest. His bodyguard to watch the door. His announcer to stay savvy in case he was needed. His toga draper to stand in the street and look pleasing. His messenger boy to stay out of trouble. Finally, his meat carver to go find something to do. After this exhausting litany of orders, Epaphroditus ascended the stairs.

* * *

Philo was waiting for him at the top. He showed him into the kitchen, pulling out a bench for him to sit at the enormous oblong table that took up much of the room. On its surface were a number of note tablets and a scroll held open by two saucepans at either end.

"I don't have any paperweights," Philo apologised.

When Philo had worked for Epaphroditus, he'd used two coloured glass balls. The kind of flashy accessory the palace specialised in.

"Is it work?"

"I'm compiling the memoirs of Julianus who lives down the street," said Philo, rolling up the scroll and tidying away the tablets. "It's quite fascinating really, sir. He served under Germanicus."

"In Germania?"

"Yes."

"I don't suppose this Julianus would know anything about Fabius Valens and Aulus Caecina Alienus?"

Philo paused in his tidying. "The commanders of the legions in Germania Inferior and Germania Superior?"

"Those are the ones. I'm hoping you can tell me why the name Fabius Valens is keeping me awake at night. But sit down first. I came to see how you are as well."

Philo sat, then popped instantly up again. "Refreshments! I'm sorry, sir, I didn't think to offer. I believe we have some bread left from breakfast. We could have that with honey, I suppose, or … Well, that's it really, I'm afraid, sir. Teretia's out shopping for supplies. We don't even have any wine. Pompeia has, or I should say had, a brother-in-law who drank to excess. She doesn't like it in the house. I could go down to the fountain, draw some water, sir."

A fountain? The only fountains Epaphroditus' home possessed were of the purely decorative version.

"I don't need anything and I can't think that you are quite fit enough to be fetching water. Though you do look considerably better than when I last saw you."

Philo's hand went up to his left eye which retained a slight swelling.

"I am, sir. I am fully recovered."

"Really, you don't have to call me sir. Sadly you are no longer my employee. Though if you ever fancy—"

"I don't," Philo cut him off. "Sorry, sir. I mean. Teretia wouldn't like it, sir."

"And you, what do you think?"

Fiddling with his stylus, pricking the point into his thumb, Philo told him quietly, "I wouldn't like it either. The palace was not a happy place for me."

The palace had not been kind to Philo. Aside from his recent arrest and interrogation, Philo had been the sexual plaything of a particularly gruesome specimen of slave overseer by the name of Straton. That Epaphroditus had somehow managed to miss his own assistant's torment was ever so slightly damaging to his reputation as the man who knew everything.

"You mentioned Fabius Valens," said Philo.

"Please put me out of my misery and tell me why his name is so familiar."

"I can think of two reasons why, sir. Though the second, we only got word of after your retirement."

A tactful way of putting Epaphroditus' retreat from public life. After Nero's demise, he faked his own death to avoid Galba's hit squads.

"Fill me in."

"The German legions, as I'm sure you're aware, sir, proclaimed loyalty to Nero when Vindex began his revolt in Gallia Lugdensis."

"Yes, I recall."

"Obviously events moved on. Nero died and Galba was declared emperor. So they were rather on the wrong side of things. There was a nasty incident involving the previous governor, Capito. I guess you'd call it a lynching, sir. Capito did not survive it."

"And Fabius Valens was behind it?"

"Oh yes. He wrote a letter to Galba claiming the deed."

"How extraordinary."

"He said that Capito had been planning to declare himself emperor and that he, Valens, had foiled the scheme just in time. He even asked Galba for a reward."

"Any evidence Capito was for turning?"

"Absolutely none. In the light of his other actions, it appeared nakedly craven. Galba certainly thought so. He was planning to make an example of Valens."

Epaphroditus smiled. "Now we uncover the man's motivations! Though it still doesn't explain how I know him."

"Do you remember the Juvenalia, sir?"

Of course Epaphroditus did. Having reached the age of twenty-one, Nero had decided to celebrate his maturity (doubtful) and the first shaving of his beard (a straggly disappointment) by instigating the Juvenalia. This was a riotous festival involving dance, tragedy, comedy, drama, pantomime, ballet, and pretty much everything else that the older generation considered degenerate Greek practices.

Epaphroditus remembered it as a lot of fun. Held in the days following the death of Nero's mother Agrippina, the secretary was feeling particularly jovial. So jovial, he'd decided to treat his new assistant to a day out at the mime.

Since Philo's appointment, the petitions department had become noticeably slicker, Epaphroditus' workload noticeably leaner, and the emperor noticeably impressed by these improvements. Naturally Epaphroditus had taken all the credit for this, but he'd not forgotten Philo's input. A day at the mime seemed a worthy reward.

It had never occurred to him to check which mime was being performed. The subject matter of a beautiful girl kidnapped and heroically rescued by her brother was so standard as to be clichéd.

It began well. Philo, open-mouthed in awe at the crowds, the stadium, and being within gobbing distance of the emperor himself. Epaphroditus was later to learn that this had been Philo's first trip outside the palace.

And then the action began. Epaphroditus thought it was a hoot, a jolly romp of a mime with just the right amount of heroics, funny foreigners, and fart gags. The story involved a beautiful young woman (weren't they all!) dressed in an outfit as flimsy as the plot, who found herself kidnapped by barbarians, in this instance Indians. This slightly clad heroine unconvincingly managed to fight off their lecherous intents until the appearance of her hero brother.

The key dramatic rescue scene involved the brother plying the kidnappers with wine. The inebriated Indians then performed a wonderfully comic drunken dance that had Epaphroditus holding his aching sides. While the villains slept off their excesses, the brother was reunited with his lost sister, and the two of them headed for home on a boat improbably crewed with clowns who produced the necessary wind for sailing from their rear ends.

Wrapped up in the merriment, Epaphroditus had failed to spot the discomfort of his assistant. It was only in the final act, with the reprise of the drunken dance, that he noticed Philo remained straight of face, wearing an expression of some pain. He'd been about to enquire as to the cause when he saw it for himself. The pointing, the comments, the jeers from the crowd, all aimed firmly at Philo, who cringed and squirmed unhappily.

He'd cursed himself for his insensitivity. Though from their very first meeting, Philo had been extremely keen to inform his new boss that he wasn't Indian, physically Epaphroditus couldn't distinguish between an Indian and the Tarpobanian Philo said he was. And neither could the audience.

Stood among the emperor's elite staff who were overwhelmingly Greek or Italian in origin, with a German or two thrown in as bodyguards, Philo's dark skin stood out like a Praetorian at a poetry recital. Anyone else would have cashed in on such exoticism by using his uniqueness to propel himself up the palace career ladder. For Philo, however, who suffered from chronic shyness and who wanted nothing more than to be left alone to do his work, standing out was a source of perennial embarrassment. Particularly so when the spectator of a performance that portrayed his near countrymen as loud, drunken buffoons.

There was nothing to be done to alleviate his suffering. As the emperor's petitions secretary, Epaphroditus couldn't leave Nero's side without a damn good explanation. Men had been known to collapse with burst bladders from the exertion of holding in their natural requirements rather than leave the emperor's side. So they'd stood, side by side, both cringing their way through the remainder of the performance.

But back to Fabius Valens, what had been his role in that vulgarity? Epaphroditus searched his memory and—click. He smiled.

"Gods, he was, wasn't he?" he exclaimed, marvelling. Given the roles on offer, you'd have thought Valens would have seized on heroic brother, but no.

"He was the farting clown!"

"He was quite good as I recall," said Philo, ignoring the unpleasantness of that day.

"He wasn't good. He was genius. I don't think I've ever seen a better rendition of bottom wind. What an artist."

Now he had the measure of the man. Grey Fabius Valens from an ordinary equestrian family plodding his way up the ranks. But impatient, ever so impatient, for glory. So impatient he'd attempted to catch the imperial eye by entering the Juvenalia. So impatient he hadn't waited to distinguish himself in Germania but manufactured a distinction by way of murder. And now that impatient man had command of thousands of men.

"And Caecina?"

"The handsomest man in the empire," reported Philo. "Glowing admiration from all quarters. Galba thought much of him when Caecina served on his staff in Spain. Until he checked the books that is. There was money missing. Quite a lot of money missing. More money than could ever be a mistake."

"Let me guess. Galba was intending to make an example of him."

"Sort of thing he was keen on, Galba. He was virulently anti-corruption."

Epaphroditus was left wondering how the late emperor had proposed to run a bribe-free palace, let alone a bribe-free empire. In Epaphroditus' experience, money was the moving force in all important projects.

"So", he began, "we have two men, both facing public disgrace and possible prosecution. Certainly the end of their careers in the short term. In more normal times, they'd have called upon the usual network of sycophants who'd plead with the emperor for anyone given the right amount of coinage. But these are not normal times. And the precedent has been set, hasn't it? Don't like the current emperor, then do a Galba and use your army to remove him for someone more palatable."

"Actually, sir, wasn't the precedent set with Julius Caesar? When the senate told him to step down as governor of Gaul and return to Rome. But Caesar, knowing he was facing certain prosecution—"

"He crossed the Rubicon," said Epaphroditus thoughtfully.

"With his army," said Philo with factual correctness.

"Well, it gives me something to work with. Fear combined with greed and ambition. The usual mix in a Roman official."

They both gazed into space, thoughtfully. Just like old times in Epaphroditus' office in the palace. Philo broke the contemplative silence.

"You haven't asked about Vitellius."

"Oh, I know him of old. There's nothing you could tell me about Aulus Vitellius that I don't know already. Hang on, what's that?"

It was the sound of running feet up the stairs. The door swung open to reveal a rather attractive blonde-haired girl. Her breathless stance suggested she'd run quite a distance.

"Philo!" she huffed.

"Oh, hullo Verenia."

Epaphroditus leaned back on the bench, staring out the window to the ground below. He saw his announcer chatting up a local girl. His four bearers leaning against a food stall tucking into what appeared to be grilled sausages. His meat carver showing off at the same sausage stall, slicing at speed to a growing crowd of oohing housewives. His messenger boy and toga draper sat on the ground playing dice and arguing furiously over who owed what to whom.

"Hey!" yelled their master. "You useless bunch! Some security contingent you lot are. You, announcer bod, up here now!"

Epaphroditus turned back. Smiling at Verenia, he told her, "He'll be up in a moment. Then we can do the introductions the proper palace way."

Verenia looked slightly unsettled by the pause in proceedings. Unsure as to whether to stand or sit while they waited for the announcer. She decided to sit right opposite Epaphroditus.

Her bosom resting on the table top, revealing a nice show of plump cleavage.

When he could pull his eyes away, Epaphroditus found Verenia looking directly at him. There was more than a hint of suggestion behind those summer-sky blue eyes. Did Philo realise what a minx she was, he wondered, as he turned up his flirt level from force of habit rather than any particular attraction to the girl.

"Sir!" gasped the announcer. One arm leant against the door frame, the other across his doubled-over stomach as he attempted to recover from the exertion.

"Honestly! Do you think you'd get away with such dereliction of duty at the palace? Lysander would tear strips off you. Now get on with it."

The now pained-looking announcer took three deep breaths, stood up straight, and opened his mouth. Epaphroditus' many titles, honours, and good deeds were projected across the kitchen. At the final all hail, he bent his head low and stepped back.

Epaphroditus crossed his arms, "What do you think to that, Philo?"

A cringing Philo replied that he didn't really believe himself qualified to comment.

"What would Lysander make of it?"

Here, after thirty years of close proximity to Lysander, Philo was qualified to comment.

"Well, sir, I rather think he might query the volume."

"Quite. Far more suited to a banqueting hall than a kitchen."

"It rather distorted the actual words."

"Yes it did, didn't it?"

The announcer visibly quivered under Epaphroditus' green-eyed glare.

"But I thought the words were very prettily announced," smoothed Philo, who hated unpleasantness of any kind. "And there was a nice flourish on that final syllable."

Epaphroditus lifted a hand. "You're forgiven but work on it. Work hard, boy, or I'm reporting back to Lysander on your failings."

"Yes, sir" murmured the miserable announcer.

"It is a jolly hard job," consoled Philo. "It took Lysander years to perfect the art."

"Pah. Now I'm fully introduced, let us hear about you," dripped Epaphroditus to Verenia.

Shaking back her hair in a movement that caused a quiver of her breasts, Verenia began. "I, Verenia, daughter of Gnaus Verenius, a merchant who is currently travelling in the East, have no great honours conferred on me yet, but I am still young."

"So you are Teretia's…?"

"Cousin. Five years her senior." Stressing the importance of those years in a manner that Lysander definitely would have approved of.

"A lovely girl, Teretia. I am so very pleased she and Philo have married. And now a baby is on the way. It is all most gratifying."

"Quite," said Verenia, lips pursed.

"Alas, Verenia, though it is lovely to make your acquaintance, I am afraid I must be making a move back to the palace."

A quick flash of displeasure crossed those pretty features before the smooth, pleasant smile returned. "I will make sure to tell my cousin that you visited and how kind you were to me."

It was said very nicely but Epaphroditus was a man with five daughters and he sensed a bite beneath those words. Getting to his feet he said, "Nice to meet you, Verenia. And Philo, it is wonderful to see you looking so well. Do keep in touch and if there is anything, anything at all I can do for you…"

"I'll let you know, sir."

"Promise?"

"Promise."

SEVEN

Flavius Sabinus was sat at a desk crammed with towering scrolls and tablets. The job of city prefect was a busy one. Perhaps not for everyone. Plenty had relaxed through its duties barely raising a sweat. Delegating to the clever little clerks that came with the post. Not Flavius.

Here was not your usual patrician stepping lazily through mundane positions en route to financial enrichment. Flavius was a worker. He threw himself fully into every job, determined to give it his absolute best. He considered it his civic duty and took great pride in his work. His favourite homily, repeated tediously often to his brother, wife, sons, and nephews, was that he had never knowingly started something without finishing it.

This work ethic was no doubt connected to his relatively humble childhood spent in the town of Rieti. Though far from poor, his family were undeniably undistinguished. Flavius had arrived in Rome without the benefit of a name. Everything he had achieved, everything his family had achieved, had been down to Flavius' studious hard work.

The Flavian name now stood for honesty and graft. And who could begrudge him that. For Flavius, though a trifle long-winded and occasionally self-important, was a pleasant and decent man. Qualities sorely lacking in the upper rungs of Roman society.

He was scribbling away by the light of four terracotta oil lamps placed dangerously near his pile of scrolls, when a slave slid in and announced, "Antonia Caenis to see you, master."

Flavius looked up from his work, a smile forming across his face. "Make her comfortable in the green lounge. I shall be with her shortly."

The slave nodded and slid out again.

Flavius finished off the scroll he was working on. He signed it with a flourish before rolling it up, melting a blob of wax on the outside, and pressing his seal ring into it. Satisfied with another chore completed, he stood and rubbed his hands together.

He found his guest reclined on a couch chatting to his head steward as she nibbled on stuffed vine leaves. On seeing him she got to her feet, embracing Flavius warmly and kissing him on both cheeks.

"My dear Flavius," she said.

"Caenis, how wonderful that you are back," smiled Flavius.

Antonia Caenis was in her sixties, close to Flavius' own age. They had known each other for forty years. He'd been a city aedile and she had been private secretary to Emperor Claudius' mother, Antonia. Caenis had given him some truly valuable tips on how to win imperial favour. More importantly, she had taught him all those complicated court rituals that had so baffled the country lad. It was a kindness he had not forgotten and they had formed a respect for each other that the years had not dimmed.

Caenis had also performed one vital function in Flavius' life. One without which he truly had no idea what he would have done: she had dealt with the issue of his younger brother Vespasian.

"The troublesome one," as Flavius had moaned.

"Oh come on, he can't be all that bad," she had smiled.

"I don't know what to do with him. He seems determined to spoil everything he does. Look at the hash he made of the aedileship I procured for him. He let the streets deteriorate to such a mess that the plebs pelted him with dung in protest!"

Caenis had laughed. "An inventive complaints procedure, far more effective than a nicely worded petition."

"It is not as if he is stupid even! He has a keen mind alright." Flavius had tapped his temple "He just doesn't employ it."

"I'd like to meet this hopeless brother of yours."

So Flavius had introduced the two of them, never suspecting what would happen. But the moment Caenis and Vespasian met, even Flavius could not fail to spot the instant attraction that fizzled between them. If Flavius and Caenis possessed an easy, relaxed friendship, Caenis and Vespasian talked as if they had known each other for years. Finishing each other's sentences and accidentally touching hands with a blush and coy hesitancy that made Flavius smile.

If it had been any other slave, Flavius would have considered it yet another dubious liaison to drag down the family name he'd worked so hard to establish. But Caenis was different. Caenis was special. Flavius was absurdly warmed by the relationship that formed between his brother and the imperial slave. Seeing them together, it was clear this was no easy liaison, this was the real deal.

Of course, they could not marry, not with the difference in their class. Yet Caenis remained by his side, consoling him as she had once done Flavius. She supported him in a typically womanly way and quietly moulded him. With Caenis' love, Vespasian prospered, and to Flavius' pride, actually began to take his work seriously. The hopeless case was now governor of Judaea, and Flavius had Antonia Caenis to thank for that.

When she had settled back on her couch, he asked eagerly, "How are you, my dear? How was Judaea?" Then a thought struck him. "And what are you doing back here?"

"Judaea is such a long way away," began Caenis. "News travels slow, particularly this time of year."

"You have heard of Rome's troubles then?"

"When I left the East, Nero had fallen and Galba was emperor. Dear Titus accompanied me."

Flavius sat up. "Titus?"

Titus was Vespasian's elder son by his legitimate and now deceased wife, Flavia Domitilla.

"Don't worry," smoothed Caenis. "He has headed back to be with his father."

"Wise, very wise. Things are very uncertain, and much has changed. For one, Galba is no more. Otho is emperor."

Caenis' eyes widened. "Marcus Salvius Otho?"

Flavius gave a wry smile. "Indeed, and surprisingly he is not making too much of a hash of it. Of course he has great advisors," hooking his thumbs in his toga, "myself and Celsus. Epaphroditus is on board as private secretary."

"Now that doesn't surprise me." She had known Epaphroditus nearly as long as she had known Flavius. "What a torrent of news."

"And that's not the half of it," said Flavius. "Wait till you hear about Vitellius—" he stopped, distracted by a shuffling noise.

A stocky youth with red cheeks and a headful of dark unruly curls was stood by the door. He held onto the frame as if deciding whether he should enter or not.

"Hello Domitian," greeted Caenis. "It's very good to see you. How are you?"

"Is my father back in Rome?" he asked, still hanging onto the doorframe.

"No, he is not."

"Come, come nephew. Sit yourself down and greet Caenis properly," implored Flavius.

Domitian shuffled in and sat on the edge of a couch looking distinctly uncomfortable. A fondness for wrestling had given

Domitian a stocky build which contrasted with his rather small head and weak chin.

"Did he …" began Domitian, his fingers lacing in his lap. "Did he give you anything to give me? A letter?"

"No, he didn't, love."

"Did Titus?" persisted Domitian.

"They are both terribly pressed. The Judaeans are revolting, there is a war on. It eats up their time."

Domitian unlaced his fingers and stood. "I see," he said.

Flavius stood up and put an arm around his nephew. "Now then, not so glum, Domitian. I am sure your father and your brother sent warm words with Caenis."

This perked Domitian a little and he looked at Caenis with hope forming in his eyes. Caenis shifted awkwardly.

Domitian shook his uncle's hand from his shoulder. "I thought as much! I may as well be dead for all they care!" he cried and departed, head cast down.

"Oh dear," said Flavius. "I apologise for my nephew's shocking behaviour."

"Please, Flavius, there is no need."

"He's always been on the moody side but recently he's graduated to new depths. My wife is finding him quite trying. I don't think he's even left the house these last two months."

"I'll have a word with him," she promised. "But first, I want to hear all about this surprising new emperor of ours and how he is dealing with this Vitellius situation."

EIGHT

Prone on a couch, feet under a warming blanket, one hand dipping into a tray of entrées, the other holding a glass of fine wine, Otho relaxed after a hard day imperialling, as he called it. There'd been a dinner, starring some of the performers Nero had favoured: a comic tumbler, a singing bird, those dancing eunuchs in their colourful loincloths.

Galba had not enjoyed such entertainments. He preferred his guests to converse amongst themselves. Occasionally, he allowed a recital of some dry, improving work. Though those had been tedious evenings for Otho, he'd made the best of them. Otho could converse with anyone. Even folk he'd sat with the previous seven dinners.

His abilities were such that one drunken evening, back in the early days of Nero's reign, propping up some god-awful bar in the Subura, Otho had enjoyed a right good natter with, he thought, a fellow drinker. Squinting through a particularly throbbing hangover the next morning, Otho was told by an annoyingly sober Epaphroditus that he'd spent the previous night engaging the bar owner's pet monkey in conversation.

"But he was wearing a cloak!" he'd protested.

"The monkey was wearing your cloak. You gave it to him because you said he looked chilly."

"Ah, well, that explains where my cloak went. Now if you can explain to me why I woke up hugging a small figurine of Juno and how I came to be wearing this Vestal's veil then I'll be a happy man! Though one suffering dreadfully from the wine sickness."

"Do you want me to retrieve Onomastus?"

"Onomastus?"

"You swapped him for the monkey." Epaphroditus had pointed to the end of Otho's bed where there did indeed lie a monkey snuggled up under the blanket.

Obviously he'd taken the monkey back, though with some regret, and reclaimed Onomastus. But it often struck him during Galba's dry dinners what a fun chap that monkey had been.

Emperor Otho was determined his dinners would be sparkly affairs. Not too sparkly, as Epaphroditus consistently warned him, but sparkly enough for his guests to leave with smiles.

"Good evening, hey?" Otho asked his companion.

Onomastus, his tiny frame taking up a quarter of his couch's length, nodded. "Good eunuchs."

"Yes they were, weren't they? Damn hard to find a good eunuch. I don't know how the palace has so many of them. I hear they've formed their own guild!"

"So they have, Imperial Majesty. They supplied me with a full list of what they will and won't do in the nature of their performance."

"Intriguing, and there I was thinking eunuchs were game for anything."

One particular eunuch popped into his mind. One slender, lithe, brown-eyed, curly-haired, cross-dressing, ex-empress-impersonating, ball-less boy.

Epaphroditus was very down on Sporus, calling him nothing but trouble. He failed to see that it was exactly Sporus' delightful mischief that Otho found so alluring. Not tonight though, the day wasn't quite over. The imperialling must go on.

"Tell me, chum, what do we make of Vitellius?"

Onomastus flicked a grape across the room. It pinged off the lamp stand with a satisfying ding. "I thought Epaphroditus gave you a file?"

"Yes, he did. He gave me facts, lots and lots of facts. It didn't tell me much of the man himself. I want, no I need, an honest view of the man. I trust no one greater than you to give it to me."

The dwarf considered. "He's like that gap there between those two cupboards."

Otho followed his pointing finger. "His floor needs a bit of a dust?"

"Vitellius is a space waiting to be filled. I believe Epaphroditus referred to him as the perfect courtier in that file he gave to you. Well, he's right. Vitellius is to each emperor whatever they need him to be. To Caligula, he was the fastest charioteer in the city."

"You'd never fit him in a chariot these days. I hear he's so fat he can't even straddle a horse."

"To Claudius, he was an expert gambler skilled in dice. To Nero, you must remember what his particular function for Nero was."

Otho did. "He was the one who ensured the crowd demanded an encore from the emperor."

"The first to shout."

"Never failed, did he?"

"Not once."

"So he moulds himself to appeal to the man in charge," said Otho thoughtfully. "But what if he was the man in charge?"

"That's the question, isn't it?" said Onomastus. "Who is Aulus Vitellius really?"

A thought that was interrupted by a messenger.

"Tiberius Claudius Epaphroditus requests Your Imperial Majesty's presence for a meeting."

"Does he now? I guess there must be news from Germania."

"The meeting is being held in the Map Room."

"There's a Map Room?" asked Otho brightly.

"Yes, Caesar," replied the messenger. "It's where they keep the maps."

"Amazing, isn't it?" Otho said to Onomastus. "They have a room for everything!"

The dwarf gave a wicked grin, asking, "The eunuch room?"

The messenger blinked. This was outside his usual remit of delivering messages. Still, he replied, informing Onomastus, "New palace, third corridor, fourth door along, sir."

* * *

The Map Room lived up to all expectations. It was a small chamber whose walls were covered with cartographical examples. Onomastus nudged Otho. "Lusitania," pointing to a representation of Otho's former province.

The emperor peered at the colourful picture of the terrain. "Makes it look almost habitable, doesn't it?"

In the Map Room were gathered Celsus, Flavius, and Epaphroditus. None of them looked terribly happy, which rather killed Otho's jolly mood.

Celsus took the floor. "They're on the move."

Otho raised an alarmed eyebrow. "I thought we'd agreed that they wouldn't even attempt to march until the spring."

"That is the traditional start of the campaigning season but it appears that the winter in Germania has been much milder than usual. They are prepared to assume it'll stay that way."

"Keen, aren't they," noted Flavius.

"If Caesar would care to examine the map."

Celsus directed them to a round marble table.

"Our scouts report that they have split the force in two. Fabius Valens will take his troops down through Gaul towards Narbonesis via the city of Vienne."

He traced the route across the map with his finger. "Caecina has set off with his men from Vindonissa; he's heading through Raetia." Again he traced the route, halting his finger at the Alps at the top of Italy.

"And Vitellius?" queried Epaphroditus.

"Not with them according to the scouts. So probably still in Cologne."

"Awaiting their success or failure, no doubt," mused Epaphroditus.

"Did they not get your letter?" asked Otho. "The one you phrased so nicely telling them that I was emperor now. How much better I was going to be at it than Galba. How I was on the look-out for talented men to reward?"

"It's possible our message has not reached them yet, Caesar," suggested Flavius.

Otho held his hands apart. "So, then."

Flavius cleared his throat. Celsus stared at the floor. Epaphroditus averted his eyes.

"What is it that's making you all so damned evasive?"

Flavius cleared his throat again. "Caesar, once a legion gets marching, it's difficult to turn it around."

"They will have expectations," translated Celsus. "They'll have been promised spoils."

"Of war?"

"Of the countless badly defended towns they were intending to pass through."

"But I thought they wanted to stay in Germania!" protested Otho. "I thought that was why they turned on Galba in the first place, because he wanted to resettle them in another province."

"Quite," said Epaphroditus. "If we can catch them before they get too far and offer them a bounty, a thank you for their loyalty to Nero. Caesar?"

"Whatever it takes," said Otho. "Whatever it takes."

NINE

The morning mist was still at knee height when Antonia Caenis reached her destination. A thin layer of drizzle fell from the grey sky, coating her face and slowly permeating into her woollen clothing, a seeping dampness against her skin. Caenis pulled her cloak around her and gave the door three sharp taps.

It opened instantly to reveal the doorman. He was a better-looking specimen than usual. Most doormen were ugly brutes employed for their fists and surly tempers, ideal to deter the most persistent of pests. This doorman was certainly burly. A broad, muscled chest was on full display, despite the winter chill. Below he wore a white pleated skirt and black boots. Gold cuffs were clamped on his wrists. A matching golden headband sported a single diamond in its centre, a look clearly designed to resemble an Egyptian pharaoh of old. And this was just the doorman!

But then, thought Caenis wryly, she would expect nothing less of Nymphidia Sabina's staff.

"Tell your mistress that Antonia Caenis is here to see her."

"The mistress sees nobody."

Feeling the cold ache in her toes, Caenis had no intention of trekking all the way back to Flavius' house.

"Kick her out of bed. Whatever she was up to last night we can discuss over a light breakfast."

"The mistress goes nowhere. She sees no one."

He was so insistent, so implacable on that point that Caenis had no option but to believe him. Which meant that something truly terrible must have happened, for Nymphidia was a social creature. She adored parties, banquets, festivals, soirées, orgies, any occasion at all. Caenis had known her to partake in a party of some description every night for a year and her energy had never flagged.

"Would you mind if I sat in your lounge for a moment? I am an old woman and I have walked far. Whilst I am recovering you can bring Hercules to me."

Sitting in Nymphidia's elegant lounge, Caenis could sense an atmosphere, a certain muteness. The slaves were moving slowly about the place in absolute silence. There was nothing of Nymphidia's natural spark present.

"Madam."

"Hercules."

Hercules was another of Nymphidia's underdressed slaves. This time in the guise of a Gallic chieftain: long yellowish hair woven into thin plaits and attired in only a pair of patterned trousers. He was Nymphidia's most trusted attendant and undoubtedly one of her lovers.

"Hercules, what in the great mother's name has happened?"

"You did not hear, madam?"

"I've been away in the East. News has reached us very slowly and then there has been such a lot of it! I fear our friends have edited out some of the lesser tales in all the excitement."

Hercules gave a solemn nod. "You did not hear about the mistress' son?"

"Sabinus? I heard he was made Praetorian prefect."

The pride had glowed through Nymphidia's letter, rightly so. It was quite a promotion for the son of a former slave, even an imperial slave.

Hercules sighed, then sat in front of Caenis. She was not surprised by this unusual stance. Nymphidia's staff, just like their mistress, were wholly unconventional.

"I presume you heard about His Imperial Majesty, Nero."

"Yes, that news did reach us."

"The two tales are but one," began Hercules gravely.

The story he told, of Gaius Nymphidius Sabinus' involvement in Nero's fall, of his taking over of the city, and his gruesome death at the hands of his own men, shocked Caenis.

"Has the world gone mad?"

"It appears so, madam. The mistress was grievously affected by the boy's death."

Sabinus was Nymphidia's only child and she doted on him with an intensity that Caenis remained unconvinced was healthy. It reminded her in a worrying way of Agrippina's attachment to Nero, and look how that had turned out. But Sabinus was no Nero. Caenis recalled him as a rather serious little boy, possessed with terrors and frights that despaired his grandfather, the arch palace manipulator Callistus.

In Caenis' opinion, Sabinus' sensitive nature had ruled him out of a palace career like those of his mother and grandfather. He lacked the sharp mind and manipulative bent that the palace demanded. The army had, at the time, seemed to be the best place for him. Though she knew Nymphidia, in fear for her son's life in the barbarous provinces, had vehemently disagreed.

"The mistress, madam, she collapsed in both mind and body. She sees no joy, no hope in anything."

"Take me to her, Hercules. Let us see what we can do.

* * *

The shutters were pushed closed. A single bronze lamp hung from the ceiling offering a dim glow in the gloom. On the vast four-poster bed, Nymphidia lay on her side, staring at the wall. Her hair was unbound and untreated. The grey streaks she normally dyed out of existence twisting to the small of her back.

Whereas Caenis had worked her way through a series of clerkish posts to her height as Antonia's private secretary, Nymphidia had gained an equivalent power in the competitive palace factions by lying down a lot. For Nymphidia Sabina had been a whore. A highly trained and highly successful palace prostitute.

She'd been a lover to emperors Caligula, Claudius, and Nero. And had slept with every powerful freedman from those reigns. This had given her enormous influence. This she used to promote her son primarily, but also those she considered friends.

She had watched Caenis' back on more than one occasion, and Caenis had returned the favour. In the heated world of palace politics, a true friend was a rarity to be treasured. It hurt Caenis to see Nymphidia in such distress.

She waved Hercules away and quietly sat on the bed beside the prostrate Nymphidia. Stroking her hair gently, she said, "Nymphidia, it's me. Caenis."

Nymphidia rolled over. Her face was streaked with tears and there was a blackness under her eyes as if she had not slept for days. She pulled herself upwards into a seated position.

"Caenis? I thought you were in the East."

"I have returned. I'm staying with dear Flavius."

"Did Hercules tell you?"

"He did. I am so sorry." She grasped her friend's hands. "That such a fine boy should end so."

"He was fine, wasn't he? I knew it from the first time I saw him, his little fingers grasping onto my thumb. I knew he would be something, someone."

"I hear he was an exceptionally good prefect."

"He was, he was," nodded Nymphidia. "He marched them into shape. They are a proper force now because of him. Can you believe, Caenis, that they even turn up at their allotted hour, on the dot!"

The Guard pre-Sabinus had a reputation for laxness on a grand scale.

"And he was so popular with them. They'd have done anything for him. Anything!"

"He was their commander, naturally."

"A great commander."

"The best they'd ever had."

"Better than they deserved!" spat Nymphidia, breaking her hands free.

"When was the last time you left the house?" she asked gently.

"What does it matter? What does any of it matter anymore?"

"So you don't know what's happening out there?"

"Why should I care? After what they did. What they all did to my Gaius. Beasts!"

"Aulus Vitellius is marching to Rome with seven legions to dislodge Otho from the imperial throne."

Nymphidia's eyes widened. "Galba is emperor though."

"Galba is dead."

"And Otho is emperor? Marcus Salvius Otho?"

"Yes."

"Better than Galba, I suppose. Otho has always been a pet," mused Nymphidia. "And you say Vitellius has an army?"

"A large one. Intent on making him emperor."

"Good gods! Has everyone gone mad?"

"It appears so. Coming home has been somewhat of a surprise for me."

"I'll bet. But what makes Vitellius think he's emperor material. The man never gets out of bed before sundown."

Neither did Nymphidia in her prime. All the better to enjoy the night's parties and other events.

"Someone is egging him on."

"I should imagine so," Nymphidia muttered, her attention waning.

Keen to keep Nymphidia's mind active and away from the fate of her beloved son, Caenis threw in her latest gossip.

"Oh, and Epaphroditus and Aphrodite have split up."

That certainly animated Nymphidia, who squawked, "What! No, that cannot be true."

"I had it from Flavius. He's back as city prefect and tells me Epaphroditus has moved into the palace. Apparently Aphrodite wants a divorce."

"But they belong together!"

"I know, I know. Flavius says he's gone to pieces over it."

"Because he adores her."

"I know. It's all terribly sad."

"What can we do to get them back together?"

Caenis smiled. "I do have a plan which I intend to implement."

"I want in. They are perfect together. Like you and your project."

Which was how Nymphidia always referred to Vespasian. She would never understand Caenis' love for the squat, bald-headed patrician. Yes, he was good company, and clearly anyone who loved Caenis was worthy of Nymphidia's respect, but he was a lousy courtier. His dry sardonic wit had found no favour with any emperor. Nymphidia could only assume that Caenis was working to better him. Hence, "project".

"How is he, your project?"

"Fighting the Jews."

"Sounds ghastly. Now, what is this plan of yours for reuniting Aphrodite and Epaphroditus? And what can I do to help?"

"I thought you'd better sit this one out, given your history."

"With Epaphroditus? That was nothing."

Caenis doubted Aphrodite would see it that way. Epaphroditus' estranged wife was staggeringly conventional. It was difficult to believe she'd ever been enslaved, so well did she play the role of the Roman matron. Nymphidia with her scores of lovers and Caenis, who'd been Vespasian's unofficial wife even during the years he was officially married to Flavia Domitillia, could not compete with Aphrodite for virtue.

"Gods, I wish I had someone who loved me so completely as Epaphroditus loves her. Perhaps things would have been different if I had."

"Nonsense, Nymphidia. You know perfectly well you are totally unsuited to fidelity. Can you imagine just one man for the rest of your life?"

Nymphidia imagined. She screwed up her nose. "No variety. Like eating cabbage every day. Though you seem to manage it with your project."

"The foreign travel helps."

Nymphidia could not help but laugh. Her first laugh in the five months since her son had been killed. It cheered Caenis: she'd known some hot gossip would rejuvenate her friend. Nymphidia lived for gossip. For causing it. For spreading it. For, on occasion, inventing it. But Caenis had use for some other skills, more specialist skills, that she knew Nymphidia possessed.

"I have a quite different mission for you. One that uses the best your father taught you."

Nymphidia's brow rose. Caenis leaned forward. "Tell me. Have you ever been to Germania?"

TEN

Otho knew he shouldn't. He knew how annoyed Epaphroditus would be. The endless lecture and hectoring he'd receive from his secretary. And truly that paused him. Because the gods knew how Epaphroditus could go on. Then he thought, "Fuck it, I'm emperor!" and he'd gone and sent for the eunuch.

It had been a most enjoyable night. It had cheered him up enormously after the dispiriting news that the German legions were on the move. They certainly trained them well at the palace. Otho didn't think he'd ever been quite so delighted. Well, maybe with Poppaea, but there was always a sting with Poppaea that took off the gleam. The eunuch lacked sting, thankfully.

There was no reason why anybody should know about it, he reasoned. Being emperor was hard work. He needed. No, he deserved a treat every now and then. Of course once he married Statilia Messalina, he'd knock it on the head. The act that is, not the eunuch. There was no need for that kind of brutality, even against slaves. But until the wedding there was no harm in it. It wasn't as if he were doing a Nero, dressing the eunuch up as Poppaea and publicly displaying him/her. No, it was a private thing. A private treat. His business. Nobody else's. That was it.

Had Otho bothered to get to know Sporus in any other capacity than the bedroom, he would have realised how utterly implausible that was.

The brief moment Otho took in emptying his bladder was all Sporus needed. Popping out into the corridor, wrapped in a bed sheet, he affected a pose of fatigued joy. Happily, two cleaning slaves were pottering by to witness the spectacle and deliver the news to the slave complex. This gave Mina time to order in the wine and nibbles for the expected post-match debrief.

* * *

Cassandra, eyeing up the honeyed almonds, roasted dormice, and assortment of pickles, groaned. "Not Sporus?"

"And what of it?"

"Is he going to be here all evening?"

"He has important news of the most crucial kind."

Even Cassandra, who never partook in gossip, was fully versed on what news Sporus was due to share.

"I'm going to the library," she said, banging into Sporus in the doorway.

"You always seem to be leaving whenever we meet, Cassie," observed the eunuch. He lacked the mental faculties to link the two together: his arrival, her departure.

"Indeed," she mumbled.

"Sporus!"

The eunuch pivoted. Remembering what had brought him there, he upped the performance. He didn't so much faint as slowly descend to the floor in a puff of chiffon, which somehow draped itself artfully around his prostrate form. Mina dutifully feigned shock, then concern. "Oh Sporus! Sporus! Are you well?" she cried, gathering him up in her arms.

Opening his eyes, fluttering his (fake) eyelashes, he declared in a voice as deep as his eunuchisation allowed, "Mina, my dear,

dear friend. I shall never be the same again. Something quite amazing has occurred."

Of course Mina knew exactly what that amazing occurrence was. But it didn't do to beat Sporus to a punchline (not unless you wanted a shrill exclamation and a flounce out) so she feigned ignorance. She helped her friend to the couch. Under his direction, she placed a goblet against his lips so he might take but a drop of wine (he downed the entire lot). Finally, she put before him some canapés, so he might recover his strength a little.

Crunching on a dormouse, he told her, "I am in love and I am loved! By—"

Pause for effect. Rather a long pause. Irritatingly long for Mina. She tapped a fingernail on the arm of the couch until the eunuch managed to expel breathlessly (though Zephyr knew he'd had long enough to inhale sufficiently), "The emperor himself!"

"Oh!"

"Indeed 'Oh'. And what an 'Oh' it was."

It took an aeon for Mina to get the full story. What with all the swooning. The break for tears of happiness. The pause for just a drop more wine to recover his senses. And the cry that he couldn't possibly reveal any more. Mina's begged pleases kicked the tale along. It was at times like these that Mina ached for Alex. Sporus was a burden that shouldn't be borne alone, and Alex had always known the correct way of handling the eunuch. But sadly, Alex had been killed the previous year and Mina had taken over full ownership of Sporus.

So drawn out was Sporus' tale that he'd not even reached the moment of consummation when Cassandra returned from the library. She visibly gritted her teeth on seeing him still there.

"Hullo Cassie," he greeted her cheerfully. "Good study was it?"

Which was as far as Sporus could interest himself in anyone other than himself. Turning back to Mina he continued, "And then—"

Mina leant forward for what should be the actual juicy bit.

"It is very late," said Cassandra pointedly.

"Is it? I have no idea. Time has no meaning for me anymore. I live in the moment."

"Do you think you could live in the moment in your own room? You might find it more comfortable."

Mina bounced to her feet. "No, he could not. Because he is my friend. And tonight something special occurred for him. And he wants to share it with me, his friend. If you had any friends, you'd know what it is to share your thoughts and feelings with someone special!"

In that way that so infuriated Mina, Cassandra showed no reaction to her outburst. She stated slowly and reasonably, as if talking to a pair of children: "You see it is very late and I wish to go to bed. So I may sleep and be refreshed in the morning."

"Gods, it's not that late!" declaimed Mina. "You are so, so, so—" flapping her hands as she tried to find the perfect adjective. She failed, ending with a less than cutting, "boring."

"And tired," replied Cassandra and blew out the lights.

"Keep talking," Mina insisted to Sporus. "She's not going to win this one!"

So Sporus did. Whether it was the late hour, the pitch darkness they were sat in, or just the squeaky melodrama of the eunuch's voice that did it, Mina could not say. Either way she found her eyes begin to close, her head nodding downwards.

"And Otho, my darling Otho says—" he paused. The pause was filled with two snores.

Thankfully both Mina and Cassandra slept through the ensuing hissy fit and flounce off.

ELEVEN

"Hmmm."

"You like, sir?"

Caecina swirled in one direction, then the other. His eyes fixed on the mirror.

"It has good movement," he said, feeling the fabric of the cloak.

"You like, sir?" repeated the little tailor, clutching a handful of pins.

A full twirl. "Fabulous colours. A most fabulous plaid. It favours me greatly. You have done well."

"I am glad, sir."

"Reward this man," Caecina instructed his slave. "Handsomely," he added, as his fingers smoothed the fabric down.

The now smiling tailor escorted out, Caecina was left alone with his mirror. A state he enjoyed immensely. He spent a very pleasurable hour practising his fierce face. His strike stance. And his addressing his victorious troops, arm outstretched pose. All very satisfying. All the more so because of his new cloak, he felt.

"Sir!" A call breaking into his revelry.

"What is it, soldier? Can't you see I am busy?"

"A chief, sir. A Helvetii chief."

"Helvetii?"

"We are passing through their territory, sir."

"Are we?"

Caecina had rather lost track of where they were. He left that sort of business to his tribunes: they understood the maps. Still, a genuine tribesman. That he had to see. It was Caecina's belief that he should have been born a Celt. More particularly, a German Celt. He admired their straightforwardness, their lack of guile, their bravery, and their concentration on the important things in life: war, women, and drink. His birth nationality in comparison seemed dull. There was an awful lot of talking involved in being a Roman. And paperwork. Why was there always so much paperwork?

The Helvetii chief was a stark disappointment. He was wearing a toga for a start. And he spoke Latin as perfectly as Caecina did. Which led to the odd situation of a toga-clad Helvetii tribal chief addressing the trouser-wearing Roman official.

"Chief. Do I call you Chief?"

"My name is Gaius Tullius."

Caecina deflated further. "Really? Well, Chief Gaius Tullius, what can I do for you?"

Gaius Tullius, a middle-aged man who'd have fitted nicely into a law court, so staid did he appear, cleared his throat. "There has been an incident that I must bring to your attention."

"An incident? I don't like the sound of that. Sit, do sit. Manus bring refreshments, some beer."

"I prefer wine," said Tullius.

"Of course you do," muttered Caecina.

"Some of our men were transporting a pay wagon when they were intercepted and robbed by some of your men," Tullius explained stonily.

"Were they?"

"They were. Your men took the wagon of coins with them."

"How enterprising of them," declared Caecina brightly.

"They stole from us."

Caecina pointed a finger at Tullius. "They did not steal from you. They plundered from you. It's what it's all about, the army; fighting and plundering. We've done a fair amount of plundering so far. The men are rather good at it. Not much fighting alas. But that'll change when we face old Galba."

"But the Helvetii are allies of Rome."

"These are strange times, chief. Who knows who is what? Slippery times. That's what I call it, slip-pery times."

"We want our money back."

"Can't be done, I'm afraid. It was honestly plundered."

"Stolen."

"Plundered."

Helvetii eyes met Roman eyes.

"You are in Helvetii territory," informed Tullius.

"I think you'll find this," Caecina stamped his foot on the floor, "is Roman territory. All of it. Every last yard."

"The Helvetii were granted certain rights, certain privileges, by Julius Caesar."

"Who is very dead."

Gaius Tullius had been tutored by a pedagogue of impeccable virtue. He had been taught rhetoric, mathematics, and law. His knowledge of the latter he applied now. "We have them written down, codified. I can show them to you. They are carved into the walls of our town."

Tullius' deep respect for Roman law took a huge dent when Caecina responded, "Oh, I can't be bothered with that. The fact is, this is Roman conquered land. We are Romans marching through it. Therefore, we are entitled to take whatever we need. Whatever we want." Caecina stood. "I think that clears up the matter. There is nothing left to be said."

Tullius rose to his feet. "The Helvetii are a proud people. I warn you that we will not stand for this. You should know that Julius Caesar himself granted us privileges for our peace because he feared us. We will take back what is rightfully ours."

Caecina shrugged. "Well, you can try."

Which is how Caecina managed to invoke a war with a Gallic tribe who'd done nothing but build bathhouses, drape togas, and give each other nice Latin names for the past century.

* * *

The Helvetii had quoted Julius Caesar the practical negotiator. Caecina was quoting Julius Caesar the warlord to his men.

"When they were brought back, he put them to death. But all the rest were allowed to surrender after handing over the hostages, deserters, and arms."

Pacing up and down, he recited to the waiting men. He was particularly pleased by the way the wind caught at his cloak, causing it to flap behind him like some great torrenting plaid river.

The Helvetii, with a century of peaceful existence, were no match for Caecina's legions. Tricked into an ambush, with the legions on one side and the Raetian cavalry on the other, the Helvetii had no chance. They were cut to pieces. The survivors taken into slavery, despite their citizen status, which should have saved them from that fate.

* * *

They held a triumph as best they could. But Caecina felt, as he trotted through the streets of Avenscium on his white horse, that it was less than he'd hoped. The spectators for instance were a miserable lot. None of them cheered. None of them threw rose petals or yelled his name in admiration. He held onto his smile until he reached the safety of his tent. There, it drooped with disappointment.

A slave pulled off his boots as he slumped into a chair reflecting on the day's events.

"Sir, a messenger from Rome."

"Really? Send him in."

Could Galba know of this triumph already? Caecina's strength had never been geography or distances. What would that flint-hearted old man think of his protégé now? A delicious thought for Caecina: to picture Galba reading of his victory, of the great battle he had won. Would he quake then? Would he realise what a mistake he'd made in upsetting Caecina? Realise how he'd underestimated him?

A man as beautiful, as spoilt, as vain as Caecina was used to being patted and petted and told how attractive he was. And so it had proved initially with Galba. One steamy Spanish night sitting side by side, pouring over the accounts, eyes aching from the dull glow of the oil lamp, Caecina felt Galba's hand come to rest on his knee. There the hand had stayed as they leant their heads together discussing budgets and rations and other such mundanities.

The hand had moved higher up the thigh. When it was not shaken off or repulsed in any way, it gave Caecina's firm, young flesh a squeeze. Caecina spread his legs ever so slightly offering an entry point of just the appropriate size. Here, any further discussions of dockings and payments and quartermasters were abandoned. Galba's gnarly old hand, delighted to discover no impediment of a loincloth, grasped hold of its target, thrilled to find it in a semi-aroused state.

All in all, Caecina felt he'd given a good performance. He'd sighed. He'd quivered. He'd stripped off pretty darn quickly so Galba could enjoy his perfection in all its sculptured glory. The old man had gasped in admiration. An appreciation that sent Caecina further upwards.

Yes, old Galba had fully enjoyed Caecina and Caecina had been happy to oblige. For who knew how many years the old goat had left. He probably wouldn't even complete his governorship. When he did die, having no offspring of his own, he would no doubt remember Caecina handsomely in his will. Perhaps he might even adopt him. That Servius name would certainly elevate him beyond his unimpressive rank. He'd return to Rome a new man. With a new name and money of his own for once.

He'd got his promotion to Germania and a position that was usually bestowed on those many decades his senior. Galba had even given him a little money. To help him display the necessary prestige the old man had said, before moving in for a far from fatherly embrace. It had all looked very promising for the beautiful young man.

However, there was one thing Caecina had not factored in: jealousy. He supposed he should have queried why his couplings with Galba only ever took place in the office. The reason, Caecina later discovered, was that Galba's freedman Icelus was the one keeping his master's bed warm. And he guarded that privilege fiercely.

Icelus waited but a couple of hours after the protégé's departure to bring his master's attention to the irregularities in the accounts that were Caecina's job to manage. Galba was not a forgiving man. In fact, Caecina would go so far as to describe him as vengeful. Very vengeful.

Facing certain prosecution and ruin, Caecina dared to write directly to the now Emperor Galba recalling his loving embraces and the joy he had found in them. It had no effect. The emperor was unmoved. The emperor had been fooled by a common thief.

All had seemed lost until the day he met a man in similarly desperate straits and they hatched a plan together. Who was the vengeful one now?

Caecina smiled as he broke open the sealed scroll. Was Galba going to beg him to turn back his legions? What could that scrawny old man give him now? Nothing. The upper hand was his. And Caecina could not wait to employ it.

His smile dimmed, then fell, as he read. Galba was dead. There was a new emperor in Rome. Dizzy with shock, he slumped back in his chair. What now?

TWELVE

While Caecina was busy undertaking his own less ordered version of Caesar's Gallic conquest, Valens' progress had been considerably smoother. He had no need to take any towns by force. They opened their gates willingly. The town elders were positively keen to give Valens' men anything they required. Their commander fared particularly well in this generosity.

Valens called the coins and women handed over to him gifts. They were bribes, absurdly overgenerous bribes that fed the invading army, and left the town starving. That the towns Valens passed through were so willing to give away their winter supplies was linked to an event at the start of their long journey to Rome.

The town of Divodurum had not resisted the troops. In fact, they had been welcomed with a cool civility, offering what scant provisions they had. They had even barracked the soldiers in their homes.

Two nights into their stay, from somewhere, and nobody could determine where, a rumour began: this was a trap. Galba's men had infiltrated the town. The townspeople were waiting until the troops were all asleep and then they would be slaughtered in their beds.

Clearly, action needed to be taken. And fast, before such a dastardly plan could be enacted. The death toll from the legionaries' action had been in excess of 4,000. A sizable proportion of the town's citizens.

Though an unpleasant incident, Valens could not regret it. It had made their progress all the smoother. Fear of a similar event led to women and children lying prostrate by the sides of the road before the marching army. It had led to riches Valens had never known. And they hadn't even left Gaul yet.

What treasure the Italians would bestow upon him was something Valens looked forward to with glee. And then there were the women. The beautiful, supple women presented to him in every town they passed through. Valens had altered their route ever so slightly to pass through a particular town where he'd heard rumours that the fairest girl in all of Gaul resided.

Her name, utterly unpronounceable, had been discarded. To him, she was Helen. This Helen possessed waves of blonde hair that by oil lamp shone like the gold that filled Valens' store chest. Her eyes were of the palest blue he'd ever seen. Almost translucent in colour and mesmerising. Her figure was just as he preferred: small pointed breasts that demanded to be bitten and a thinness that was nothing beneath his weight.

That she was the daughter of a local tribal chief was of no matter to Valens. Nor that she already had a husband. He was similarly unconcerned that she was resistant to him to the point of violence. He liked them unwilling, fighting him the whole way. It made their inevitable conquest all the sweeter. Valens found himself attracted to her. Probably it was her spirit. Her angry, spitting spirit that refused to be broken no matter how evilly he used her. Even after so many forced couplings, she resisted violently. Kicking and scratching at him. Valens' back was striped with nail marks. His shoulder was the victim of a hard bite. Riding on his horse bound for the next unfortunate town, he could feel his wounds sting. This made him smile and yearn for more of the same.

Of course she was a flight risk, so he was forced outside the bed to tether her tightly. He couldn't wait to present her in Rome, his Gallic princess. What a return home that would be for Fabius Valens. Victorious general. Right-hand man to the emperor. The best-looking woman in all the empire his alone. Valens' Gallic adventure had even put a smidgeon of colour back into his grey features.

It was quite a transformation for him. The man so poor he'd been unable to marry. So lacking in coinage he couldn't bribe his way up the usual round of positions. How he'd smarted watching those men, younger men than him, rise ever upwards. He smarted at it now, even though his chest was overflowing with gold and any woman he wanted was his for the taking. He needed to get to Rome. He needed to show them. To show them all!

"Sir, news from Rome!"

The messenger handed him a scroll and clicked his heels. Valens broke the seal and scanned the contents.

Marcus Salvius Otho was emperor, apparently. Whatever had happened to Emperor Galba was clearly extremely nasty since it was excised entirely from Otho's account. Instead this emperor promised Valens a role in his administration, and dished out some trite sentiment regarding the past being past. Though whether this was a reference to Otho's racy past or Valens' own misdemeanours was not clear.

What was clear was that Otho would not hold it against Valens that he had declared Vitellius emperor and raised an army to claim the latter's throne. It was all a terrible misunderstanding. Valens couldn't possibly have known that the despotic Galba was no more. How could he, all that way away in Germania? Much better for all if he turned his men round. Back to Germania where Otho would ensure they could stay.

Unlike that Galba who'd wanted to resettle them away from their families. No, Otho was very amiable to the German legions, very amiable.

A figure was mentioned as to exactly how amiable Otho was feeling towards the German legions. A month previously that figure would have seemed like all his dreams come true. A chance finally to shake off his grossly unfair poverty. But that was then. This was now. His men had collected double that figure during their march and they were only a third of the way to Rome.

Valens screwed up the scroll. He placed it in the brazier, watching the flames blacken Otho's words to ashes.

THIRTEEN

Asiaticus, freedman of Vitellius, watched his master sleeping. The emperor had hit doze midway through a meal. The food remained on the low table in front of him. The slaves would not dare remove it. Vitellius expected morsels within reach at all times of the day. It was rare to see him without at least a chicken leg in one hand.

Asiaticus had heard it told that an Anatolian man had eaten himself to death. Gorging until his stomach burst and its contents spilled to the ground. A fate Vitellius was in danger of emulating.

"Go on, wake him," he nudged the slave.

Looking up, the boy gave a shudder. Taking in Asiaticus' features and, most particularly, the livid scar that dissected his face. It cut from his temple, across one eye forcing it shut and slicing his nose almost in two. His lip was pulled upwards by its torc, giving him a permanent sneer.

Asiaticus ignored this, putting down the slave's terror to a fear of waking up his master. A prematurely woken Vitellius was like a bear, lashing out at all. Asiaticus had witnessed small boys fly across the room, propelled by a direct hit. The boy crept forward, kneeling on the floor. He spoke. "Imperial Majesty, Imperial Majesty."

Asiaticus was unsurprised when this produced no effect. The amount Vitellius had drunk so far that day would knock out an elephant.

"Imperial Majesty," spoken louder. Nothing.

Asiaticus took pity and waved him over, handing him a silver serving dish.

"Drop it, then run," he ordered.

The boy nodded. He went back to the couch, held the plate above his head and then threw it downwards onto the marble floor. The force reverberated around the room, dishes clattering together on the table. Vitellius opened one eye. It swivelled round taking in the room. The boy took this as his cue to leg it as instructed.

"An important message, Imperial Majesty," barked Asiaticus.

"Is it? Is it really?" growled Vitellius.

"I believe it will astound you, Imperial Majesty."

"That's quite a promise," said Vitellius hauling himself upward.

Not terribly upward, he merely replaced his elbow on the arm of the couch to a partial recline. His usual stance. Adopted, so Asiaticus believed, because his master could no longer fit his enormous bulk into a standard chair. "I hope you can deliver."

"Otho has declared himself emperor."

Vitellius' jaw fell ever so slightly open. Then he laughed. "Has he now? What a stupid enterprise. I thought more of Otho than this. He only has a single legion. At least Macer's machinations had the additional boost of disrupting the corn ships and even that did him no good. Send a man down to Lusitania to remind Otho that he has only 5,000 men and I have ten times that number."

"He's not in Lusitania. He's in Rome."

"He's in Rome?"

"Apparently, he travelled down with Galba when all this business kicked off."

"And Galba is?"

"Dead, Imperial Majesty."

Vitellius considered, scratching at his groin. "That certainly was worth waking me up for. So we are marching 70,000 legionaries—"

"Against the wrong emperor," finished Asiaticus.

Vitellius' chins wobbled as he laughed. When he could finally speak he said, "Strange times, Asiaticus. Strange times."

"What is your command, Imperial Majesty?"

"I've nothing against Otho. I always rather liked him. You can't help but admire a man who can convince his wife into a threesome with Nero. Of course he came out the worse of it. Probably a lesson in that for us all. But a likeable man. Very likeable."

"Imperial Majesty?"

Vitellius grinned, a small sliver of saliva escaping from the side of his fleshy mouth. "You see, I like that 'Imperial Majesty'. I've grown used to it. Be a shame to throw it all over, and for Otho of all men! The man who lay with Nero like a woman. I'm not sure he's emperor material."

"Imperial Majesty, we need to get notice to Valens and Caecina before Otho does. The gods know what he'll offer them."

"Valens is not for turning. He's far too hungry for glory. There's no glory in graciously backing down. And he's promised his men bounty aplenty. There's nothing a soldier loves more than a good sacking. That's the one thing we've got that Otho can't offer them. Unless he throws open the gates of Rome."

"And Caecina, Imperial Majesty?"

"Vain as a peacock. And stupid as one too. He'll follow Valens' lead." Vitellius scratched at one of his chins, the remaining chins wobbling around his finger. "Much as I have full faith in the craven nature of Fabius Valens, it can't hurt to make sure that he is as venally self-serving as we know him to be. Deliver my message personally, Asiaticus. It'll make the bastard feel loved and trusted by his Caesar." Vitellius gave a belly laugh that ended in snorts not unlike those of the warthog.

"Yes, Imperial Majesty."

Vitellius grinned. "These times get more and more interesting."

FOURTEEN

Over and under, over then under. The blonde strands moved at a pace that was dizzyingly fast as the pattern flew downwards. This was Philo's favourite part of the day: when he and Teretia had retired for the night and finally they were alone together. He would lie on the bed watching as Teretia plaited her hair and they would discuss the day's events, their hopes for the future, their greatest wishes and darkest fears. Though in recent days, these seemed to all revolve around Verenia.

"And then Verenia says, 'Should you be carrying the shopping in your condition? Is that sensible?' And then she hands her bag to Doris. Just to show off to Tadius that she has a slave and I don't. Not that Doris does anything useful anyhow! All she does is follow Verenia around. Which I'm sure I would find quite annoying."

"Oh," said Philo.

This seemed the only practical response. Any other sentiment, Philo had learned, tended to exacerbate Teretia's tirades against her cousin. Tonight he had quite definite plans, for which he needed his wife in an amenable mood.

"*And. And,*" she continued, "she's been going round telling everyone that the emperor's private secretary came to see *her*. When it was *you* he came to see. Epaphroditus had never even heard of her before he came to see you. Why would he? Because she's not really very important at all. I have much better cousins, nicer ones, who don't try to better me all the time. Because that's what she's like. When we were both little, my mother made me this lovely dress with pretty ribbons on the arms. Verenia went out the next day and got her slave to make her exactly the same dress. Except the material was of better quality than mother's and of course her ribbons were shinier. So it does not surprise me at all that because I marry the emperor's private secretary's secretary, she should try to go one better and throw herself at the emperor's private secretary just to spite me."

"Epaphroditus? You think she wants to seduce Epaphroditus?" asked Philo, snapping out of his plait reverie. "I don't think that will work."

Teretia spun round on her stool. "You don't?"

"Epaphroditus doesn't like freebies. Sorry, freeborn girls. He only likes palace girls."

"Really? So she has no chance whatsoever?"

"No, I shouldn't think so."

An answer that pinkened Teretia's cheeks with glee as she tied a ribbon around the end of her plait. "Serves her right. Now let me see how your bindings are."

The bindings in question were the white bandages wound round Philo's torso to protect his broken ribs from any further damage. Teretia unwound them carefully. Philo gritted his teeth in anticipation of a sharp pain that did not materialise. Teretia gently pressed a finger against his chest to check for tenderness.

"Does that hurt?"

"Not that much," he replied, surprised. "It smarts a little, that's all."

"The bruises have faded quite well."

She placed a palm on the soft dark hair that covered Philo's chest.

"My jaw feels a lot better too. And I haven't had a headache all day. Well, not one worth mentioning. I am feeling much better. Which made me think. Made me wonder whether you. Only if you want to of course. If you'd like to engage in some err, well, you know, lovemaking. If you felt like it. If you don't feel like it then we won't. Because we can another time. When you feel like it. Though I suppose, does the baby make you feel less like it? No, we probably shouldn't, should we? We'll just go to bed and sleep. Because you need some rest now that you are—Oh you're naked."

Indeed she was. Teretia had flung off her nightgown during Philo's monologue.

"Are you sure you—?"

A question rendered mute by Teretia pressing her lips against his.

* * *

It was an almost cheerful Philo who lay in bed the next morning listening to Teretia potter around the kitchen. Linking his fingers behind his head, he replayed the previous night's exertions. A smile formed on his lips as he remembered the delicious softness of Teretia's flesh against his. The way she sighed, "Vima," his pre-palace name, gently into his shoulder at her point of pleasure. How they had snuggled up together afterwards, falling asleep in each other's arms.

Such tender lovemaking was still new for Philo. Teretia was the first and only woman he'd pursued such pleasures with. Prior to meeting Teretia, Philo had held the firm opinion that sex was something to be suffered and endured. In Philo's case, at the hands of Straton.

There had been nothing enjoyable, nothing pleasurable, nothing soft or kind in any of his encounters with Straton. It had been searing and hard. A tearing rawness that he would never have wished to recall afterwards. Philo had pressed such memories deep inside himself never to be accessed. The very opposite of his relations with Teretia, which were to be savoured and replayed in his head.

She really was marvellous wasn't she? His wife. He was still getting used to the idea that he had a wife, that he was married. Philo had never thought he'd marry. It seemed the sort of thing that happened to other people. If he'd pictured his future, it was one of diligent toil and perhaps a nice apartment with a library, where he would read into the night until it was time to go to work again. Nowhere in these musings had a wife and family featured. With the looming ever-present Straton, Philo had believed such things were not meant for him.

Yet here he was, thirty-one years old, married to the most lovely woman in all the empire, and there was going to be a baby too! Most important, he was happy. Truly happy.

He should do something nice for her. To thank her for marrying him. For nursing him back to health. For participating in such satisfying lovemaking. For improving Philo's prior rather miserable life to something worth living. He knew exactly what it was; the perfect gift for his perfect wife. He would go up to the palace and invite Epaphroditus and Aphrodite round for dinner.

Teretia was fond of Aphrodite. And undoubtedly she had lots of questions regarding pregnancy and babies that the seven-times mother Aphrodite could satisfy her on. Philo was also keen to see his former boss again. He wanted to know what the situation was with Vitellius and his German legions.

Perennially the insider, Philo was finding it odd to be on the outside with as little knowledge on events as any gossip monger on the Viminal. Which was all rather different and a little unsettling for him.

But more than the prospect of a pleasant evening with people she liked, Philo was gifting Teretia the chance to comprehensively put Verenia's nose out of joint. The attendance of the emperor's private secretary at their Viminal abode underlined the connection was with them rather than Verenia. The attendance of the emperor's private secretary's wife exposed the fantasy of Verenia's "close" relations with Epaphroditus. It was perfect.

* * *

Philo set off full of determination, strutting down the Via Longus with a firm step. Perhaps it was the previous night's pleasant activities. Perhaps he was still not fully recuperated. But soon after he began his trek, his ribs began to ache dreadfully. It seemed a terribly long way to the Palatine. Much further than he remembered. He did not recall ever on his route to work having to stop and lean against a wall to catch his breath or sip from a fountain to ease his swollen tongue.

Of course when he'd worked for the palace he'd been terrified of being robbed and would not have paused at any point lest some villain jump out on him. Maybe it was the weather. Possibly his cloak had soaked in some of the rain. It did feel uncomfortably heavy. But he strode onwards towards the forum nonetheless.

Once he'd chatted to Epaphroditus and invited him and Aphrodite round, he rather fancied he'd nip into the archives. He knew there was some correspondence housed there from the actual Germanicus that would be perfect for Julianus' memoirs.

He cut through the busy forums of Augustus and Caesar, avoiding the street hawkers with their trays of goods, narrowly missing being hit by a wobbling sedan chair. Reaching the bottom of the Palatine Hill, standing beside the round Temple of Vesta, he stared up at the imposing arches of the old palace.

There he halted, feeling his heart up the speed of its beats until he felt sure they could be heard even above the Roman street din. Despite the winter chill he felt uncomfortably hot, his palms slick with sweat.

The old palace loomed above him. It looked like it might fall on him. Crush him to pieces. He took a deep breath, attempting to slow his frantically beating heart. Looking down he saw his hands were trembling.

This was ridiculous. He just had to keep moving. Walk up the hill, past the guards ... guards. The last time Philo had seen Praetorians, they had been punching him repeatedly. Only ceasing to allow Laco to bark more questions at him.

What if it were those two guards on the gate? Would they recognise him? Even if it weren't those two guards on duty, any of the other guards would know about it. The Praetorians liked to boast about their brutality. And even when he'd got past the guards, there'd be everyone else. Looking at him. Knowing. Gossip was the favourite pastime of the imperial household, the more gruesome, the quicker it spread. Everyone would *know*, would know what had happened to him that day.

Another tremble to his hands. Another glance up at those huge arches.

And Straton. What about Straton? What if he ran into Straton? He hadn't even considered that when he'd set off from the Viminal. If the last time he'd seen Praetorians had been unpleasant, then the last he'd seen of Straton was truly horrible.

That moment had taken place at Epaphroditus' house as he lay recovering from his interrogation. Straton had walked in on him and Teretia and had not taken the discovery that "his boy" had fallen in love with a girl terribly well. Had Epaphroditus not sent in four of his slaves to dislodge the overseer, Philo had no doubt that Straton would have succeeded in his attempt to bludgeon him to death.

He couldn't go in. It was a stupid idea. A terrible idea. Born of love certainly, but he felt sure that Teretia would rather he came home alive. He'd just go home now. Maybe he could send a note to Epaphroditus and Aphrodite. In fact, that was what he should have done in the first place. Why didn't he think of that? Philo rubbed at his head. Maybe he hadn't recovered as well as he thought he had. Maybe the injuries to his head were still affecting his thinking.

"Philo!" A voice, loud and deep, carried across the forum. Philo snapped his head up to see Lysander walking towards him, smiling broadly.

"Have you come to see me?"

Philo nodded. It seemed the easiest answer.

"Excellent. Let's get some lunch. I know this little wine shop round the corner."

Philo followed him. Once the palace was out of sight, he felt his heart return to its natural rhythm and his hands ceased to tremble.

FIFTEEN

The little wine shop that Lysander knew of was a rather salubrious dive off the Via Sacre. The owner, new as was proudly displayed on a board outside the door, had made some efforts to increase its charms: a lick of cream plasterwork with a fresh fresco that was very nearly decent, a large sign announcing a plethora of wines available, and some rather incredible claims regarding its food menu.

Lysander ordered without consultation. Two bowls of steaming stew, a black hulk of bread, and a couple of beakers of yellowish liquid were placed before them. Lysander tucked straight in, using his bread to mop up the sauce. Philo pushed the grey meat around with his spoon.

"It's good to take a break. My protégés are driving me mad today. Ruddy useless the lot of them. They don't understand that announcing is an art. You can't just plough in and hope for the best. You must train your voice for the necessary gravitas and volume. You must work on your lip movements."

This was familiar stuff for Philo. He had spent many years listening to Lysander gargle with his homemade vocal potions and watched as his roommate practised a series of painful-looking grimaces into a bronze hand mirror. "They moan like anything when I correct their diction or push them into the correct pose. Useless. Ruddy useless."

He took a long draught of the liquid before telling Philo, "I almost wish they'd died during Otho's coup. At least I'd have fresh bodies to work with. Untainted by that rubbish they teach at the imperial training school. Felix brought in a job lot of Britons, I think they are. Tall and blond. Good attributes for an announcer."

Lysander was both tall and blond.

"Some of them would look extraordinarily good standing by a door, but they can't speak Latin yet, so no good to me! I need Latin and Greek at a minimum. Right old tension there is between these Britons and the others. You are well out of it, Philo. There's been a scrap or two already. Felix is dishing out whippings like bowls of gruel. Well out of it," he stressed, spooning a large piece of grey meat into his mouth. "And course now Straton's gone, Felix hasn't got much to threaten them with."

Philo placed down his spoon. "Straton's gone? Where did he go?"

Lysander gave him a disdainful look as if he should already know the answer. "He died. He died the day Galba fell."

"He died? Straton died?"

"That's what I said," replied Lysander, blowing on his spoon.

Philo's eyes moved one direction, then the other, then fell back on Lysander. "Straton died?"

"Gods alive," swore Lysander through a mouthful of stew.

Philo pondered as Lysander chewed through a particularly gnarly piece of meat. "I don't think that can be right," he concluded.

Lysander swallowed down the gristle and took a large sip of wine. "It's true. I was there. I was with him when he died. He took a dozen arrows to his body." He gave a shudder. "It was horrible. That whole day was horrible. I don't think I'll ever forget it. There was blood running down the guttering in the forum like a rain storm and bodies everywhere. You had no choice but to step on them. There was no other way to get out of that massacre. And the soldiers were parading round with their javelins held up high." Lysander lifted his arms to demonstrate. "So everyone could see the heads they'd spiked on the tips. I know Straton was, well, what he was. But that day he was a hero. Without him I'd be dead. We'd all have been dead. He saved us. He gave his own life to save us. Incredible isn't it?"

For Philo, it truly was incredible. Though not for the same reasons Lysander found it so. He was gone. Straton was gone. It was incredible. Too incredible surely?

"Epaphroditus didn't say anything about it when he came to see me."

"He probably forgot about it. He's got a lot on his mind."

Philo could well imagine. Epaphroditus must be working all hours to stop the march of Vitellius' soldiers.

"What with his wife slinging him out and everything."

A statement that had Philo gasping, "No, that's not right."

"It is," insisted Lysander. "They're divorcing. Everyone knows about it."

Philo leant back against the wall struggling to absorb this information. He'd only left the palace a month before. In that time the emperor he'd served had been killed along with all his associates. Another emperor had declared himself and sent 70,000 men ahead to claim his prize. The man who'd tormented and abused him for most of his life was dead. And the couple he'd always thought had the perfect marriage were now divorcing. It was a lot to take in.

"You're not eating," commented Lysander. "It's good, honestly. Might not look it but the bread complements it perfectly."

Philo pushed his bowl forward. "You have it."

Lysander shrugged and then tucked into Philo's stew. "I came to see you, lots of times. Teretia wouldn't let me in," he said in-between mouthfuls.

"I wasn't very well."

"Teretia said that you'd got married."

"We did."

"How come I didn't get an invite?"

Philo shifted on his stool, answering without looking at Lysander. "We didn't have a party in the end. I wasn't well enough."

Squishing a bean with the back of his spoon Lysander said, "I'd say you look better, only I wouldn't know. Given I wasn't allowed to see you."

"It wasn't Teretia. It was me. I told her not to let you in," admitted Philo. Then catching the hurt in Lysander's eyes, he added, "I'm sorry. I didn't want to see anyone. Not then. I wasn't ready."

"I'd walked all the way from the Caelian in the sodding rain," complained the announcer. "And then I had to walk all the way back again."

"The Caelian? Why were you walking all the way from there? You only live round the corner."

"Not any more I don't. My bastard landlord turfed me out."

"Why?"

"We had a disagreement over the rent. He thought I should pay it. Which I was going to, obviously. But he didn't give me the chance."

Taking in Lysander's red-braided tunic and heavy, gold chain bracelet and matching torc, Philo had a fair idea where his friend's rent money had gone.

"So where are you living?"

"At my mother's. Except she's not there because she's nursing some sick friend in Baiae. So it's just me and him."

"Oh," said Philo, knowing the "him" in question to be Lysander's stepfather Gaius Baebinus. The two did not enjoy an easy relationship.

"It's just temporary," insisted the announcer. "Until I get myself sorted again. Whenever that might be."

He looked rather dispirited. Philo handed over his bread to him in sympathy, and guilt at having avoided his friend during what, it transpired, was an awful time for him.

"I am sorry," he said. Suddenly, an idea hit him. "Pompeia's looking for a lodger."

Lysander looked up from his food. "So?"

"You could lodge with us. It's the perfect solution."

The perfect solution for the homeless Lysander. The perfect solution for Pompeia, who needed the extra coinage. And also the perfect solution for Philo. Lysander could fill him in on all the news at the palace. That way he'd no longer feel so bereft, so estranged from his previous life.

SIXTEEN

Epaphroditus scanned the scroll before groaning and tossing it across the room.

"Sir?" voiced his assistant Talos.

"Nothing, nothing." Epaphroditus waved him out impatiently.

The scroll that had caused him so much displeasure was a report from one of his intelligence agents. Though "intelligence" was one facet the agent definitely seemed to lack. Epaphroditus had sent him off to infiltrate Valens' forces which were currently camped at Trier. His mission was to get in with the troops and find out who exactly it was who had leant on Vitellius. Was Valens senior partner in this extraordinary venture or was it Caecina?

Either way, the ringleader needed to be neutralised by violence or by bribery. Epaphroditus did not care which. Once the leader was gone, the remaining two would naturally feel their loyalty to the cause falter, and they too could be bribed not to be so troublesome in future.

However, agent Marcinius had failed totally in his information-gathering. According to his report, he had tried his very hardest to makes pals with the soldiers. He'd spent every evening drinking with them at the local bars, visiting two or three each night. He'd joined in the ruinously expensive dice games that they favoured. He'd even resorted to buying them drinks in an attempt to get them to trust him. But the troops had proved extraordinarily tight-lipped, even when drunk, and had offered nothing of any use apart from a few tips on how to brew German beer.

The crux of Marcinius' report was a request for further funds in order to ingratiate himself.

There was not a chance Epaphroditus would comply. If he couldn't squirm information out of a drunk German by such insane generosity, Epaphroditus failed to see how further bonhomie funded by him was going to help. Clearly Valens' troops had seen through Marcinius' attempts at friendship and were fleecing him for their own amusement. Damn Marcinius! They would be extra vigilant now for any further incursions. No doubt a warning was riding its way towards Caecina's forces.

The question weighing on Epaphroditus' mind most heavily was: where were Vitellius' spies? Because he would have them too.

If there were a spy in the palace, or even the potential for one, really the Praetorian Guard should be notified. A thought that made Epaphroditus shudder. The Praetorians were the emperor's own bodyguards, sworn to protect him and his family. They even had a fancy oath full of solemn promises that ended with the initiate thumping his fist against his chest with a "Ha!" No doubt amongst themselves, they had devised some more extreme, degrading initiation ceremonies. Epaphroditus did not want to know.

What he did know was that in the last nine months the Praetorians, for all their swearing of loyalties and thumping of chests, had forced one emperor into suicide, murdered one would-be emperor, and looked on as a second emperor was hacked to pieces by a mob in front of their eyes.

At protecting the emperor, the Praetorians were about as capable as a eunuch in the breeding programme.

The nod that there might be an interloper lurking in the palace was unlikely to heighten their senses or indeed improve their performance. More likely, they would treat it as a gleeful opportunity to frisk down all female visitors and search the private possessions of any luckless fool they'd taken a dislike to.

There were times, not often admittedly, where Epaphroditus could almost miss Nymphidius Sabinus. Sabinus would have taken a threat to the emperor's life extremely seriously. He'd have double-drilled the Guard in preparation, and no doubt presented Epaphroditus with an enormous scroll listing all his improvements. A scroll Epaphroditus would have simply chucked Philo's way without distressing himself to read. Sabinus would have been all over this. But alas, Sabinus was no more.

It was time for more surreptitious methods of locating Vitellian agents. Epaphroditus opened the bottom drawer of his desk and pulled out a small scroll. He placed it on his desk and unfurled it. Philo's neat handwriting faced him. This was a list they'd had to resort to many times while working for Nero and very useful it had proved. The former emperor had been driven mad with paranoia. Forming daily irrationalities that certain senators were plotting against him. So much so that Epaphroditus and Philo, struggling under a mounting backlog, were forced to outsource the evidence gathering.

This small scroll contained the names of the agents they had used in that task. They were all excellent at weeding out disloyalty and deception. Any one of them would be perfect for locating and disposing of Vitellius' agents in Rome. He ran his finger down the list and settled on one name in particular.

SEVENTEEN

Not one to baulk at unpleasant truths, Cassandra had debated the optimum moment and words to reveal Otho's bed sparring with Sporus to the empress. Because she'd have to be told. There was no debate on that point in Cassandra's well-ordered mind.

If it had been the usual type of patrician engagement, two men wanting to consolidate their considerable fortunes by wedding their children together, she might have reconsidered. In such an arranged marriage, there was no wriggle room, no protest that would be heard. But the engagement between Otho and Statilia was one freely entered into without cumbersome negotiations. It was that rare thing: a love match.

Cassandra knew her mistress to be dizzyingly in love with Otho. She found it rather touching to see her usually barbed mistress reduced to a mushy, lovelorn girl. One would have thought that her previous three marriages would have put Statilia right off men. But, no, she still possessed a romantic core that believed in Otho. That she should find out after the marriage that her beloved was enthralled to the most hated of her late husband's bedfellows was a humiliation she wished to save her mistress.

Better she find out now. Before the fancy wedding where hundreds of guests would all mutter to each other that of course they'd known Otho was a bit like Nero in his tastes. Let her know now and consider her options. She could gracefully bow out of the engagement, claiming all manner of believable excuses. That it was more expedient of Otho to marry a relative of Vitellius' to ease the political situation. That at her age she worried over her abilities to produce an heir. That as a rich widow, she did not wish to be beholden to any man. Any number of reasons that people would understand. To break an engagement was not so scandalous as breaking a marriage.

So she told her. The moment was not quite as optimum as she had hoped. Really, she'd have preferred Mina absent, but the words were well chosen. She began with, "Mistress I have an uncomfortable truth I need to inform you of—"

It was not a pleasant thing to do. But it was done, reflected Cassandra later as she dealt with her washing.

The door flung open it banged into the stonework creating a flurry of white plaster chips. There entered a fiery Mina, eyes glowing through the slits of her helmet. A sight that caused Cassandra to momentarily cease folding her laundry.

"How could you?" she screeched, lobbing her helmet onto her bed. "How could you tell her about Otho and Sporus? Sporus told us that in confidence."

Cassandra raised an eyebrow as she added another perfectly folded gown to her pile. "Confidence? Sporus never does anything in confidence. His whole life is a public display. It's right round the palace because Sporus spread it out there."

"You could have put his life in danger. The empress could have him executed."

"I doubt Felix would let her despatch such a valuable piece of merchandise."

"Felix could sell him!"

"I think you're being a touch overdramatic, Artemina. I am the empress' personal secretary. It is my job to bring to her attention events that affect her."

Mina was open-mouthed in rage, which was the choice moment Sporus decided to skip in. He failed to pick up on the atmosphere or notice Mina's clenched fists as she squared up to Cassandra. Depositing himself on a couch, he asked cheerfully, "What news, oh girlies of my acquaintance?"

"*She* told the empress about you and Otho!"

"No!" cried Sporus, throwing an arm across his eyes. "No! No!" A pause and then a peek from under the arm. "How'd she take it, Cassie? Was she devastated? Really was she? Or was she all stoic but inwardly devastated? Well…?"

Loyal Cassandra did not reply. Less loyal Mina certainly did. "She made a sort of urgh noise in the back of her throat. Then said she was going for a lie down and she was not to be disturbed."

Sporus sat up, triumphant. "Devastated!"

* * *

The musicians had been playing the same tune for two hours, over and over again. There were callouses starting to form on the fingers of the water organist. The skin was flaying off the lips of the trumpeter. But still Statilia insisted they play.

She lay on a couch, staring up at the ceiling. Wondering why she was as bad at choosing men as her parents had been when setting up her first two marriages. Perhaps it was a family curse. Some spiteful client scribbling horrors onto papyri and stuffing it in the hollows of the temple wall that prevented her from ever being fulfilled.

And Otho had seemed so promising! So charming! So handsome! So besotted by her! But yet he was infected with the same disease her latest late husband had suffered from: that damned eunuch! That eunuch was the source of much humiliation for the proud Statilia, culminating in a very public wedding in Delphi between it and her husband. A spectacle she'd had the misfortune to witness with her own eyes.

Statilia had found her inner shrew after that event. The eardrum bashing that Nero was subjected to afterwards ensured that *it* was kept far, far away from her. She could almost pretend it didn't exist. When her husband had fled, his throne stolen by that traitor Galba, it had gone with him. Statilia assumed it had perished with Nero. But no. Months later, it had crawled back out from whatever lair it had hidden in and immediately seduced Otho. To Statilia, this was beginning to feel personal.

The musicians paused, hopefully, at the end of the song. Statilia lifted up her hand, and they began all over again. Drifting off into their rendition, Statilia was abruptly woken by a discordant trumpet blast which was far too cheerful for her mood.

"Calvia Crispinilla." The announcer put such an emphasis on the last syllable that Statilia thought him about to burst into song.

Calvia Crispinilla. Nero's former party planner. The mistress of his wardrobe. The woman who'd put the "oh" into orgy. She entered in a bustle of red and gold. A shawl combining the colours pinned to one shoulder, draping artfully down. She did not look happy, but then she never did. Despite a career spent creating wonder and delight, she possessed a short temper and an exacting standard that few could live up to. Certainly not the announcer who was given a hard glare.

"Standards have dropped markedly in my absence."

It was her absence that Statilia most wanted to know about. "Calvia! Sit! Tell me all about Africa."

Calvia positioned herself, barked some orders at the slaves, and then greeted the empress.

"My dear! I have missed you. Barbarians," she hissed. "The heat is abhorrent and the wind and dust! My dear, never go."

"Did you not go to Egypt? We heard you were in Alexandria."

"Don't believe the stories that there is civilisation in the East. It's all lies. There is nothing civilised about Egypt."

"And Clodius Macer?"

Clodius Macer was the governor of Africa and a former lover of Calvia's. She'd fled to Africa when Nymphidius Sabinus had deposed Nero, putting Galba in his place. Rumours in Rome said that it was Calvia who'd been the driving force behind Macer's war against Galba. Certainly nobody thought Macer capable of coming up with the idea of stopping the grain ships leaving Egypt for Italy. Given enough time, that action would have starved Rome into submission.

"Pah," said Calvia in answer to Statilia's question. "He always was a fool. I should have remembered that before throwing myself on his mercy." This was injected with a heavy dose of sarcasm. Calvia needed no one's mercy, no one's sympathy. "He's dead," she added.

"And you're back?"

"I am."

"How?"

Meaning, how on earth had Calvia, who'd sided with a known enemy of Rome, a man who'd been executed as a traitor by Galba, managed to return home and stride into the palace like none of it had ever happened.

Calvia popped a grape into her mouth, gave a wicked smile, and revealed, "I got married."

"You did? Who to?"

She then unveiled a name that had Statilia choking on her wine. A flurry of slaves rushed forward to pat her on her back and wipe her mouth.

"Him?" she coughed.

"Him," smiled Calvia.

"Isn't he about seventy?"

"Nearer eighty."

Statilia leaned forward, lowering her voice. "Does he exercise his conjugal rights?"

Calvia picked a pip from between her teeth. "Of a fashion. Put it this way, my dear. He achieves satisfaction but there is no danger of pregnancy." She raised her elegantly drawn-on eyebrows.

A particularly squishy picture formed in Statilia's mind. Reflected in her pursed lips and sudden greenish tinge.

Calvia patted her arm. "It's fine, my dear. It could even be the happiest of all my marriages. My husband gets his very specialised needs fulfilled and I get all the protection his name offers. Nobody can touch me," she grinned, showing tiny sharp teeth. "But what news from you? Word reached us that you and Marcus Salvius Otho—"

Which was the cue for Statilia to break down and reveal all of her latest discovery. When she'd concluded, Calvia asked, "Sporus?"

"Yes, that's it. What is it with that thing? Why must it wreck all my marriages? I can't marry Otho now. Not knowing what I know. I thought he was different, Calvia, I really did. I'm going to call it off."

"Do you love him?"

Statilia closed her eyes. "Yes."

"Does he love you?"

"Yes."

"Then you'll not call it off."

Statilia's eyes opened, "Calvia—" she protested.

"I know Sporus of old."

She did. She'd been his dresser when Nero was emperor. Responsible for transforming the eunuch into an approximation of the late Poppaea. So she knew of his very particular weakness.

"Statilia, you need to invite him to every banquet. Every feast. Every single event at the palace."

Statilia looked distinctly sick at the thought. "Not a chance! The next time I catch sight of that thing, I'm going to kill it. I would have succeeded last time if it hadn't been for the damn guards." A reference to the dinner party held the previous spring that had been greatly enlivened by Statilia trying to claw out Sporus' eyes.

"Invite him to every event. Let him see you and Otho together. Let him see the love between you," continued Calvia. "Trust me. He'll absolutely hate it."

That had Statilia smiling.

EIGHTEEN

It was the ides of February and thus the first day of Parentalia. This was a nine-day festival where good Roman citizens remembered their deceased friends, relatives, and ancestors by gathering together at their tombs with picnics ready to share with the dead.

Like everywhere else in the city that day, preparations were in full swing on the Viminal Hill. Pompeia stood by the kitchen table busily packing up a picnic basket of goodies for the shades of her relatives with the assistance of Philo and Lysander.

"Did you want to come along with us to my late husband's tomb? You'd be more than welcome to, Lysander," said Pompeia.

Her latest lodger shook his head. "I promised my mother that I'd visit the graves of her husbands because she's still nursing her friend so can't get back for Parentalia this year."

Pompeia ceased her packing. "Husbands? How many times has your mother been married?"

Stood beside them cutting up pieces of pie, Philo averted his eyes to avoid revealing any of his thoughts. Lysander's mother Lysandria had been a hairstylist to Nero's mother Agrippina. Now retired, she had got through a surprising number of husbands since her freedom. To be widowed once was a misfortune. Twice a tragedy. Five times bordered on the suspicious.

Particularly when Lysandria's wealth increased greatly with each sadly demised spouse.

A clatter on the stairs announced a visitor.

"Is that you, sister?"

"No, it's Verenia, Aunt Pompeia," came the cry back.

She appeared moments later. Her slender figure draped in a floaty cream gown with matching veil pinned to her blonde hair. This was twisted in plaits above her ears that coiled into a bun at the nape of her neck. Around her shoulders she wore Teretia's pink shawl. Behind her followed her slave Doris.

Philo noted Doris take a very familiar position by her mistress. To be handy if needed, but not too close to be a noted presence. It was a position that Philo himself had often taken up during his career at the palace. Though, Philo also noted, she was within kicking distance, suggesting Verenia could not be quite as unkind as Teretia claimed.

Philo was about to comment on this to Lysander, who like him had learnt the importance of standing a good leg-length away the hard way, when he spotted his friend's expression. He was staring intently at Verenia, his lips twitching upwards into a smile, his posture unconsciously straightening.

"Mother, I found the blanket you wanted," said Teretia, walking into the kitchen with the item draped over her arm. "Oh, it's you," she said at the sight of Verenia.

"Hello, my dearest cousin," said Verenia, sweeping Teretia into a surprisingly warm embrace.

"We'll go check that we haven't forgotten anything," said Lysander. Grabbing hold of Philo's arm, he dragged him out.

* * *

"What am I looking for?" queried Philo, staring blankly around Lysander's bedroom. The shelves that had once held Teretia's animal-shaped oil lamp collection, he noted, now stored the announcer's extensive range of voice tonics.

"You're not looking for anything," said Lysander. "I need you to tell me everything about her."

"Who?" asked Philo.

"Doris."

"Doris?"

"No, of course not Doris. Verenia. Tell me everything about Verenia."

"She's Teretia's cousin."

"And?"

"Her father is Teretia's mother's sister's husband."

"Oh come on, Philo. You can do better than that. I know you'll have stored all manner of pertinent facts here." Lysander tapped his temple.

Reluctantly Philo divulged his knowledge. "Her mother, I understand, died when she was a young girl. Her father Verenius is a trader of some description. It appears he likes to supervise his business since he travels a great deal. At the moment he is in Alexandria but I gather he and Verenia have visited most of the major trading ports in Greece and some further east. His business appears to be sound as he owns a home further up the hill as well as a small country estate."

"An estate?" queried Lysander, picturing a rural idyll with pleasantly baaing sheep and several hundred acres of vineyards or perhaps olive trees, complete with full slave chain gang, making sure the profits were healthy.

"Estate might be pushing it," admitted Philo. "Pompeia's travels outside the city have been few. I suspect it might be more of a farm."

"But with land?"

Philo gave a shrug. "I suppose."

"She's available, though?"

Philo failed to hide his look of horror as he finally caught onto the reasoning behind his friend's questioning. "I really don't think you should, Lysander. It wouldn't be right."

"Why?"

"It just wouldn't," began Philo vaguely, before inspiration hit. "She's only recently divorced."

"She's divorced? So she's not intact?"

Philo was lost. "Intact?"

Sighing, Lysander told him, "A virgin."

Philo supposed not.

Lysander scratched his chin. "That's a shame because I really wanted an intact one."

Philo gave a relieved exhalation that stopped mid flow when the announcer interjected, "Still, I suppose it won't shock her then. Some of these freebies are terrified of men. I blame their mothers. They don't prepare them properly. How can they, when they won't even let them speak to men. One of the few things that can be said for slave girls is they're not green. Come on, we best get back to the girls."

Saying that final word with more precision than Philo liked.

* * *

They returned to the kitchen to find Teretia holding up her wrist to show off the narrow gold band that encircled it.

"Philo," she smiled. "Verenia was asking about the bracelet you got me for Parentalia."

"It was my mother's," said Philo. "I thought it might cheer Teretia," he added, holding onto his wife's hand.

This was Teretia's first Parentalia without her father, Teretius, who had been killed back in the autumn. Though she had entered into the festival's jollity of family gatherings and picnicking, it was not without a tinge of sadness.

"How thoughtful of you, Philo," commented Verenia. "It is perfect for your delicate bone structure, Teretia."

Taken aback by the compliment, Teretia's cheeks went pink. "Thank you, Verenia. I intend to wear it always."

Her cousin gave a sweet smile, saying lightly, "I wouldn't do that, Teretia dear. It's well known that plated copper turns your skin green if you wear it too long." She added, "Not like real gold," fingering her own bracelet.

The blush rose up from Teretia's throat to her face, her eyes filling up. Then she hitched up her skirt and ran from the room, Philo following her.

"Oh dear," said Pompeia.

"I am so sorry, auntie. I didn't mean to upset her. She is rather sensitive. Perhaps it's all the excitement or her being pregnant. I've heard that pregnancy can have terrible effects on the mind."

Lysander gave a knowing, "Hmm," that seemed to growl from the back of his throat into a perfectly pitched agreement.

This drew Verenia's attention to him. "You must be the latest lodger!" she smiled.

"Servius Sulpicius Lysander," he smiled back, holding out a hand.

She shook the hand with a firmness that impressed the announcer, and had him imagining all manner of scenarios involving those slender fingers.

Verenia leaned into him. Lowering her voice she said, "I should be wary of my cousin, Servius Sulpicius Lysander. Look what happened to the last lodger. She jumped on him before he'd paid his first rent bill. I would so hate to see the same happen to you."

She placed a hand on his shoulder. A small touch that had the heat rushing up Lysander's neck. He was set to utter something wildly inappropriate when he was saved from social disaster by the arrival of Pompeia's sister and her large brood of children.

NINETEEN

Philo's arms were held tightly around the sobbing Teretia.

"It's not gold. I'm sorry. I'll buy you a gold bangle if you'd like one. We'll go look after Parentalia when the shops are open again."

"I don't want another bangle," she sniffed on his shoulder.

"Are you sure? I don't mind if it's not quite what you like. I'd rather you be happy than pretend to be happy to make me happy. Honestly."

She wriggled out of his embrace. "I love it," she said caressing the metal with her fingers. "It was your mama's and it came all the way from Tarpobane with her. And you gave it to me. You chose to give it to me. And that means everything to me, everything. I wouldn't swap it for a solid gold bracelet a hundred times its size."

Gently pressing his thumb against her wrist, he said, "What does it matter what Verenia thinks if you like it."

"It doesn't," said Teretia quietly and then with more certainty, "It doesn't."

Philo smiled. "Would you like your other present now?"

"My other present?"

"I thought I'd save it for when we were alone, in private."

"What is it?" she asked wide-eyed.

Such a set-up in the hands of Lysander would probably have continued with a call of, "Have a look at this!" and the presentation of something best left tucked away in a loincloth. But this was Philo. He reached under the bed and produced a box tied up with a pink ribbon.

Teretia undid the bow and opened the lid. "Oh, Philo!" she gasped, and gently lifted out the box's content.

It was a terracotta oil lamp in the shape of a boar's head. Its wide-splayed nostrils acted as the wick holes.

"I saw you didn't have a boar one," said Philo, glancing at the basket in the corner where they had packed away Teretia's animal-shaped oil lamp collection.

She had claimed that now she was married she would put away her girlish past times but Philo had caught her on more than one occasion gazing wistfully at particularly fine examples of the craft in the local shops.

"It's wonderful," she gushed. "And I don't have a boar one! How clever of you."

She threw her arms around his neck. When she released him, she offered Philo a smile of such warmth, such love that it wiped out all his anxieties regarding Lysander's interest in Verenia.

* * *

Epaphroditus' Parentalia began with him opening a single eye. It swivelled over the red décor, fearing that if it lingered on the garish colour, it might bring on another headache. There was something to be said for the plain greyish walls of the slave complex. He was in his own quarters at the palace, which was promising. When he opened the other eye, the anticipated blinding shot of pain to his head did not materialise.

Seeing him awake, a slave appeared by the side of the bed armed with a glass of cordial. Epaphroditus sat up and took it from his hands with gratitude. The cool liquid went a long way to descaling his tongue from the previous night's indulgence.

Had he? He turned his head to the right. Yes, he had. Lying beside him was a red-haired girl. Searching his memory, he finally managed to place her as one of the empress' dressing attendants. Penelope, was it? Or Phaisne? Something like that.

The slave whose name began with a P was awake.

"Happy Parentalia," she said, sitting up in bed, letting the sheet fall to expose a cleavage that was more nipple than breast.

Gods, how old was she? He'd say young enough to be his daughter. But Epaphroditus had reached the age where practically everyone was young enough to be his daughter. Even the empress. It was deeply dispiriting.

As was the girl clambering across his lap, thrusting her slight mounds into his chest and squirming her hips about like some Persian dancer.

Epaphroditus gently lifted her off.

"I have to get to work."

She snuggled into him. "I could please you any way you like. I'm very good," she purred. "I could bring you to your pleasure quicker than you can slip your sandals on."

Such confidence in her abilities gained his interest. He reached over and rolled a nipple between his thumb and finger. It hardened instantly, which was pleasing. Placing a hand between her thighs, he discovered a satisfactory wetness. Ah well, if she really wanted it, he was happy to oblige. And of course, secure her the desired promotion that undoubtedly lurked behind her lustfulness.

"We'll have a competition," he told her. "My slave will count the time it takes you to bring me to my peak. Then, likewise, the time it takes me to bring you to yours."

"And the winner gets?" she asked.

"Whatever they desire."

He made sure she won. He kept her on the brink of climax moving his tongue away when he saw the muscles in her thighs tense. As the slave counted past 257, he returned to that point and brought her to a shuddering conclusion at the count of sixty-nine.

After she'd recovered her breath she claimed her prize, a promotion to keeper of the empress' bracelets. A deal he sealed by mounting her from behind, his hands pinching at those tiny little breasts.

* * *

He left her dressing, a smirk of satisfaction evident across her features. He made his way to his office reflecting that Penelope or Phaisne had been rather pleasing. Perhaps he'd keep her on as a mistress. It would be interesting to test her skills and find out exactly what she was willing to do to become keeper of the empress' necklaces.

He found his desk was, as ever, overflowing with correspondence.

"I put the one from Vitellius on top, sir," Talos told him.

"Thank you."

He cracked open the seal and unrolled it. Having digested its contents, he rolled it back up again and placed it on his desk.

"Sir?" queried Talos.

"It is Vitellius' response to the emperor's offer of a comfortable retirement in a location of his choice."

"What does he say, sir?"

"He offers the emperor a comfortable retirement in a location of his choice."

"Oh."

"Oh, indeed," sighed Epaphroditus. "Why don't you knock off for the day. Enjoy a little of Parentalia."

"Really, sir?"

"Really," replied Epaphroditus waving him out.

With Talos departed, he picked up Vitellius' scroll. Had he really expected Vitellius to take up their offer? To lay down his arms and army? To slip quietly away to some Mediterranean island to live out his days?

No, he hadn't. But he'd held onto a tiny smidgeon of hope that he might, he realised. And with that refusal, that standing of his ground that he was the true emperor and Otho an imposter, that smidgeon of hope withered. For he already had Valens and Caecina's responses to the same offer.

Valens' reply had come via the Praetorian Guard. He'd promised them a generous bounty when he reached Rome if they swore their allegiance to Vitellius now. Luckily for Otho, the Guard retained a fierce loyalty to him and had brought the message straight to Epaphroditus. The Praetorian tribune Antonius Honoratus had handed it to him with a look of disgust on his face.

Caecina's response had been a straightforward rejection of Otho. Vitellius was the only true emperor, properly ratified by the legions of Rome. Which showed a distinct lack of knowledge of the proper procedures. But then, what did procedures matter when you had 30,000 men marching behind you?

That was the new reality: men with armies fighting it out. Just like Caesar and Pompey, Marius and Sulla, and all those other republican generals who had waged war throughout the empire and nearly destroyed Rome.

Though he knew it to be pointless, Epaphroditus couldn't let go of the thought that had Otho ascended to the emperorship in a more orderly fashion, none of this would be happening. Becoming emperor by way of such a bloody coup and by having murdered the previous holder of the title gave Aulus Vitellius of all people the moral high ground. And wasn't he bloody loving it! Pah!

Epaphroditus threw the scroll across his office. It landed a few feet from his desk. A failure that for some reason had him overwhelmed with rage: at Vitellius, at Valens, at Caecina, at

Otho, at his damn self. So he picked up his paperweight and lobbed that too. It hit the door with a satisfying thwacking thump.

Talos stuck his head round. "Sir?" he asked, noticeably concerned.

"I'm fine. Go enjoy the festival." He bounced his other paperweight in his hand, eager to thwack it at the door too: surely that would relieve him of this rage?

"Oh, sir, I meant to say, your wife dropped by."

The paperweight fell from his hand. It thudded onto the floor, narrowly missing his toes.

"Dite? Dite was here?"

"She wanted to know if you intended to participate in Parentalia. She said she couldn't wait for you as she had lots to organise. So I promised to pass it on."

Epaphroditus' mind hit whirl mode. This was promising, wasn't it? She wanted to see him. That had to be good. Had she forgiven him?

He glanced down at his very ordinary tunic.

"I need to get changed," he decided. "Talos, get my chamberlain to eject a girl from my quarters. I want her gone by the time I get there."

TWENTY

Epaphroditus tried to keep a check on his temper as he paced the atrium. It was outrageous. He was being forced to wait here, in his own home, by his own slaves.

Portius, his doorkeeper, had squirmed with embarrassment as he'd told him, "The mistress bids you wait in the atrium until she is ready to receive you."

He had responded to this with a withering glare that promised the doorkeeper a hard thrashing. Otherwise, he made no comment. He would play Aphrodite's game for the time being.

Parentalia had always been of special meaning for them. Epaphroditus and Aphrodite used the festival to honour their son Iugarthus, who'd died shortly before his sixteenth birthday. None of his siblings had met Iugarthus. Yet they talked eagerly of their unknown brother and he remained central to the family's life.

He was certainly central to Epaphroditus. He held onto his memories of his son as uniquely precious. Time had not lessened his grief as everyone had promised him it would. There was a hole in his centre that would never be filled. The only person who truly understood this was Aphrodite.

He had just balanced a buttock on the edge of the gurgling fountain when the door opened. In walked his wife, as beautiful as ever in a dark blue gown. Surrounding her were a gaggle of children who ran forward with cries of "Daddy!" and threw themselves at their father.

Epaphroditus gathered as many as he could onto his lap. Tickling Julia until she squealed. Kissing the older children on their heads.

"Daddy," said Julia, cuddling into Epaphroditus. "Mummy says we're going to see Iugarthus."

"That's right," he said, hugging her close and putting his other arm around Perella who snuggled into him. "We're going to take a picnic for Iugarthus."

"Does he like pickled eggs?" asked Perella. "Because we packed pickled eggs."

"I am sure he will."

"If he doesn't," worried Perella, "we do have some grain and some wine."

"Iugarthus always liked pickled eggs, didn't he, Dite?"

Aphrodite extracted Perella from her father's arms. "He used to eat five for breakfast."

"Five!?" gasped Perella. "Didn't he get sick?"

"He had a very strong stomach," smiled Epaphroditus.

Iugarthus had the oddest diet. Yet, he never put on weight, remaining slim and handsome until his death. Epaphroditus looked to Aphrodite in an attempt to share the memory but she looked away.

Clapping her hands together, she said, "Come on children, let's go."

* * *

They walked in an ill-ordered gang towards the city gates. Epaphroditus carried Julia on his back. His next-eldest daughters, Claudia and Perella, whined that they wanted Daddy to carry them too. Alongside him walked his son Pollus, nearing fourteen, tall and gangly. Faustina lagged behind, dragging her feet and moaning, to her mother's increasing irritation.

Epaphroditus moved alongside his wife. He smiled at Rufus, the youngest of their brood, who was held in her arms and enjoying all the gaiety. "Where's Silvia?"

Silvia was their eldest daughter.

"Martinus' family sent a note yesterday asking her to accompany them to honour his shade," Aphrodite informed him.

Epaphroditus frowned. "I thought they'd cut her off?"

Martinus' family were an old patrician family but poor. Which was why they had deigned to marry their son to the daughter of former slaves. On Martinus' death they had slung their grieving daughter-in-law back to her family, making it clear how little they valued her.

"They had, but then they had good links with Galba. Now with Otho emperor, they find themselves out in the cold. But then how could they know such a man as Otho would ever be emperor?" she scorned. "So they need connections." And here she looked directly at Epaphroditus with a firm stare.

"They're trying to ingratiate themselves with me via Silvia?"

"It would appear so," she confirmed through gritted teeth. "Of course, Silvia genuinely believes in their concern for her."

"That is not my fault," responded Epaphroditus to the anger he heard in her voice.

"No, nothing ever is, is it?" She glared at him, tucking a strand of hair behind her ear.

"Dite," he pleaded, trying to take her hand.

She snatched it away. "Don't Dite me. I am not your Dite. Not anymore."

Then she yelled back over her shoulder, "FAUSTINA! Stop dawdling!" cutting off his reply.

* * *

So here it was, situated just outside the city walls. Iugathus' tomb. A marble villa in miniature, the edifices of columns carved into the stone. The door was heavy oak with a plaque that promised a dire death for anyone who dared to damage the monument. Beneath this was a large bronze knocker.

Epaphroditus nodded to Pollus. "Go on. We don't want to take Iugarthus by surprise."

Pollus gave the door a sharp echoing tap. Next, he twisted the handle, creaking open the door. Two slaves rushed forward with lit torches, which they took inside and placed in brackets. The family walked in together to the square space. Stone benches were situated down either side and at the far end was a shelf on which stood an urn. Above the urn was an inscription. It read:

> For the spirits departed of Iugarthus, employed in the Imperial Treasury.
>
> He lived 15 years and 300 days. His promise unfulfilled, he rests here. This was dedicated by his devoted parents Tiberius Claudius Epaphroditus, Imperial Freedman, and Aphrodite Claudia, Imperial Freedwoman.

Epaphroditus, on reading these simple stark words, felt a familiar pang. He glanced to Aphrodite and saw a similar passive expression on her face. The children amused themselves. Perella the worrier taking charge of unpacking the picnic. Julia and Claudia engaging themselves in a game of chase that took them in delighted circles around the exterior of the tomb. Faustina plonked herself down on the bench with a groan. Pollus sat beside her, engaged in conversation with one of the slaves, a lad around his own age.

Epaphroditus reached across and took hold of Aphrodite's hand. This time she did not resist.

"He would have been thirty," she said quietly. "He would have been free. He would have been married. He would have had children."

"We would have housed them in the north wing of the house," Epaphroditus continued. "So they could have privacy but still join the family for meals."

"Their youngest would have been a good playmate for Rufus," said Aphrodite sadly, cuddling the boy to her.

"We would have walked to work together each day." And here his throat caught.

That was the worst of it. To lose their smiling, charming teenage son was terrible. But to lose all that he would have been, left them inconsolable. Epaphroditus felt the tears sting his eyes. His wife let go of his hand. She carried Rufus over to Faustina and handed the infant to her before returning to her husband and throwing her arms around him. They clung to each other, the only two people in the world who understood the searing pain of that grief.

TWENTY-ONE

They walked back together. Epaphroditus with his arm around his wife, she resting her head on his shoulder. Perella, happy with the way the picnic had gone, had been entrusted to pour the wine libation onto the ground. She had enacted this with such careful precision that Faustina had cried out, "For Hades' three-headed dog! Just pour it out!" This earned her a slap across the head from her father and a frank admonishment from her mother.

Julia, Claudia, and Rufus had tired themselves out and were being carried back by the slaves. Pollus shuffled along, wondering how he could sneak out to the next morning's chariot race. While Faustina grumbled her way back home.

As they headed through the city gate, a great crowd passed them in the opposite direction. They were following a chain that snaked up to a small hillock. Aphrodite puzzled at the queue of happy festival goers. "Where are they going? What's on that hill? There's no tombs there."

Epaphroditus raised his eyebrows as he figured it out. "It's where we cremated Nero."

A queue of civilians honouring Nero. If Otho had any sense, he'd be down here with a casket of wine and heartfelt lamentations, thought Epaphroditus. When he got back to the palace he would— Aphrodite pushed him away and set off at a quicker pace.

"What?" Epaphroditus called after her. She ignored him. Shaking off his hand when he jogged alongside her and attempted to gain her attention. "What did I do?"

Eyes fixed straight ahead, she told him, "I am not doing this in front of the children."

They continued the journey in silence, Epaphroditus utterly perplexed by her anger. Once home she stormed into their bedroom. Epaphroditus followed her.

"You couldn't resist it, could you?" she stormed at him.

"What? What am I meant to have done?"

"On this day? How could you?"

"How could I what?"

"I'm not stupid. I saw your face when you saw those people queuing to pay their respects to Nero. You were plotting weren't you? You were thinking, how can Otho take advantage of the situation? How can we use this?"

He didn't bother to deny it. Aphrodite was indeed not stupid.

"This is our day." She pointed a finger at him. "This is Iugarthus' day. Our son. Our beautiful, beautiful son. And you're thinking of work. How could you? But then it is so typical of you. Putting work before your wife. Before your family."

"That is not true. I have always put you first. Always," he insisted, raising his voice to match hers.

"Two days after the ides, did you put me first? No, you did not. You ran to Otho's side and left your family unprotected."

"That's rubbish! I armed the slaves. You were perfectly safe. I made sure of that."

She laughed, a hard bitter scoff. "Geminius the gardener armed with a hoe? How safe would we have been if Galba had brought the legions in? If Otho had been defeated? They'd have hunted down all his associates and their families. How safe would we have been then?"

"That didn't happen. It wouldn't have happened. Everything was planned, thought out."

"Of course. That'll be why it took three days to remove all the corpses from the forum where your daughter's husband was butchered!"

It was true, he hadn't thought about Silvia or Martinus. He should have done but all had been madness. His key thoughts had been on safeguarding Aphrodite and ensuring Otho's enthused supporters did not destroy the entire city. And it was because she was right, and because it was true, that he was stung into uttering these words that should never have been spoken:

"But Silvia's not my daughter, is she?"

Aphrodite's face fell. He would have apologised instantly, for he knew when he had crossed a line, but her mouth formed an "o" as she stared at something behind him. Epaphroditus swirled round to see Silvia, returned from mourning Martinus, frozen by the door. Her hand went to her mouth and then she ran. Epaphroditus heard her cracked sobs as she departed.

Aphrodite pushed past him calling, "Silvia, Silvia!"

Epaphroditus grabbed her arm. Aphrodite shot him a look of pure venom.

"Get out!" she hissed. "Just get out!"

He felt every particle of her anger. "Dite, please."

"Get out, get out, get out!" she screamed at him, prising off his fingers and pursuing her daughter.

Epaphroditus ran a hand over his head. O gods. O gods above! Exiting the bedroom, he was confronted by his six other children gazing at him with wide eyes. Claudia and Julia burst into simultaneous tears, which set off baby Rufus and pushed the sensitive Perella into hysterics. Pollus and Faustina merely looked shocked. Epaphroditus paused, contemplated sitting them all down and explaining. Deciding that he couldn't face it, he walked past them all without comment.

TWENTY-TWO

Epaphroditus stormed through the grand atrium of the old palace, swatting away Praetorians and announcers as he progressed. He was going to get drunk. Gloriously, stupefyingly drunk. And then he would have a woman. Any woman from Felix's catalogue. He didn't care who. Just anybody. Anybody rather than be alone.

So determined was he on this task that he swept straight past Antonia Caenis.

"Epaphroditus!"

He stopped mid-march down the corridor and spun on his heels. "Caenis?"

She smiled, walking towards him arms outstretched.

Breaking their embrace, Epaphroditus commented, "I thought you were in the East with that man of yours."

Epaphroditus had never understood Caenis' affection for Vespasian. He'd never understood Vespasian, truth be told. A man who spoke his mind no matter the company or the consequences to himself. He'd even got himself deported from Nero's tour of Greece for the unforgivable act of falling asleep during one of the emperor's recitals. Epaphroditus had assumed it was Caenis' influence that had spared his life.

"I was eastward but now I'm home. You look," she paused to consider, while Epaphroditus squirmed under her enquiring gaze, "troubled," she decided.

"These are troubling times. Did the news reach you of the latest twist? Vitellius has somehow got himself declared emperor. It's the talk of the city. The wags say he's only doing it to get access to the palace kitchens. Apparently they have no talent for roasting peacock in Germania."

"Flavius filled me in."

"Of course. He is a very thorough man."

"He also filled me in on your troubles." The tone was sympathetic, kind, caring. A raw Epaphroditus bristled.

"Flavius is misinformed. The only troubles I have are fifty thousand fewer troops than Aulus bloody Vitellius!"

Caenis took his arm gently. "Come, let us take a walk in the gardens and catch up."

He let her lead him to the south side of the Palatine Hill. To a forgotten courtyard overgrown with ivy, a fountain producing a sad trickle of water into a basin thick with slime.

"We really should notify the gardeners about this place," said Epaphroditus, picking at the yellow lichen that spotted the stone bench on which they sat.

"I rather like it like this. It has a certain romantic charm. Do you remember the first time I brought you here?"

"Of course. You told me you would sponsor me through school. That you would mentor and aid me in my chosen career in any way you could."

"And what did you say to such a considered gift?"

Epaphroditus winced.

"You said, 'Does it involve sex?'" She gave a cackle of merriment. Much like the one she'd expelled at the time, all those years back.

"In my defence, I was at an age when sex dominated all of my thoughts. It was before I discovered politics."

"I've been honouring Parentalia," she told him. "I visited Flavia Domitillia."

"Vespasian's wife?"

"He asked me to. I was happy to oblige. I always liked her. Don't look so surprised. She was quite a suitable wife for Vespasian. I'll admit when he came to me and told me he must marry, I felt a pang. But of course that is life. Men marry. He couldn't marry me, of course. But of all the people he could have married, I was glad it was Flavia Domitillia."

"What did she think of you?"

"She liked me. She always said that her realm was the private sphere: the production of heirs and the management of their home. But she preferred that I aided Vespasian in his public life. She was not of that cloth, so she said."

"Would that my wife were so understanding."

"Is there no hope of a reconciliation?"

"An hour ago I would have said yes." He gave a sigh. "I've really messed up. She despises me."

"I'm sure that's not the case. Parentalia is a strange festival. Though we commemorate, we cannot help but mourn at the same time. It can bring up some forgotten emotions. Raw emotions."

It certainly had for Epaphroditus. He felt as if his skin had been scrubbed off. "I used to come here with my son," he told Caenis. "For man-to-man chats, well, man-to-boy. He never made it to man."

Caenis placed her hand over his. "And what would you tell him?"

"I told him to appreciate everyone, no matter how high, no matter how lowly."

"That's rather a lovely sentiment."

He'd left out the final coda. He recalled it now, along with Iugarthus, his clever, handsome boy, sitting right where Caenis was now.

"What do you mean, papa?" Iugarthus had asked.

Epaphroditus had told him, "Because everyone, absolutely everyone, will be of use to you one day."

Antonia Caenis had taught him that back when he had been Iugarthus' age.

She spoke now. "How fares this new emperor?"

"He is the best I've ever worked for." Then, seeing Caenis' slightly sceptical eyes, added, "No, really. He listens and he acts. He will be a bonus to Rome. To the empire."

"Yes, but for how long?"

Their eyes met briefly. Epaphroditus looked away, fearing his emotions were all too easy to read.

"Otho does know just how bad the situation is, doesn't he?" she pressed. When Epaphroditus did not respond, she continued, "I've never been one for overwhelming an emperor or empress with information. There is much they have no need of knowing. But there are some truths that need to be laid out."

There was a pause.

"I know," admitted Epaphroditus finally.

"It would be best if it came from you."

Epaphroditus looked up, and there was no hiding his emotion now as he replied, "I know."

TWENTY-THREE

Otho considered himself a pious man. He knew he had much to thank the gods for. And boy, had they got him out of some tight spots in the past! So, although there was much he'd rather be doing on Parentalia, he instead found himself on an inclement Capitol Hill watching as a Vestal Virgin made offerings by the tomb of Tarpeia.

Tarpeia was the daughter of a Roman general, back when Rome had kings. She had approached the Sabine enemy, offering them entry to the city in exchange for their gold. Instead, disgusted by her treachery, they had thrown her from the rock that now bore her name. It was from this cliff face that the Romans still threw traitors to their deaths, eighty feet below. As someone who had very recently been accused of treason, Otho was finding being this close to the drop a not-altogether pleasant experience.

So it was with some relief that the imperial party moved onto the Temple of Jupiter for the usual sacrifices. This party had been carefully selected by his secretary to visually represent Otho's government. It included enough elderly patricians to suggest Otho's respect for the wisdom of age, a smattering of men who'd held high posts under Nero to show Otho's desire to continue the Julio-Claudians' work, and Salvius, to show there was an heir apparent. Completing the picture was Statilia Messalina, currently linked onto Otho's arm providing the suggestion of a dynasty in the making.

Stood on the steps of the temple, Otho gave her a smile. Statilia smiled back, giving the crowds a salute and moving closer to the emperor; a move that caused a wave of cheers. She was, thought Otho fondly, exactly the sort of woman he should marry.

It had been rare in Otho's zingy life that, whilst knowing the correct path, he'd actually followed it. Rather, he'd start off on the path, veer into a flower bed, crash through a hedge, and appear floating in a fountain blowing water out of his mouth. Not this time. This time he was going to do the right thing. The honourable thing. The sort of thing a good emperor would do.

Glancing over his shoulder, he caught sight of a particular member of the party he'd added to the guest list personally. A dazzlingly glorious figure draped in a green gown of shimmering material, with silver sandals and a fur-lined cloak. A beautiful creature with kohl-ringed eyes behind long, dark lashes at odds with her red hair but somehow complementing it. Adding to the allure were those plump, red lips. Very kissable lips. The tip of a pink tongue poking between them, adding moisture, a certain wetness to their surface—"O gods!"

"Marcus!"

An elbow to his ribs awakened the emperor. "Yes, my dear?"

"It is time for your speech," said Statilia, glancing behind and seeing that creature dressed up like some tarty freedman's wife, make-up plastered on like the first layer of a fresco. No doubt to disguise its distinctly masculine jaw.

The thing gave her a beautiful smile. Statilia glared back. The sort of glare she'd once used on Nymphidius Sabinus when he'd suggested she marry the aged Galba. The sort of glare Medusa used to turn men to stone. The sort of glare Juno gave Jupiter every time he arrived home with yet another lame excuse for his lateness while picking swan's feathers from between his teeth.

Would that Statilia had Juno's power to turn that thing into a weasel, as the great goddess had done to Galanthis! Instead, remembering Calvia's words, she sucked up her anger, leaned into Otho and whispered in his ear. Clearly it was something very pleasing. For when the surprise had left his face, he full-on beamed and whispered something back in her ear that brought a flush of red from the base of her neck right up to her cheeks. She giggled, girlishly.

From five paces back came an anguished screech. Mina, on empress-protecting duty, pushed a shoulder in front of the wailing Sporus.

"Oh no you don't," she warned.

"Don't what?"

"I know that look. You're going to fake a faint. A very unconvincing swoon to the ground in the hope that Otho will scoop you up into his arms."

Sporus stuck out a petulant lip. "And what if I am! What's it to you?"

"I am the empress' bodyguard. And if I know you, and the gods will declare that I do, O half boy whom I knew when he was fully intact boy, you will aim your swoon straight into her to push her out of the way. Which might well result in an injury to the empress. So I am not allowing it."

"You used to be so much fun. I suppose I shall just have to stand here and radiate attraction. I'm very good at that. Drop me into some eastern king's harem and I'll be his chosen partner. Every. Single. Night."

On the final "t", he bolted for it, leaving Mina just a split second to decide whether to go for her whip. Her mentor, Straton, had taught her never to whip in anger, for you would never hit your target. You must be in control, measured, calm. He'd mentioned nothing as to whether it was acceptable to whip your oldest friend to stop him wrecking a very carefully choreographed religious ceremony. It was the sort of question Mina would have very much liked to ask him. Straton-less she had but a beat to decide. One calming breath then—

Sporus was surprisingly nimble, even in strappy heeled sandals. He was within swooning distance of Statilia Messalina when—crack! The thong of the whip wrapped itself round one of his heels.

If he'd had a chance to speak, Sporus would have mouthed a very filthy line on what would happen to Mina if her whip should damage his favourite pair of shoes. Instead, he was pulled to the ground.

Alerted by the sound that even a slight eunuch makes when he hits a stone floor while wearing enough jewellery to cover a petite Babylonian princess (less of a thud and more akin to the noise a drunk party guest makes when he careers into the tambourine players), the imperial couple turned round.

Otho looked down upon the prone figure at his feet. Sporus raised his head (wig now slightly awry) and smiled his very best, knee-quaking, emperor-seducing beam of teeth. The smile cracked into a yelp as Statilia brought down her heel on the back of his hand.

"You bitch!" squeaked Sporus.

He grabbed hold of her ankle and opened his mouth to bite down hard, when he was removed by Mina with the help of Honoratus and a couple of his men.

As Sporus was dragged down the temple steps, Statilia made sure she gave him a nice cheery wave. This action produced a series of insults from the eunuch that had the front five rows of the crowd gasping in shock.

* * *

"Well, that is quite a battle!" exclaimed Caenis.

"Hmm, isn't it," murmured Epaphroditus.

They'd found a good spot at the very front of the crowd by the bottom of the temple steps. Epaphroditus had been impressed by just how well Otho wore the purple tunic. Just how well-suited he was for the garland pinned to his toupee.

Even from a distance, his natural charm was apparent. The crowd had responded to it, helped by the presence of Statilia Messalina. Though Epaphroditus had never particularly gelled with Statilia, due to a personal dispute between them concerning his Esquiline home, he couldn't deny she'd been a fine empress. She would again inhabit that position if events went Otho's way and that damned eunuch could be contained.

"I'm tempted to sell the creature."

"Sporus? You wouldn't."

"I would. He's been nothing but trouble his whole life."

Caenis grinned. "Well, of course, he's a eunuch! I've never encountered a trouble-free eunuch in all my years in the palace."

"I'd sell him tomorrow."

Caenis linked onto his arm. "You could try but I doubt the emperor would let you."

Unfortunately, Epaphroditus suspected, Caenis was entirely correct in this analysis.

They were making their way back to the palace when a gasp from a nearby woman caught Epaphroditus' attention. The woman was nudging at her companion, urging him to look upwards. The secretary followed their gaze to the roof of the temple and the statue that adorned it. It was of Victory standing in a chariot, her hair flowing behind her to suggest great movement. Epaphroditus couldn't see what was so attracting the woman's gaze: it looked exactly as it always had.

"The reins," the woman insisted to her companion. "Look!"

Epaphroditus took a second look. Victory was standing in her chariot alright but the reins that were usually clasped in her hands, had vanished.

"It's a sign from the gods," the woman continued agitatedly. "It's a bad omen."

"It's no such thing," Caenis assured Epaphroditus. "It's a statue in need of repair, that's all."

He knew that. But it didn't matter what he knew. It mattered what the people thought. Seeing the woman's horrified expression, he felt sure she'd be passing on this tale to all she met: that Victory was no longer being steered.

TWENTY-FOUR

"It's not fair!" wailed Sporus as Mina escorted him down the corridor.

"Oh for Hera's girdle, stop your moaning! It is so completely your own fault. If you hadn't gone for the empress then I wouldn't have had to restrain you and you would be at the Parentalia feast."

She'd debated tying him up in chains like a slave at the market to prevent further escapades. In the end, she gained Sporus' compliance extremely easily by pointing out the heel to his sandal was starting to wobble and there was a stain on his dress. Horrified, he'd fully concurred with accompanying her back to the palace.

"And if it hadn't been for that bitch the emperor would—" began Sporus but was unable to finish. Mina grabbed his arm and pulled him back round the corner they'd just taken.

"What was that for?" squeaked the eunuch.

Mina pressed a finger against his lips. "Sshh."

Such an action was far too subtle to silence him. Behind the finger he enquired, "What is it? And gods, do you need a manicure!" Holding up her finger for inspection, he added, "Look how brittle that nail is, it needs shaping and polishing. Ooh, I have the perfect red varnish that will totally suit you."

"Will you shut up!" hissed Mina, back pressed flat against the wall, daring a darting glance round. "He's still there."

"Who is?"

"There's a man."

"And?"

"And what is he doing here? He's not a guard. He's not in white, so he's not a slave. He's not the emperor's family because they're all still at the temple. So who is he? And what is he doing unescorted outside the empress' private rooms?"

Sporus applied his meagre intellect to the situation. After a pause long enough to squeeze in a good stanza of Virgil, he said, "Maybe he is a friend of that cow, come to visit her from far away, which is why he doesn't know its Parentalia."

"Or maybe he's a Vitellian spy."

Sporus' heavily kohled eyes widened. "In the palace?" he squeaked.

"In the palace."

"The fiend! Mina, you have to kill him. He's plotting against my beloved Otho. He must die. Very horribly."

"Or I could demand he tell us what his business is," was Mina's milder suggestion.

"And then kill him."

Mina patted him on the shoulder. "We'll see. You'd better stay here. It could be dangerous." She unhooked her whip from her belt, uncoiling it to its full length. "If I shout for help, run and get someone. Not a Praetorian. Someone useful like Felix."

Sporus nodded, imbuing his nod with what he felt was additional gravitas. This could well be the last conversation he and Mina shared. On that thought, Sporus felt there was something that needed to be said. Something that needed clearing up. A final matter that required resolution before his dearest friend in all the world faced off against the evil Vitellian spy.

"Mina," he began solemnly.

"Yes, Sporus."

"You know that pinky dress the empress gave you after you flattened those two Praetorians to entertain her?"

"Er, yes."

Sporus took her hand gravely. "It doesn't suit you. I thought you should know."

Mina's lips twisted upwards. "Stay here."

As a surprise attack, it was undoubtedly successful. Though perhaps in retrospect, Mina accepted, she probably should have given him more time to respond to her barked command of, "State your business now!"

The red-tunic-attired man, taken unawares, was visibly shocked by Mina's sudden apparition. His mouth opened and closed without speech. At which point Mina let crack her whip. The man moved swiftly from the vertical to the horizontal with a smack on the marble floor that had Sporus wincing on his behalf (from a safe distance).

Again retrospectively, Mina realised the fall had probably winded him. Thus, it was unlikely he would have been capable of supplying answers to the yelled questions the shouty woman standing with one foot pressed on his throat clearly expected. All in all, with hindsight, Mina felt she'd got the tiniest bit overexcited. Something Straton would never have done.

"ARTEMINA! Get off him!"

Mina swivelled her foot, causing an agonised gargle from her captive, to see a fuming Cassandra.

"Get off him right now!"

"He's a Vitellian spy," provided Sporus, popping round the corner.

"No, he's not," said Cassandra, helping the man to his feet. "He's my boyfriend."

TWENTY-FIVE

"Boyfriend?"

"Yes," replied Cassandra with monumental patience. This was the fifteenth time she'd been asked this same question.

They were, all four of them, holed up in Cassandra's and Mina's room. Sporus sat cross-legged on the floor between the two girls. Publius (for that was the boyfriend's name) was sat on the chair drinking a calming cordial. He appeared overwhelmed by both his surroundings and his companions. His eyes darted nervously about, settling on Sporus then flitting away. Yet to be initiated into the mysteries of the eunuch, what Publius saw was a well dressed, clearly very wealthy lady sitting on the floor of a slave's room. It was incongruous and deeply puzzling.

"Why didn't you tell me you had a boyfriend?"

"Because it was no concern of yours."

"Surely it's a concern of mine. What if I'd returned later? I'd have walked straight in on you two at it."

"It would have scarred her mentally for the rest of her life," provided Sporus.

"We were going out to mark Parentalia."

"We can still do that, Cassandra," interjected Publius. "The day isn't over yet."

149

Mina raised an eyebrow at her roommate. It's high arch intimidating Publius back to his cordial.

"Quite," said Cassandra. "I'll get my cloak."

"We'll come with you," said Sporus. "So we can all get to know each other better. We need to know everything, and I mean everything, about you, Publius. We need to assess if you are worthy of our Cassie."

"I would hope I was—"

"No," said Cassandra fastening up her cloak.

"Oh come on, Cassie, it'll be fun!" persisted Sporus.

"No, I don't believe it will be."

"Oh go on."

"Yes, do go on," said Mina, fixing her roommate with a stare. "I think it will be jolly fun. You can commemorate your dead while Sporus and I grill Publius. And the empress doesn't get to hear that you faked a stomach bug so you could spend the day with your lurverrrr," rolling her eyes at that final drawn-out word.

Cassandra blinked first, a low moan forming in her throat. "I don't suppose I have a choice, do I?"

"Absolutely not," beamed Mina.

* * *

Getting to know Publius was easily achieved. There was not much to know. Not much of any interest that is. He was the proprietor of a bookshop on the Aventine Hill. The shop had been his father's and his father's before him, so Publius felt duty-bound to keep it running though it was a constant struggle. Sporus, despite never having read a book in his entire life, gave a sympathetic "Mmm."

Publius had been undertaking some research on the competition, those bookshops in the Argentum that were always teeming with customers, to see what he could learn, when he'd first seen Cassandra.

"She was ordering a copy of Livy. So I knew right there she was a clever lady." He smiled at the clever lady, who to Mina's surprise produced a flush on those usually pale cheeks.

Apparently they'd got into a heated discussion of Livy versus Polybius, discovered they had much in common (a general dullness? a lack of humour? wondered Mina uncharitably), and from there a deep friendship had formed.

Mina managed to extract that Publius had been excused military service on account of his feet. They looked pretty normal feet to Mina. According to Publius, they were no good for the type of marching the army insisted upon, and he would only have been a hindrance to them. Coward, thought Mina. Though an understandable one. Publius' meek personality would have been crushed in a day by a centurion barking commands.

All in all, Publius was exactly the sort of uninteresting, intellectual, book-obsessed man that Cassandra would end up with. Though Mina had not anticipated the moles. He was very mole-y—brown spots dotted across his cheeks like some careless fresco painter had accidentally given him a quick spray from his brush. One large blob of brown had taken refuge from further assault by the side of his nose.

And his hair was annoyingly neat. There was no style to it at all. His clothes were similarly nondescript: a brown sensible tunic with practical belt, no patterns or garish shades. Nothing to indicate any form of personality.

As a couple, they were perfectly suited. No doubt when Cassandra was freed they'd get married. Her no-nonsense common sense would turn his struggling bookshop into the most respectable and frequented bibliophiles' paradise in Rome. Perhaps they'd open a second or third bookshop. Mina could see it all now, Publius being just the right side of mushy to present a project for Cassandra.

Urgh, thought Mina as she made her way through the darkened palace. There was one very important task she needed to complete before retiring for the night. Thus, she had left before ascertaining whether Publius would give Cassandra a farewell kiss. No doubt Sporus would fill her in tomorrow with his own embellishments.

She stopped at her destination, the shrine to the Lares that was dug out of a singular wall in the slave complex. A small shrine but that was all that was needed. There were no tombs for Mina to visit and offer food and drink to her dead. She had no idea where Felix had placed the ashes of her friends: of Alex, of Daphne, of Straton, of everyone she knew who had perished in the last year since Nero fell. All she had was this shrine.

She laid three objects in the shrine: a square of blanket, a studded leather knuckleduster, and a wooden elephant.

The blanket had been knitted by Daphne, her former roommate, for the baby she was carrying. The baby had never been born. She had died along with her mother during Otho's coup.

Straton had been the owner of the studded knuckleduster. Mina recalled with a smile the time he'd used it to aid their escape from the palace dungeons the night they'd rescued Philo.

The elephant was one that Alex had carved himself, for he'd been a talented carpenter. Honoratus, the Praetorian tribune, had wanted to adopt him as his son. Alex had a future. A promise of great things to come. That he had never lived to escape his life as a messenger slave. That he had never been Honoratus' son. That he was not around to offer comfort and gossip to Sporus and her. These were all things that Mina struggled to believe.

She rubbed at the tears that formed in her eyes. Her voice trembling, she recited a prayer to all of their shades.

TWENTY-SIX

With Caenis' words echoing round his head, Epaphroditus reluctantly went to find the emperor. He found Otho relaxing in one of the rooms of the new palace. It was a pleasant, cosy room. Black walls overlaid with red squares. Each held a minature scene of such delicacy, they compelled you to get up close. Once there, you discovered the marble panels beneath. Only when you inspected them further did they reveal themselves to be also painted, so perfect was the effect.

Otho sat enveloped in a purple dressing gown. His feet propped up on a stool as a slave washed his feet.

"Ah, Epaphroditus. I know exactly what you're going to say."

The secretary froze in the doorway.

"You're going to say that the events at the temple earlier are exactly what happens when one involves oneself with eunuchs."

"Actually," began Epaphroditus, shooing the foot-washing slave away and sitting himself down on the stool, "I would have merely phrased it as 'damn eunuch'."

"I know, I know. I'm a fool for a well-turned ankle."

"Marcus."

"Now I know I'm in trouble if you're dropping my official titles."

"Imperial Majesty," he corrected himself. "As your advisor, I advise you to stand down as emperor."

Otho blinked. "Stop being emperor?"

"It's not too late. The senate haven't officially handed over all the powers. You can step aside without any loss of honour. You can say you were holding the position temporarily to ensure the city was safe."

"It's not so desperate yet, surely," protested Otho. "I know Vitellius turned us down but there is still Valens and Caecina. They're the ones with the power. You said so yourself."

"I had a letter from Valens some days back," admitted Epaphroditus. "He is not for turning. And Caecina is on the move south again."

"Days ago? I'm pretty sure that's the sort of thing I should know about, being emperor and all. Does Celsus know?"

"Not yet. I was," he stared at the floor briefly before looking up again. "I was hoping that Vitellius' answer would be different. Let him have it, Marcus. Let Vitellius be emperor if he so desires it."

Otho got to his feet. "But this is what we planned, you and I."

"I didn't think it would go so far. We didn't know about Vitellius when we started this venture."

Otho latched onto the first part of that sentence. "You didn't think you'd make me emperor? Then what was it all about? Our plotting and planning? All those meetings? Those decisions? That crawling I did to every patrician man and boy?"

Running a hand through his hair, Epaphroditus evinced a rare moment of honesty. "I thought Galba would make you his heir. What I didn't anticipate was him dying so soon. I thought, Marcus, I assumed he'd soon discover the true you and appoint another more suitable candidate."

Otho blinked, absorbing this information. "You never believed I'd be emperor?"

"No," admitted the secretary, meeting Otho's blue eyes, noting the hurt in them. "Please, Marcus, step aside. Let Vitellius have the garland."

"Is that what you advised Nero? Step aside, let Galba have your throne?"

"That was different. Nero was the blood heir of a dynasty. Things are different now. Unique. There is no bloodline. Whoever has the biggest army wins. Vitellius has that. Let him win."

Otho leaned against a black wall, elbow obscuring the art work. "If Nymphidius Sabinus hadn't caught up with Nero, what were you planning to do?"

"Does it matter?"

Otho looked up. "I believe it does."

"I was going to take him east and unite him with the legions there."

"Why?"

"Because they'd have beaten Galba's sole legion."

"No, I mean, why keep fighting when Nero had lost the palace, the city, the western provinces?"

"Because he was Caesar," responded Epaphroditus instantly.

Otho straightened his back, pulling his dressing gown cord tighter. "Exactly," he said. Then, quieter, "Will you support your Caesar?"

"This isn't going to go away, Marcus. Valens and Caecina are marching here with 70,000 men."

Otho held up a hand. "Will you support your Caesar?"

Epaphroditus looked at his friend. "Of course."

"Good. Then we both know where we stand." Then he smiled, a beaming Otho smile that could not but lighten the mood. "If there is one thing I am superbly good at, it is beating overwhelming and death-causing odds. Look at me, Marcus Salvius Otho, I'm emperor! Who'd have ever thought that?"

"Certainly not me," said Epaphroditus, feeling a smile twitch at his mouth.

"We'll treat Vitellius like that Sumerian gladiator. Remember?"

"The one who threatened to disembowel you?"

"That's the one! I still have a red mark on my stomach, right here, from the point of his scabbard," said Otho cheerfully, as if recalling a pleasant family meal or a particularly inspiring festival day. "Gods, did I think I was a goner that time!"

"It was close," conceded Epaphroditus. "So close I believe I even had to close my eyes at one point."

"You were wincing the whole time. How little faith you had in my survival." Their eyes met with mutual understanding, mutual affection.

"Old friend, let us crack open an amphora, get drunk till sunlight and reminisce on how Onomastus disarmed that gladiator by a flying head butt to his crotch."

"Still rates in my top five of the most astounding things I've ever witnessed."

"Who'd have thought dwarves could fly like that?"

"I imagine it was the throw that provided the trajectory."

"Yes, but who'd have imagined Poppaea could fling a dwarf like a javelin?"

"Astounding."

"Astounding girl," grinned Otho.

TWENTY-SEVEN

Caenis pressed a coin into the messenger's hand.
"Thank you. Discretion as always."
"Yes, mistress."
The messenger exited, colliding with Domitian in the doorway.

"Were there any messages for me?" he asked.

The hope was so naked on his face that Caenis winced as she told him, "There's nothing from Judaea."

"Oh." Hope died.

He shuffled round.

"Come back in," implored Caenis, placing her scroll down on her desk.

Domitian scuffled in with all the enthusiasm of a sacrificial bull visiting the temple on festival day. Gods, how he reminded her of his father!

She indicated the chair and he lowered himself down as if expecting the arrival of the knife-wielding priest.

"We've not had a proper catch-up yet, have we? Tell me all that you've been up to since I've been away all these months."

A pause, then, "Nothing really."

A dourly spoken comment that could have stopped the conversation dead. However, Antonia Caenis was palace trained. She could wheedle an anecdote out of the most taciturn presence. A reputation she'd earned after managing somehow to inspire a smile out of the famously miserable emperor Tiberius. Domitian, for Caenis, was sadly reminiscent of dour old Tiberius, a fate she was determined to alter.

"Come on. You must have done something. How do you like living with your aunt and uncle?"

"S'alright."

"Flavius says you're doing well in your studies."

"I failed rhetoric."

This did not surprise Caenis in the slightest. "But gained great marks for your literary appreciation," she continued cheerfully.

A "Yes" muttered at the floor was the response.

"Apparently Gaius Silvianus Junius is having a bash for his younger son's coming of age. We should go along, it will probably be lot of fun."

"No, I don't think so," said Domitian.

"Flavius tells me you haven't left this house since the last nones," she said with concern. "He says you haven't seen any of your friends."

Though he'd never been overburdened with pals, unlike his affable elder brother Titus, he'd been part of a tight friendship group of similarly aged boys. They'd visited the gym or watched the wrestling together. According to Flavius, these friends had drifted away recently. By quizzing the slaves, she learned that Domitian spent most of his time alone in his room. They suspected him of a very teenage habit. Their comment to Caenis: Flavius needed to have a talk with his nephew before the thing fell off.

If that were truly Domitian's hobby, it didn't appear to be improving his mood. He sat sulkily, shuffling his feet back and forth on the floor in an action that was beginning to set Caenis' teeth on edge.

"Come on. It'll do you good to get out."

"I want to stay home."

"Oh, you are so very much like your father!" she smiled.

Domitian raised his eyes slightly, regarding her through soft brown lashes. "How so?" he asked.

She saw in him, for the first time in their rather tortuous conversation, a spark of interest.

"You are both stubborn as mules! He was always a terrible partygoer too. It would take me ages to persuade him to go out, and then he'd ignore the host and concentrate on the snacks! And he is utterly useless at small talk. He can't even feign interest!" she smiled at the memories. "He is so frustrating!"

Domitian looked thoughtful. "Dad is more of a doer than a courtier."

"That he is," she agreed. "Though he'd put that far less nicely than you have."

Another smile as she recalled Vespasian's disastrous attempts at the imperial social scene. The culmination: not only dozing off during one of Nero's poetry recitals but actually snoring. Loudly.

So very different from his eldest son Titus. Titus possessed the ability to talk absolute reams of nothingness to the most inhospitable of emperors with a smile.

No, Domitian and Vespasian were truly two of a kind: awkward, lacking in sociability, but both hardworking. She knew that underneath his teenage moodiness, Domitian had a hint of his father's talents too. If she could just draw it out of him. Domitian, for Caenis, was another project.

"Who was your message from, if it wasn't from Father or Titus?" he asked.

Caenis was caught unawares by this abrupt change in subject. "Just a friend," she told him.

"The one who writes from Aventicum?" he asked, surprising her. "I saw the messenger arrive," he explained. "I heard what he said to the doorman."

So he wasn't spending all his time knocking one out while dreaming of Valeria Messalina or whoever was the great beauty these days.

"Yes, it is. She is having a rather difficult time of it, sadly."

"Is that why you've been corresponding so frequently?"

"Yes, it is."

"My uncle says Caecina and his army are stationed at Aventicum."

Caenis regarded her stepson. He watched, he noted, and in his head formulated a theory. Oh yes, he had his father's intelligence too.

To him, she said, "Is he really? I must write to her and ensure she is safe. You know what soldiers are like."

Domitian averted his eyes to the floor.

TWENTY-EIGHT

Epaphroditus awoke with an unthumping head and a space beside him in bed. There was not a single naked floozy to be seen. Nor one flagon of wine. It had been that way ever since Parentalia. Gone were the maudlin evenings spent drinking and fornicating and then regretting. Epaphroditus didn't have time for such hobbies any more. He had but one task, saving Otho's throne.

There was nothing he could do now to turn Valens and Caecina over to Otho's side. The now-sober Epaphroditus recognised there was something to be gained from the speed Caecina's forces were now progressing. At his present rate of movement, Caecina's army would cross the Alps far ahead of Valens' army. That meant less men for Otho's inferior numbers to face. Which gave them just a pinch of a chance.

It was imperative to keep the two armies apart for as long as possible to take full advantage of this pinch. To this end, he'd sent an envoy to Valens. He had no hope of success. Otho had nothing to offer the commander. But it might, just, hold up Valens for an extra day or two.

With this on his mind, he reached his office a little after the first hour. Talos stood to attention. That was one thing to be said for his assistant: he was punctual.

"Your post, sir," he indicated.

Epaphroditus followed the direction of the hand. There were scrolls everywhere: piled on his desk, fallen on the floor, placed carefully on his chair. The problem with a letter-writing habit: people tended to write back.

"Is there anything of note?"

"I didn't open them, sir!" exclaimed Talos, shocked. "They were addressed to you!"

"Oh good Jupiter's thunderbolt," murmured Epaphroditus.

If the secretary was forced to read every letter, every report, every plea addressed directly to him he'd never leave his office. That was indeed the point of employing an assistant. He gave Talos a narrow look. Philo would have pre-read each scroll, dealt with the minor correspondence himself, and presented only the most crucially important letters to his boss. Even then, he'd have given Epaphroditus a potted description of their contents, saving him the trouble of actually reading them. Oh for a Philo!

"Perhaps you could leave me in peace with my letters, Talos."

"Yes, sir."

Left alone, he gazed at the pile again, then he rolled up the sleeves of his tunic. Best to get on with it. How did he used to do this in the old days when he was the assistant to Callistus, Caligula's private secretary?

He stretched back into his memory.

1) Scan for seals of notable persons and separate them out.
2) If they couldn't put their most important news in the second sentence then it was not of any importance.
3) Pull out a selection of good and bad news to report to the emperor, making sure that the final report was good news to ensure a happy emperor.

And so to it.

First up: correspondence from Vitellius. He cracked open the seal, unfurled and read. By the end, his bad mood had all but dissipated and a smile had formed on his lips. It really was rather good.

Since Vitellius had rejected Otho's offer of a noble step down and a comfortable retirement, the correspondence between the two emperors had degenerated from sensible suggestions of a practical solution to their problem to an exchange of ever more entertaining insults. Mainly this was due to Otho's insistence that he answer the letters personally.

Presumably Vitellius was doing the same. His letters reeked of someone fully trained by some top pedagogue in the mysteries of political rhetoric. Otherwise known as how to publicly ridicule a rival while keeping the crowd on your side.

Today's list of accusations included Otho's supposed effeminacy. This was confirmed by his habit of bathing his feet in perfume and having the hairs individually plucked from his body. Tame stuff compared to the accusations against Nero that Epaphroditus had regularly fended off.

The only accusation of any note was the recurrence of that old tale of Otho prostituting Poppaea out to Nero. This could be easily spun away given Otho was the injured party in the story. Nobody would believe that a governorship of Lusitania of all places was a reward for handing over his wife.

He jotted down a few suggestions on his tablet for the reply, though he doubted he could compete with Vitellius' vividly entertaining description of Otho's toupee: "It is fashioned from the pelts of minks kept hostage in his palace and force-fed on a diet of wine-soaked lampreys to ensure their coats are as glossy as possible. Then they are cruelly skinned while still breathing, the tiny corpses left out for the birds to peck at while the emperor proudly displays their skins as a fashion! It is said that if you look at the toupee above the emperor's left ear, you will see the eyes of one of the unfortunate creatures looking back at you with great sadness."

Classic.

He jotted down the name of Vitellius' wife, Galeria. She, with her young son, was currently under house arrest in Rome. There was no need for threats, at least not yet. But a reminder that they were fully at Otho's mercy was probably worth stressing.

Next in his pile was a report from a scout he'd sent out. He broke the seal and scanned the contents. It was an account of Caecina's entrance into Novaria.

"The citizens welcomed Commander Caecina."

Epaphroditus didn't blame them. The appearance of three legions at your gates tended to make you very accommodating.

"Caecina however quite disgusted the townsfolk by his adoption of German dress and his haughty attitude. He rode into town on a white stallion and acted if he had conquered the town by force rather than being freely welcomed. His wife, Salonina, similarly caused disgust by wearing a gown of purple silk as if she were empress. Some say that she, being a woman of mature years, has bewitched Caecina with potions. The troops of Caecina, too, offended the citizens by their barbarous behaviour and their maltreatment of young girls."

Epaphroditus' scribe training kicked in. The pertinent point was not the joyous rapture given to Caecina. Nor was it the detailed description of his men. No, the pertinent point was the wife.

"Talos!"

The scribe was instantly present with a worried, "Sir?"

"Caecina's ridden into Novaria with his wife. There's been no mention of Caecina's wife in previous despatches."

"No, I don't believe there has, sir. She must have joined him recently."

"From Rome? You're meant to have all of their families under house arrest!"

He didn't mean to hurl his stylus at Talos. It was an unfortunate accident. His finger had slipped during a particularly wild gesticulation. It flew across the desk smack into Talos' forehead. The slave gave a yelp and bent over rubbing at his head.

"Are you alright?" asked his boss, getting out of his chair. "I didn't mean to—"

"It's fine, sir," gulped Talos. "I will go and re-check that list of relatives."

Noting the small trickle of blood running from his assistant's head, Epaphroditus suggested, "Why don't you go have a sit down, Talos. I'll go find that list."

"No, no, I'll do it, sir. It's my error to fix." Using a finger he wiped the blood from his head.

Watching Talos depart, Epaphroditus winced as the guilt kicked in. It wasn't Talos' fault that he wasn't Philo. When Talos returned, he'd apologise and then give him the afternoon off. He wasn't so bad an assistant. Looking back pre-Philo, all his assistants had been generally useless. But they were generally useless with one eye on Epaphroditus' job, and quite happy to do whatever it took to push their kindly employer out the door.

Talos in comparison was a much better companion. Not once had Epaphroditus entered his office to find a suspiciously cloudy glass of water on his desk, or a loose asp hissing on his chair. And not once had he found himself facing claims of treachery with a charge that contained information that could only have come from his own office.

Actually, Talos was a star performer, reconsidered Epaphroditus. He deserved a reward. And Talos would have received his reward had he not returned with such an insufferably triumphant expression on his face. He told his boss, "I have the list of Caecina's relatives in Rome. There is no mention of a wife or a Salonina. Just as I thought."

The omitted "sir" lost Talos his afternoon off. Epaphroditus clicked his fingers impatiently. Talos handed over the scroll, his smug smile drooping down at the edges. He was dismissed by a waved hand.

After reading the account through for a second time, Epaphroditus mused, "So where did this wife spring from? She can't have accompanied him to his German post or we'd have heard of her before now. And she can't have come from Rome, as proved by Talos. So where in Hades has she come from?"

TWENTY-NINE

It had been in Aventicum that Caecina had first stumbled upon Salonina. She had wandered into the camp one afternoon looking for directions. The soldiers all provided clear directions, accompanied by a thrusting of their groins.

Most well-bred ladies, as Salonina clearly was, would have been shocked and scared by such bawdiness. Not her though. She'd laughed and informed legionary Taurus that she really didn't feel she could spare the time to coax such a worm out of its hole. The men loved her instantly. As did Caecina when he went to uncover the source of the merriment and first set eyes upon her.

That Caecina and Salonina should come together surprised no one. He was a jaw droppingly handsome man. She was a stupefyingly attractive woman. Such beauty naturally gravitates towards itself. That she had at least a decade (she'd admit to) over Caecina was no impediment. Indeed, Caecina's first sexual experience had been with a friend of his mother's: the stately, elegant wife of an established equestrian. A woman of impeccable dress and morals.

On the day in question, Caecina had been sent to her house with a note from his mother. Gaia Merella, after regarding this tall, beautiful youth, had suggested they adjourn to a more comfortable space. A dutiful boy, who'd always been taught to obey his elders and betters, Caecina had followed her into what turned out to be a bedroom.

It was in this bedroom that she slipped off her modest, sensible gown to reveal the curvy womanhood beneath. Standing naked before the rather surprised boy, she instructed him in much the same tone he'd heard her order her slaves about. Like them, Caecina obeyed every direction. By the fall of light, he had been comprehensively initiated by the voraciously appetited Gaia. It was a training that had served him well.

Not that Salonina reminded him in any way of Gaia Merella. She was a quite different woman. There was nothing staid and respectable about Salonina. She was a woman of tantalising seduction. She possessed such invention in the bedroom that he never tired of her. Away from their furious and satisfying ruttings, he discovered her other attributes: her unfailing support towards him and, what he came to recognise as, her wise counsel. It was Salonina who'd persuaded him that the only way was forward.

After receiving news of Galba's death and Otho's ascension, Caecina had vacillated on what to do. He had no argument with Otho. He'd never even met the man. And as his letter had eloquently explained, Otho had no argument with him either. In fact, this new emperor sounded a very reasonable man, forgiving even. Which certainly distinguished him from Galba.

If he lay down his arms, Caecina would not want for money or distinction, so Otho promised. There was no need for him to commit to a war with the legitimate senate-sponsored emperor. A war that had no certain conclusion. Everything Caecina wanted, everything Caecina desired, he could have right now. He had no need to fight for it. It seemed such an extremely sensible recourse.

Valens wouldn't like it, Caecina knew, but Vitellius he felt sure would feel the same way he did. Why expunge all that effort when they'd been granted all they'd wanted. Galba was dead. There was no impediment to his and Valens' career. In fact, Otho promised to sponsor the two of them. Though poised to accept, Caecina felt it prudent to wait for word from Vitellius.

It had been Salonina who owned no doubts, no hesitations, who had convinced him to press on.

"Well of course you must go on," she had said, one hand gently stroking Caecina's smooth, hairless chest.

"Your men expect it. You have raised them with such stirring speeches. You can't unstir them once they are stirred. They believe in you, darling."

"But what if Vitellius decides to bend to Otho. What if he relinquishes his garland?"

"But why would he? He has so many more soldiers than Otho, my darling."

She made it seem so simple, so obvious, that Caecina troubled himself no more. The next morning, Caecina and his men packed up and marched onwards.

* * *

Valens saw the appearance of five senators and their entourage as an admission of failure. If Otho was reduced to relying on these old windbags with their polite entreaties of peace and common sense, then he truly knew he was beaten. Still, he listened politely as they bored him with their speeches.

Sitting on his ample chair, with a soft cushion to aid his old ailment, Valens raised a finger towards Regulus. The senator stepped forward. Unlike his colleagues, he had no script, no prepared list of dull sentiments to repeat. He looked directly at Valens and said, "This is madness."

Well, it was an intriguing start, if a trifle disrespectful, thought Valens. He kept his grey face straight, betraying no sign of his inner thoughts.

"And you know it," continued Regulus.

Valens retorted calmly, "Any madder than a battle in the forum? I have distinctly less blood on my hands than Otho."

"For now," said Regulus. "But you'll pull Rome apart, pull the empire apart. Our enemies will take advantage of this confusion. Even now, the Jews massacre our troops whilst our eyes are on this matter. It can only be a matter of time before the Parthians make use of our disunity. I knew your father, Fabius Valens."

Valens shifted uncomfortably.

"He was a noble man, a good man."

"Oh spare me!" said Valens. "Spare me yet more tedious speeches on honour and duty. What honour has Otho? He who was Nero's catamite and Poppaea's jester! He who murdered your senate-approved emperor. Who made the streets of Rome drip with blood."

"I do not agree with what Otho did that day. But he is emperor. Vitellius needs to step aside for the sake of our city. For Rome."

"For Rome," sneered Valens. He indicated to the soldiers stood behind him. "I am Rome now. And Rome offers you twenty thousand sesterces for your loyal allegiance to Vitellius. The allegiance you are about to swear." Valens templed his fingers together. "The money is a sweetener to make it less bitter for you. You will swear. You will swear now or those soldiers behind you will unsheathe their swords."

Regulus turned his head. The five soldiers by the tent entrance grinned and placed their hands on the hilts of their swords.

Four senators fell to their knees. "Emperor Vitellius," they quaked.

Regulus stood beside their cowering forms. "I will not bow," he said.

Valens didn't doubt his resolution. He nodded to a soldier. The legionary took hold of Regulus' shoulders and pushed him down onto his knees. The senator, half kneeling, half heaped on the ground, balancing on one elbow said, "I will not swear, no matter what you do to me."

Valens yawned. "Then you are of no use to me."

The soldier walked round behind Regulus. He grabbed a fistful of hair, pulling up the senator's head. His sword slashed across Regulus' throat. The gush of blood spurting across the pristine white togas of the other senators.

THIRTY

Epaphroditus was being dressed by his body slaves when the announcer arrived.

"Yes, what it is?"

"A young girl to see you, sir."

As his body slaves went about their business, Epaphroditus enquired, "Any other details you'd care to share? Anything helpful at all? Answer wisely or I'll see you cleaning pans."

The announcer, name of Ampelius, liked to big up his role by holding back information. "She claimed to be your daughter, sir."

Silvia? Had she come to hear his side of the story? What had her mother told her about the revelation at Parentalia? Surely not the truth? Caught between his desire to see his daughter and his dread at what she might ask of him, he ordered the slaves about with cross impatience. They flustered under such criticism, fumbling with fastenings, neglecting to tighten his sandal straps tight enough. This earned them a full dressing down, leaving them all staring at the floor. Bar Ampelius, who loved a good drama, and indeed causing them.

* * *

Outside the door to his ample atrium, Epaphroditus enquired, "Any reason why you are following me?"

"So I can announce you, sir."

"To my own daughter?"

"She might need reminding of your titles. It'll foster respect, sir. I hear the younger generation is lacking in that, sir."

Ampelius himself was twenty-one or twenty-two, perhaps twenty-five. Nobody was quite sure. Least of all Ampelius, who considered himself most likely a seasoned twenty-seven.

"I'll manage," Epaphroditus told him, throwing open the great doors.

He managed to disguise his disappointment behind a tight smile as he spied not Silvia, but Faustina settled on a cushioned bench.

"Father!"

Faustina was his second daughter. A freckled girl with green eyes and a great wave of brown hair, which without the aid of curling tongs veered towards gorse bush. Aged thirteen, she looked unlikely to manage her mother's regal height. But what Faustina lacked in stature, she made up for in personality. For Faustina was currently going through a difficult stage of life. In her case, it had begun shortly after birth and continued unabated.

Her mother had suggested they hold off from marrying her for a few years. Her optimistic hope that Faustina's more fractious elements would settle into something resembling wife material. In anticipation of that failure, Epaphroditus had been putting aside a significant proportion of his wages as a dowry for her.

Leading her through to the more comfortable dining room, he enquired, "Did you come here on your own?"

"I tried to get one of the slaves to accompany me, but they are too slow and I got bored waiting. And then I invited Silvia but she's crying all over the place." This was said in a tone that suggested Silvia's grief was invented merely to thwart her. "And I would have asked Pollus but he spends all his time locked in his room playing with his toy chariots. Mother says she never wants to speak to you again. And the others are babies and so totally useless."

Epaphroditus did not know where to start with that one. "Silvia?" he asked tentatively.

"I always knew she wasn't one of us," began Faustina smugly. "She's always been a bit weird and she looks weird, not like the rest of us." Faustina helped herself to a honey cake. "She has blue eyes and I have green eyes, like you. Who is her father?"

Epaphroditus didn't answer, demolishing a honey cake of his own by flaking it between his fingers.

"Did you know?" persisted Faustina. "Was it that groom we used to have? The one with the squint? Because he always eyed up mother as if he wanted to …"

"What groom?" asked Epaphroditus, stiffening. This was the first he'd heard of any lecherous horseman!

"You know, the one with the limp. He used to drag his leg behind him in a sort of shuffle, and he really stank of horse doings and he only had one hand. Is he Silvia's father?" she asked hopefully.

"Let's change the subject, shall we?"

But Faustina was not so easily distracted. She commented with Ampelius-style glee, "If you'd caught them at it, legally you could have killed them both."

Technically, he supposed he had caught them at it. He'd been present at Silvia's conception, but as a spectator rather than a participant. It did not rate as one of his happiest memories.

To Faustina he said, "Did you want to see some of the sights while you're here? There's a dining room where the ceiling rotates with pretty pictures and a pond with the largest fish you'll ever see."

He held his hands apart to demonstrate.

Faustina considered, "Are they killer fish?"

"Who knows. We could collect some dormice from the kitchens and test it out."

* * *

The large white fish swam past the sinking dormice, unconcerned. They had comprehensively been proved not to be of the killer variety. Epaphroditus and Faustina, lying on their stomachs by the edge of the pool, had plopped the mice in one after the other.

"That's disappointing," commented Faustina, watching the last mouse descend slowly into the water.

"Perhaps they just don't like mice," consoled her father.

"We could try a cat," suggested Faustina with a dangerous spark in her eyes.

"Sir!"

"Ampelius, if that's you!"

"No, sir. It's Talos, sir."

"Talos?" Epaphroditus stood, brushing down his tunic.

"Is that the new Philo?" asked Faustina as her father helped her up.

"No, it's Talos. What is it?"

"Some post you need to see, sir."

Epaphroditus held out a hand for the expected scroll.

Talos, failing to hand anything over, looked rather embarrassed. "It's in the map room, sir, with the emperor. He requests that you come and decipher it."

"What is it you are trying not to say, Talos?"

Talos gave a cough. He inclined his head towards Faustina, who brightened immediately, after the disappointment of the non-killer fish.

"I'll come!" she declared. "I'd love to see a map room. I'm sure I've never, ever seen a map room before."

"I'll get a chair and a slave to take you home."

"Aww. At least tell me what it is. Then I'll go quietly. I promise."

There was a familiar hint of mischief in her eyes. A spark that Epaphroditus knew could ignite a room and scorch everything in a three-pace orbit.

"Go on, Talos. Tell her."

Talos, looking very uncomfortable, informed Faustina gravely, "It's a head."

Faustina's eyes opened very wide. "Father, you knew who Silvia's father was the whole time! And you've had him killed already!"

THIRTY-ONE

Fingers pinching at his chin, Otho considered. He considered very hard. His eyebrows met across the bridge of his nose. His cheeks reddened with the strain. He expelled a hiss of breath.

"Nope. Still no idea."

The head looked at the emperor blankly from the centre of the table.

"Imperial Majesty."

Otho spun round. "Good, good. Epaphroditus. Come here. We need you to identify this fellow. At least we think it's a fellow, we're not entirely sure."

A yeughh from the corner alerted Epaphroditus to the presence of Salvius vomiting noisily into a bowl. Onomastus was rubbing his back.

"It's his first head," the dwarf informed them.

"Well, you never forget your first."

"No, you don't," replied Otho wistfully. "I saw my first at the games during the gladiator round, a fierce battle between a Thracian and a secutor. What a blow though. Never seen the like. Unfortunate that I was on the front row. Thing landed right in my lap. Ruined my toga. You know they say urine gets out a blood stain? Onomastus can tell you it certainly does not."

"No," confirmed the dwarf. "It does not."

"So I picked it up and lobbed it back into the arena."

Yeughh, yeughh.

"But back to this head. Who in Pluto's three-headed dog is it?"

"There was no note?"

"There was but they put it in the bag with the head. It rather soaked up the juices."

Yeughh, yeughh.

"Illegible. Though I sent your new Philo off to try and decipher it. He reckons if he dabs the scroll with urine it might dislodge the worst of it."

"He's wrong!" interjected Onomastus with feeling.

"We did warn him but he seemed uniquely interested in spending his afternoon in a fruitless task."

To avoid the glaring eyes of the head, translated Epaphroditus. It was not a pretty specimen. It had clearly travelled some distance for it owned a green tinge and the lips were decaying fast. He bent down to examine it more closely.

"Clean cut of the neck."

"Yes, we noted that."

"Man, clean shaven, middle-aged, looks quite unhappy."

"Well, you would, wouldn't you?"

"Shame the eyes are so damaged, you can't get the colour."

"I don't know what it is about heads. The moment they're popped off, all features become uniform. It's like Galba all over again! How many heads did we have that day?"

"Many."

"And we never even found Galba's!"

"I heard there's a guy on the Aventine using it as a plant pot," was Onomastus' contribution. One that inspired another wet splash from Salvius.

Otho pinched his chin again. "Very puzzling. Who would send me a head? And is it a warning or a gift?"

"Gift!" shouted Onomastus. "We could do with a plant pot. It'll be a talking point."

"That it would," concurred Epaphroditus. Peering at the head, he searched for a mole, a cleft lip, a tattoo, anything that made it distinguishable.

"Marcus Celsusssss."

Rather too much emphasis on the final "s", thought Epaphroditus, wiping the spittle from the back of his neck. But he was glad to see the man.

"Celsus—" he began, but Celsus' information was too pertinent to be interrupted.

"Caesar! I have news! The Pannonian, the Moesian, and the Dalmatian legions have all sworn allegiance to Your Imperial Majesty. And word has come in from the east. They are all to a legion on your side."

They'd heard nothing but bad news since January. This sudden burst of the good variety stunned the room into silence.

Epaphroditus was the first to speak. "That's a lot of men."

Salvius looked up from the pot, his eyes brighter. "Uncle Marcus."

"Also, Caesar, the Corsicans have come over to our side. Word has it their governor, Picarius Decumus, was planning to rally his islanders to join the Vitellians. However, he was killed by some loyal citizens before he could embark on his scheme."

Otho bent down, staring at the head, eyeball to rather dead eyeball.

"Hello Decumus."

Decumus did not reply.

To Celsus, Epaphroditus asked, "Where's Caecina, do we know?"

Celsus cleared his throat. "He's moving as fast as ever. The scouts have come back to say he's crossed the Alps."

"In winter? He is bold," said Epaphroditus.

Otho straightened back up. "What do we do?" he asked.

"We have to face him, Caesar, before he can make too many gains in the north of Italy. The good news is that Valens is nowhere to be seen. He's not moved in weeks."

"How curious. Surely it's not to do with our envoy?" pondered the secretary. "The wording from Valens was quite clear in its failure, as we expected."

"The legions, the other legions you mentioned," pressed Otho. "How near are they?"

"Close but not close enough to assist us now."

Otho chewed at his lip.

"It's what we wanted, Imperial Majesty," stressed Epaphroditus. "To face Caecina on his own. If we can stop his journey, if we can keep him in the north for just a few extra days, it'll give the other legions a chance to catch up."

Otho looked to Celsus, who gave a nod. "He's right. Now is the time."

"Right," said Otho with enforced brightness. "Then that is what we shall do. How long will it take to arrange our departure?"

"A few days, Caesar."

"Then we'd better get organised," replied Otho. "If you'll excuse me, there is someone I need to go tell of this decision."

THIRTY-TWO

Statilia had known it would be bad news by the way the emperor had appeared at her chambers unannounced. Usually when visiting her, he would send a chamberlain ahead to give her time to call in her army of beauticians. Then she would test out various lounging positions, Cassandra advising her of the most flattering to her figure, before she was draped to perfection at his arrival.

Otho had appeared accompanied by just three slaves. An impractically small number of attendants for an emperor. Then he had sat on the edge of her couch, taken her hand, and spoken words she did not want to hear.

"Leave? But where are you going?" she had squeaked, failing to hide the distress in her voice.

"To meet Vitellius, my love," replied the emperor softly.

"Meet Vitellius? But why would you want to do that? Especially after all the lies he's been spreading about you."

"Meet him in battle, my love," Otho clarified, kissing each knuckle of her fingers one by one.

"But surely that doesn't have to happen. Surely that man can fix it. That's what he does, isn't it? Fix things?" meaning Epaphroditus.

"Some things aren't fixable. Some things have to be faced."

"But surely, surely there must be something that can be done to stop this."

Her hand began to tremble. Otho placed it down gently. "Believe me, all roads have been explored. This is how it is. The good news is that the eastern legions are on their way. But, Caecina, unfortunately, is going to beat them to Italy. So we must face him now."

"But I don't want you to go!"

"Can't say I'm too keen on it either," Otho admitted. "Celsus is a good man. He tells me we have able commanders and I'll only be a few days away from Rome."

Statilia felt her heart tear. With desperation she pleaded with him.

"We could run away, Marcus. Together. You and I. We'll go to Sicily. Live out our days in some small villa," she begged. "If we go now Vitellius need never know. Let him be emperor. What does it matter? What does any of this matter?"

Otho cupped his hand on her cheek, cradling her chin on the palm of his hand. Bringing his face close to hers, he kissed her gently on the lips.

"When I return, we'll get married," he told her. "If you concur, of course."

"Of course I concur. Of course I do. Of course I'll marry you."

On the verge of tears, she snuggled into him.

"I will be back, Statilia. Please believe that."

She looked up at him. His warm blue eyes were for once, sad.

"I need your faith," he told her.

Pressing down her pain, Statilia told him, "You have it, husband."

THIRTY-THREE

Caecina, one hand across his brow to protect his eyes from the winter sun, asked, "So where is he?"

His tribune gazed across the lush valley. "He's not here," he concluded after a good study, as if Valens and his 30,000 men might be hiding behind a hedge. The horses approached, bearing the scouts Caecina had sent ahead.

"Well," he demanded.

"He's not here," they said in unison.

"He said to meet him in the Po valley. He distinctly said that. We are supposed to reunite our forces and take on the Othonians, or Galbians as it was back then. That's what he said," insisted Caecina, scouring the landscape one last time. "He is definitely not here." Then he looked to Salonina who sat on her horse beside his.

"No, he's not," she said.

This clinched the matter for Caecina. He scratched at his chin, made his horse trot around the place for a bit, the trotting abruptly halting when a thought noticeably struck his perfect features. "You don't think he's fallen foul of some Gallic tribe? Should we go rescue him?"

He could picture his army sweeping in and saving the day for his colleague. How annoyed would old grizzling guts be when he, Caecina, gained all the glory?

Not that he disliked his colleague, far from it. They'd shared some most enjoyable evenings in Germania. Sort of. Valens being a sparse drinker rather inhibited their jollity. And, of course, all he ever wanted to talk about was politics and to gripe about Galba.

The gods knew Caecina liked a good moan about his former boss but really, after an hour or two on the topic, he was done with it. Not Valens though, and he'd never even met Galba! If anyone should take against the man, it should have been Caecina. But then that was Valens all over: bitter.

Caecina could see why. After all, how old was Valens? Forty something? And what had he achieved in that time? Precious little. So short of coinage that it was inevitably Caecina who paid on their nights out. And unmarried too. That generated all kinds of gossip in the barracks, gossip of the unpleasant sort. Nasty rumours had circulated about Valens' sexual habits. Even Salonina had heard of them, that's how well known they were.

"Men are men," she'd purred. "But I'll admit, my darling, that Valens makes me uncomfortable. If any of what they say has the smallest truth in it, then I doubt any woman is safe from him."

Caecina kissed her lips, assuring his love that he would protect her from Valens' lasciviousness.

"Oh I know you shall, darling. But really, how should a man like that be taken in Rome? It's all very well forcing your desires on some Gallic peasant but what's he going to do in Rome? Such things are not tolerated. Caligula had a fondness for other men's wives and he wasn't one to take no for an answer either. He took them away from their husbands over dinner and then returned them sullied by the dessert."

"So they say," muttered Caecina.

"All I am saying is that there are rules in Rome that govern behaviour. Rome does not tolerate such behaviour: look what happened to Caligula!"

He'd told her that Valens was no Caligula but the analogy stuck in his head. Hadn't there been that incident at their previous night-time haunt? The landlord's daughter. His very young daughter. Valens had denied it absolutely. Denied that he'd ever touched her, claiming the girl was looking for a Roman husband and lying to secure one.

Caecina had believed it at the time. The girl was but a child. A scrawny creature, with pretty eyes to be sure, but she'd yet to reach her prime. Seeing Valens beside her, the charge was ridiculous. Her head only came midway up his chest. They looked so wrong together. And of course she'd want to escape that hovel of a bar. And with all these Romans about, Romans with money, expectations, they presented the perfect opportunity for any girl ambitious to better her circumstances.

But Valens? Of all the thousands of Romans she could have settled on for her plot, why him? Why not a dishy legionary with only a few years on her? Surely a far more likely match than Valens with his pitted cheeks, his clammy skin, his greying, greasy hair, and gruesome reputation.

What manner of man was Valens? Likes them young, likes them fighting—that's what they said. Should Caecina really be tying his name, his unblemished name, to such a pervert?

"I believe the tribes are friendly on his route," said Salonina, pulling Caecina from his musings.

"I suppose they would be," he replied, thinking it was typical of Valens to choose the easier path for himself away from the warring Helvetii (conveniently forgetting it was he who'd provoked the Helvetii into warring in the first place).

"So what now? Do we wait for him?"

"And lose our advantage, darling? Surely not."

"Hear, hear," cheered the tribune.

THIRTY-FOUR

The reason Valens had failed to make their rendezvous was in the main due to the sheer speed of Caecina's army. They'd descended upon Gaul like a swarm of locusts, demolishing a town's supplies and then swarming off to the next unfortunate settlement. The victory over the Helvetii had given them further impetus. Eager for more fighting, they could not wait to encounter the Othonians.

Valens' journey had been more measured, controlled. Unlike his colleague, Valens had given some thought to the battles upcoming and he wanted his men suitably rested, ready to meet their enemy. The appearance of that ridiculous envoy from Otho had given them that respite.

They had been making extremely good progress until Ticinum where Valens had fallen ill. And there he lay on his couch, a dull ache in his stomach which beat a horrible rhythm, leaving him greyer than ever, a sheen of sweat coating his forehead. He lay staring at the ceiling, biting his lip, and willing himself better. What a time for his old ailment to hit.

On his sickbed, he'd had plenty of time to catch up with his colleague's exploits.

"Stupid boy," he cursed as he read through a detailed commentary on Caecina's war with the Helvetii. The "boy" had claimed a magnificent triumph far out of kilter for what amounted to some minor skirmishes with untrained locals. Valens had little faith in Caecina's generalship. His confidence lay in Caecina's battle-scarred men and what he could do with them once the two forces were combined.

Where Caecina's talents lay, even Valens would admit, was in the performance. Looking every inch an Alexander the Great, even in his ludicrous trousers, Caecina cut a dashing figure on his horse. His handsome looks and fine speech-making were perfectly complemented by Valens' own talents in the commanding of men.

What was the stupid boy thinking? Was he thinking at all? Probably not. Caecina was all about action, possessing minimal skills in strategy and planning. What kind of mayhem would he unleash in Italy should he get there first? Valens had plans for Italy, carefully thought-out plans that would maximise their opportunities for a swift victory. Plans that the idiot, headstrong Caecina would trash all over.

It wouldn't do. He had to get to the Po valley first. Screw resting his men, they'd have to march at double pace. He got up from his couch ready to lay down orders for their movement but completed the move far too quickly, his eyes spotting over as a sharp gasp of pain shot through his stomach. Staggering, he managed to grip hold of the back of a chair for balance. His hands grasping tightly as the pain racked his stomach. His knuckles turning as white as his face.

Once the worst of the horror subsided, he called out shakily, "Crito!"

His body attendant rushed over and helped him back onto the couch.

"Master, you must rest."

Through gritted teeth, Valens violently disagreed. "Need … to … move … the … men."

The slave shook his head. "Not today you don't, master. Even the wagon will pain you in this condition."

Picturing the juddering transportation, Valens was forced to agree.

"Master, let me get you a tonic to soothe your stomach a little."

Through another terrible wave of cramps, Valens managed a nod.

* * *

"Persephone's pomegranate! I think he's actually going to die," said Crito.

His fellow slave, Ephesus, shook his head sadly. "And who will lead this army then? No one, that's who. They'll run riot through the villages, there will be no one left from here to Rome."

Crito shuddered at Ephesus' bleak analysis. He was right though. Without Valens, these brutish soldiers would be uncontrollable.

"Is that wise woman about, do you know?"

Looking up from his polishing, Ephesus told him, "I saw her earlier with Decian. She was giving him something for his blisters. He reckoned he could feel it working already."

* * *

Her name was the wonderfully foreign sounding Gwencalon. One that sounded odd on Latin tongues, so they'd taken to referring to her as the wise woman. Which made her sound like some druid hanger-on, complete with a repertoire of evil magic to wither penises. This she was not. Rather, she was a woman with a knowledge of herbs that aided all manner of illnesses. Such was her skill that magic, evil or otherwise, was not required.

The army's own doctors, superior at knitting bones and trepanning heads, had little time for their charges' dodgy tums or aching shoulders. "Come back when the arm is hanging from the socket, then we'll talk about it," was nearer the mark.

So the wise woman had found a niche to occupy. It also helped that she had a calm, soothing voice and was a patient listener to all manner of woes.

Crito found her using a funnel to carefully pour liquid into a small glass bottle.

"Hello there, Crito," she said.

A woman of middle years, her one great feature was her hair, which she wore in a most unusual style. Her blonde locks were fixed in curls that towered upwards one on top of the other in the shape of an arch some seven curls high. The remaining hair was tied neatly in a bun behind this edifice. Gwencalon was very much a woman ahead of her time.

"What can I do for you today, Crito?"

"That tonic, the one you gave me before for the commander. I need more."

Gwencalon placed the funnel on the table. "Is he really that bad?"

"Madam, I believe he is dying."

She rolled up her sleeves and turned round to face the shelves of bottles. "Not if I can help it," she told Crito with all the enthusiasm she had shown so far for the legionaries' ingrowing toenails, boils, and nasty lice infestations.

These were her boys and she was determined to fix them all, from commander to slave.

Valens was certainly grateful. He took the mixture with some desperation. This tonic was the only substance that had offered him any relief in the last few days. It was to him a precious liquid, a thing more precious to him than his Helen, and he gulped it down eagerly.

"Master?" asked Crito as Valens sank back into his bed.

Using his hand to wipe away the stray liquid from his lips, Valens told him, "I feel sure I shall be well enough to move tomorrow. We'll catch that idiot boy up."

THIRTY-FIVE

The organisation involved in moving an emperor, his advisors, his slaves, and all the necessary adornments that gave him an imperial gleam was hefty. Epaphroditus was working long hours to ensure nothing was forgotten. Celsus was taking care of the army side of the party, gathering together as many men as he could to accompany the emperor northwards.

The number of reported omens was ever increasing in the city as these preparations took place. It cast a blanket of gloom, even as Epaphroditus bribed his way round the temples to produce superior and positive auspices. Though to the secretary's appreciation, Flavius was making a good job of keeping the streets calm prior to their departure.

The emperor himself was keeping his mind occupied from the unstoppable approach of Caecina's forces by organising a dinner party to mark his official engagement to Statilia. Though they'd always had an understanding of sorts, Otho had now committed himself publicly to marrying her. It seemed fitting to celebrate this happy event prior to his departure to face the Vitellians.

* * *

It was this planned party that was troubling the usually untroubled Lysander. More particularly, whether he dared to invite Verenia to the party.

Verenia—the very name had Lysander sighing as he recalled, with an inner joy, their conversation at Parentalia. The way she'd listened to him, and then responded with words of her own. And then listened to him again, and then responded and then listened. She was quite unlike any other woman he'd met before.

He loved her. He knew he loved her because every time he thought about her, a strange reflex kicked in and he smiled without even realising he was doing so. Thoughts about Verenia hit him at the oddest moments and not all of them, to Lysander's surprise, were sex related. Such as that morning over breakfast when Teretia had been sick in her porridge bowl, and he'd immediately thought how much Verenia would enjoy hearing all about it.

Inviting her to the party seemed like a good first step in convincing her to love him back. Only, unusually for Lysander, taking this step had filled him with doubts. Doubts over whether Verenia would accept. Doubts over whether it was permissible to even ask her. Like Philo before him, Lysander had discovered that the freebie world operated in quite a different way to the palace. All that seemed normal in the palace was considered quite differently in the outside world.

This Lysander had discovered when he'd commented over supper one night on how Apollonius had paired Ampelius with Penelope in the breeding programme, and what a duff match it was because everyone knew she hated him. She'd been so keen not to be sown by him during the last round that she'd shoved a vinegar-soaked sponge up her— Which was the point at which Philo abruptly, and rather rudely Lysander thought, changed the subject.

Philo had taken a similar stance on Lysander's tale of a whipping dished out to Doricus, which had Lysander protesting,

"What, what? Teretia asked if anything interesting had happened during my day! That's what happened during my day! Doricus dripped blood all over the banqueting hall floor, passed out, and smacked his head on a lamp stand on his way down."

In the palace, that would have been the gossip of the day, and jokes would have been spread endlessly about Doricus' fall. Especially the bit when Otho's dwarf had slipped on the blood pool and skidded right across the floor. That had certainly made Statilia Messalina laugh. But Teretia and Pompeia seemed bizarrely more concerned about Doricus and whether he had recovered from his misfortune.

It truly was a strange world. And gallingly for Lysander, it was a world he needed help from Philo to navigate. However, finding the apartment empty, he decided to spend the afternoon depilitating his body until Philo returned home. He found depilating a calming process, and it was of course a useful preparation should he manage to get his end away with Verenia. Everyone knew women abhorred a hairy man.

He'd reached a particularly snarly bit on his chest that was resisting even his hardest tugs, when he heard voices.

"I'm alright, Philo. Truly I am."

"Let's just get you upstairs," replied her husband, one arm around her shoulders as he assisted her up the staircase. Opening the door to their apartment, Philo escorted his wife to the kitchen where he insisted she sat down.

"I don't feel sick at all now. Honestly I don't."

Philo handed her a bowl. "Just in case," he told her.

"I think it was Tadius' display. There is something about raw meat that bothers me, and him," she said, smiling down at her now noticeable bump, which she insisted contained a baby boy.

Philo took her hand and kissed it. Then placed his own hand on where their child resided.

There came from within the apartment a call: "PHILOOOOO."

Only Lysander's trained voice could penetrate wood and plaster so effectively.

"PHILOOO, I need to talk to you."

"Later," Philo called back. "Teretia's not feeling well."

"NOW. It's important."

"You go see what he wants," said Teretia.

"No, it can wait. Let me get you some water and—"

"Philo!"

"Later!"

"Really, I am quite well now I am away from that raw flesh."

A slam and then Lysander appeared completely bereft of any article of clothing. Teretia took one look, gasped, "Sausage," and retched into the bowl. Philo rubbed her back supportively while giving Lysander a long look.

"Didn't you hear me? I need to talk to you. It's very, very important."

"I'll come see you shortly. Once I'm sure Teretia is fine."

Lysander gave a humph.

Teretia looked up from the bowl. "You go, Philo. I'm fine." She avoided any further glances at the announcer's departing nakedness.

After a few rounds of "If you're sure" and many rounds of "Yes, I'm fine," Philo was convinced enough to go seek Lysander in his room.

He entered to find the still-naked Lysander sitting on the edge of the bed, plucking the hairs from his chest.

"That's the one good thing about the palace: the depilators are on duty all night. This is hard work. I really shouldn't have left it so long."

Lysander's chest was indeed red from the effort and he winced as he pulled out another springy blond hair.

Philo sat on down on a chair, then gazed around. This small chamber had a very different feel to it than when it had been Teretia's bedroom, and also a different smell. It smelt uncannily like the room Philo had shared with Lysander at the palace.

A combination of the overpowering hair preparations the announcer insisted were necessary and stale socks.

"What is it you wanted?" he asked.

"Statilia Messalina and Otho have got engaged so there's going to be a big party. Do you think it would be acceptable to ask Verenia?"

"Acceptable?" asked Philo.

"Yes, acceptable to ask Verenia to the party?"

Philo blinked.

"You want to invite Verenia to the emperor's engagement do?"

"Yes."

"At the palace?"

"Gods above! Do you need a nap or something?" exclaimed Lysander impatiently. "You're not usually this slow. I put it down to marriage. It's mushed your brain up."

"You want to know if it's acceptable?" This was the part that was baffling Philo.

"Yes," replied Lysander, pulling out a hair with a stronger yank than he'd intended. He gave a yelp, wincing as he rubbed at his chest. "You know all about freebies. You're married to one, aren't you? You know about this stuff. How they operate. What the rules are."

Philo, taken aback by Lysander admitting for the first time in their twenty-plus years of friendship that there was a subject he knew less about than his former roommate, managed to utter a non-committal, "I suppose I do."

"So is it acceptable by their rules?"

Philo considered the matter. "As she's divorced, she's back under the authority of her father. So really you should ask his permission."

"Isn't he out east?"

"Alexandria now, I believe."

"And the postal ship takes?"

"Two days."

"The party is in three days."

"That's a shame," said Philo. "You won't have his answer by then."

Lysander placed down his tweezers carefully on the bed. "Oh," he said.

Philo rather thought he detected a note of disappointment in that "Oh".

Whatever it was, it was most unlike Lysander. In fact, now Philo thought about it, his friend's entire dealings with Verenia had been most out of character.

It was Lysander's habit to make a move on a girl pretty much the moment he met her. Usually before she'd even had chance to tell him her name. As was indeed the case the first time he met Teretia. Yet as far as Philo knew, courtesy of the Viminal gossip-vine, Lysander had not made a single sexual advance towards Verenia. Whenever she popped round to the apartment, the announcer, now Philo came to think about it, was uncharacteristically silent while Verenia pottered about and inevitably managed to upset Teretia with some small slight.

"You like her." This came out as a surprised revelation rather than a question.

Lysander looked up. "Can't I ask an aunt if I can't get hold of her father? She has lots of aunts on the Viminal."

It was clear to Philo that for Lysander this was a question of the utmost importance. There were those, including Epaphroditus and latterly Teretia, who'd wondered why Philo and Lysander remained friends. Besides the difference in their personalities and their respective palace jobs, Lysander forever spoke to Philo as if he were his idiot younger brother. As this had been Lysander's habit for their entire acquaintance, Philo was by now quite immune to his barbs, assuming them to be entirely accurate in pinpointing his deficiencies.

But much as Lysander was tuned in to Philo's weaknesses, likewise you couldn't share a room with someone for so long and not be similarly familiar with his sore spots. And Philo knew that beneath that braggart attitude, there lurked a certain vulnerability. It didn't appear often, buried beneath the overly confident, faintly odious face Lysander showed the world. But it was present now in his troubled eyes and the way he'd plucked his chest hairs all out of sequence, leaving an unsightly springy mass around his left nipple that he appeared to have forgotten about.

"You know about this stuff," continued Lysander. "What things are. Out here."

Out here as opposed to the palace where they'd both grown up. Philo had been rather surprised to learn just how controlled the lives of the freeborn could be. Marriages were arranged between families with little say from the bride or groom. And before that, daughters from good families were closely chaperoned in order to maintain their and their family's honour.

Honour was not a state that held very well in the palace for the slave girls. But you wouldn't damn a girl to spinsterhood just because of "that". Because "that" was just one of those things that happened. As Philo in his sad history with Straton could attest. Once you were free, all that was washed away and you could start anew.

Philo deliberated. It was a tricky one. "I should ask Pompeia," he finally concluded. "She'll know what Verenia's father would consider appropriate."

This answer seemed to satisfy Lysander and he returned to his depilation with a renewed enthusiasm in the groin area.

THIRTY-SIX

It was the hour of Aphrodite's flute lesson. It was a hobby she'd only recently returned to. As a child in the palace, she'd shared a room with a flute girl who'd taught her to play. Not something Aphrodite would publicly acknowledge lest Felix were to hear about it and assign her to that role. Aphrodite had far greater plans for herself than a mere flute girl who'd be pensioned off the moment her breasts developed.

No, she had her eyes set on an imperial secretarial career and she'd achieved it slowly through one position followed by another, until she reached the job as chief correspondence clerk to the empress. Then she'd got married and that had been the end of her career. She'd spent her days in this gargantuan Esquiline mansion popping out baby after baby, gradually losing touch with all her palace friends.

She hadn't meant to do so, but the children had taken over her life to the exclusion of pretty much everything else. What did she care if some secretary lost his life to Agrippina's wiles when Silvia had a fever? What did the death of Nero's baby daughter matter when her own baby was refusing all liquids? Her priorities switched and her world, she now recognised, shrank.

Since her separation, she'd had time to consider what might have been. What if she hadn't thrown away her job? She'd probably be a private secretary now; powerful and respected.

Probably more so than her estranged husband. Whilst Aphrodite's talents had been spotted early, her husband had served in a much more lowly position, as a mere wine boy, until his lucky break courtesy of Caenis.

Taking the flute up, she recognised, was a sort of revenge against the man who'd so limited her life. Plus she rather fancied the instructor, a man at least fifteen years her junior and with a very pleasing face. She'd planned to have an affair with him but ten lessons in, she'd got no closer to implementing that seduction. And today was as rigidly formal as the previous nine occasions.

After Maximus congratulated her on her improvements she'd replied, "I have a lot of spare time to practise," in a vaguely coquettish way. But he'd failed to offer to fill that time with anything other than another lesson in four days' time.

After Maximus had departed, she'd stuck her head in the schoolroom to check on her son Pollus' tuition. He waved her away with the sort of irritated embarrassment eleven-year-old boys specialise in. Then she'd talked to the cook regarding dinner, inspected the garden noting a few spring shoots, and then completely given up and gone for a lie-down. It was from here that she was awoken by a slave who informed her that Antonia Caenis was waiting in the atrium.

Caenis had been her superior in the correspondence bureau. Although, typically, she'd been commandeered by her husband as his patron. Thus, even Caenis herself had apparently forgotten she'd known Aphrodite first. Her visit could only mean one thing: a plea for her protégé.

Aphrodite, woken from her nap, was not in the mood for hearing any such plea. A fact Caenis was quick to discover when Aphrodite's opening words to her were, "I suppose you've come to beg me to take him back. You're wasting your time. I'm more likely to sprout wings than take that man back. So I would prefer that you leave right now rather than drag this ghastly meeting out."

Caenis couldn't suppress her laugh. "Actually, Claudia Aphrodite, I came to invite you to a party."

"Oh."

"Not that I don't want you and Epaphroditus to be reconciled. You are as perfectly matched a couple as I have ever met. But I'd assumed you wouldn't want any interference in such a personal matter."

"Exactly," said Aphrodite, sitting opposite her guest. "Sorry for my terrible welcoming. I'll get some refreshments arranged and we can start all over again."

"Yes, let's," smiled Caenis genially. "Salut to you, Claudia Aphrodite."

"And salut to you, Antonia Caenis. You are very welcome in my home."

"I thank you for your hospitality."

"It's offered gratefully for your presence."

"And I am flattered that my presence should invoke such gratitude."

"I do not offer flattery but only what honours my esteemed guest, which is owed due to her superior intelligence."

"I bow my head at my host's superior intelligence in noting my intelligence. And must, of course, mention her countenance which is not so lined as mine, nor as hard worn, but one of a subtle grace."

"I thank, I thank... No, I can't keep it up!" laughed Aphrodite. "I'm out of practice at palace panegyric."

"Me too. And aren't you as glad as I am about it?"

They shared a smile.

"So this party?" asked Aphrodite, as a slave laid a platter of nibbles on the round table that was positioned between them.

Delicately picking up a quail's egg, Caenis told her, "A palace event to celebrate Statilia Messalina's engagement to the emperor."

Aphrodite gave a shudder, then replied, "Thank you, but no. I don't go to palace events."

"Don't you?" queried Caenis lightly.

She'd attended the occasional banquet. The weddings, naturally. But otherwise, she'd stayed away from palace events. Again, she could pinpoint the exact moment that became the case: her marriage to Epaphroditus. He didn't like her attending palace do's. Had fobbed her off whenever she'd suggested accompanying him to one of Nero's parties with, "Not your sort of thing, Dite."

How did he know it wasn't her sort of thing? She could have missed out on many a delightful evening because of her husband.

"Actually, why not?"

"Why not indeed. Dear old Flavius will accompany us, so it will all be perfectly proper."

For once Aphrodite wasn't worried about propriety. She was a single woman for the first time in thirty years. She could be as flirtatious and flighty as she wanted. She wondered inwardly whether there were any teachers of flirting as well as flute playing.

THIRTY-SEVEN

Sporus had taken the news that Otho and Statilia were to marry surprisingly well. There had been hysterics, a lot of crying, a fair amount of fainting, a great deal of speculating that he should surely die from such pain and one threat to hang himself from the nearest available tree. When Mina had suggested the tall pine by the new palace entrance, Sporus had been unmoved.

However, compared to the fuss he'd made when Nero had married Statilia, it was notably low key. Which left Mina wondering whether Sporus possessed the great love for Otho he claimed to.

"I'm not attending this stupid engagement party," he huffed, arms folded. "I'm not seeing that smug bitch all over my darling Otho. I won't be able to bear it. I shall surely expire on the spot."

"As far as I am aware, nobody has yet dropped dead from a case of envy," said Mina.

"It's not envy! It's love. A pure and beautiful form of love you will never understand!"

Mina rolled her eyes. "So I'll tell the empress you're not attending then?"

"Don't tell that bitch anything! Tell the emperor. Tell my darling Otho that I am sickening and not well enough to leave my bed. He'll be so worried, he'll come find me."

"Of course he will," said Mina unconvincingly as she got to her feet. "I need to go back to my room to get my best whip. Publius must surely have buggered off by now."

The scent of gossip had Sporus shedding his overwhelming grief.

"Gods! Is that still a thing? Are they actually at it now?"

"Nope, not consummated."

Mina's certainty on this had nothing to do with any confidences shared by Cassandra. Rather, it was due to a series of accidental early returns to their room. These accidents had produced zero results. No walking in and finding Cassandra and Publius nakedly engaged in heaving thrusts. In fact, no one even looking slightly sheepish while fiddling with their clothing.

Rather, when she'd kicked in the door (a trick she'd learnt from Straton), she'd inevitably found Publius sitting on the chair and Cassandra sat on the bed. The two of them discussing Livy, whoever he might be. Unless this was some elaborate form of foreplay, Mina was pretty sure they'd not done the deed as yet.

"Is she frigid?" queried Sporus. "I always thought she'd be frigid. She was with Philo for ages and they never consummated it either. Once, you can understand. Twice, well, it begins to reflect on her." He was pursing his lips, nodding sagely like some wise guru.

"She's only two months off thirty and she'll have treble what she needs in her freedom fund, so I expect a marriage announcement imminently."

A thoughtless sentence that had Sporus crying, "Oh!" Then, "My love lost to me forever! Unless. Unless…"

He grabbed hold of Mina's arm, his eyes bright and eager, which could only spell trouble.

"Mina, Mina, this is my chance," he said. "My last chance to prove to Otho what a mistake it would be to marry that cow."

"Sporus, I am warning you. Do not mess up this party," said Mina holding up a finger. "Because I will take you down. Completely. In front of everyone."

"Pish, pish," scoffed the eunuch. "There's no need for me to do anything. I shall just be myself."

"And that will convince Otho to break his engagement how?"

"Because," the eunuch began smugly, "I shall be noticeably more attractive, more desirable, more glamorous, and just MORE than her. Now send in the bangle selectors, the necklace pickers, three dressers, five make-up artists, and at least seven hairstylists because the Sporus is ready to be beautified!"

* * *

"But you said I should go out more," protested Domitian. "You said that staying in the house could only be unhealthy for me. That is what you said."

Caenis had to admit that she had, and was inwardly cursing herself for it.

This decision of Domitian's to attend the emperor's engagement party had been announced over breakfast. No amount of pleading by Caenis and Flavius since had detracted him from this aim. This was her final attempt as they stood face to face in Flavius' cramped study.

"We'll go out tomorrow night together," she said. "There is bound to be another party on somewhere. But not tonight. Tonight you need to stay here."

"Why?"

"Because you're not on the guest list. You'd be turned away by the slaves on the door," she said, hoping to play upon his very adolescent fear of humiliation.

Domitian folded his arms across his chest. "You're telling me that if I turn up at the palace with the city prefect, a former private secretary to numerous empresses, and the wife of the emperor's current private secretary, that not one of you could argue with a door slave? That not one of you possesses the clout to get me placed on the guest list?" His lips pouted. "I rather think that you don't want me at the palace."

Which was absolutely true. Caenis did not want Domitian to be anywhere near the palace. Vespasian may have offered up his legions to Otho, but how long had Otho got? There might well be a new emperor shortly. Therefore, it was not wise to associate too closely with the current and probably temporary regime. Flavius as city prefect had no choice. But the attendance of Vespasian's son was a powerful message on which side the Judaean governor was on.

"It's because I'm the younger son, isn't it? I'm not going to be allowed to have a public career. You're just going to pack me off to the country house so that I don't get in the way of Titus' glorious rise!" he protested.

"That is simply not true," she attempted to placate.

"Yes it is. Look at how Titus was chosen to be a friend to Emperor Claudius' son Britannicus. Look at how he was taken into the imperial household. Meeting all the influential families and getting to make an impression on the emperor. And look at me! Hidden away here in this house. It's clear father doesn't want me to meet anyone important. He has his golden boy. What does he need me for?! I might as well hang myself!"

Caenis sighed inwardly. He was seventeen, several years into his supposed adulthood, yet still prone to these childish foot stampings.

"Very well," she said. "You may come to the party."

Wiping a globule of spit from the corner of his mouth, Domitian said meekly, "Thank you," then kissed Caenis on the cheek.

THIRTY-EIGHT

Philo fidgeted around the kitchen, straightening the saucepans that hung on the wall, lining up the chairs, and cleaning down the sides with a damp cloth for the eighth time. He attempted to sit down but sprang straight back up again, unable to bear even this brief respite from action.

The source of Philo's anxiety was linked to his plans for the evening. He and Teretia, along with Lysander and Verenia, were due to attend the emperor's engagement party. He had no desire to attend. He'd had no plans to attend. The fact that he was attending was all down to his own stupid self.

After advising Lysander on the propriety of courting Verenia, Philo had gone to check on how his wife was feeling. Naturally she'd asked what Lysander had wanted to talk to him about, and he'd explained that the announcer wished to take Verenia to the betrothal party. This seemed to upset Teretia rather a lot. She had been adamant: it was unfair for Verenia to go to a palace event when she, Teretia, was not. She had even cried a little.

And it was here that Philo had blundered. He consoled her with, "You'll go to other palace events."

He hadn't really meant it. It was just the sort of thing you said to someone who was upset by her older cousin going to a party that you weren't going to. However, Teretia had picked up on it immediately.

"Really?" she'd asked.

"There will be plenty of palace parties that Verenia won't be going to."

"We could go to other parties?"

"Of course," Philo had said. He then fell into a trap of his own making by adding, "I'm sure I could get us an invite via Epaphroditus."

"Could Epaphroditus get us an invite to Otho's betrothal party?"

Philo couldn't really claim otherwise. Which had led to a rather long speech by Teretia. She was quite sure that Verenia's father would be much happier if they chaperoned his daughter, because her uncle hadn't even met Lysander. It was the proper thing to do, she'd stated, looking straight at Philo with slightly teary eyes.

Of course he'd caved in. Anything to make his adored wife happy. It had not made Philo happy at all. He'd spent the last few days making guilty prayers to the goddess Rati to turn Otho's lustful passions elsewhere and thus break the engagement. They hadn't worked, as Philo discovered courtesy of Lysander, and the party was very much still on.

He glanced down at the table, decided it still wasn't clean enough, and was wiping it down for the ninth time when Verenia appeared.

To Philo, she looked very nicely dressed but that was the limit of his thoughts on the subject. His mind was very much elsewhere.

"Teretia is getting ready," he told her. "And Lysander too. I don't think they'll be long."

She sat down at the now extremely clean kitchen table.

"Good, that gives us a moment to talk."

Philo's stomach sank. He wondered what possible subject he could converse with Verenia about successfully, before remembering that they had at least one thing in common: their plans for the night. Overjoyed at having something to say that would fill the already awkward silence, Philo said, "It should be a nice evening." He smiled at her. She did not smile back.

"The emperor will be there," stressed Philo.

"I need to ask you about Lysander. I believe you are the person to ask," she said with a faint hint of disbelief.

"Lysander? Oh. Well, he's, erm, he trains announcers at the palace."

"I know that. He told me when he invited me out. He told me all manner of things, but nothing I needed to know." Meeting Philo's eyes, she went on, "I've been taken in before. I'll not let it happen again. You and I, we're different. You may look like you've just fallen off the latest boat but I'll wager Doris that you're not as naïvely dim as you appear."

Behind Verenia's rather insulting rhetoric, there was a truth. Though Philo had maintained an expression of benign mystification during every conversation Verenia had struggled through with him, he had worked for Nero. It had been a rare month when he hadn't been asked to source a good assassin or explain to an acrobat trainer exactly what the emperor expected his contortionist to be able to perform.

"I know," she continued, "that you will tell me the truth. Unadulterated."

Philo glanced over his shoulder towards the back of the apartment where both Teretia and Lysander were preparing themselves for the party. "What do you want to know?"

"Start with his father."

This was one of the odd things about life on the outside. The obsession with who your father, mother, uncle, grandfather were. It was not something discussed at the palace, where a large contingent of the slaves had no idea of their parentage. Philo, though he'd had a mother, lacked for every other category of relative. Verenia was in luck though. Lysander was a verna, that is a palace-born slave, and thus Philo was able to tell her with confidence:

"He was a singer."

"Was?"

"Yes, he was…" Philo trailed off.

"Was?" repeated Verenia.

"He died."

"Yes, he was died?" Her scepticism at Philo misusing a verb was well placed and the freedman shuffled awkwardly on the bench. "What happened to him?"

"Well, he was … He was … Well, he was executed." Then to Verenia's rather shocked expression, "But it wasn't really his fault."

"What did he do to have such a fate?"

"He was a very good singer."

"I'm sure he was, but you're avoiding my question. Why did he get executed?"

"Because he was a very good singer," repeated Philo. "And Nero was a singer and he wasn't as good." He shrugged. "That's all there was to it, really. His mother was pretty keen that Lysander not become a singer after that."

"His mother? She is?" asked Verenia rather cautiously.

"Oh, she's alive," brightened Philo. "She was a very high-ranking attendant to Empress Agrippina. She's currently married to Gaius Baebinus. They have a very nice house on the Caelian Hill. He is a most successful and well-respected businessman," he supplied more happily.

"Currently married?" asked Verenia. "What does that mean? Is she contemplating divorce?"

"Lysandria would never divorce Gaius Baebinus."

She had a much cleaner method of disposing of husbands.

Verenia, with clear difficultly, let this pass, saying, "You've known Lysander for many years."

"Yes."

She fiddled with her bracelets again, before asking, "He is a good man?"

From her tone, Philo could tell this was very important to her. Crucial. Therefore, he deduced, she'd be wanting a cracking answer.

"Er," began Philo, inwardly weighing up the relevant criteria to measure Lysander against. He'd decided on several factors in his list before his thought processes were interrupted by Verenia.

"Oh for Juno's sake," she swore. "Is he emotionally cold?"

Philo blinked. "No."

"Is he cruel?"

Another blink. "No."

"Is he violent?"

"Gosh, no."

"That'll do," she said, standing up.

"Philo! Do you have any scent? I want to put some on my—." Lysander appeared in the doorway, freezing as he saw Verenia sitting at the table.

Unlike Philo, he paid full attention to her appearance.

She was dressed in a pink gown that floated from her shoulders over her pleasing figure and flowed onwards to her shapely ankles. A pearl necklace was worn around her long neck, matched by earrings and, most arousing of all for Lysander, a single string of the jewels around her left ankle. She had not dared to ape the elaborate court hairstyles of the day, but rather her blonde hair was held simply in a bun like those imperial ladies of old, Livia or Octavia. It flattered her greatly. As did the white gloves warming her slender hands. And the white cloak that was draped around her shoulders.

It was fair to say that Lysander gawped at this vision. He even sweated a little. A sudden tightening in his groin forced a hasty sit-down on the bench beside Philo. The table top hid his appreciation as he gazed up at the loveliness that was Verenia.

He opened his mouth ready to greet her and vocalise some of this appreciation.

In Lysander's defence, it came from the heart, which was how Philo described it later to an unimpressed Verenia. With a lusty breath, the announcer launched into possibly the most ill-advised pre-first date compliment ever uttered in the history of the empire.

"My gods! You're looking gorgeous enough to be a palace whore!"

THIRTY-NINE

"I've blown it, haven't I?" gloomed a miserable Lysander as they trudged through the forum.

Verenia had decided that the litter was not big enough for all four of them and made Lysander walk alongside it. Philo had joined him out of sympathy.

"Not necessarily."

"I meant it as a compliment," protested Lysander for the umpteenth time. "It is a compliment. Those sex slaves are luscious. You couldn't be a sex slave if you weren't utterly gorgeous."

Philo offered a, "Hmm," in response. As he spotted the familiar arches of the old palace ahead, his hands began to tremble.

"I wasn't suggesting that she was a palace whore. I was trying to be nice—what's up?"

Philo had halted by the Basilica Julia, fists clenched by his side, staring up at the old palace. The bearers kept moving. The swaying red litter that contained Verenia and Teretia disappeared from view.

"Philo?"

Lysander tapped him on the arm. He flinched away. The announcer took in Philo's shaking hands and wide eyes. He gently placed a hand on each shoulder and manoeuvred Philo into the Basilica's colonnade. He sat Philo down on the plinth of a column.

"What's the matter?"

A muttered, "Nothing."

"What is it?" persisted the announcer.

Philo, winded by the frantic race of his heart, stuttered out a "I can't—I can't do it."

"Do what?"

Philo looked at Lysander with panicked eyes and a wobble to his bottom lip. In a trembling voice, "I can't go to this party. I can't do it. I never wanted to go, only Teretia…" he tailed off miserably at his mention of his wife. "I can't do it."

"Of course you can. You've done it hundreds of times in the past. I know you hate parties but this isn't going to be like the parties Nero used to throw. There isn't even an orgy planned!"

"I can't do it," repeated Philo, his eyes fixed on the cobbled pavement.

Lysander sat down beside him. "Is this because of what happened to you? Being arrested and beaten up and then left for dead in the cells? Is it because of that?"

The shiver that wracked Philo's meagre frame answered the question for him.

"But nothing like that is going to happen tonight. It's just a party. With food. And drink. And probably a bit of singing and stuff," said Lysander. "It's Otho's party for Jupiter's sake! He doesn't even like to have slaves whipped! He's pretty much banned it since that Doricus incident. Nothing is going to happen to you. Nothing."

"I know," said Philo softly. "I know that. But I can't. I just can't."

Lysander pondered. They couldn't just sit here in the forum. What would the girls think when their litter reached the summit of the Palatine Hill, the curtains were opened, and they realised their escorts were gone? Lysander, despite his horrible faux pas, still harboured a smidgeon of hope that he might make significant progress with Verenia. That wouldn't happen if they went home. Verenia would slope off to her Viminal mansion, even more miffed at him after failing to deliver on the promised imperial banquet.

He glanced at Philo sat on the plinth, pulling his fingers through his hair in agitation. Lysander had known Philo near-on his whole life. He had been his best friend always. Thus, he knew that if there was one thing Philo couldn't stand, it was letting people down. So he said casually, "What's Teretia going to say? Hey?"

Philo looked up.

"She's been looking forward to this banquet for days."

He let that hang for a moment. Philo stood up and they continued their journey.

* * *

The first room in the old palace was a huge entrance hall with marble columns twenty feet high that rose to an arched ceiling studded with gems and liberally applied with gold. It was meant to both impose and impress. To Lysander and Philo, it was merely home.

They'd negotiated the ample space so many times over the years that they barely even glanced at the expensive finery. Teretia had nipped through this space to visit Philo at work frequently enough to be unfazed. But for Verenia, this was all new. And though she may have wished to hold onto the image she projected as a mature, travelled, experienced woman—faced with the hall, her jaw dropped as she gazed upwards.

The word, "Amazing," fell from her lips. Teretia jumped on the opportunity this afforded her. "Oh, this is nothing. You should see the new palace. The ceilings there actually rotate and the walls squirt perfume onto visitors. Don't they, Philo?"

Her husband didn't answer, being distracted by the sight of Praetorians lurking by the walls. Lysander attempted to thaw Verenia by way of an extended explanation of some of the art work contained in the new palace. His description of the statue of Laocoön and his sons fighting off a terrifying serpent had Verenia almost smiling.

"I should like to see that," she said.

"I can take you," said Lysander quickly. Then, with an affected nonchalance, "I pass by it every day while working for the emperor."

"What is the emperor like?" asked Verenia looking up at Lysander.

"Well …," began the announcer.

Verenia linked onto his arm.

* * *

Narrow-eyed, hand placed on the handle of her whip, Mina observed the party guests with suspicion. Any one of them could be a Vitellian agent vowed to kill the emperor, maim the empress, and ruin what should be a nice evening. Any one of them. Though probably not that one, thought Mina, eyeing up an anxious-looking Philo across the hall.

Mina hadn't seen Philo since the night she and Straton had rescued him from the palace cells. His injuries had been so grievous she'd fully expected him to die. Yet here he was, out for the night with that wife of his hanging off his arm. Blonde, blue-eyed, large-busted, and young, Teretia was the very antithesis of Mina's flat-chested, brown-haired, and creakingly aged twenty-nine-year-old roommate who'd also been the subject of Philo's affections some years back. Once you added Straton into that mix, you had to seriously wonder what Philo's type was. Mina certainly did.

Catching Philo's eye, she gave him a cheery wave. He froze and looked away. Which was both rude and ungrateful in

Mina's view. A view, she decided, that needed to be shared. She would have done so if Cassandra hadn't appeared by her elbow.

"The mistress is asking for you."

Mina straightened her helmet and hooked her thumbs into her belt.

"Party time," she growled.

FORTY

Epaphroditus was in even less of a party mood than Philo. He had a stack of correspondence to work his way through. Plus some worrying correspondence from an agent of his which proved that, as he had feared, a Vitellian spy had infiltrated the palace. He would have bowed out and let Talos attend on his behalf, had he not known Philo was attending.

He was keen to catch up with his former assistant to pick his brain on a number of topics that were bothering him, and to check on his health. From their last meeting, Epaphroditus was not convinced that Philo was as well as he claimed to be. So he'd let his body slave deck him out in a braided tunic of a shade of red that was apparently the very thing. Epaphroditus sat through his barber's ministrations in silence, his mind on other matters.

"Alright, that'll do," he waved away the slave bearing down on him with a pair of tweezers.

"But your eyebrows, master," the slave exclaimed in horror.

Epaphroditus assured him he'd survive, even with slightly overgrown eyebrows.

He entered the winter dining room via the back, across a deserted banqueting hall and through a discreet entrance. This allowed him to reach the emperor without having to go through all the rigmarole of a formal announcement, or having to force his way through the inevitable guests keen to make his well-connected acquaintance for their own advantage.

He found the emperor settled on a couch with Statilia Messalina. The other two couches in the arrangement were taken by Salvius and Onomastus.

"Ah, there you are," beamed a very sprightly looking Otho. "Doesn't Statilia look glam."

The empress wore a golden necklace with a glowing ruby the size of an egg in its centre and a gown the exact same shade as Epaphroditus' tunic. Clearly his body slave was correct, it was the very thing.

"Is the bodyguard really necessary though, Imperial Mistress?" he asked, indicating to where Mina stood behind the couch, her eyes just visible through the slits in her helmet, scanning the party guests for any dangers.

"I can't be without her," said Statilia. "Unlike most, she has my best interests at heart." She was looking with faint accusation directly at Epaphroditus.

"Sadly Calvia couldn't make it," said Otho. "Apparently that new husband of hers is feeling a bit dicky. She's staying home to nurse him."

Calvia as a nurse? An image that had Epaphroditus shuddering. Calvia had all the bedside warmth of a damp octopus.

"Still, it should be a good night, hey Salvius?"

His nephew nodded, distracted by the arriving guests, the busy slaves, and the all-out fabulousness of the décor. This was dining done imperial-style. A lavish extravaganza of food, drink, and entertainment with no account taken of cost.

"Titus Flavius Domitian and Claudia Aphrodite," the announcer drawled at terrific volume.

Epaphroditus' head snapped round.

"Oh, is that your ex?" asked Statilia sweetly, peering towards the door. "And she's brought a toy boy. How very fashionable of her."

Otho placed a restraining hand on his fiancée's arm.

"If you'll excuse me, Caesar," said Epaphroditus, avoiding Statilia's gaze, unable to trust himself not to respond to her bite.

* * *

She looked beautiful. Of course she did. Because she always did. Even when she'd just woken up or was in a fury with one of their children, Faustina generally. He hadn't seen her since that scene during Parentalia. Hadn't dared even to write to her. He was terrified that if he did, she would respond with finality: I am divorcing you.

His heart stepped up a beat. His throat tightened. For a man as poised as Epaphroditus, these were uncomfortably raw feelings. He knew that he had to talk to her, but on the route over he'd failed to devise any speech. Thus, when he reached her, rather than complimenting her appearance or telling her how wonderful it was to see her, he eyed up the curly-haired youth on her arm and demanded, "Who's this?" It was said with such naked hostility that Domitian instantly broke the connection.

Aphrodite grabbed Domitian's arm and re-hooked onto it. "What's it to you who I decide to venture out with?"

He would have responded with a proprietorial, "You're my wife."

But luckily, for it could only have inflamed her further, Caenis, who had been quietly standing beside Aphrodite, interjected, "This is Flavius' nephew."

Epaphroditus took another look at the boy. "I have heard much about you. Your heroics at the siege of Yodfat pleased Nero greatly. He had you marked for a good position when you returned to Rome. This new emperor, I am sure, will be willing to recognise your successes."

"I've never been to Judaea. I've never been anywhere. I've not done anything. You're thinking of my brother."

"Oh," said Epaphroditus. Then, to Caenis, "Am I?"

"You are."

"You look a lot like him."

A platitude that failed to placate Domitian, who said, "He's eleven years older than me."

"I was going to say you look like him when he was your age," Epaphroditus attempted to soothe.

Domitian did not look soothed.

Caenis put an arm around her stepson. "Come, let us join Flavius. They'll start the entertainment soon."

Aphrodite went to follow but was stopped by Epaphroditus grabbing hold of the top of her arm.

"Dite."

"What?" she hissed. "Do you want me to secure another adolescent for you to humiliate."

He removed his hand. "We need to talk."

"Do we? Strange, I've not seen much of a need for chatting from you recently. She's fine, by the way. Silvia. Not that you've bothered to enquire."

"Because you made it very clear I wasn't welcome."

"You could have sent a letter. A note. Anything to show you care."

"Of course I care."

"Then tell Silvia!" she cried exasperated. "See it from someone else's view for once. She discovers the man she thought was her father isn't. And how does he respond? He cuts off all contact with her!"

Stung by this perfectly true statement, he demanded of her, "What have you told her about her real father?"

Aphrodite couldn't stop herself from glancing over to where Otho, Silvia's father, reclined, nattering away, oblivious, to Statilia.

"I couldn't tell her the truth, could I? It would put her in terrible danger."

"So what did you tell her?"

"That I was brutalised."

"Dite—"

"Well, what would you prefer her to know? That I cuckolded you? That I am some dreadful trollop who's been putting it about the entire city?"

"No, of course not. Look Dite, can we go somewhere quiet? We need to talk. I need to talk. There are things I need to say."

Seeing the plea in his eyes, she almost wavered. But at that point, the gentle song of a flute chorus drifted over and all her grievances came back to her.

"These last few months have been a revelation. I can see clearly now. I can see just what a despot you are."

"Despot?" a baffled Epaphroditus queried.

"Yes, despot. You've kept me locked up in that house these past fifteen years as some kind of animal set to breeding your spawn. It's been relentless! And whilst I've been suffering through endless birthing pains and swollen breasts and no sleep whatsoever, you've been orgying it up here like a sexually incontinent Lothario. You do realise that you're not obligated to have sex with everyone you meet. You're not a wine boy anymore," she spat. "I had a job. A career. I was somebody. Somebody important. People trusted my opinion. Empresses relied on my consul. And then I married you and all that was snatched away from me, along with my friends. What friends have I now? No one. I'm shut up in that house all day and all night, with no one but the slaves to talk to."

This was not a description of his marriage that Epaphroditus recognised. "You kicked me out!" he managed to interject.

"I was talking about when we were together," she retorted angrily. "Though together is overstretching it because you were never at home. Hardly ever. Too busy dipping your penis into every passing slave whore!"

"I was working," stressed Epaphroditus through gritted teeth. "I was working to secure our home, our future, our children's futures."

"Because we didn't have enough money five years ago or even ten years back," she scorned. "I begged you to retire after Nero died. And you lied to me. You lied to me over and over again as you and that man schemed his way to power. And for what? For a reign that is crumbling before your eyes! Ask yourself, Tiberius. Ask yourself honestly. Was it worth it?"

FORTY-ONE

Teretia stood on her toes, trying to see above the heads of the guests in front of them.

"What's this room, Philo? I don't think I've been in this room before."

"Winter dining room," her husband replied as they shuffled forward in the line.

"Ooh I can see water! There's water between the couches," she cooed, bouncing up on her toes again.

"They'll float the food dishes on the water," Lysander added. "With fish-shaped oil lamps floating in-between so you can see what you're eating."

This enthused the animal-shaped oil lamp collector Teretia, who beamed with excitement. "I wonder if they have a whale. I've never seen a whale-shaped oil lamp before and I've searched everywhere for one."

Even Verenia was impressed when she spied the arrangements. "How romantic," she sighed.

It gave Lysander additional hope in the freebie-scoring. As they got nearer, they could hear the announcer doing his stuff. Lysander cocked an ear, then tutted.

"Ampelius," he told Philo. "Useless idiot. He's got the inflection wrong in Titianius Labienius."

He pronounced the name smoothly, deeply, and with the correct emphasis (in his experienced opinion) as they shuffled to the front. Catching sight of his boss, Ampelius straightened his back.

"Sir," he barked crisply. Then, noting Verenia on Lysander's arm, his eyes opened very wide.

Lysander waved his spare arm, "Go on then, impress me."

Ampelius, checking the guest list cleared his throat.

"Servius Sulpicius Lysander and Verenia," he projected across the banqueting hall.

"Your volume needs work," tutted Lysander.

"Lysander," said Philo, tugging at his friend's tunic sleeve. "I don't want to be announced," he pleaded. But in vain, for Ampelius had taken a lungful of breath and imparted in double his previous volume, "Tiberius Claudius Philo and Teretia."

He pronounced it Fee-lo rather than Fy-lo but nevertheless heads poked up. Not the esteemed senators. Not the equestrians. Not even the assorted eastern client kings who'd been sent to Rome in a sort of cultural exchange that was in no way a hostage situation to keep tricky monarchs under the Roman yoke. Rather, it was the imperial slaves dotted about the hall who lifted up their heads.

It even managed to pique the attention of the rowing Epaphroditus and Aphrodite.

"Philo?" they both said, looking at each other without a hint of anger or reproach for the first time that evening.

Philo fidgeted under such attention. He lowered his head, missing the smiles and cheery waves that were aimed in his direction. He hung tightly onto Teretia's arm, keeping his eyes down as they were led to their seats.

There were three couches arranged around a low table. Between the arms of each couch were rectangular ponds with plates floating on the surface containing small titbits. Teretia and Philo shared one couch, Verenia and Lysander being unmarried got a couch each.

"It's a whale!" proclaimed Teretia with joy pointing at an oil lamp. "They have a whale!"

Verenia peered around. "So where's the emperor then? We seem to be in a very poor spot to see him."

"There's a prescribed etiquette as to who sits where. Like at the games," explained Lysander, leaning forward and helping himself to a crispy slice of pork.

Verenia gazed at the couches nearest them. "I thought you had impressive imperial connections," she said to her cousin.

"Philo used to be the emperor's private secretary's secretary," piped up Teretia.

Verenia delicately picked a titbit off a floating plate. She nibbled it gently before stressing, "Used to be."

Teretia's cheeks went pink. "I've met the emperor," she insisted hotly. "Otho came to our home, actually came inside. Didn't he, Philo?"

Philo caught in his own private misery muttered, "Yes he did. He came in."

"So you see, Verenia, we are very much acquainted."

"Is that so?" smiled Verenia. "Well then, I'm sure the emperor will be sure to come over and say hello to you, seeing as you are such good friends."

"Philo."

The sight of the approaching Epaphroditus and Aphrodite had the well-trained Lysander and Philo on their feet, heads bowed.

"Sit, sit," instructed the secretary.

Aphrodite sat on the edge of Teretia and Philo's couch. "You are positively blooming Teretia. Pregnancy seems to suit you."

Teretia's hand went to her stomach, though not before she managed to shoot Verenia a smug look.

"Thank you," she said shyly, adding, "I have started to feel a little sick though."

"Argh, tell me about it. When I was pregnant with Pollus I vomited all day long. For some reason just the sight of raw meat set me off."

"That's like me! I can't bear to eat prawns and I used to love them so. But I can't bear to look at them or even think about them because it makes me sick."

She didn't look sick. She looked, as Aphrodite had commented, positively blooming, with pink cheeks, a clear complexion, and hair that seemed thicker and blonder. Her husband on the other hand, Epaphroditus noted, was the opposite: paler, thinner than he remembered even from his last visit, and looking distinctly unwell.

"Philo, how are you?" he asked kindly.

He didn't answer so Epaphroditus touched him lightly on the arm to get his attention. A gesture that had Philo jumping back as if burnt.

"Philo?" asked Teretia.

"I'm fine. I'm well," he responded briskly. "Much weller than I was. I'm—" his eyes fell on a nearby Praetorian.

A nauseous lump formed in his stomach, grumbling and growling until it pushed upwards into his throat. He got to his feet. "Excuse me, I think—"

He retched, holding his hand across his mouth.

Epaphroditus took one arm, Aphrodite the other. "Alright, alright, let's find somewhere—"

"Philo?" Teretia sat up.

"We'll get him some air," said Aphrodite. "You stay here. You won't want to miss the entertainments."

FORTY-TWO

They rushed Philo out through the adjoining banqueting hall that was being used as storage space and then through a side door into a small courtyard. Philo ran over to the basin of a fountain and was noisily sick into it. Aphrodite rubbed his back gently. Seven retches later, he sat up.

"Sorry," he muttered to two concerned faces. Then gazing back into the fountain, he said, "I think they'll have to drain this." Wiping a hand across his mouth, he repeated, "Sorry."

"No matter," assured Epaphroditus. "The cleaning slaves live for this kind of adversity. They love a challenge."

"Perhaps we should arrange for a litter to take you home."

"No, no! Don't do that. Teretia. Teretia will miss out and then Verenia will be the winner."

"Verenia?"

"Teretia's cousin," explained Philo.

"The girl accompanying Lysander," said Epaphroditus with a raised eyebrow.

Aphrodite failed to stop the smile. "Most unusual and surprising." Lysander's lack of success with women was legendary.

"Teretia was upset that Verenia was coming to this dinner and she wasn't. She thought Verenia would be mean about it or something. I don't really understand it."

Epaphroditus and Aphrodite had five daughters. They perfectly understood the fierce competition that raged between girls with all the intensity of a battlefield engagement and twice as bloody.

"I didn't want to come," said Philo, shuffling his feet on the ground. "But Teretia—"

"Didn't want Verenia to win," completed Aphrodite.

"Yes, I think that's it."

"I'll admit I was surprised when I got your note requesting an invite. I didn't think you were much of a partygoer."

Philo hated gatherings of any kind. Epaphroditus had only ensured his attendance at the event of the decade, Nero's and Statilia's wedding day, by pretending it was a work assignment. Philo was to make notes on the behaviour of the guests. He presented his findings during one excruciatingly long morning the next day as Epaphroditus lay horribly hungover on a couch.

"I couldn't let Teretia down."

Epaphroditus pressed a finger to his lips for a moment. "There is one way we can please Teretia and comprehensively best Verenia, in a way she'll struggle to match ever."

Philo looked up with interest. Aphrodite was similarly intrigued.

"I'll get the emperor to pop over to her couch and say hello. Maybe make some vague reference to the great favour she did him last year in looking after Sporus."

Aphrodite clapped her hands together. "Oh yes, that's it! Verenia will be mad with jealousy."

"He'd do that? The emperor? For you?"

"Not for me. For you. Naturally he'll be pleased to help. You know what Marcus is like, he can't bear any upsets. I'll get onto it now."

Placing palms on his thighs, he got to his feet. As he did so, he exchanged a look with Aphrodite, angling his head towards Philo. She nodded her assent in return.

With Epaphroditus gone, they sat side by side on the rim of the fountain. Philo's sickness seemed to have passed. Aphrodite said softly, "It must be strange being back here at the palace."

She knew she'd hit the spot by the way Philo instantly averted his eyes downwards. Extracting confidences from Philo was a slow process. Aphrodite knew him well enough not to push, but rather she sat and waited. Eventually, he admitted quietly that it was indeed a bit odd for him.

"I imagine your memories of the palace have been tarnished by the last time you were here."

Philo rubbed at his knee with the heel of his hand. "I wanted to thank you for looking after me when I when... When I was ... ill."

"You've already thanked me. Nearly hourly as I recall," she smiled. "Of course your memory was a bit messy in those first few days at my house. How is it now? Your memory?"

A hand went to his head. "I can store facts away and reference them like before."

Interesting, she thought, that Philo was casting his life as "before" and "after". A clue to how deeply he'd been affected by events.

"I am much better now though. Much better."

"Hopefully my nursing helped a little with your recovery."

"I'm sure it did, thank you."

"That's all in the past, Philo. You need to put it behind you. You have so much to look forward to with Teretia and the baby."

Philo turned his eyes upwards. "Epaphroditus told me when I was freed that my life was a blank tablet and I could start afresh. I really wanted that. I wanted to be new and different. But everything was just the same with ... with Straton. And then I was arrested. And I hadn't done any of what they accused me of. I worked hard for Galba. I've always worked hard. It's all I've ever done and it didn't help me at all. Not with Straton or Laco or Icelus or Galba."

Aphrodite reached over and squeezed his hand. "I know," she said.

And she did. For she had been a "Philo". A quiet, diligent secretary who'd never wavered in her loyalty and dedication. That hadn't saved her either. Not from Agrippina's machinations. She was hit by a memory of the day she now knew Silvia had been conceived. The day that Otho under Agrippina's instructions had raped her. She remembered the humiliation that burnt into her skin, the willing for it to be over.

And then afterwards, lying on a bed in a dark room, facing the wall as Epaphroditus swore that nothing like that would ever, ever happen to her again. Promising her that he wouldn't let it happen. That he would save her from the palace.

"You have Teretia and the baby and your life on the Viminal. That's worth far more than anything that came before. My husband is right. You have a blank slate. We just need to give it another wash down. There are so many wonderful times to be noted on that slate. I can see you now, surrounded by your children, and Teretia of course, opening a school on the Viminal."

"A school?" queried a puzzled-looking Philo.

Aphrodite smiled. "Yes, a school, I think. You don't want all that palace training to go to waste, do you?"

"I suppose not."

"There must be a lot of folk on the Viminal who'd like their children to learn some of those skills we have drilled into us here."

Philo thought for a moment and then replied with a brighter tone, "I think you might be right. Tadius is always going on about how he can never add up his takings from his shop. And there are plenty of people who'd like to write better. They are always saying so."

"Well, there you go," she said warmly. Then, in a quieter voice, "With time, these memories that are hurting you now will fade."

Philo looked at her with pleading eyes. "Will they?"

Another memory. This time of moving into the Esquiline house and how she'd felt as she'd sat in their courtyard for the first time. A deep sense of release, of shoulders relaxing, of the anxiety that had hung over her constantly lifting. She'd felt free. She was safe. Finally, she was safe.

"They will fade, become less raw, but they will always be there, Philo. It's important that they are because they will make you appreciate all that you have, all that you have achieved, from out of your bleakest moment."

It was a touching, private moment between two people who'd both suffered. It was interrupted by a call of, "Philooo!" as Mina stomped her way across the courtyard. She came to a full stop directly in front of them, her hands placed on her hips.

"Well," she said.

"Hello, Artemina."

"Is that all you've got to say for yourself, Tiberius Claudius Philo?" She made his prestigious imperial name sound like an insult.

Philo, confused by her hostility, asked, "How are you?"

It did not lighten her mood and she positively glowered at Philo.

"Is there something we can help you with?" interjected Aphrodite in a pleasant tone.

Addressing her, Mina said, "He totally blanked me." She thumbed at Philo.

"I'm sure he didn't mean to. Did you, Philo?"

A confused-looking Philo mumbled, "Sorry."

He fidgeted on the edge of the fountain. Sitting beside him, Aphrodite could feel his springy energy. A sign of his desire to escape the situation.

"Right, Philo, shall we get you back to Teretia?" She made to stand but Mina interrupted.

"I thought it rude. Very rude indeed. Especially after what I did for you."

"Did for me?"

Mina gave an exasperated sigh. The sort of sigh Lysander frequently resorted to during conversations with Philo. "I rescued you from the cells at great risk to myself. I saved your life."

Philo looked at her blankly.

"You could at least be partly grateful. A thank you would be nice."

"I don't," he began, then faltered, a hand rubbing at his jaw.

Aphrodite picked up his thread. "Philo took several nasty blows to his head. If he hasn't thanked you for all you did that night, it's not because he isn't grateful. It's because he doesn't remember."

"Oh." Mina's fiery eyes softened. "You don't remember what happened?"

Philo shook his head. "You rescued me from the cells?"

"Yes, I did. Minerva's trident, what a battle it was! There were Praetorian scum everywhere, all stabby, stabby. Then there were the other prisoners going mental all over the place. And I had hold of you and I dragged you across the floor between them. I still can't believe we got through that chaos. It was like some bacchanal orgy. But with killing rather than sex."

Rubbing at his jaw, Philo continued his questioning. "You took me to Epaphroditus' house?"

"She did," said Aphrodite gently. "You were flitting in and out of consciousness. That's why you don't remember."

"I was sure you were going to die," continued Mina brightly. "You were gasping and heaving all over the place. But here you are!"

"You saved my life?"

"I did."

A pause, and then Philo put to her the question that was perplexing him most. "Why?"

"It wasn't my idea," confessed Mina. "Not that I wouldn't have saved your life on my own. I could have. Easily.

Well, maybe not easily because it needed two of us to get into the cells. And, actually, thinking about it, without Straton I probably couldn't have got out either. It was definitely a two-person job."

"Straton?"

Aphrodite placed a hand on Philo's trembling fingers. "Artemina and Straton brought you to my house."

Mina plonked herself down beside Philo. "He died. Straton died. Did you know?"

Shuffling away from her, he muttered, "I heard."

"I miss him," sighed Mina. "I miss him every day. I can't imagine how you must be feeling. It must be devastating. He really loved you. I mean, really loved you." She gave a wistful smile. "Maybe one day someone will love me like that." Missing the incredulous look that Philo shot her way, she continued, "Felix gave me some of his stuff, trinkets to remember him by. Did you want any of them? So you can remember him too?"

On the other side of Philo, Aphrodite pressed her leg against his. It was a warning to be careful what he said. To verbalise, to confirm, that he'd been Straton's victim was social suicide. It would damn him as one of "those" imperial freedmen. The likes of Pythagorus, who had given his body to Nero well into his freedom.

To submit to such degradation as a freedman was unacceptable. If such a charge became linked to his name, Philo would no longer be received at the palace with the respect his former rank deserved. The emperor and his inner circle would not wish to associate with him.

If word reached the Viminal Hill, Philo's promising new scribing career would be destroyed. For who would want to put their words into the hands of such a creature? An invert. A cinaedus. And then there was Philo's family, Teretia and her mother. The scandal would destroy their lives too. Pompeia's standing on the Viminal would be called into question by letting her daughter marry such a man.

What Philo said now or didn't say would determine his future. Aphrodite willed him with everything she had to remain silent.

"I have his whip." Mina fondled said article, which was attached to her belt. "What about the stylus case? The one he had your name engraved on. Would you like that?"

"I feel quite sure Philo doesn't want anything that belonged to Straton," said Epaphroditus, appearing by the colonnaded section of the courtyard and walking towards them. "Honestly, Artemina, the man was a complete pest. He wouldn't leave Philo alone, no matter how often I told him Philo had not the slightest interest in him that way. I mean, why would he? Straton was hardly a catch for the emperor's private secretary's secretary. But that was Straton all over, delusional. I couldn't tell you the number of times he formed such unsuitable crushes. The only thing I was thankful for is that I managed to keep it from you, Philo." To his former assistant, he said, "I am sorry. Possibly I should have told you about Straton's feelings towards you, but I didn't want to distress you."

Philo looked at Epaphroditus blankly.

"I told him not to tell you," said Aphrodite, catching onto the tactic. "Not when it was limited to him hanging around, wanting to catch sight of you."

"It was too benign to unnecessarily upset you," continued Epaphroditus.

"Hang on," said Mina. "Straton loved Philo."

"From afar," said Epaphroditus.

"No, that's not right. He told me himself that they were lovers. He said so."

"*He* said so," stressed Epaphroditus.

"They were moving in together. I helped Straton get his room ready for Philo to move in with him," insisted Mina.

Epaphroditus arched an eyebrow. "Philo was moving in with Straton on the Palatine while marrying Teretia and living with her on the Viminal? Even for an efficient man like Philo, it's quite an act to be in two places at the same time!"

Mina shook her head looking baffled. Suddenly, she brightened. "Presents! He bought him presents."

"Like the stylus set you mentioned?"

"Yes!"

"The stylus set you have possession of. So clearly, he didn't give it to Philo, did he?"

"But he said," she insisted.

"He was wrong," said Aphrodite softly.

"Yes, he was," stressed her husband. Then to Philo. "This must be quite a shock for you."

"It is," Philo managed to croak.

"Come, let's get you back to Teretia," said Aphrodite, standing up and assisting Philo upwards.

"Good idea," said Epaphroditus. "I'm sure Teretia will want to tell you all about the emperor's visit to her couch."

Philo looked at his former boss. "Thank you," he said.

"Not a problem. The emperor was most keen to renew his acquaintance with your wife."

"Thank you for the other too," said Philo, quietly angling his head to where the confused Mina sat.

"Not at all."

"Lysander said you were divorcing," said Philo.

Aphrodite looked at Epaphroditus, the man who had married her despite knowing the child in her belly was probably not his. "A rumour," she said. "With no foundation."

FORTY-THREE

"You're not on the guest list," insisted Ampelius.

"Yes I am. You spell it S., P., then some more letters that make it Sporus."

Ampelius scanned down his list again. "Nope," he said, looking up.

"Alright, alright, look for That Eunuch."

Ampelius looked down at his list, his finger poised on a scrawled name. "Aha!" he beamed. "Found you: That Eunuch."

He opened his mouth, ready to announce. Sporus gave him a quick kick in the shin. "Don't you dare announce me as That Eunuch. Don't you dare."

"It's what it says here," he replied, holding up the list with one hand while the other massaged the dent Sporus' sandal had caused in his leg.

"You know nothing. You are a fool. Go get Lysander. He's a proper announcer."

"He's not working. He's attending the party as guest," Ampelius informed him. Then, unable to resist, he added in a hushed tone, "He's brought a woman."

"Nooooo," breathed Sporus. "He never has."

"He has."

"He never has. It's one of you trainees in a dress."

Ampelius looked Sporus up and down. "Well, you'd know all about that. Men in dresses."

"I AM NOT A MAN. I AM A SPORUS!"

And here the eunuch gave Ampelius' other leg a sharp kick. Which was probably why he announced him as, "A Sporus, whatever that is!" to the entire dining room.

Alright, thought Sporus, it wasn't quite the introduction he'd envisaged as part of his grand entrance, but there was still plenty of opportunity to make up for such an abysmal arrival. Sporus had spent all day plotting this moment. The moment that would lead to the abrupt termination of that cow's and his darling Otho's engagement.

Being spectacularly more beautiful than that bitch by his estimation, Sporus didn't need to do much to outshine her in looks. But he'd been stunningly more gorgeous at the last three dinners, and so far that had inexplicably failed to break them up. Even though Otho had bedded him immediately afterwards. Clearly, he needed to do something more.

As his manicurist worked on his nails and a small girl massaged his feet in perfumed oil, Sporus applied his meagre intellect to the problem. Compared to that bitch, Sporus was both more desirable and beddable, but neither of those attributes had persuaded the emperor to commit to him. So what was it that Otho wanted? And then it hit him: Otho wanted an empress.

I mean, it was obvious when you thought about it. A bachelor emperor, with a rival in that man in Germania that everyone in the palace kept talking about. Otho needed an heir to prove to that German man he was of dynasty-making material. Naturally Otho, being a busy man, would fall upon the empress who was still haunting the palace to save time. So all that Sporus needed to do was to demonstrate that there was an alternative.

To this end, he shot off to Mina's room for a very particular reason that had nothing to do with catching up with his friend.

Mina's room rather handily conjoined to that cow's dressing chamber. Through the gap in the door, Sporus could peek at Statilia Messalina dressing for the party. That was how he knew she was dressed in a shade of red that was all the rage, with gold trimming and a gold cord tied beneath her saggy breasts.

Sporus made his way through the dining room, gloriously satisfied that all eyes were on him. Partly, he accepted grudgingly, this was due to Lysander's useless underling's announcement. But mostly, he knew it was because of his gorgeous dress in a shade of red that was all the rage, with gold trimming and a gold cord tied beneath his perky (and fake) breasts.

As Statilia had placed Sporus on a couch near to her own in order for that creature to bear full witness to her and Otho's love, she was forced to watch the eunuch walk the entire length of the hall and see her guests' expressions as they clocked his attire.

"That damned eunuch!" said Statilia, through clenched teeth.

Sporus gave her a cheery wave, then blew a kiss to Otho.

Statilia, looking at her fiancé, was enraged to find the word "Wow" stuck on his lips.

FORTY-FOUR

The Praetorian barracks lay on the Viminal Hill. A large fortified edifice with spikes topping the walls. The story went that these spikes were less to keep people out and more to keep the Praetorians contained. The long-suffering residents of this part of the Viminal had been known after particularly gruesome Praetorian-inspired disasters, to park their wagons against the gates, trapping the lot of them inside. It gave them a few hours respite until the cohort stationed at the palace returned from duty.

Tonight the Praetorians, aside from that singular cohort, were all at home. This was no cosy domestic scene of helmet polishing, boot cleaning, and uniform folding. Tonight was "dice night". An all-out, no-holds-barred evening of hard-core gambling with no limits placed on bets or, indeed, losses.

The previous dice night resulted in one guard losing not only his own worldly goods, but also those of his well-positioned merchant brother-in-law and toothless grandmother. Another guard drank himself into such a stupor that he fainted the next morning on palace duty. Right across the table in the middle of a committee meeting, scattering paperwork and smashing two glass paperweights. This enlivened the meeting beyond all measure. Guardsman Fuculus was even more unfortunate.

He awoke with a black eye, a broken nose, and the little finger on his left hand missing. Such was the standard casualty rate of dice night.

This evening, it was early enough for everyone to be mildly intoxicated and nobody's losses had outstripped his inflated monthly wages. All was therefore relatively peaceful. It would not stay that way.

The instigator of what came to be known colloquially by the Praetorians as "the party fuck-up" was their very own tribune Crispinus. It was later pointed out that Crispinus had merely been following orders. Thereby demonstrating to the Guard just how dangerous such job-worthiness could be.

Crispinus' job was at the behest of Celsus. The 17th Legion were being moved from Ostia to Rome in preparation for Otho's assault against the Vitellian advance. Naturally, they would need to be armed sufficiently for the campaign. Therefore, Crispinus had been entrusted to take these weapons by wagon from their storage point at the Praetorian barracks to the agreed rendezvous point with the legion. It was just unfortunate that this task happened to coincide with dice night.

Stood before the open armoury, Crispinus and his clerk ticked off the relevant items on the inventory as three slaves loaded up the wagons. All was going well until guardsman Paulus, having lost his monthly wage to an incredibly lucky dice throw from Proculus, went outside to take in some fresh air. Leaning against a wall, he heaved violently, splashing the ground with the red mixture that provided a carpet of colour the morning after each dice night. Once he'd got most of it out, or enough to facilitate fitting some more wine in, he leant back and took in fresh gulps of cool air. This was when he spotted Crispinus.

Paulus' wavering, drunken eye failed to recognise his own tribune and added double the number of helpers to the scene. Thus, it no longer resembled a small party at work, but something more akin to a mob. And what was this mob up to?

This was where Paulus' limited brain took on a life of its own. A palpable sense of déjà vu had him scanning his memory. Hadn't there been a raid of the armoury before? He recalled weapons being handed out one by one. Once they'd run out, they'd ripped apart the wooden latrine and handed out planks instead. It had made that midnight bladder-letting much chillier than it needed to be ever since.

The memory that Paulus had hit upon was Otho's coup back in January, which the Praetorians had instigated. Unfortunately, he failed to recall this aspect.

A coup! A ruddy coup! Against the emperor! Organised from their very own barracks! What treachery! What epic treachery, thought Paulus.

But they hadn't started yet, had they? Because they were still arming themselves. So there was still time, wasn't there? Time to stop them. Time to save Otho's throne! Paulus wondered what kind of reward they'd get for such heroism. Here his thoughts diverted into a list of how he'd spend his share of the coinage: a horse. He'd definitely buy a horse. Snapping back to the present, he resolved they had to be stopped.

To this end, Paulus staggered back to dice night and flung open the doors of the barrack room. In a suitably dramatic flourish worthy of Sophocles, a sudden gust of wind followed him in, blowing over two stools with a crash. All eyes fell on Paulus who cried, "It's a coup! They're going to kill our emperor!"

Given the sheer level of drunkenness at dice night, it took three more yells of, "Treason, dark treason," from Paulus before anyone responded. And when they did respond, they did so in the traditional Praetorian way: with no actual forethought, foresight, or forward planning.

"Let's get 'em!" said Proculus.

"Let's," agreed Lucullus.

And off the Guard went en masse, swords drawn, to wherever it was that whatever it was was happening.

To Crispinus and his clerk, happily ticking off the last batch of javelins, what followed made absolutely no sense at all. One moment Crispinus was congratulating everyone on their hard work, the next a series of yells announced the arrival of a hundred of his own men. Armed. Clearly very angry. Clearly very, very drunk. And now circling him and his clerk.

"What is the meaning of this? Stand down legionary! Stand down all of you!"

All was lost among the general clatter of, "Traitors," "Treason," "Emperor killers."

The clerk moved closer to Crispinus. Unfortunately for the clerk, that one step towards his tribune was also one step closer to the wagon of arms. His intent was completely misread by the growling Praetorians. Tribune Crispinus was treated to the spectacle of his clerk, whom he really was quite fond of, being hacked to death before his eyes. Stupefied and appalled, Crispinus failed to respond to Paulus' demands to know, "Who else is in on it?"

"He says nothing," said Paulus, fairly unnecessarily to the watching guards, as Crispinus' mouth opened and closed like a fish gulping for air.

"Who are you arming?" Proculus tried. "Who are these weapons for?"

This was the moment Crispinus found his voice. "The … the legion," he responded.

A hush. Then an intake of breath as a hundred guards all got the same thought simultaneously. It was verbally expressed by Proculus, who with horror exclaimed, "The legion are going to kill the emperor!"

"No—" began Crispinus.

"Yes," insisted Proculus, with the sureness of the drunk. "And we must… We must—"

"Get to the palace to save him!" declared Lucullus.

Crispinus' protests that they had to listen to him, that they had got it all wrong, were silenced by a sword thrust to his gut courtesy of Paulus.

So keen were the Guard, they abandoned the traditional march and instead ran through the streets of the Viminal. By the time they'd reached the bottom of the hill, they were rather short of breath and five of them had been sick. Thus, they switched back into a normal marching pace, if slightly out of sync.

FORTY-FIVE

Epaphroditus and Aphrodite had deposited Philo back with his wife. Teretia instantly garbled out in excitement that the emperor had especially come over to greet her.

Walking away from that happier party, Epaphroditus dared to ask, "Did you mean what you said to Philo? About rumours of our divorce being unfounded?"

"I am very grateful for what you did for Philo. And for Teretia. And for their future," she said.

"Philo is an excellent scribe, a thoroughly decent man. He doesn't deserve to be tarnished by acts forced upon him."

Their eyes met with mutual understanding and shared memories.

"What you said to Philo, did you mean it?" he asked again, visibly anxious.

"Come home," she said.

Epaphroditus' gaze faltered. "Do you mean that? Really?"

She kissed him on the cheek. "Yes, I do."

"What about?" He looked over to the emperor's couch.

Aphrodite followed his gaze, giving a shudder. "I don't like him. I never will. Not just for— Well, you know. But for what he leads you into. But I know you and I know you have to see this through, whatever the outcome is. And I have one thing to thank him for: Silvia."

He took her hand to his lips and kissed it. "She is my daughter."

"Yes, she is," said Aphrodite, leaning into him.

* * *

"Are you enjoying yourself?" Caenis felt duty-bound to ask Domitian.

If he was, it was not outwardly visible. He wore the habitual cloak of a disappointed adolescent, whatever his surroundings.

"I liked the monkeys," he said finally.

Flavius gave a conspiratorial wink, grinning. "Not the dancing girls then?"

"Not really," was his nephew's sparse reply.

Despite his age, girls did not appear to be one of Domitian's interests. Or more likely, Caenis concluded sadly, rather he did not consider himself worthy of them. Most unlike his amiable older brother. He was always playing one girl off against another, and the more scandalously unsuitable as wife material, the better. His father could hardly complain when his own long-term companion was an ex-slave. Caenis was of the opinion that some slave common sense might actually be of use to the struggling Domitian.

Looking about, Domitian commented, "I can't see Claudia Aphrodite or her husband. Do you think they've gone off to argue?"

"Or the other," said Caenis lightly.

"Hey ho there. Have you been matchmaking again, Caenis?" enquired Flavius.

"I might just," she smiled. "Ahh."

She pointed over to where Epaphroditus and Aphrodite stood hand in hand, Aphrodite leaning against her husband.

"You've done it again, old girl!" exclaimed Flavius.

"I knew that if they encountered each other on home territory they couldn't keep up this silly separation. They've far too much history. And less of the old, Flavius, you aged goat."

They shared an affectionate laugh.

* * *

Statilia could not take her glare off that eunuch. Look at it instructing the slaves to fetch its own special meal! Who did it think it was? And look at it now, dangling its leg off the couch to show off a golden ankle bracelet just like her own! When she was empress, she'd deal with that thing once and for all!

"Uncle, who is that girl?" Salvius asked Otho.

The emperor gave a twisted smile. "Less of the girl, Salvius. But very much a woman." Raising his eyebrows, he patted his nephew's arm. "I'll tell you about it someday." Glancing to his right to where the infuriated Statilia reclined, he added, "But maybe not tonight."

FORTY-SIX

The news that a large contingent of Praetorians were on the loose failed to reach the palace. The simple reason: every citizen who saw them coming immediately ran back home and bolted the door. So it came as a complete surprise to the two Praetorians guarding the main palace entrance.

"Hey up, what's going on?" said one as they spotted the jogging purple plumes in the forum below.

The second guard didn't wait to find out but instead sent a message straight to their tribune.

Tribune Martialis, who considered he had better things to do, nevertheless dragged himself to the main entrance. He reached it just as the contingent of Praetorians, led by Paulus, approached.

"What are you doing here?" snapped Martialis. "Change-over isn't till another three hours. Go back to camp. It's not time. Honestly! Useless, the lot of you. Don't we employ an hour slave to shout out the time for you idiots?"

This dressing-down caused a pause in the guards' momentum. Possibly, it might have impressed some sense into their heads. Their drunkenness was such that many in the group had forgotten the reason why they'd run all the way to the palace. Unfortunately, guardsman Paulus had not.

"Murderrrr!" he cried.

The guards behind him gave a rumbled roar, waving their spears above their heads.

"What?" queried Martialis, with all the impatience of a man who was aware he'd left a good dinner unprotected from sneaky slaves.

"The emperor is going to be murdered," insisted Paulus.

You'd have thought that this was the sort of threat the Praetorian Guard lived for. Goodness knows they had precious little else to do. Martialis would now leap into action to investigate Paulus' claim.

However, it was a really good dinner he'd left. Also, it was dice night, which Martialis knew to be a night of madness in which all kinds of odd things occurred. So he dismissed them outright.

"Rubbish," he said. "The emperor is relaxing with friends. He is quite safe. Now go back to your camp."

This was not the response Paulus and his followers had been expecting, and it took them a moment to digest it.

"I said, back to camp. That's an order."

From three lines back Proculus had a revelation. It was the first revelation he'd ever been inflicted with, and he felt a burning need to share it with his pal Lucullus.

"I reckon the tribune's in on it. That's why he won't let us in."

"Oooh, do you think?" responded Lucullus, and then without waiting to gain Proculus' consent to sharing his personal revelation, he yelled, "Paulus! Proculus reckons the tribune's in on the murder. That's why he's ordered us back to camp."

This was when all thoughts of his steaming dinner were abandoned.

"That's nonsense," Martialis attempted. But he could see that the guards were in no mood for reason.

"We're going in," stated Paulus.

Martialis took a step backwards. The two door guards either side of him did likewise.

"Charge!" yelled Paulus.

"Run!" yelled Martialis.

The two door guards belted into the palace followed by Martialis. In pursuit of them were Paulus' gang of Praetorians.

Martialis was not as quick as the two guards. Stumbling, he fell and was crushed beneath boots as the Praetorians broke into the palace.

The two door guards skidded round a corner and straight into Honoratus accompanied by five other guards.

"What the—?"

"They're coming!"

Hearing the trample of boots, Honoratus quickly assessed the situation to be verging on the critical.

"Sallustus, get more guards. Quickly! You four with me. We need to shut the inner doors and get behind them."

They all ran to the spot where two huge wooden doors were folded against the walls. They heaved these doors shut, throwing the bar across them.

"Get behind them! This bolt won't hold for long."

A marching group of Praetorians brought by Sallustus added their bulk to the makeshift barricade.

"You want to tell me what's going on?" asked Honoratus.

"They think the emperor's going to be murdered. They won't listen to anyone."

And then came the cry of a charge as Paulus' band of gloriously drunk Praetorians ran full pelt at the doors. The ensuring thump wobbled the bolt.

"Hold steady men, hold steady."

FORTY-SEVEN

"And he was ever so kind. He specifically asked after you, Philo," said Teretia in-between mouthfuls of sliced fruit. "He said that Epaphroditus has been keeping him up to date on your recovery. Which I think is lovely of him because he must have so much else to do, being an emperor."

Verenia rolled her eyes at this, but said nothing.

"That is very thoughtful of him," agreed a far perkier Philo.

On his way back to the party, Philo had passed many palace slaves and not one of them had made any reference to his arrest. Rather, they were keen to ask after his health and update him on all the latest gossip, such as how useless Talos was. It had left him worrying over the state of the filing in his old office, which in turn had led him onto happier memories of his life at the palace. Like the time Epaphroditus had let him reorganise the way they handled the post. Or that day he'd spent in the archives researching whether any scribes of old had better ways of cataloguing, and the satisfaction he'd felt when he'd concluded they did not.

It hadn't been all bad, had it? He'd had a job he enjoyed, a boss he respected immensely, and a friend in Lysander.

"And I asked him about Sporus, and the emperor said that Sporus is very well," continued his wife cheerfully.

"Well, he'd know," interjected Lysander with a laugh.

"Oh," sparked Verenia. "It's like that, is it?"

"Like what?" asked Teretia.

"It's like that every night," supplied Lysander, popping a fig in his mouth.

"Like what?"

Verenia gave a condescending smile. "Oh my dear cousin, you must know, surely. The eunuch is, ahem, servicing the emperor."

The vagueness of servicing meant it was a moment before Teretia caught on. With heated cheeks she said, "No, that's not right. Sporus loved Nero. There could never be another in his heart. He told me so."

"I don't think it's his heart that Otho wants," said Lysander.

The distance between their couches meant that Philo was unable to deliver a sharp kick to silence Lysander. Instead, he had to settle on shoving a plate of cakes under his nose in the hope he'd stuff his mouth so full he couldn't speak. Once Lysander had taken a cake, Philo handed the plate to Verenia hoping for the same result. However, she waved it away, commenting, "I simply couldn't eat any more. I don't have the excuse of pregnancy to hide my excesses."

"I believe," said Philo with uncharacteristic volume, "that there may be some dancing next."

"Here," said Lysander, spitting crumbs out of his mouth, "What's that noise?"

* * *

Contrary to appearances, Domitian was enjoying his expedition into palace life. It certainly beat being stuck at his uncle's house, lying on his bed, staring at the ceiling brooding.

Seeing the colourful entertainment and the gaiety of the guests, Domitian rather regretted cutting himself off so completely from society.

Perhaps tomorrow, after he'd slept off this late night, he might venture out to the gymnasium and see if there were any wrestling bouts on. It would certainly beat the muffled tedium Domitian had found himself in.

It would also give him something to write about in his letters to his father. Recently, he'd struggled to write anything beyond the usual greeting and pleasantries. Instead, he'd resorted to a series of complaints, which he suspected his father skipped over. He certainly never made any reference to them in any of the scant messages he sent to his younger son.

Popping a date into his mouth Domitian wondered whether to write to his brother with a juicy description of the party. His eyes scanned about, looking for a girl he could include for an imaginary assignation.

His eyes fell upon the emperor's couch, and then onto Statilia Messalina who lay beside him. She was a truly beautiful, refined woman. Titus would never believe it of his little brother. Domitian moved his gaze upwards to the slave girl standing behind the empress' couch. The Greek helmet she wore obscured most of her face, true, but Domitian admired her slim figure.

He was pondering whether the slave girl would be keeping her helmet on or off during the encounter he would describe to Titus, when he heard it.

"What's that noise?"

"What noise?" Flavius asked.

It was audible, just, above the general din and chatter of the party. A discord of shouts? Yells? A bang or two?

Caenis felt her skin get goosebumps.

"Flavius," she said carefully, slowly. "Flavius, we need to leave. Now."

Flavius' eyebrows knitted together above his nose. "What is it?"

Domitian, hearing a further bang, louder, closer, got to his feet.

"What's going on?" he asked.

* * *

Domitian was not the only one feeling the tension. Several other guests had got to their feet. Even the normally self-obsessed Sporus paused from throwing flirtatious looks Otho's way to listen.

Otho signalled to Onomastus. "Go find out what's going on." Then to Statilia, "I'm sure it's nothing.'

Standing behind the couch, Cassandra pursed her lips. Mina's hand fell to her whip handle.

* * *

Caenis, stood beside Domitian, placed a hand on his arm. "Stay with me. Whatever happens."

"What's going to happen?" he asked, alarmed.

FORTY-EIGHT

Onomastus threaded his way through the dining room into the corridor outside. This he followed to the source of the commotion. Rounding a corner, he came across Honoratus and his men, desperately pressing against the eight-foot-tall wooden doors. Whatever was on the other side of those doors appeared very keen to get in.

"What the—?" he voiced.

Honoratus, unable to turn his head, yelled, "Dwarf, is that you?"

"Yes, what's going on?"

"There's no time. Get moving. Get moving now. Secure the emperor. You need to get everyone out. We can't hold them back much longer."

Onomastus recognised that this was not the time for questions. He ran with surprising speed for a man so short in the legs. His first port of call was Epaphroditus. He whispered a succinct explanation in his ear.

Squeezing Aphrodite's hand, Epaphroditus told the dwarf, "The banqueting hall that adjoins this room has multiple exits. Get two Praetorians to escort the emperor and empress safely through and stick with them. I'll instruct the chamberlains to see the other guests through. If we can do this calmly and efficiently, we'll avoid a panic."

A sudden bang made him jump. "Now, Onomastus."

The dwarf sped off.

Aphrodite turned to her husband. "Do we have Felix?" she enquired. "He'll safeguard the slaves on duty."

Epaphroditus kissed her forehead. "Good idea."

The chamberlains, professional as ever, approached each couch. They defined the situation as an unavoidable but necessary change of venue. Claiming, if asked, that the noise was a thunderstorm occurring overhead, and that they feared the roof was not as watertight as it needed to be for such an expected deluge. Worried for their fancy frocks and folded togas, this soon got people moving.

Teretia and Verenia, ignorant of the calm, politely-worded palace speak for an imminent disaster, shuffled along with the other guests to the doorway that led through to the banqueting hall. Lysander and Philo cast worried gazes backwards.

"Are you armed?" Lysander asked him.

"Of course not."

"Me neither," admitted Lysander.

"Will the banqueting hall have the ponds with the little fishes and the floating lamps?" asked Teretia. "Because I thought that was particularly lovely."

"I'm not sure," said Philo, a hand on her elbow, trying to hurry her along.

As they'd been at the back of the dining room, they were also at the back of the evacuation. That, to Philo, did not seem a happy place to be.

A trotting band of Praetorians heading in the opposite direction wasn't a great omen either.

* * *

In the banqueting hall, Onomastus told the emperor, "This way, master." The dwarf gestured to the door that would take them to the outside world and safety.

"No," said Otho. "I'll stay here."

"Caesar—"

"These are my guests. I am their host. I shall not leave them." Then to Statilia: "You go with Onomastus, my darling, and make sure you put Mina outside your door."

"I'm staying with you."

"Statilia."

"I'm staying." She gripped hold of his hand to show her intent.

"I'm staying too, Uncle," insisted Salvius.

The boy was trying so hard to be brave. He was given away by the sheen of sweat on his forehead and his constantly darting eyes. Statilia took pity on him.

"Go, Salvius."

"No, no, I'm staying."

She took hold of his shoulders. "You're his heir, Salvius. You can't put yourself in danger. Go."

"Go," repeated Otho, pushing the boy forward.

"Uncle?" he bleated, looking over his shoulder as he was pushed along by a slave.

Otho turned to Statilia. "You guessed how much Salvius means to me. Thank you."

He kissed her gently on the lips. Sporus shot past the pair of them, having abandoned his sandals for a speedier exit. As his red-covered frame disappeared out the door, Otho gave a scoff of a laugh. "He didn't even look back!"

FORTY-NINE

The banqueting hall had never been intended for use that night. It was stacked full of random furniture: old wardrobes, couches lain on their side, stacked units of chairs. The chamberlains winced as they led the guests through the mess to the exits.

Otho attempted to lighten the atmosphere in this crowded space by cordially saying his farewells to the guests. Wishing them a pleasant evening and suggesting that perhaps they should avoid the forum side of the Palatine Hill just at this moment.

Statilia, in full empress mode, did likewise. Telling panicked senators and their wives, "How lovely it was to see you. You simply must come again, soon. Do make it soon."

Mina stood one pace behind her mistress, gripping a nail-studded cudgel. There were too many people crammed into too tight a space for her whip to be an effective weapon. She'd as likely slash an aedile across the face as whoever was out there wanting Otho dead.

Instead, she was geared up for some targeted smashing of noses, knees, stomachs, and, of course, that most effective of targets, male genitalia. Oh yes, Mina was fully geared up for some scrotal smashing. It just might take her mind off Epaphroditus' claims regarding her hero, Straton.

"Don't panic," she told Cassandra. "I'll protect you. Though obviously my main aim will be to protect the empress, then the emperor, but you're third in line."

"Thank you, Artemina. And if Sporus hadn't run away?"

"Fair point. Fourth in line."

* * *

Epaphroditus and Aphrodite had managed to weave their way through the crowd to the connecting doorway between the dining and banqueting halls. Here they encountered Caenis, Flavius, and Flavius' nephew, who was clearly not the hero of Yodfat, given his absolutely terrified expression.

"What is it?" asked Flavius.

"Drunk Praetorians," explained Epaphroditus. "They've got it into their heads that the emperor is in some kind of danger and are most keen to protect him."

"Can't we wheel him out to prove to them he's absolutely fine?"

"A sensible suggestion, Flavius, but, alas, the Guard are not in such a sensible mood. They've killed two of their own tribunes who dared to point out their error. The gods know what they'll do if they get hold of the emperor."

"Take him to the Praetorian camp and wage war on the city on his behalf?" suggested Caenis.

"A not unfeasible scenario," admitted Epaphroditus. "Which is why we need to get everyone out of here, including the emperor, and let them rage at the walls for a bit until they get bored, go home, and sleep it off."

* * *

Lysander, standing on his toes, announced, "We're not far from the doorway now."

"Good, good," said Philo, looking about. "We'll head down the Oppian Hill way."

"We're leaving? But I thought we were just changing venue?"

"We are, Teretia," said Lysander. "We're changing our venue to home where we'll bolt all the doors and sit it out."

"Sit out what?"

Teretia didn't get an answer. At that moment there came a thunderous, splintering crash. Lysander and Philo exchanged panicked looks as they scanned the dining room for alternative exits, finding none.

* * *

"Caenis," said Domitian, his voice shaking. His stepmother gripped hold of his hand.

* * *

At the back of the banqueting hall, the fall of the doors was audible.

"O gods alive!" swore Onomastus under his breath.

Mina climbed up onto an overturned couch and bent low, holding onto her cudgel.

FIFTY

"Out, out, out," Otho urged his guests. "Quickly, quickly." He had to resist the urge to slap them on their bums to hurry them up.

Statilia assisted with hurrying. "Go, go, go," she entreated them.

* * *

Back in the dining room, there came the sound of thumping boots on marble, of shouts and cries. It was this that truly set off the panic.

"We have to get out of here!" yelped Lysander, pushing at the people in front of them, trying to get through.

* * *

In the adjoining doorway between the two rooms, Domitian and Caenis found themselves forced forward. Domitian tried desperately to keep his feet on the floor as the panicked guests crushed around him, pushing him into the furniture-stacked dining room. His hand was wrenched from Caenis' and he lost sight of his stepmother in the confusion of movement.

A stack of chairs began to wobble, then fell with a crash onto the marble floor. A wide-eyed Domitian gave a gasp of horror as another stack smacked downwards onto the head of a nearby woman. She stood for a moment, dazed as the blood poured from her forehead down into her eyes. Raising an arm to the wound, she gave a moan and then crumpled to the ground. Her slave looked down at her mistress, bloody and still, and screamed and screamed. She was silenced by the fall of a wardrobe, which obscured her completely.

That was all Domitian saw before a rush behind him had him tripping forwards.

* * *

Philo's desperate scanning of the room produced results.

"Quick, this way."

"But they're coming from that way," panicked Teretia.

"There's an alcove," explained Philo. "If we crouch down, they'll not spot us. Don't you think, Lysander? Lysander? Where is he?"

"I believe he ran that way," said Verenia. "Coward."

Philo grabbed hold of their hands and pulled them through the crowd, heading away from the banqueting hall doorway to a small alcove on the right-hand side of the dining room. It was just wide enough for the three of them. Philo told them to crouch down.

"Flatten your backs against the wall. Amongst all these people, they'll not see us." He left off the "hopefully".

Verenia did as instructed. Teretia too. Cuddling into Philo she asked, "It will be alright, won't it?"

He kissed the top of her head. "It will be fine. We'll be fine."

And that was when the Praetorians burst in.

FIFTY-ONE

The Praetorians' aim was to protect the emperor from a foe within the palace. On arriving in the dining room, they found a mass of panicked citizens trying to push their way into the banqueting hall, not much caring who they knocked over in the process or who they trampled over to reach that doorway. The guards paused for a moment, trying to decipher this strange scene of panic.

"Where's the emperor? Where's the emperor?" shouted Paulus at the terrified guests.

In the alcove, Philo pushed the ladies back against the wall. He crouched in front of them, covering them both with his own body. Looking into his wife's terrified eyes, he pressed a finger against his lips. Teretia nodded in understanding and took hold of her cousin's hand, squeezing it tightly.

Getting no sensible answer from the guests, even after holding one up against the wall by his neck, Paulus, the unlikely instigator of this whole disaster, had a moment. He called it realisation. Epaphroditus, in his subsequent report to the emperor, referred to it as a "fatal miscalculation".

"It's already happened!" shouted Paulus. "It's already happened! We're too late! They've deposed the emperor!"

It would have been helpful had Paulus clarified who "they" were. But he didn't. So the Praetorians took "they" to be the fleeing party guests, and took it upon themselves to punish them.

Ahead of the Praetorians in the banqueting hall, all was chaos. The guests struggled to navigate the fallen furniture and the immobile forms of those crushed in the stampede. Such was the panic that some senators not only left their very expensive cloaks behind but their slaves as well. They ran into the night, alone for once in their pampered lives.

* * *

On his knees, buffeted this way and that by fleeing guests, Domitian struggled to get onto his feet. One hand pressed on the floor, he tried to stand up but was knocked back down again. A passing knee crunched against his cheek.

"Domitian!"

He gazed upwards to see his stepmother trying to get to him, pushing her way through the people. Beside her was Flavius.

"Caenis! Uncle! I'm here!" he yelled.

"Oh, thank the gods!" she swore, holding out a hand to him.

Flavius took hold of the other hand and hauled him to his feet.

"Let's get out of here."

"Caenis!"

The three of them turned to see Epaphroditus and Aphrodite heading their way. The couple were halfway across the banqueting hall, only a few feet from an exit, when a discord of screams announced the arrival of the Praetorian Guard.

Having cleared a path through by way of a massacre, their bloodlust was fully raised. In their minds, they were on a battlefield exacting revenge on an enemy that had killed their emperor. They charged this enemy at full pelt, swords raised, with such a speed, there was no time to react.

A thump of an elbow to Epaphroditus' back knocked him off his feet. Hitting the floor, he took a kick to his stomach. On the ground, with feet running past him in every direction he saw the danger he was in. Spotting a wardrobe to his left, he managed to half crawl, half roll his way to it, tucking himself underneath it, away from the drama unfolding.

* * *

"Domitian! Quickly!" said Caenis, pulling him along. "Domitian!"

His gaze was backwards. A look of horror playing across his features.

"Domitian, we've no time to stare. We need to get out of here."

He slipped his hand out of hers and began pushing his way back into the banqueting hall.

"DOMITIAN!" she yelled. "Where are you going?"

He didn't respond, just kept moving back the way they'd come, against the flow of people.

"Domitian!" She grabbed hold of the arm of his tunic.

"I can see her. I can get to her," he said, struggling to break her grip.

* * *

As the torrent of bodies approached the emperor, his Praetorian guards stepped in front of him and Statilia.

"Well," said Otho to the empress with a tight smile. He took both her hands. "It's been marvellous. Truly marvellous."

"Marcus—"

"I would have enjoyed being married to you, Statilia Messalina," he told her. "I think we would have had many children."

Cassandra turned her eyes upwards to entreat the gods.

To Mina, Onomastus asked, "You got any other weapons?"

Mina took off her helmet. "The crest on this is pretty sharp. You could throw it at them."

Onomastus weighed it up before saying, "Nah."

The dwarf picked up a nearby chair, smashing it down hard on the ground, splintering two of its legs off. These he held in either hand growling, "Let's be 'avin' you!"

A sentiment a geared-up Mina fully concurred with. Bouncing on her toes, she spotted the enemy bludgeoning and slashing their way through the guests. Purple-plumed helmets and scorpion-embellished breastplates caught her eye.

"They're Praetorians!" she exclaimed.

"What?" said Otho and Statilia in unison.

Onomastus dropped his chair leg. "They're loyal, the Guard, they always have been."

Otho turned to his guard escort who looked as puzzled as he was.

"We are sworn to you, Imperial Majesty," one told him.

Otho pulled his toga back over his arm. "Bring me that chair," he instructed Onomastus.

"Marcus, what are you going to do?"

"Trust me," was his response.

With a little bit of help, he climbed up onto the chair.

"Oh for a trumpeter," he muttered. "Or even better, Lysander. Or Felix!"

Cupping his hands round his mouth, he yelled to the fullness of his lungs, "GUARDS! GUARDS! YOUR EMPEROR LIVES! YOUR EMPEROR LIVES! YOUR EMPEROR LIVES!"

He paused for a breath. "YOUR EMPEROR LIVES!"

Statilia hitched up her skirts and climbed onto the chair beside Otho, yelling, "YOUR EMPEROR LIVES!"

Mina, Cassandra, and Onomastus added their voices to the chorus. "YOUR EMPEROR LIVES!"

Epaphroditus slid out from his hiding place and similarly stood on a chair, yelling, "YOUR EMPEROR LIVES! YOUR EMPEROR LIVES!"

Soon it reached such a crescendo that it was audible even above the chaos. The guards slid to a halt, crashing into one another.

"Did they say the emperor's alive?" Paulus asked Proculus.

"YOUR EMPEROR LIVES!"

Then they saw him. Marcus Salvius Otho Nero, His Imperial Majesty stood on a chair. His cheeks ruddier than usual. His beringed hands cupped round his mouth.

"YOUR EMPEROR LIVES!"

"He's alive," said Proculus.

"We've saved him!" decided Paulus.

FIFTY-TWO

Epaphroditus watched from afar as the guards gathered before Otho, their heads bowed. The secretary wondered what tack Otho would take with them. What the guards deserved was a tongue lashing of such ferocity that it melted their helmets. But now was not that time. Not when their swords were still dripping blood, their veins still intoxicated with murder. Epaphroditus hoped Otho recognised that.

"My guards," began the emperor, stepping down from the chair. "My guards, you can see that I am well. That I am unharmed. Your concern for your emperor does you all justice."

A few guards broke into smiles at such praise.

"I understand that you feared for your emperor. It does you credit that you acted so promptly on such fears."

More smiles.

"I believe that the best recourse is that I, your emperor, accompany my Guard back to your barracks." The suggestion produced a gasp of horror from Statilia.

"Then you can be assured your emperor is safe whilst there is a thorough investigation here at the palace into this heinous conspiracy."

Inspired, thought Epaphroditus. Taking himself away from the palace ensured an end to the violence. With Otho at the Viminal barracks, the Guard would be duty-bound to stay there to protect him. Well away from the mess they'd caused.

And what a mess it was, thought Epaphroditus, staring round at the stacks of broken furniture. The guests sat on the floor staring dazedly into space. Then there were those who did not sit, who lay on the floor unmoving.

"Epaphroditus?"

"Flavius," he greeted the city prefect. "Quite a speech from the emperor. And entirely the right thing to do, given the circumstances."

Flavius did not respond.

"You are well?" asked Epaphroditus. Noticing the red stain blobbed across the chest of Flavius' tunic, "You're injured? Come, sit down. I'll get a slave to see to you."

"I'm not hurt," said Flavius. "You need to come with me."

* * *

"I think it's safe now," said Philo.

He stepped out of the alcove, offering a hand each for Teretia and Verenia. "Are you both unhurt?" Philo asked, his arm now around a shaking Teretia.

"I think so," she said, looking down at her stomach. "I should think it's given the baby quite a shake."

"But no pain?"

"No."

"Verenia?"

"I'm fine." And then, "You saved me," looking at Philo anew. "Unlike some." Her eyes now on a sheepish Lysander walking towards them.

"Don't be too hard on him, Verenia," said Philo. "It's what you do here." He meant the palace. "You run."

"You didn't run," she pointed out.

Philo didn't answer. But the look he gave Teretia was an answer in itself.

Verenia felt a pang in her chest at the sight of such mutual adoration and love. Her reflective mood she soon shook off with the arrival of Lysander.

"Hullo," he said. "What a brilliant speech from the emperor. Stirring, very stirring. We should probably call it a night, though, now. Draining, that's what it's been."

He held out his hand to Verenia.

The look he received in response would have pickled a walnut.

* * *

Flavius led Epaphroditus to a spot at the side of the banqueting hall between two standing stacks of chairs. There he found Caenis hugging tight to Flavius' sobbing nephew, his legs splattered with blood. Behind them, on the floor, he could see a pair of feet.

"Domitian saw her fall," said Flavius. "He tried to get to her. But all was… Well, it was—" Flavius threw his hands up. "He couldn't get there in time. I'm sorry. We tried to stem the blood flow. But it was too late."

A creeping dread took possession of Epaphroditus. He froze at that spot. He did not want to move any further forward. He did not want to know why that boy was howling, why his legs were spotted with blood.

Caenis, seeing him, handed Domitian over to Flavius. As she did so, Epaphroditus was given a full view of the body on the floor. It was his wife.

She lay on her back, one leg bent at the knee, her eyes open, staring upwards at the ceiling. She did not blink. She did not move. Her fingers were absolutely still. Her neck, her beautiful, elegantly long neck that he had covered in kisses so many times, was soaked in red. A cloth was pressed against it.

Epaphroditus bent down and removed it, revealing a gash of such depth it had almost cut straight through.

"I'm so sorry," said Caenis.

A near half-century of mastering his emotions to display the exact demeanour required, no matter how he truly felt, counted for nothing. Instead, he managed to croak out a "Dite" before falling to his knees and collapsing into noisy, rib-aching sobs that would have made a professional mourner proud.

Claudia Aphrodite would have been proud too. She would have seen it was a rare moment of absolute honesty from her husband and loved him all the more for it.

FIFTY-THREE

The curtains of the litter were firmly pulled shut and had been ever since they'd dropped off Philo and Teretia. Verenia had been very clear that she did not welcome Lysander's company. But he had been equally adamant that she needed escorting back to her home. So he'd trotted alongside the litter, talking away to the curtains with no response from within.

"So it wasn't quite the evening I'd planned for us. The announcers were atrocious. I'll be having stern words with them tomorrow, don't you worry. And the flute girls were rather lacklustre. The food was tepid in bits and of course the Guard bursting in like that and all. Still, I promise next time it'll be better. Perhaps we could go somewhere else, a non-palace event. My mum throws nice parties. Lots of palace people there obviously, but not too palace, if you know what I mean. I'd like you to meet my mum and I know she'd love to meet you. She's always going on at me to settle down, especially now Philo has."

Inside the litter, Verenia was not asleep. She wished she were: it might have saved her from Lysander's drivel. Instead, she sat bolt upright, unable to relax back upon the pillows, grinding her teeth in a similar motion to the litter. Her cheeks were flamed, not with anger but with, she came to realise, shame. Shame and embarrassment.

Shame and embarrassment that the man who'd desired her presence at the big event of the year had, at the very first sign of trouble, abandoned her to save his own skin. Demonstrating so very publicly how little he cared for her. A shame made so much worse by her cousin witnessing the whole thing.

Pretty, sweet Teretia with her happy marriage and husband who so nakedly adored her: Verenia almost cried to see it. It took her back to her marriage to Lucanus. Had he ever looked at her like that? All she remembered was the loathing he'd felt for her. How else to explain his cruelty?

"I'm sorry, Verenia, truly I am. I didn't mean to—"

A slap on the roof of the litter brought the bearers to a dead halt. The curtains were yanked apart from inside.

"You didn't mean to what? To run off? To leave me to be cut down by the guards? It's only because of my cousin's husband that I'm still alive!" she raged. "Because, of course, Teretia's husband would be brave. Unlike some." Lysander was treated to a particularly withering glare.

"Perfect little Teretia with her perfectly adoring parents who let her pick her own husband," continued Verenia. "Not like mine. My mother dead before I could form any memories of her and my father who cares so little for me that he left me to be raised by slaves while he went off travelling. The only time he bothers with me is to marry me to an absolute brute. Not like Teretia. No, she gets to choose her husband and she manages to choose a nice one. Because she would. Because everything goes right for Teretia. Whilst I swim against the current smashing into rocks, she just glides past me on a barge with sails and a navigator. So of course her runty foreign husband would play the hero while my partner runs away as quickly as his legs will carry him. Because everything, absolutely everything turns out perfect for her!"

Lysander's expression at the end of this rant was a sort of slapped silence. Eventually he managed to say, "She's not that perfect. I don't rate her leek broth. It's far too watery."

Unexpectedly, Verenia felt a laugh bubble inside her. It escaped from her lips and she found her all-encompassing fury dissipating. When she'd ceased laughing, she told him, "Thank you for that. It helped."

She banged on the litter roof again, the signal for the bearers to lower the litter onto the ground.

"Sit beside me."

They were but a few feet from Verenia's home in a narrow street that was only the width of the litter plus half again. Lysander sat beside her.

"I'm sorry I ran. It's a sort of instinct you pick up, growing up in the palace."

"Philo didn't run," she said in a quiet voice, deliberately moderating her tone to be non-accusatory.

Lysander, eyes still on the ground, smiled a little. "Philo can't run. Have you ever seen him try? I don't think he has the muscles for it," he shrugged. "Or the inclination. He wouldn't have left Teretia anyhow."

"No," agreed Verenia sadly. "He wouldn't."

Lysander raised his head. "Was your husband really a brute?"

"He beat me."

"Beat you? Why?"

Verenia threw her hands up. "Because the asparagus at dinner was too hard. Because the apartment was not clean enough. Because the colour of my dress was garish and tarty. Because I spent too long getting ready for the festival. Because my look was not demure as a wife's should be."

"He sounds a lot like an emperor."

She'd been so caught in the misery of those memories that his reply caught her by surprise.

"Just like an emperor," continued Lysander. "You can never please them either. Not Otho, he's alright, but the others…" He lifted up his fringe. "Can you see this?" he asked, placing a finger on his forehead.

Verenia leaned forward to examine. By his finger, she could just see in the darkness a white scar, maybe an inch long.

"Nero threw a tray at my head," he explained.

"Why?" she had to ask.

Lysander gave a wry smile. "Because I was too tall. The time he threw a cup of boiling water at my feet was because I was too blond. The yellowness of my hair was distracting him from his lyre lesson. And one morning I was too straight. It was making the fresco painter's work look wonky, so he made me stand with one leg bent. I've been whipped for not projecting the arrival of the empress loudly enough, so the emperor was taken by surprise. I've been whipped for being too loud and worsening the emperor's hangover. Then there's the empress and her tendency to throw her shoe at your head whenever you displease her. Some days, nothing you do is right."

Though Lysander held onto his smile, Verenia remembered Philo's tale of his father. The man who'd been executed because he could sing.

She felt a lump form in her throat and it was in a tightened voice that she said, "You understand."

Lysander dropped his hand to his side, his fringe flopping down onto his forehead, obscuring the scar. "I understand what it's like to be the butt of someone else's frustrations, if that's what you mean."

"My father refused to believe me when I told him. So I showed him my bruises and then he believed me. I clearly hadn't been a good enough wife, he said. I tried so hard," she told Lysander, tears beginning to form in her eyes. "And nothing, absolutely nothing I did, ever pleased Lucanus. In all the time we were married, he never said a single kind word to me." Verenia rubbed her eyes with the sleeve of her dress.

"Then it's a jolly good thing that you're no longer married," was Lysander's matter-of-fact response.

For Verenia, who since her return to Rome had suffered the knowing looks and comments of the Viminal Hill regarding the failure of her marriage, this was a precious gift. Lysander understood and, more importantly, he approved of her actions.

It made her look at him afresh. He really was quite good-looking with that blond shaggy hair and sideburns and those warm blue eyes. Verenia felt the second unexpected impulse of the night. She leant in and kissed him gently on the lips.

It was an action that seemed to take Lysander by surprise, for his lips were entirely unresponsive. She'd been about to pull away humiliated, when something kicked in and he realised this was real and happening to him.

Lysander, not being the sort to dawdle when given an opportunity, had her lying back on the litter's pillows a mere five beats later. Ten beats later Verenia gasped, "The curtains!"

Lysander broke off momentarily to tug them shut. The bearers, lined up against a wall, rolled their eyes and groaned as the litter began to shake.

FIFTY-FOUR

"Do you think we should call a doctor?" Flavius asked Caenis.

They were stood in the doorway of Domitian's bedroom. The teenager was lain on the bed, his limbs still visibly trembling.

"Get some wine, unmixed. I'll try to get him to drink it. Maybe it'll steady him.

Flavius nodded and departed to fetch the necessary medicine.

Kneeling beside the bed, Caenis addressed Domitian softly, "Not quite the relaxing evening out we hoped for, was it? You did a brave thing trying to save Claudia Aphrodite."

"I didn't succeed though, did I?" said Domitian. "I couldn't get to her. There were too many people," he lamented. "I'm sorry, Caenis. I'm so very sorry that I was useless. As ever." He began to cry.

"Listen to me," she said. "You've seen palace politics up close for the first time. You've seen it at its worst. I don't blame you for feeling shaky. Your brother was much the same after Nero's stepbrother Britannicus was poisoned beside him at dinner. But you need to do as he did. You need to swallow down that fear, that terror, because there are going to be more shocks, I'm afraid."

Domitian looked at her enquiringly.

"What you did tonight was noble, but promise me you'll never do anything so stupid again."

Shocked, Domitian said, "But she was your friend."

"She was," admitted Caenis. "But you are more important. Much more important than you realise. Your father sent me home to keep you safe, and nothing, absolutely nothing, is to happen to you."

"Keep me safe from what? I don't understand."

"Nor will you, yet. Promise me, though. Promise me that you won't ever put yourself in such danger again."

"I promise, but Caenis—"

"Wine for the patient," announced Flavius.

Caenis pressed her finger against Domitian's lips. "Between us, yes?" she whispered.

Domitian nodded his assent.

"Flavius, my dear, what vintage have you raided from the cellars?"

Domitian took his medicine as instructed, keeping one eye on his stepmother. She was joking along merrily with Flavius, his uncle oblivious to all. Domitian was torn between curiosity and dread. Something was definitely going on and he clearly had a part in it. Whether he wanted to or not.

PART II

WAR

"The Othonians spoke scornfully of the enemy as a lot of foreigners and aliens"
—Tacitus, *The Histories*

FIFTY-FIVE

The mountains were behind them, forbidding peaks of darkness that climbed into the clouds. They had proved no obstacle to the legions. They'd laughed as they ascended, recalling that Hannibal had done the same with a troop of damn elephants. Camped in their tents for the night, they fancied they could hear the trumpeting of those long-dead creatures carried on the winds.

30,000 men filled the lush green valley on the other side of those dark crags. The terrain they faced now offered nothing more challenging than a burbling stream and an endless carpet of soft grass.

Caecina stood before them, dressed as usual in his trousers, tunic, and plaid cloak. What had seemed fitting, sensible even in Germania and during their route through Gaul, was out of place in the landscape on this sunny day. It made Caecina appear all the more extraordinary: the handsome giant ready to crush all in his path.

"Italy, men! Italy! Home!" cried the giant to his troops, casually forgetting that the majority of them had never set foot in the motherland before.

"We are here! And now there stands only sixteen days' march between us and our beloved Rome!"

This caused a wave of cheers, of chest beating, of some distinctly Germanic battle cries from beneath Italian leather and steel.

"I have written to Otho giving him one last chance at reconciliation. One final opportunity to lay down his arms."

The silence that greeted this was attributed by Caecina to his inspiring rhetoric. In fact, it was the stunned silence of 30,000 soldiers who'd marched twenty miles a day for three months to reach an epoch-deciding battle, only to be told a peace treaty was being sought.

Thankfully for Caecina, he didn't drag his dramatic pause out too long.

"But he refuses!"

Cheers.

"He thinks he can beat us!"

Boos.

"He thinks he can beat the best of the best. The best of the empire!"

Cries of, "Never, never!"

"We shall show him. We shall show this circus-loving, eunuch-chasing fool of a so-called emperor our might, the might of the German legions!"

* * *

"So," said Otho, clapping his hands together. "These are my troops. My men. The brave fellows who are fighting for my throne."

"Some of them," replied Celsus, unable to entirely suppress the apologetic note in his voice.

They had travelled to the Campus Martinus, an open piece of land where in times of old, soldiers had exercised their horses and suffered agonisingly long drills. These days, the city had encroached upon the space, adding temples, baths, and the imposing tombs of emperors past.

Before Otho were arrayed not seasoned, well-trained, well-polished soldiers but instead five cohorts of Praetorians. They'd put in the extra effort. They were very nearly in a straight line and had given their purple plumes a bit of a brush. As Otho walked past, each one puffed out his chest and attempted not to smile at the emperor they now considered one of their own. They'd even presented Otho with his own Praetorian uniform, which he promised to wear the very next time the occasion demanded it. Perhaps the first dice night after this business with Vitellius was done. A suggestion the guards had heartily agreed with.

They moved on from the Praetorians, walking down the line.

"And these are… Well, they are… They're…" blustered Celsus. "They're gladiators. That's what they are."

The gladiators did not stand to attention. They lolled. It was a keen loll, but a loll nevertheless.

"I'm hoping to get some proper armour for them," apologised Celsus as Otho took in their skimpy attire of loincloth, and cloth-padded arms and legs.

Present were the murmillo gladiators with their rectangular shield and crested helmet, the Thracians with their brimmed helmets topped by a striking griffin head, and the Retiarii, who wore no protective headgear, dependent entirely on their skills with the net and trident.

The emperor waved a hand. "No need. I think they are perfectly terrifying as they are. They are more than a match for some bare-chested German barbarian."

Onomastus nudged Otho. "Look, it's Brutus."

The dwarf pointed to a particularly fearsome specimen of secutor in a smooth helmet that covered his entire face aside from two tiny slits for his eyes. His chest was at least three times the width of the dwarf. His leg muscles so developed, he was forced to stand with his feet two hand-widths apart. His arms were bulging with strength even in this lolling state.

"So it is," said Otho. Then, noting his freedman's dreamy stare, "Oh go on then, get his autograph. You know you're dying to."

"Thank you, Imperial Majesty," replied the dwarf, fishing out a slither of wood and a pen from his bag.

As Onomastus trotted off to meet his hero, Celsus led Otho down the rest of the line-up. Sensing the emperor's distraction, Celsus told him, "The 17th Legion are but half-a-day's march away and our advance party of Pannonians are excellent men."

"Hey?" said Otho distractedly.

"I was saying that there are some good fighters on our side, Caesar. It's by no means a foregone conclusion."

"No, it's no good," began Otho.

Celsus, thinking this was a criticism of the army he'd raised, began to speak but was cut off by the emperor.

"I have to have Brutus' autograph too. You know they say he is going to beat Cyprian's total of kills in his next bout. Legendary!" And he trotted down the line back to the gladiators.

FIFTY-SIX

There was a large crowd of the populace gathered in the forum, ready to hear their emperor's farewell speech. They were not terribly lively but perhaps that was to be expected. Recent heavy rains had washed part of the Aventine district away and many locals with it. Then there were the food shortages. With two armies battering their way towards them, the farmers of northern Italy had fled, leaving their crops to rot.

And of course, this was no celebration. Many of those waiting for the emperor were shortly to watch their sons march off to war. Most fearing they would not return. So perhaps it was not so surprising that the cheers for the emperor were rather lacklustre. This despite Otho's supremely rousing speech and a spirited and booming introduction from Lysander.

* * *

Escorted down the line of wagons by Onomastus and the usual flurry of slaves, Otho was surprised to find a familiar face standing beside one.

"Epaphroditus?"

The secretary bowed his head. "Imperial Majesty."

"We didn't expect you back so soon."

Epaphroditus' didn't answer. His attention was drawn to Otho's outfit. "You appear to be wearing armour, Caesar."

"I know!" beamed Otho, giving a small twirl, his leather skirt lifting upwards as he did. "Marvellous isn't it?" Stroking the breastplate with pride, he added, "Menachus knocked it up for me. Turns out hairpieces aren't his only talent."

Taking in the distressed state of the leather—the bald patches, the bashed leg pieces, and the sort of brown, sort of black, sort of something else colour—Epaphroditus had to ask, "What in Jupiter's name kind of cow did it come from?"

Following the secretary's gaze, Otho admitted, "He may have had to bounce up and down on it a bit to make it appear worn. It seemed more fitting than the comedy armour my dresser offered me. Which, apparently, Nero liked." Otho's tone made it clear that he did not.

Epaphroditus knew exactly what "costume" he meant. "Nero wore it when he wished to play at being one of the gods. Ask Statilia Messalina. I'm sure she has some eye-popping stories connected to it."

"Best not to know," he decided. "She likes this, though. She likes this outfit very much." A glint appeared in his blue eyes.

"Best not to know," repeated Epaphroditus with a smile.

"I'm sorry I didn't make the funeral," said Otho. "Emperor's business and all that."

"It's what I would have advocated," said the secretary, his smile sticking to his face with difficulty. "Thank you for the mourners though."

"They were good, were they? Onomastus set them up."

"Proper specialists, best in the field," butted in the dwarf.

"No, they were good. I think they expressed what we were all feeling."

"The children?" enquired Otho. "How do they bear up? Of course, it is such a blow when one's mother passes. It draws a line between childhood and the adult world."

"Does it? I wouldn't know. I sent them down to Baie. I have a house down there. I thought it would be safer for them. But what news here?" asked Epaphroditus, changing the subject so abruptly it took the others a moment or two to catch up.

"I spent a very enjoyable few days in the Praetorian camp," supplied Otho. "Nice bunch of fellows really, aside from—" He waved a hand in Epaphroditus' direction to indicate their murder of his wife. "Paranoid, though. But who can blame them after the last couple of years."

Epaphroditus could blame them. Wasn't it the Praetorians under Nymphidius Sabinus' command who'd forced out Nero and started this whole mess?

"The emperor made a very moving speech," said Onomastus.

"I did," concurred Otho. "I had them weeping in the ranks. They are sorry. Genuinely so, I believe." He was looking straight at Epaphroditus.

The secretary averted his gaze. "How much did you have to pay them?"

"5,000 each. It seemed reasonable given their insistence they'd saved my life."

He had expected it. How else did you pacify the only marauding army within the city walls? Still, it was still a rancid gollop of garum sauce for Epaphroditus to swallow.

"But we won most of it back at dice night," smiled Otho.

"Really?"

Epaphroditus, well-versed on Otho's history of calamitous gambling, found that hard to believe.

"It was Onomastus. He is a killer thrower."

The dwarf mimicked the action.

"'Course, I had killer dice."

That made Epaphroditus smile a little. "You played the Praetorians with loaded dice?"

Onomastus shrugged. "They're not terribly bright."

Now that, Epaphroditus definitely agreed with. But enough of the small talk. It was time for work.

"Caesar, if you follow me, I shall take you to your wagon to start your journey."

Epaphroditus held out an arm, ready to direct the emperor.

No need. I'm going to walk."

"You're going to walk?"

"With the soldiers. Actually, in front of the soldiers. Except the standard bearers. I shall be walking in front of the soldiers, but behind the standard bearers."

"I think the word you are looking for is march," supplied Epaphroditus. "You cannot be serious. Have you any idea of the distances we'll be covering?"

"What is good for the soldiers is good for the emperor," insisted Otho.

"Yes, but they drill them every damn day. When was the last time you marched anywhere? You don't even walk if you can avoid it. I've known you take a sedan chair to the latrine."

"Only when I was extraordinarily drunk," admitted Otho. "I'll not hide away in some wagon sipping wine. My men need to see me. Caesar needs to endure their hardship. It'll earn me their respect."

Epaphroditus, sensing Otho was not to be moved, said, "For Apollo's sake, put a steel breastplate over that ridiculous garb lest some passer-by gets happy with a slingshot."

"Will do, O loyal servant of mine."

"I bet a thousand sesterces you don't make it to the Appian Way before you catch a lift."

"Agreed," said Otho, and they shook hands on it.

FIFTY-SEVEN

Leaving Otho practising his marching steps, Epaphroditus went to see to the final arrangements for their departure. Though he tried to keep his mind on the multitude of tasks he needed to complete, he couldn't stop his thoughts wandering onto his recent bereavement.

He'd told Otho that he'd sent the children away for their own safety. This wasn't wholly true. He couldn't bear to witness their grief. Pollus had run off on hearing the news and hadn't emerged from his room. Faustina and Silvia had brokered a rare truce and holed themselves up in Dite's room, fingering her gowns and jewellery, desperate to maintain a connection. Perella sobbed and sobbed, clinging to her two younger sisters. Rufus, the baby, sat on his knee, looked up at his papa and asked innocently, "Mama?"

It was too raw, too uniquely painful to be borne just yet. So he'd sent them away to the coast, pushed his own feelings down, and returned to work. Because what else could he do?

Before they departed to meet Vitellius' forces, there was much to be done, which suited Epaphroditus fine. Anything to fill the gap, even if it were a dull morning checking off supplies for the baggage train.

Moving down the line of transportation, he groaned as he saw Felix, head of slave placements and chief overseer, lounging against a wagon. His adopted son Ganymede stood beside his father, imitating the same stance. Fabulous. That was all he needed, an earful of Felix.

Felix had been a loud, sweary presence in Epaphroditus' life. He'd spent his childhood having "Green Eyes!" bellowed at him. This was Felix's way of distinguishing him from all the other slaves named Epaphroditus that littered the palace. Later, Felix had refined this to "Fuckin' Green Eyes". A title he'd continued to use right up to the point Epaphroditus entered the petitions office and became the only Epaphroditus of any note.

In quieter moments, when Felix was therefore far, far away, he'd reflected on how lucky he was that it was his eyes that were his most distinguishable feature. Unlike the hapless "Big Nose", "Flabby Thighs", and "Fat Head" (respectively Phaon, Crenus, and Doryphorus).

That Felix had stuck to "Fuckin' Green Eyes" throughout Epaphroditus' tenure as Agrippina's chief enforcer said much for his bravery and couldn't-give-a-fuck demeanour.

"Felix," nodded Epaphroditus. "Is everything in place? I heard the kitchens were slow in preparing the hams."

"Sent a couple of my boys to whip 'em into shape."

"Good, good."

"Got you a travelling assistant," said Felix.

A confused Epaphroditus asked, "What did you do with Talos?"

He'd meant it as an innocent enquiry but Felix apparently took a darker meaning. A grumble growled its way from the back of his throat.

"I didn't have 'im fucking killed! Minerva's arse! What do you take me for! Think I'd waste fuckin' good merchandise like that? 'Coz he were good merchandise, Talos. Good fuckin' lad."

"He can write and everything," contributed Ganymede with awe.

Felix ruffled the boy's hair affectionately.

"That he could. Right star fuckin' performer, Talos. Wasted on some people, apparently. That lad will be much happier in accounts. It's well away from you for a start."

Keen to get on with things and get away from Felix, Epaphroditus asked, "This travelling assistant, does he write Greek? Notices will have to go out across the empire, after… After this is settled."

"He means this civil war," Felix translated for Ganymede. "They'll be a living emperor and a dead emperor. People will have to know which is which."

"Greek?" persisted Epaphroditus.

"'Course. And a ton of other stuff you'll find useful." He grinned, hooking his thumbs in his belt. "He's in wagon number ten. You'd better go fuckin' settle him in, fully brief him on all the horrible things you want 'im to do for you." Then to Ganymede, "Dirty work scribing. Best off out of it, lad."

Ganymede gave a nod in agreement and, Epaphroditus fancied, a dirty look thrown straight at him.

"Thank you, Felix," he said, turning his back on them.

A cough and then the overseer said to Epaphroditus' back, "I'm sorry about Claudia Aphrodite. Right sorry. Sad news it is. Right fuckin' good worker she was. And a nice lady with it."

The secretary turned round in shock. He'd had nothing but abuse from Felix his whole life, so this sympathy was as unexpected as a troop of dancing girls in the Senate House.

"Yeah, right nice lady and clever too. Would have made a good empress' private secretary too. Only she got married and her fucker of a husband took her out of the workforce."

And thus straight back to the Felix he was much more familiar with.

"I'll go check out wagon number ten," Epaphroditus said.

Felix gave a nod. One distinctly lacking in respect, Epaphroditus fancied.

* * *

Against wagon number ten was a most intriguing sight. An entwined couple, resting their heads on each other's shoulders, looking in need of crowbarring apart.

"Philo?"

Philo let go of a teary-looking Teretia.

"Sir," he said crisply. Stance straight. Tunic sensible. Satchel strap slung over his shoulder.

Epaphroditus swallowed his surprise. "You're back?"

"I am, sir."

"Teretia?"

The girl, her eyes red from what must have been many shed tears, responded, "It was my idea. I felt you needed a friendly face, and Philo has so missed the palace."

Her husband looked away.

"You have," Teretia insisted. "You're always quizzing Lysander on what's been happening."

Philo gave a reluctant nod. Then, to Epaphroditus, "I'm coming with you. Talos has briefed me fully on the situation and I've had a chance to read through the correspondence. I've separated out the most pressing."

He reached into his satchel and retrieved two scrolls.

Epaphroditus squeezed his shoulder. In a tight, quiet voice: "Thank you. This means a lot to me. Dite was very fond of you."

"And I of her," replied Philo in a similarly tight voice.

Teretia took hold of Philo's hand. "We've decided that if the baby is a girl, we'll call her Claudia after her."

It was a gesture of such thoughtfulness that it was some time before Epaphroditus was able to speak. Embracing Teretia, he told her, "You are an extremely kind woman to lend me your husband at this time, when I'm sure you'd rather have him at home. I promise you that I will take good care of him."

Teretia folded back into Philo, her eyes filling once again with tears.

FIFTY-EIGHT

Domitian read the first letter again. Then the second letter. After a slight pause to gather his thoughts, he read them both once more. They were still just friendly letters. One from Claudia. One from Julia. Both sent from Gaul. Both addressed to his stepmother. Which was puzzling, very puzzling.

His curiosity had been piqued by Caenis' strange words on the night of the banquet. Domitian was a man on a mission. He wanted to know what was going on. Part of this drive derived from frustration and anger at being excluded from events. No doubt his father was merrily sharing everything about Caenis' activity with his favourite son, Titus, while he was being kept in the dark.

His father, he knew, still considered him a child. Despite Domitian having donned the toga virilis of manhood a clear three years previously. He'd begged his father to be allowed to join him in Judaea and play a role in the ongoing war. His father had refused to even consider the idea. Caenis had tactfully and kindly told him it was because his father feared for his safety. Domitian knew otherwise: his father thought he'd get in the way.

He read the letter from Claudia again. It was important. He knew it was. Not just because it had arrived from a part of

Gaul suspiciously close to where Vitellius' armies were passing through. But also because when he'd sneaked back into Caenis' study for a further search, he could not locate the original. Nor could he find the original Julia letter either. Just as well he'd made these copies.

Caenis had clearly destroyed the letters. But why? Why obliterate such outwardly benign messages? Because, Domitian had concluded, they weren't benign messages. They were something altogether different. Something Caenis wouldn't want to be found in possession of.

But what? He read them through again. The first was a note from Caenis' dear friend Claudia, who was nursing the sixth of her seven sons. He picked up the second message, a letter from Caenis' most blessed friend Julia, who was glad she'd managed to gain passage on the seventh of the eight ships she'd tried.

Sixth of seven. Seventh of eight. A similar phraseology from two different letters from two different writers.

Domitian grabbed his note tablet. Sixth of what? Seven what? Sixth letter of the seventh line? That letter was an F. Which meant? He counted on a further six letters to find a C, a further six letters revealed an S and then a further C. Not a word, not an anything. He threw his pen onto the desk. Then picked it up again when a thought hit him, maybe it was the sixth letter on each line starting from that seventh line.

That led him to the F and a V. FV?

He flung his pen down again. There was nothing there, was there? It was all in his head. His stupid thick head. Thank the gods he hadn't shared his suspicions with his uncle Flavius.

Something clicked in Domitian's head. Flavius? F. Not Flavius though: Fabius. Fabius Valens. FV.

With some excitement, Domitian counted out the remaining letters in Claudia's message, noting down each on his note tablet. FVSTALLEND.

Fabius Valens. Stall. End.

Domitian scratched his head with the sharp tip of his pen, still none the wiser. Putting that letter aside, he picked up the other message, counting out the seventh letter on each line from the eighth line onwards.

CITIID.

Which meant even less.

He split the letters into clumps.

C must be Caecina but that left IT and IID. Sitting back in his chair, his eyes caught the calendar on the wall. Flavius used it to remind himself which days were deemed inauspicious for work. Not that his diligent uncle actually paid any attention to that. Then Domitian saw it. Not ii. II. Two. And D? Days! Two days.

Caecina IT two days. IT? What might be IT? Oh, of course, Italy! Caecina was due in Italy in two days' time. And Julia had been helpful enough to date the letter.

Domitian turned back to the first code. If Caecina was on the move, then Fabius Valens wasn't. Stall = stalled. Fabius Valens stalled. And end? End what? End his stalling? Domitian's brooding adolescent brain in all its pessimism got it: Fabius Valens stalled. End. End him? It was a question.

Palace politics at its most deadly, Caenis had said to him. And here it raised its head once more. His stepmother had an assassin in Valens' company and a spy in Caecina's. He knew from his uncle the vast odds stacked against Otho, the huge number of soldiers marching to Rome. Except they weren't all. His stepmother's agent had somehow stalled Valens. Caenis was deliberately keeping the two armies apart.

The revelation gave a spark to Domitian's brooding mind. He knew his stepmother had once been a secretary to an empress but he'd never given it much consideration. He'd assumed, wrongly he now knew, that she'd been a transcriber of letters to the empress' friends or helped compile dinner party guest lists. She hadn't been that type of secretary at all, had she?

And she hadn't really retired either. She was still working for the palace as a runner of spies.

This was all too incredible for Domitian to swallow. The question, of course, was what was he to do with this information?

FIFTY-NINE

It had been an odd sort of journey. The last time Epaphroditus had travelled outside Rome with the imperial household was when he'd accompanied Nero on his tour of Greece. The crowds had lined the Via Appia, sitting on top of the tombs, throwing handfuls of rose petals and screaming the emperor's name till their voices were hoarse.

The Via Appia had been empty for Otho. Travellers stood to one side watching the soldiers march by. No cheers. No sound at all. Just boots. Clumping boots. And the trundle of wagon wheels on the cobbles, splashing through puddles.

They reached their camp just as the sun was beginning to sink through the grey clouds into the murky ground. Epaphroditus examined his quarters, a wooden hut with two beds placed either end.

"It's a bit basic I'm afraid," Epaphroditus told Philo, completely unaware that they squeezed eight soldiers into a similar-sized space. And they certainly weren't allocated the plump mattresses and flea-free cotton bedding that Philo and Epaphroditus warranted.

"It's fine, sir," replied Philo, sitting on his bed scouring through the latest dispatches.

"Be sure to write to Teretia. The mail is leaving in less than an hour."

"Thank you, sir. That's very kind of you. I shall write her a quick note to say we have arrived safely."

"Did you have a chance during the journey to read those reports on Caecina I gave you?"

"Yes, sir, I did."

Epaphroditus sat on a chair positioned in front of Philo's bed. "Your thoughts?" he asked.

"Well, sir, I thought it odd about the wife. This Salonina."

Epaphroditus couldn't help but laugh. "You saw it too," he smiled.

"There's no mention of her until Aventicum," puzzled Philo. "She must have joined him there. Given her behaviour at Novaria and the other towns they've passed through, she would have garnered talk if she'd been with him earlier on his route."

"But from where did she come? Talos swore not from Rome."

"Caecina went straight from his appointment in Spain to that in Germania. He certainly wasn't married in Spain."

Something in Philo's tone caught Epaphroditus' attention. He raised an eyebrow at the scribe.

"His missives to Galba passed across my desk," admitted Philo with some awkwardness. "He was clearly very worried about Galba's intention to prosecute him over matters in Spain. His letters became rather desperate. I think if he'd had a family, he would have brought it up as mitigating circumstances. He certainly brought up everything else, including his own, erm, 'relations' with Galba."

Epaphroditus' eyebrow arched higher. "Really? Now that is interesting and worthy of a discussion, but it won't get us any closer to Salonina."

"No, sir. But what is interesting is that it's from Aventicum onwards that he really picks up speed. I mean, he was always moving fast, sir. But from that point onwards he moves faster. He should never have reached the Alps this soon."

Epaphroditus pinched his chin. "So what are we saying? That true love has spurred him on?"

Philo gave a shrug. "I don't know, sir. Sorry. I just felt it was interesting and unusual."

"And worth mentioning," Epaphroditus finished for him. Getting to his feet he said, "Right, we'd better go see how the emperor has fared this long journey."

Philo stood up, slinging his satchel strap over his head.

Just like old times, thought Epaphroditus with a smile.

"Did the emperor really march the whole way?" asked Philo.

A question that Epaphroditus repeated to Onomastus.

"He did," supplied the dwarf as he lifted up the emperor's bare feet and placed them gently into a trough of hot water.

"Owww," winced Otho. "I think I've got a blister."

"I think you'll be lucky if you can walk tomorrow," said Onomastus, pouring salt into the water.

"I think you were magnificent, Uncle Marcus," breathed Salvius. "He did march the whole way. The soldiers loved it. They made up songs about him. It was inspiring!"

"It was stupid," countered Onomastus.

Epaphroditus knelt in front of Otho's nodding head. "Imperial Majesty!"

The head jerked upwards.

"I'm awake. I'm awake!" he insisted, his eyelids heavy, his face streaked with dirt.

"Celsus is waiting outside. He has the latest dispatches on Caecina and Valens."

Otho, using a finger to extract dirt from his ear, gave the nod. "Send him in."

He winced a little as he shuffled his feet in the water.

Celsus strode into the emperor's quarters, unable to stop his head from turning and taking in the luxury. It included a full-sized marble bath and a bed laden with fat, plump imperial purple cushions. "The good news is that Valens is still holed up at Lucus," he informed them. "There's no sign of him moving."

"How peculiar," puzzled Epaphroditus. "What's he waiting for?"

"Perhaps your envoy idea worked."

"Valens' letter seemed to suggest it very much hadn't," mused Epaphroditus, recalling Valens' choice words of rebuttal.

"Who cares? It's what we wanted, isn't it? The two armies not to meet."

"Caecina has sent word," Celsus waved a scroll in the air.

"Oh yes? What does our brave young buck have to say?" asked Epaphroditus.

"He offers terms for surrender."

"Would I be right in supposing they are not favourable?" queried the secretary.

"They'd have to be outside this room with swords drawn before I'd consider accepting them. I would advise not putting pen to parchment, Caesar. Let him wonder whether we're fool enough to lay down our arms to him."

"Noted, Celsus," said Otho. "And our plans?"

"Imperial Majesty, the legions Caecina controls are a hard lot. A tough lot. Even without Valens' legions, they will annihilate our Praetorians, gladiators, and raw recruits in open battle."

"I'm hoping you're about to follow that with a soooo," said Otho.

Celsus broke into a grimace, the nearest he got to a smile. "Soooo, Caesar, we don't give them the opportunity." He unfurled a map on the ornate, mosaic table top. "This is his likely route."

They all bent over the sketched terrain. "I say we put a cohort of our legionaries here, in this bit of woodland. It'll take them by surprise. And I say we keep bothering them like that. It'll cut down their numbers and hold off their travelling."

"Until the other legions get here?" asked Salvius brightly.

Celsus gave a humph and changed the subject. "The only issue is Placentia." He pressed a thumb over where the town was marked on the map. "It's right on his route. It's the first major Italian town he'll pass."

"Who have we got at Placentia?" asked Epaphroditus.

"Spurina," replied Celsus. "If we start off tomorrow morning, we can get reinforcements to him before Caecina gets there. We are a day closer than him."

"Do it," said Epaphroditus.

Otho pinched his chin between his fingers. "We should send a note to jolly him up. To make it clear that we have every faith in his ability. Throw him some gifts of money or whatever he desires."

"Lest Vitellius present him with a better offer," inserted Epaphroditus drolly.

"So cynical in one so young!" smiled Otho.

Epaphroditus gave a laugh before getting back down to business. "Don't throw fripperies his way. It'll look too much like a bribe for his loyalty. He'll feel undermined, distrusted."

"He's a straight-up man," confirmed Celsus. "A fortifying message, as you say, Caesar, shows our confidence in him. Such hopes placed on him may be the dissuading factor from treachery, should he waver when Caecina's superior forces gather outside his town."

"Philo," called Epaphroditus.

The freedman stepped forward. "I'll start composing the words immediately, sir."

"I'd like you to deliver the message personally."

"Sir?"

Epaphroditus turned back to Otho. "Sending a close member of your court will show the esteem you hold Spurina in, rather than the usual dusty recruit from the messengers section. It sets it on an important personal footing."

"True," agreed Otho. "And you do have such a lovely speaking voice, Philo."

Their attention drawn back to maps and legions and formations by Celsus, Philo's look of dismay remained unseen.

SIXTY

Antonius Honoratus, Praetorian tribune, looked the small freedman up and down.

"Can you ride?"

The look Philo gave in return was one of utter surprise. "I went to scribe school."

"You can ride in one of the baggage wagons," decided Honoratus. "They're back that way."

He pointed beyond the three cohorts of Praetorians lined up and ready to march. Philo shuffled his way past them, dragging his feet along. Epaphroditus, seeing his assistant's miserable expression and begrudging attempt at breakfast conversation, had been at pains to stress that there was no chance of him being caught up in any actual fighting.

"You saw the map, Philo. We are a day closer than Caecina. He'd have to march his men at double pace to get to Placentia before you. Besides, he has several towns on his route, no doubt he'll rest his men at one of them ready to face Spurina. There's no need to fret at all. You just have to deliver the emperor's message to Spurina. You don't even have to stay the night if you don't wish to, though it might be wise."

None of which calmed Philo's nerves in the slightest. What was troubling Philo in particular had little to do with accidentally being caught up in battle. Rather, it had everything to do with travelling with three cohorts of Praetorians.

Philo had grown up surrounded by Praetorians. The palace slaves were an easy target for the Guard's casual cruelty. Philo had been the subject of numerous jibes about his appearance.

"Oi, Guru, where's your elephant?" was a particular favourite. Along with loud musings on whether it was true that Indian man-seed was black in colour. There being an unspoken threat that they might seek to confirm the story by any means necessary. Philo had always scurried past them with his head down, his face burning, and his hands shaking.

Then there were the legs deliberately thrust out that had him thumping onto the floor, bruising his knees. How they laughed as he scrabbled about on the floor collecting up his scrolls, taking the time to kick his paperwork out of his reach over and over again to their continual amusement.

As a man, he recognised he'd got off lightly. Felix was forever storming to the prefect's office to complain about the rapes and injuries inflicted upon his female stock.

So no, Philo did not like Praetorians. And that was before two of them had cracked his jaw, bruised his ribs, and held him down while his former boss Icelus had inflicted a very Straton-like humiliation on him. The thought of travelling with such brutes, whose number no doubt included those two particular guards, had inspired a terror in him that no amount of placation from Epaphroditus could remove.

Probably the best thing to do was to stay out of their way as much as he could. He'd remain in the wagon and write letters to Teretia. He didn't even need to come out for food. He could cope one day without it. He hitched himself up into the wagon, pulled the leather curtains shut, and proceeded to settle himself down in the very back of it, squeezed in-between amphoras of wine and oil. If he stayed here hidden by the supplies, they might forget all about him. Which in Philo's mind was the very best possible outcome for his mission.

SIXTY-ONE

It was an odd sort of an atmosphere in the imperial palace. Without an emperor many daily tasks were suspended. Chamberlains pottered around empty rooms. A surfeit of announcers with far too much time on their hands had taken to elaborate drinking games involving penalties for any dropped syllables or slurs in their diction. Scribes sharpened, then resharpened their styli into lethal weapons.

Of course, they'd been without an emperor before. Nero had spent two years touring Greece. Galba had dallied for months in the provinces before reaching Rome. But this was different. This time they had no idea which emperor would be returning to the palace. Which was unsettling for an institution that prided itself on forward planning.

Statilia was filling this quiet time with an excessive amount of piety. All gods were to be properly venerated. The temple priests were overjoyed by the fabulous votives appearing at their doors. She had ordered the reading of the auspices every morning and insisted upon a full report.

And then there were the omens. The strange and fantastical. The disastrous and tragic. The empress desperately tried to read their meaning. Was the flooding of the Aventine district and the collapse of a bridge a good or bad omen? Did it foretell disaster for Otho or disaster for Vitellius? Statilia was meeting with an ever-growing group of interpreters.

"She should join in the announcers' drinking game," Mina told Cassandra one evening as she greased up her whip. "It would be far more productive than all this religious stuff. What does it matter if it's a bad omen? There's nothing she can do about it, aside from wind herself up further. She's going to ping like a ballista bolt any day soon."

Cassandra agreed, the mistress was becoming ever more anxious. That morning she'd berated Phaon, the head of the messengers section, that there wasn't enough information coming through.

Phaon had told her, "The thing about messages, Imperial Majesty, is that someone actually has to write one and then send it."

Her own letters to Otho, as dictated to Cassandra, were a jumble of thoughts that the secretary worked hard to transform into coherent paragraphs. Cassandra didn't blame the empress. The uncertainty was affecting her too. Cassandra liked order. She liked structure. She flourished when her day was planned down to minute detail. The last year's events had pulled those foundations from under Cassandra's feet. She was left in a world where nobody knew who was going to be the boss from one day to the next.

During all this uncertainty, Publius had been brilliant. He listened to her outpourings of fear. He held her hands, promising her, "You've got two months left till you can buy your freedom. Only two months to stick it out. Then I'll take you away from here to my bookshop and we can start your new life together."

She smiled at this. Inwardly, she wondered when the best time was to break it to Publius that she had no intention of giving up her job once she was free.

To Mina she said, "I'd like to have the room this evening. Publius is coming round."

Mina paused in her greasing. "Oh, oh! Is this going to be the night?"

That she and Publius had yet to consummate their relationship was one fact Cassandra bitterly regretted sharing with Mina.

"The night he takes you roughly from behind and shouts 'Bona Dea!' You know you should get Sporus in. He's ace on sex tips. He pretty much trained up Teretia and now she's pregnant. A Sporus course is well worth paying attention to," said Mina. "I should take notes or draw little pictures of his suggestions."

"I don't need tips of that nature, thank you, Artemina. I would just like some time alone with Publius."

"To do the humpy rumpy," decided Mina. "No, that's fine. I don't want to stand in love's way. It's actually nice to know that someone is getting some, because I am certainly not. And everyone else, even Sporus, seems to have gone wildly celibate."

She placed down her whip, and put the top back on her grease pot. "I hope you have a lovely time."

"Thank you, Artemina, it is appreciated."

"And check his todger for lice, because you do not want those!" was her parting shot.

* * *

Kicked out of her room, Mina decided to seek out Sporus. She found him, to her surprise, lying on a couch, dressed in a male tunic and distinctly clumpy footwear. She couldn't remember the last time she'd seen the eunuch in male dress.

"Didn't feel like it," was his dismissal when she questioned his outfit. "I'm not feeling sparkly, or shiny, or even silky today."

Helping herself to a handful of nuts, Mina enquired, "Is it because of Otho? Because you're worried for him?"

Sporus gave a sigh. It was a small sigh, completely lacking in induced drama or hysteria.

"Do you remember when the palace was fun? When it was all about the parties and the orgies? And all we cared about was the gossip and the scandal?"

"Yes, yes I do."

"I miss it," admitted Sporus. "I miss it all. I wish things were back the way they were. The way they should be. My darling Nero singing his heart out. Tigellinus being sick in a fountain. Calvia being all bitchy. And Alex—" He paused.

This was the first time he'd mentioned Alex since their friend had died.

"And Alex here on this couch with us," he continued, holding a fist against his chest, "moaning about his job, and lusting after you but never getting anywhere. I want him back. I want them all back!"

Mina put her arms around him. Sporus quietly wept on her shoulder.

"I know, I know," she said, rubbing his back. "I want things back the way they were too. I want the empress to be bitching about you, not mourning a man who isn't even dead yet. I want Nymphidius Sabinus being all stern and shouty and strange. I want Tigellinus to squeeze my bum and laugh about it, as if he's not done it every single day for the entire time he's known me. I want Nero back, plinking-plonking on his water organ and having ideas for poems mid conjugal visit. I want to be inconsequential and flighty and fun. I want Alex and Daphne and Straton. I want my friends back!"

"Me too!" wept Sporus. "I want them all back!"

Mina hugged her friend tightly to her. "Otho will be back," she told him. "You'll see. He'll come back. And everything will be jolly again. And there'll be parties and fun and everything will be back to normal."

Sporus looked up at her. "Do you promise?"

"Nobody wants Vitellius to be emperor," she insisted. "Why would they, when we have a perfectly good emperor already?"

"Exactly," said Sporus. "That's exactly how I feel. It's going to be alright, isn't it Mina?"

Though she felt nothing of the sort, Mina replied. "Everything is going to be fine."

SIXTY-TWO

"I shall be toasting Mars tonight, now that you're here," said Spurina, handing Honoratus a beaker of wine.

He tapped this against Spurina's own cup before taking a sip. They were sat at a rectangular table in Spurina's command building. Spurina and his young tribune, Cossius, sat on one side, Honoratus and an awkward-looking Philo on the other.

"You sure you don't want a drink?" Spurina asked Philo.

The freedman shook his head. "No, I'm fine. I'm not thirsty. Though, actually, do you have anything to eat? I'm a bit peckish."

Spurina gave a glare at a standing slave. All that was needed for the boy to rush off to fulfil Philo's request.

"You should see what they've left me with! Tomorrow morning we'll do a line-up so you can wonder at what they thought they were doing! I tell you, I could defend this town better if I armed all the housewives rather than the wet whelps they've given me. I swear they've emptied the schoolrooms and sent them all my way. I took one look at them and told Cossius to bolt the gates."

Though he appeared to Philo's eyes like one of the wet whelps mentioned, Cossius gave a sage nod at odds with his tender years. "The general decided there wasn't a chance our troops could survive a battle with the enemy."

"The young whelps thought differently though," said Spurina with a grim laugh. "They decided they wanted to face the enemy eyeball to eyeball and so off they went."

"A mutiny?" said Honoratus.

"Pah!" spat Spurina. "A load of boys getting overexcited."

"How did you regain control, sir?" asked Philo.

"Easy. I let them march," grinned Spurina. "I said, 'Alright, if you want to fight the enemy, let's go do it.' They were keen enough for the first three miles. Then they began to flag. By the tenth they weren't nearly so excitable."

Spurina's eyes sparkled. "I was kind though. I said, 'Let's make camp here.' That pleased them no end until I told them they'd have to build it themselves."

Honoratus smiled. "Let me guess, they thought slaves did that sort of thing."

"Ahh, Antonius Honoratus, I gather that spoilt little boys are no novelty to you."

"It's why centurions were invented," quipped Honoratus.

"Well, to cut a long story short, we'd only got a foot or so into the earth before they decided I was right the whole time, that really we should hold onto the town. And back they marched. Fools. Caecina's Germans could build a fortress in the time it took me to march my boys three paltry miles."

He held his hands apart. "Tell me, Honoratus, what have you brought me?"

Philo happened to be looking at the tribune and he saw his cringing stance as he was forced to admit, "I brought Praetorians. Three cohorts of Praetorians."

The smile dropped from Spurina's face just as the food arrived. Philo dived a spoon into the steaming cauldron before its bottom hit the table.

* * *

Salonina was catching up on her correspondence when Caecina stormed in. She put her letter aside when she saw his rage.

"My darling, what is it?"

He huffed about their quarters. Rearranging items on the desk. Slamming down an ink pot. Flinging down a stylus. Salonina came up behind him and put her arms around him, pressing her body onto his back.

"Darling."

She placed a kiss on the back of his neck and was gratified when his skin goosebumped. "Darling," she repeated in a slightly more husky tone. She turned him round. His lips were pursed in a sulky pout. His brow was furrowed. He looked like Apollo after another unsuccessful nymph-catching exercise.

"Why the frown, my love?"

"Urgh," was the reply she received. Then, "Argh."

Caecina scanned the room. His eyes fell upon a silver jug placed on the table. He picked it up and threw it across the room, spraying them both with water. Still unsatisfied, he picked up the table and lobbed that too. The resulting thump brought in the sentries. Salonina waved them away as Caecina overturned the desk and then kicked his feet through the resulting debris.

Salonina watched this display calmly. Eventually there was nothing else to fling about.

Caecina gave a roar not unlike that of a dying lion in the arena. "Where are they?" he demanded of the walls. "Where are these damn Othonians? Why do they not march to face us? How are we meant to be victorious if we have no one to fight? I promised the men a battle. A proper battle this time, not some soft Gallic fools. Proper soldiers to fight! We need to conquer!"

Pulling his fingers through his hair, he turned round. Salonina was stood absolutely still, her eyes wide and her lower lip trembling. Her expression was as anxious as a virgin about to lose her maidenhood. It was a look Caecina found instantly arousing.

He kissed her hard, forcing her mouth open and pushing in his tongue. One hand squeezed at her breast and as the nipple hardened she gave a small cry. He could wait no longer. He threw her onto the floor, pushed her skirts above her waist and then thrust himself into her. She screamed at that first thrust but by the third, her hips began to join in his rhythm and then the moans came. A joyous Caecina thrust harder and harder, her moans increasing until he reached a grunting, roaring climax.

His chest heaving from his efforts, Caecina threw an arm around Salonina. Gods, she was marvellous, wasn't she? How did she do it? How did she play the part so successfully, so convincingly? Her entrance had been as tight and hard as a virgin's. How had she done that when it was usually so warm, so plush, so soft?

During the months they'd been together, he hadn't touched another woman, or a man. He didn't need to now. Not when Salonina could be anything and everything he needed. The Germans took one wife for life and Caecina had always admired them for their fidelity. It was quite at odds with the bed-hopping and divorcing that went on back in Rome. And now he had a woman he could commit to for life, he couldn't imagine a life without her. He loved her.

He kissed the top of Salonina's head.

"We have passed through villages and middling towns so far," she told him. "They're not worth defending. That's why we've not found the Othonians. But Placentia is only a half day's march away."

"Placentia, you say?" Caecina propped himself up on one elbow. "It's an important town?"

"They'll make their stand there. They'll not want you to get any further south."

"A half day?" Caecina sat up.

"We can set off tomorrow," smiled Salonina.

"Tomorrow?" queried Caecina with a sudden energy. "Why tomorrow? There is still some light left."

"An hour or two, maybe—"

"That's enough. I'll march the men double pace. That way we'll reach Placentia all the quicker."

"But darling, the men are having dinner."

"Good. Hungry men are useless fighters."

Salonina leaned in and kissed his lips. "You are so right, my darling, and so clever. Why don't you announce it to the men right now?"

* * *

It was an order that the legionaries, who'd been itching for a decent enemy to fight, were happy to follow. With total belief in their superiority of numbers and experience, doused with a good meal and accompanying beer ration, the legionaries felt sure they could take down Placentia within the hour.

Such was their confidence, two miles into the march when it was noted that they hadn't brought any siege equipment with them, a general sense of bravado triumphed. Every man of them felt fully confident that they could scale walls without ladders and break down the city gates by pounding on them with their fists.

SIXTY-THREE

"Let's go see these men of yours," Spurina had said, with all the enthusiasm of a man visiting the latrine in the middle of the night and discovering there was no bum sponge.

Honoratus did his best. He walked Spurina quickly past the less impressive of his troops to the Praetorians. They at least fitted into their uniforms without any unsightly bulging. Honoratus talked about Nymphidius Sabinus' improvements, listing the accomplishments of the deceased prefect in increasing the Praetorians' fighting ability. He even mentioned their recent success in protecting the emperor from danger (whilst at no time mentioning that this threat was entirely born of their own imagination).

Spurina made no comment. Not one. Not until they returned to his quarters where they found Philo tucking into his third bowl of stew.

"You boy!"

Philo got to his feet still chewing.

"Tell me how many legions has the emperor got back at camp?"

Philo swallowed a chunk of carrot. "The I Adiutrix and a forward party of the XIII Gemina."

Spurina wiped a hand across his forehead. "A forward party? And as for the First, I've never heard of them. What is this I Adiutrix?"

"It was a legion put together by Galba," interjected Honoratus. "Of sailors."

"Sailors," repeated Spurina. After a moment letting that sink in, he dared to enquire, "And who else?"

"He has the Praetorians, the ones that aren't here that is. And some, er, miscellaneous troops."

Spurina turned to Honoratus. "What does he mean by miscellaneous troops?"

Honoratus took to looking at the ceiling, a tiny corner of it, well away from Spurina's glare.

"So that's how it is, is it?" grumbled Spurina. "Boy! You go back to the emperor and you tell him that I shall hold this town. But I'm going to need some of those 'miscellaneous' men of his as well as what we have of the XIII Gemina."

This was an order to gladden Philo's heart and now-full stomach.

"Yes, sir. I shall go back right now."

Spurina indicated to Cossius who led Philo out.

"If you could arrange my—"

But Philo never got to finish that sentence. There came thundering through the main gates: a horse. It pulled up in front of Cossius, its rider leaping off.

Spurina appeared through the door. "Speak!" he demanded.

"They're coming!" gulped the messenger. "The Germans are coming!"

Spurina looked around and then yelled, "CLOSE THE GATES!!! CLOSE THE GATES!!"

Men ran towards the city gates.

A panicked Philo bleated, "But I have to get back to the emperor."

"Not today you won't," said Honoratus, before marching off to organise his men.

Philo approached Spurina. "Sir, I have to get back to the emperor to get your reinforcements."

"There's no time for that now, boy. Didn't you hear? The Germans are coming. We've got to bolt the gates and man the ramparts. Nobody can leave."

Philo, seeing Spurina's attention fall on Honoratus' attempts to get the Praetorians to form some sort of suitably military stance, turned to begging. "Please, sir. I have to go."

"Cossius, we need to be sure we have a decent supply of ammunition on those ramparts."

"Yes, sir!"

"Sir! Sir!" Philo interrupted.

Spurina didn't hear him and he marched off leaving Philo staring into space. Cossius gave the freedman a tight smile. "It's my first time in battle too," he confessed. "But it's going to be absolutely tremendous, you'll see."

Philo did not share the young tribune's excitement. He watched with a pit of dismay forming in his gut as the city gates were swung shut. The bars lowered across those huge wooden doors, trapping him inside.

SIXTY-FOUR

To Philo's eyes, it was a barrage of manic activity. Wagons were pushed with little directional skill against the gates along with anything else with any weight. There was a clambering of soldiers and Praetorians up onto the ramparts of the town's walls, where centurions yelled them into their positions. He could see the archers pulling back the strings of their bows as they tested the tautness in preparation.

The townspeople of Placentia had vanished. They'd barricaded themselves in their homes, leaving Philo with nowhere to hide and wait out the siege. Reluctantly, he had taken up position somewhere near Spurina's left elbow. He figured that at least he would be able to give a full report of the general's actions back to the emperor. Assuming the Germans didn't storm the town and kill everyone in it, of course.

He wondered if he should pen a farewell note to Teretia. And one to Lysander asking him to take care of his widow and child. And finally, one to Epaphroditus informing him where he'd put the key to the stationery cupboard.

He was so wrapped up in his thoughts that it was a moment before he realised the roaring trundle of wagon wheels, the yells of centurions, and the complaining grunts of Praetorians had ceased. All was quiet.

Philo looked to Spurina. The general's eyes were closed. Beside him, Cossius sported a similar look of concentration. Then Philo heard it. Singing. Unmistakable singing from beyond the walls of the town.

Spurina opened his eyes. "That's them." To Cossius, he said calmly, "Let us man our positions and keep our heads. We have the advantage. We already hold the town. It's up to them to displace us."

"We'll not let them! We'll defend to the death!" cheered Cossius.

"Well, let's hope it doesn't come to that."

Spurina climbed up a ladder onto the ramparts. Honoratus stood with one hand held above his eyes to block out the glare of the setting sun.

"Mars almighty, there's thousands of them!" exclaimed Cossius.

And so there were. Thousands and thousands of Germans dressed in Roman uniforms rapidly filling up the flattened ground in front of the town. In the twilight gloom, they were but shadows of men.

A squinting Philo enquired, "Is that forest made up of shrubs? Because the trees seem rather small."

"They're giants!" gasped Cossius, completing Philo's thoughts.

* * *

A sentiment that was rapidly filtering through the Praetorians who stood on the ramparts.

"Gods above!" hissed Proculus to Lucullus. "Look at them! They're huge! How did they get so big?"

"They eat raw meat," replied his friend. "That's what I heard. They rip it apart with their teeth. Sometimes when the beast is still alive!"

They both gave a shudder. One that increased as the Germans moved forward and it was revealed that some of them had decided to fight in the traditional style.

* * *

"Barbarians," breathed Cossius, taking in the bare chests of the approaching Germans.

Philo, whose sole experience of soldiers was the lax and flabby Praetorian guardsmen, was shocked by the muscled Germans.

"They're as wide as bears," he squeaked.

Looking at their fists, he almost expected to see claws gripping at their swords.

They had no chance against these brutes, did they? The hysteria began to flutter in Philo's chest. He was going to die, wasn't he? They were all going to die. He looked to Spurina in desperation. The general was scanning the scene, his eyes narrowed, his expression one of surprise mixed with confusion.

"Where's their siege equipment?"

Spurina's surprising discovery was lost by a cry from Cossius.

"Ye gods, is that Caecina?"

The tribune pointed to the left side of the amassing Germans and a figure riding a pony up and down the ranks. As he got nearer, Philo realised the pony was no pony and its rider no ordinary man.

He truly was a giant to diminish the scale of such a stallion. He was a giant clad in a tunic and trousers with his plaid cloak flapping in the wind behind him. Even though Philo was extremely familiar with Caecina's entire life story and knew him to be as Roman as a crumpled toga stained with garum sauce, his first thought on seeing the rider of that stallion was, this man could not have a single drop of Italian blood in him. He was a German barbarian.

A shudder ran the length of Philo's back just at the moment Caecina waved his sword in the air and yelled, "LET THEM HAVE IT!"

Which was the signal for the Germans to run full pelt for the city walls.

Philo's natural instinct, born of his palace upbringing, was to run. Except there was nowhere to run to. The freedman looked to Spurina for guidance.

The general was gazing at the 15,000 Germans belting towards the walls with an expression of amazement.

"Sir?" pressed Philo.

Spurina shook off his astonishment and turned to Honoratus. "Let's do this."

Honoratus gave a grin. Like Spurina he had noticed the gap in Caecina's army.

"I reckon we've got the edge today."

Spurina gave a nod. "Let us take advantage of it then."

* * *

A whoosh alerted Philo to their archers' opening shots. The arrows headed upwards and then arched downwards onto the Germans. Some threw themselves beneath their shields, hearing the ping of the deflected arrows. In a post-dinner, beer-enthused bloodlust, many were not so quick thinking. Their screams reached the ears of those stood on the ramparts. Philo winced as the archers released a second round that was quickly followed by further screams.

"ANOTHER!" yelled Spurina. "Get as many in before they can get themselves organised. Faster!"

Philo wanted to put his fingers in his ears. He wanted to close his eyes. He wanted anything not to be there. He wondered what Teretia was doing back home. At this time of day she'd probably be getting ready for bed, plaiting up her hair and complaining about Verenia.

He was pulled out of his thoughts by a tug at his arm from Cossius.

"We need to get the sheets up," the tribune told Philo.

"I'm sorry, what?"

"Sheets up!" yelled Spurina. "Now! Quickly!"

Philo watched two Praetorians hoist up wet linen sheets on poles.

"We need to repel their arrows," Cossius told him as he struggled with the pole. "The linen is wet to put out the flaming arrows. If the town catches fire, we'll have no choice but to open the gates."

"Oh. What can I do?"

"Help me with this bit."

With some awkwardness, they managed to hoist up the wet linen.

"Cossius!" addressed Spurina. "You boy! Get behind the sheets now."

The two crouched down beside the general as a whooshing noise assaulted their ears.

A cowering Philo, expecting the thud of arrows against the sheet, was surprised when none came. Glancing at Spurina, he saw he was not alone in his surprise.

"Sir?" queried Cossius.

"Let's take a look."

Spurina got to his feet and put his head round the sheet cautiously. Then he laughed. "Oh my. Come see, Cossius. You too, boy."

Philo stepped round the sheet, followed by Cossius.

Spurina pointed to the right. To the amphitheatre that stood outside the city walls. It was now on fire.

"They missed! They missed an entire town and hit that instead!"

Philo didn't know much about archers, but he'd always assumed they could hit a target. Otherwise, surely they were a fairly pointless addition to the legions. He dared to gaze over the ramparts and spotted a blazing line of flames on the plains outside the walls. This was the result of those archers who'd truly indulged and whose arrows had fallen a few feet in front of them. It provided a barrier of sorts to the Germans' assault on the walls. Slowing them down. And giving Spurina's slingers and archers a chance to launch further assaults, cutting into their numbers.

Philo watched mesmerised as the Germans were felled. Those behind tripping over their fallen comrades and falling to the ground, making them easier targets for Spurina's archers and slingers. Caecina didn't look too pleased either. Philo could see the general waving his arms about as he rode back and forth behind his advancing soldiers.

It was all so very different from the terrifying reports he'd read on the German legions. They were meant to be the best trained, the meanest and baddest of all the legions. Yet even to Philo's distinctly untrained eye, they seemed to be making a bit of a hash of besieging Placentia. A thought that was instantly challenged by a THUMP.

Philo shot three inches in the air. THUMP, THUMP.

"What's that noise?"

"Some of them have made it to the gates, it appears," Spurina said calmly.

THUMP, THUMP, THUMP, THUMP.

"Will they get in?" THUMP, THUMP, THUMP. "They seem rather eager."

"Of course they won't!" decided Cossius firmly. "We're going to stop them!"

Though the tribune seemed so very sure, Philo didn't see how they could stop the Germans from gaining entrance. If they were at the walls of the city, that was a very hard angle for the archers and impossible he supposed for the slingers. All they could do was wait and listen to that horrible thumping until the gates splintered and cracked open and in they all ran, swords pointed and ready for slaughter. Philo's stomach flipped over.

Spurina, taking pity on the freedman's panicked face said, "They've got no spades to dig under us. All they've got is crowbars, swords, and their fists to get through the gates. If we keep them distracted, we can hold them off."

"Distracted how?"

Spurina indicated the young legionaries who were lobbing down pebbles and grit and anything else they'd managed to collect. In-between barrages of falling debris, Honoratus and his Praetorians leaned over the turrets of the ramparts and flung their javelins downwards.

"MORE!" yelled Honoratus to his men.

* * *

Caecina, watching his brave Germans fall by the walls, felt like crying. Really he did. He wished Salonina were there. She would know exactly the right thing to do. She'd have some brilliant innovation that would make the Othonians open the damn doors to that city! But she wasn't there. He debated about sending a messenger back to ask for her help. But then he heard the screams as yet more of his soldiers were pierced by arrows or by javelins or blinded by slingers. He knew there was only one recourse.

"RETREAT!!!!"

* * *

"They're running the other way," said Philo vacantly. "Why are they running the other way? I don't understand."

"They've given up, boy," Spurina informed him.

"They're fleeing, sir. They're fleeing!" bounced Cossius.

"We won?" queried Philo as the Praetorians broke into cheers.

"For now," said Spurina. "But they'll be back, boy," he said as the Germans ran into the darkness. "They'll definitely be back."

The relieved smile faded from Philo's face.

SIXTY-FIVE

The sun was only just in the sky, the mist still hanging, when the Germans began filling up the plains again.

"Well, they've been busy," commented Spurina dryly, noting the towers, ballistas, ladders, and battering rams the Germans had brought with them.

Spurina had also kept his men busy during the night. While the Germans had been constructing siege equipment, they'd been collecting absolutely anything that could be used as ammunition. They had quite an arsenal of pebbles, stones, great slabs of rocks, iron horse shoes, even pots and pans. But the heaviest, and anticipated as the most lethal, were the millstones they'd had to use ropes to hoist up to the ramparts.

Philo for his part had been given the job of sharpening up posts of wood on the basis that he was a scribe and the technique required was surely similar to sharpening a stylus. Though he'd spent all night at the task, his customary thoroughness meant Philo had actually only managed to produce two such stakes. Spurina, gently touching the tips and watching the blood trickle down his hand, had seemed impressed nonetheless.

"You want to throw these lethal beauties down yourself, boy?"

A weary Philo had shaken his head, "I'm not much of a shot."

"The size of those Germans, you don't need to be."

* * *

Viewing the artillery the Germans had managed to build, Philo felt the panic his night's work had distracted him from. It was evident in his face for Spurina said kindly, "Remember that these are the same drunken idiots from last night. Except they've had no chance to sleep it off."

That might have soothed Philo's frazzled nerves if Spurina hadn't immediately turned to Honoratus and said, "The townspeople are citizens. So there's no point in those Germans capturing anyone alive if they can't sell them on. If they get through those gates—"

Honoratus gave a bow of his head. "My men will do whatever it takes," he promised.

Beyond the walls, in the field there came a yell and then a whooshing noise.

"Brace yourself," said Spurina. There came a thump against the walls that vibrated beneath their feet.

Philo didn't have a chance to ask what it had been for there came another whoosh. And this time a crash that made his teeth shudder.

"Ballistas," said Cossius, steadying himself by leaning a hand on the wall.

Another whoosh. Then a smashing, cracking sound and the space in front of Philo was suddenly a cloud of dust.

He ducked down, coughing as there came another hit that shook the ground. He reached out and hit something warm. As the dust evaporated, he could make out what he was touching. It was Cossius. The tribune was lying on one side, his lower half a mashed mess of blood. He stared at Philo, his mouth fell open to expel a rush of red, and then his body was wracked with tremors. After that he fell still, his eyes glassing over and fixing at a singular point.

Philo scuttled backwards on his bum to the cover of the hoisted arrow-repellent sheets. He gulped at the air, his hands shaking.

Spurina was on his feet, yelling. "It's cover for the battering rams. Archers, slingshotters, let rip!"

The whirling and whooshing came from their side this time but it didn't stop the pounding of further ballista hits. Philo kept himself crouched low as Spurina paced and Honoratus dashed back and forth with further commands for his Praetorians.

He heard screams but could no longer work out from which side they came. He heard grunts, from the Praetorians presumably. The whooshing of arrows. The whirling of slingshots. The air was thick with smoke and dust. Beneath his feet, the blood of Cossius pooled in thick red puddles.

The shuddering of the walls alerted Philo that the Germans had reached the city. The repetitive crashing could only be their battering rams splintering the gates. Surely it was only a matter of time, despite their reinforcements during the night, before those gates fell. Philo screwed his eyes shut and silently prayed to his gods.

He was midway through a plea to Kali, the black one, when he felt a hand on his elbow. Opening his eyes he saw Spurina. The general hauled him to his feet.

"Get down into the town, boy. They're putting up ladders against the walls. We're going to have to fight them hand to hand, and I don't want to be worrying about the emperor's favourite scribe whilst I do it."

"You want me out the way?"

"And Cossius too. Where is he?"

Keen to get out of the way of angry Germans, Philo dropped the niceties he usually employed when breaking bad news.

"He's dead."

Spurina blinked, then shook his head. "Shame. Now get out the way."

Philo ran to the ladder. In his haste, his feet missed a rung and he slid the length down, hitting the ground with a bone-jarring thump. Above him on the ramparts, a bloody fight for survival was about to take place.

SIXTY-SIX

The sky was a warm blue. The air already hot, even at this early hour. Quite at odds with the miserable damp they had left in Rome. Such was the change that Epaphroditus found himself pondering whether it was an omen. A thought he quickly squashed: since when did he believe in omens? If he ever had, it had been crushed during his years working for Callistus and the merry band of priests, auspice readers, and soothsayers who had trotted up to the palace each month for their bribes.

Epaphroditus settled himself on a bench outside his quarters, a note tablet resting on his lap. It was a much nicer place to work than his stark quarters with its bare walls and earthen floor. No wonder legionaries were so ill–tempered, forced to live in such dreary surroundings. He'd prefer digging ditches, fighting barbarians, and marching endless miles to escape those walls.

He flipped open his note tablet and tried to concentrate. In front of his bench was the wide road that ran down the centre of the camp. A group of gladiators had taken to practising their moves each morning and a group of star struck legionaries inevitably came to watch. Their number this morning included the emperor's nephew.

Salvius stood transfixed by the dives and shouts of the muscled, loinclothed fighters. Oh dear, a love of gladiators was not a suitable hobby for an emperor. He'd advise Otho to have a word with his nephew after he'd dealt with the issue at hand.

Epaphroditus stared down at this tablet and the one word inscribed into the wax: Salonina.

She was important. He'd known it from the very first report he'd received of her existence. But who was she? A careful examination of the papers Philo had helpfully arranged for him shed little light. Rather, they pinpointed a series of inconsistencies. There was no agreement even on whether she was Caecina's wife. In some reports she was described as his mistress, in others as a consort, and in a few as his wife.

Whatever she was, she was constantly by his side. And ever since meeting her, Caecina had moved his army at incredible speed. Which meant? Epaphroditus scratched his forehead with the end of his stylus.

It meant either that Caecina was overly keen to impress his new lady love with victory, or that she was egging him on.

Another scratch to his forehead. The first Epaphroditus could well understand. He'd once been a cocky young man desperately trying to impress a girl. Hadn't everyone?

The latter made no sense. For if Salonina was egging Caecina onwards, what possible purpose could she have? The faster they moved, the further they moved away from Valens' army and certain victory.

Valens was another mystery. He was still camped up at Lucus with no sign of moving. Conflicting reports suggested he'd either fallen ill or fallen down dead. Which should have made Epaphroditus happy. For it meant Otho's distinctly inferior force only had to meet Caecina's army. But it didn't cheer him. It troubled him. It was all too convenient. The very thing he'd been desirous of, keeping the two armies apart, had occurred. But it was certainly not down to his machinations.

The bench dipped as Salvius sat beside him. "They are wonderful, aren't they?" he said, indicating towards the gladiators. "I thought Brutus was for certain defeat too! Yet somehow he makes it back to his feet and Glyax is the one on the floor. Incredible!" The boy's eyes were agleam with the passion of a genuine enthusiast.

"Many years back, I used to work with a man named Ariston. He was mad for gladiators," said Epaphroditus. "Of course, his interest went beyond parries and thrusts," he continued, his eyes falling on the blushing Salvius. "Ariston developed a passion for the topmost gladiator of the time. He used to drag me out every morning to watch this gladiator train. And of course we attended every bout he took part in. Ariston used to chew his fingernails down to the flesh watching his lover. I will admit, though, as a man who loathes sport in all its forms, that I have never seen a gladiator more impressive in contest."

"Better even than Brutus?" queried Salvius.

Epaphroditus took a look at the muscled secutor, his chest marked with scars.

"Ariston's gladiator never took a hit or a slash or any mark. Though the gods knew, his opponents tried. I've never seen a nimbler man. He was untouchable."

Salvius screwed up his eyes. "Is that even possible? Surely the trainers would want to put on a good show. The crowd needs blood."

"Oh, they got that," smiled Epaphroditus. "He could despatch the opposition with enough blood to satisfy the viewing sadist. But the real show was to see if they'd get a hit on him. The stories went that there was more money placed on Straton than gold in Anatolia."

"Did he remain untouched then, this Straton?" asked Salvius, the interest clear in his voice.

Epaphroditus was distracted by the sight of the camp gates opening and the horse that rode through them. The rider was one of Otho's messengers, and seated behind him, a smaller, strangely familiar figure, his arms tight around the messenger's waist.

Epaphroditus flipped his note tablet shut. "He did indeed," he told Salvius, getting to his feet. "At least until the day Ariston slit his throat."

* * *

He hurried over, reaching the horse just as the messenger was helping his companion down from the stallion.

"Philo!"

"Sir."

The freedman's usual pristine garb was marked with dirt, his greeting smile nervous. Epaphroditus found himself clenching his fists in anticipation.

"He held it," said Philo. "Spurina held Placentia."

Then Philo's knees gave way and he fell to the ground.

* * *

Epaphroditus settled Philo, quite against his wishes, in the emperor's quarters. The freedman lay on a very comfy couch, propped up by pillows and covered in a gold bed sheet.

Otho, sat on the end of the couch, handed Philo a glass of wine mixed with water and spices.

"You look like you need this, Philo."

The freedman took a sip and then a gulp. "It's been a long journey back. I didn't want to stop too often. I knew you needed to hear the news as soon as possible."

"Spurina kept them out?" said Celsus, expelling puffed cheeks of air. "He really did it?"

"Yes, sir, he did."

"Take a few more sips, Philo. Get your breath back. There's no rush," said Otho, one knee jiggling up and down.

"No, it's alright, Imperial Majesty. I'd rather give my report now whilst it's fresh in my memory."

This made Epaphroditus smile. He knew Philo's prodigious memory meant he could repeat word for word an imperial speech made two years previously.

The report Philo delivered had Otho grinning from ear to ear.

"The army we've feared since January is not invincible it seems," said Celsus.

"And also," Epaphroditus told Otho, "we now know what kind of a commander Caecina is."

"An idiot one," said Onomastus under his breath. "Were they really all drunk?"

"That first night Spurina believed they were," said Philo. "It would certainly explain the mess they made of their siege. Looking back, their battle song was more merry than warlike."

"I look forward to hearing Honoratus' account," smiled Otho.

"Antonius Honoratus? The Praetorian tribune?" enquired Philo.

"That's the fellow."

"Imperial Majesty, I'm afraid he fell during the second battle and, er, didn't get up."

"He died?"

"Yes, I'm afraid he did. Spurina will be able to tell you more if Your Imperial Majesty wants to know the details."

"No, no, I don't think I do. Honoratus. He was the first to support my claim to be emperor," mused Otho. "Without him, the Praetorians would never have joined our cause. Without Honoratus, we'd have never succeeded. We'd have never made it to this place right now."

Otho's gaze turned upwards. Onomastus threw a look at Epaphroditus.

"Caecina's vainglorious," interrupted the secretary. "He's in a hurry to make an impact without his fellow commander Valens. And, most important, as Onomastus notes, he's an idiot. We can use that."

"Strike him while he's down," Celsus said. "We've not got the forces yet to tackle his army on open ground, so I say let's pick a few more men off him."

"What do you suggest?"

Celsus gave a brief smile. "I say, let's unleash Brutus and his pals."

SIXTY-SEVEN

It was not a palatable sensation, defeat. Caecina had never been defeated at anything before. There was no woman he hadn't succeeded in seducing. No man either that he'd failed to tempt into sex. Every position he'd excelled at. His stint at being commander of the German legions had been similarly successful until that humiliation at Placentia.

The first failed attempt to take the town he could just about swallow. They'd been foolhardy rushing in without preparation. That had been a lesson worth learning, even at the expense of a number of his legionaries. But their second attempt, that was different. They'd spent all night constructing siege equipment, and Caecina had debated for hours the tactics with his tribunes.

He couldn't understand it. He had the best soldiers in all the empire. The hardest, toughest nuts of legionaries anywhere. There was nothing they couldn't do. Except take down a town held by a load of kids and a smattering of Praetorians. He couldn't understand how they'd failed. It was utterly incomprehensible. And no amount of discussion illuminated it any further for him. They should have taken Placentia easily. Yet they had not.

Lying in bed, hands linked behind his head, Caecina made a momentous decision.

"We shall stay here, right where we are, and wait for Valens. He can't be that many days away now."

Salonina propped herself up on one elbow. "Darling, are you sure that's what you want to do?"

Caecina nodded. "That was the plan all along. We would meet up in northern Italy. I should stick to my side of the agreement. Valens is very clever about these things," he conceded.

"But darling, the scouts that came back today say there is no sign of Valens anywhere."

Caecina rolled onto his side. "What do you think that means? I can't make Valens out. He said he'd be there but he wasn't."

"I fear he may have been caught in some local dispute and not managed to extricate himself as successfully as you did, my darling, with the Helvetii." She brushed her lips against his. "He could be days and days away. Maybe even months."

She moved one hand down to a spot on Caecina's body that she knew to be particularly sensitive. Nibbling at his neck she whispered, "With Valens so far away, if you wait for him, it gives the Othonians more time to gather their army together. If you wait too long, they could build a force greater than both yours and Valens' combined."

As Salonina used one hand to caress his groin and the other hand to press at that very particular spot that lay hidden behind it, Caecina concluded she was right. Of course she was right. Hadn't that been why they'd marched so quickly to Italy? Hadn't Valens said something or other about the eastern legions and the distances and timings or something? Salonina's actions were beginning to mist over his thoughts.

Advantage. They still had the advantage. They had to use it.

"We'll move in the morning. First light," he declared.

"I think that's wise," said Salonina, straddling him. "I think that's very wise."

* * *

It was a very pretty wood. A copse of interlocking trees, fresh green leaves, and a blanket of bluebells. It was home to gently grazing deer, to softly calling songbirds, and also, this day, to Brutus and his band of fellow gladiators.

They lay hidden in long grass or crouched down behind bushy thickets with their backs pressed against trees.

Celsus' scouts had been trailing Caecina's army. They had confirmed that he and his men were heading straight through this woodland. This news caused great excitement among the gladiators: fighting was what they lived for. They were completely and totally outnumbered by Caecina's army, by thousands to one. But then they didn't intend on taking it all on.

Gladiator Hilarion skipped over a tree root and threw himself on the ground beside Brutus.

"They're coming," he told him.

Brutus raised his arm, the signal for his men to hold their positions.

A thump, thump, thump of boots broke the peaceful idyll of the forest. Accompanying that, they could make out a clip-clopping, which had to be the cavalry. They came first. As it was a narrow pathway with plenty of trip hazards, the riders' attention was on successfully navigating the road ahead. One briefly looked round but spotted nothing untoward and continued on his way.

Next up was a small band of legionaries. These the gladiators ignored. As they did the trundling baggage wagons. Which was unusual. These were generally the first target of any attacking force. Armies had been brought to their knees by the loss of that night's supper.

They even let Caecina himself, resplendent on his black stallion, and Salonina, riding beside him dressed in an imperial purple gown atop her own white horse, pass. Following Caecina was the main bulk of the force which, given the path, only allowed them to march two abreast. It took a fresco-drying amount of time to pass through. But let them pass the gladiators did. They were waiting for what followed the legionaries. Their very specially selected target: the auxiliary soldiers.

The auxiliaries were the non-Romans recruited locally to support the citizen legions. If they served their full term, they too could become citizens. If they survived to do so. For being an auxiliary meant one thing: expendability.

Usually they'd stick them at the front of the marching column to use their local knowledge to lead the way and avoid dangers. But here in north Italy, the German auxiliaries weren't local so they'd stuck them at the back. The perfect position for the gladiators to attack.

Though they'd been recruited from some of the fiercest German tribes, they weren't barbarians. Gladiatorial combat to the death was as popular a spectacle in Germania as it was everywhere else in the empire. So they were quite familiar with the heavy helmets and padded limbs of the gladiators. However, watching such muscled specimens from the safety of the eighth row of the arena was quite different to suddenly seeing scores of them running through a previously idyllic scene right towards you.

Those auxiliaries on the front line understandably panicked, dropping their shields and legging it. Unfortunately, they found their exit blocked by a line of the Retiarius class of gladiators. Their tridents made short work of the petrified recruits.

Those trapped in the centre remembered at least part of their basic training. Huddling together, they raised their shields up for protection. However, the narrowness of the path meant they couldn't huddle together in sufficient numbers to save themselves from the force of the gladiators. Their protection was ripped from their trembling fingers. They were despatched with repeated dagger thrusts to their throats and torsos.

Those at the rear, seeing the slaughter in front of them, fled back the way they came, desperate to escape, only to run into a further batch of Retiarii.

Brutus, amid the carnage and the chaos, grinned entirely unseen by anyone else behind the thick metal of his helmet. His instructions from Celsus had been clear.

"Get in there. Take out as many as you can. But don't dawdle because the rest of the legion will be sent back for you."

Advice Brutus heeded, calling for his men to retreat.

They weren't pleased. It ate into their professional pride not to finish the job but they obeyed, slipping back into the forest just as the legionary rescue force arrived.

What those legionaries found was a heap of bodies and a number of stunned survivors. Of their attackers, there was no sign. A clopping of hooves and there appeared Caecina atop his stallion. He stared at the scene and more particularly at the heap of corpses.

"My men. What happened to my men?"

SIXTY-EIGHT

The news of Caecina's disaster at Placentia reached Valens' camp some days later. Still bedridden, the commander felt his stomach heave and lurch as he read of humiliation reaped on Caecina.

"Crito!" he yelled.

"Yes, master."

"Tell me, did the messenger speak to anyone else in the camp?"

"Not to my knowledge, master."

Valens flopped back on his pillows. His men did not need to know about this. It would increase an already taut atmosphere. He knew his extended bed rest was causing friction within the barracks. The Germans were eager to fight. They were fed up being stuck in camp. They wanted to get at the enemy. Valens didn't blame them. He would be well enough to move soon. He knew he would be. The wise woman's tonic had done wonders. Just another day or two of rest and he would be well enough to go sort out that idiot boy.

* * *

Of course the messenger had talked to others in the camp, and Caecina's defeats were soon common knowledge. Strangely, for it was entirely his fault, Valens' men didn't blame Caecina. Instead, they blamed their own commander. It was Valens who'd kept them here, letting Caecina march into a dreadful Othonian trap. If they'd been there at Placentia, they'd have taken the town within the hour and sold off the population as slaves by dusk. Those men killed in Placentia, their colleagues in arms, there was no need for them to die. No need at all!

"It's obvious, ain't it?" said legionary Gemus. "We have to get rid of him."

A few shocked faces had Gemus qualifying this. "He's going to die anyway. Crito reckons it can't be long now. It would be a favour to him really, coz he's lingering now and that lingering, well, you see what it's caused. Our German comrades-in-arms attacked and beaten by those damn effeminate, circus-loving, eunuch-chasing Othonians. We can't let it be!"

"How should we do it?" questioned one.

"Mercifully. No need to be brutes about it. A pillow over his face. It won't take long. And if we do it properly, no one need know. They'll think he died naturally."

* * *

In a camp of tens of thousands of bored men, gossip is hot currency. The news that the commander was going to be murdered in his bed was the hottest of the hot. A toasted bath stone of hotness that spread right across their encampment and beyond. So much so that some enterprising locals, in anticipation of the legions moving, had set up a series of stalls en route in the hope of making a killing.

"I see," said Valens when word was brought to him of his imminent murder.

His hands shook against the table he'd balanced himself against. This could have been from fear or rage. Or it might just have been an amplification of the recent tremor that had affected him.

"I see," he repeated in a tighter voice. His knuckles whitened, the table legs wobbling from his grip. "Are they aware what the punishment is for even speaking of such an act?" he demanded.

The lictors present did not answer.

"Well, what are you waiting for? Go arrest them! Now!" yelled Valens.

The lictors disappeared, leaving a spittingly angry Valens. "It'll be those fucking Batvarians. They've been nothing but trouble since the day they joined us. Fuckers!"

He continued in this vein for some time, releasing his bile into the air. It felt good. As would the ringleaders' execution. He might even decimate the rest of those troublesome Batvarians. Why not? Galba had done it only a few months previously. And for far lighter a crime than plotting to murder a Roman commander.

His gleeful anticipation of revenge was interrupted by Crito.

"Master, master, we must run," said the slave, his eyes darting about.

"What?"

"The Batvarians, master, they've attacked the lictors. They're on their way now! We must run, master."

Valens' head shook. "They dare to attack the anointed lictors?"

"Master," pleaded Crito. "We must go. They intend to murder you."

That was the moment that Valens realised the very real danger he was in. He made to move and was afflicted with a rush of pain.

"Crito," he cried, doubling over. "Help me."

With Valens' arm round his shoulder, Crito realised they were not going to make it far. He could barely hold onto his master's convulsed and rigid form.

"Master, the slaves' quarters. We'll hide there."

Valens, teeth gritted with pain, was in no state to disagree.

SIXTY-NINE

The wise woman narrowed her eyes. "What's all that yelling about?" she wondered out loud.

"The legions! They're mutinying. They've killed their commander and they're going on the rampage. We need to flee, right now," her neighbour informed her. "They'll rape the lot of us and burn the town down."

Maybe, mused Gwencalon, maybe not. But it was certainly too hot for her. Her work was done. Time to return to Rome. She pulled down the shutters on her potion shop and calmly made her way out of town.

* * *

Failing to find Valens in his soon-to-be deathbed as expected, the eight soldiers ransacked the room. They turned over the bed, cupboards, tables, and chairs in their hunt. Helen watched all this with wide eyes.

"Where is he? Where the fuck is he?" they demanded of Crito.

The slave pressed his lips together and tried not to look in the direction Valens was hidden.

"Fuck it, he doesn't know," said one.

He pulled out his sword and thrust it into Crito's gut.

"What 'bout her?"

Helen would happily have told them where her captor was but the soldiers were in too much of a hurry to wait for her reply.

In the adjoining room underneath a bed, Valens listened to Helen's dying gasps, desperately trying to hold back the wave of nausea that hit him. If he were sick, the retching would surely alert the soldiers.

The sweat beaded on his forehead. A shiver affected his limbs. He forced himself to be still. This was not how he was going to die. Stabbed in some squalid slave quarters, cowering under a bed. No, not him. Not Fabius Valens. He had plans. Big plans. It couldn't be over now.

The sound next door ceased. Valens held his breath trying to detect the sound of a door opening and the footsteps that would spell his doom. Silence. Then, yes, there it was. The distinct sound of a door swinging open and footsteps. In front of Valens' eyes appeared a pair of legs.

O gods above. Valens' lips moved as he worded an entreaty to Mars. The legs bent at the knees as their owner leaned over.

O gods, no! He screwed his eyes shut. What a way to go, cowering under a bed!

When nothing happened, Valens dared to open his eyes. He was confronted by a horrifying vision. A face dissected by a vicious white scar that cut from the temple, across one eye forcing it shut and slicing the nose almost in two.

"Fabius Valens."

"Asiaticus?" Valens asked. Though who else could it have been with that face?

"Vitellius sent me to check on your progress, Valens. Get out from under that bed. We have much to discuss."

SEVENTY

Sat opposite Asiaticus, Valens waited for him to speak. He didn't. Instead, he leaned back in his chair and straightened out his legs in front of him, one finger tapping on the arm.

Though they both served the same man, Valens had spent little time in Asiaticus' company. The sight of that puckered white gash with its serrated edge and pinkish hue across the damaged eye turned Valens' already delicate stomach. He'd heard many stories in the bars of Germania as to how Asiaticus had gained his scar. Some said he'd been a gladiator whom Vitellius had bought to serve as his muscle. Others that he'd been a hero of the legions incurring a fearsome wound from a foul Parthian. And then there were those who said Asiaticus had won his freedom by taking a blow meant for his master. Valens thoroughly disbelieved the last, finding it hard to imagine the idle Vitellius invoking any man's hatred to such a level.

Facing him, Valens worked hard to keep his face neutral, resisting the urge to flinch. The twisted sneer of Asiaticus' upper lip made it appear as if he were fully aware of Valens' efforts and was finding it suitably amusing.

"It's a shame you caught me at such an inopportune moment."

Asiaticus ceased his tapping. "Is that what you're calling it? Inopportune?"

Due to his injury, Asiaticus' voice sounded muffled. As if he were talking with a cloth held across his mouth.

"The tribunes have rounded up the troublemakers."

"On my instructions," informed Asiaticus. "When I arrived, nobody knew what to do. And what with you hiding beneath a bed, it seemed someone needed to take control."

There was no accusation in his tone, Asiaticus was merely stating facts. "The thing about soldiers is that they like their routine, their order. So I instructed the centurions to return to their barracks. The legionaries didn't like that. No one to tell them what to do, where to go, or how they might conclude their insurrection. They seemed quite relieved when I ordered the tribunes to arrest the instigators. They seemed almost glad of punishment and the natural order being restored. Even the two I caught outside your tent."

Valens held his tongue with difficulty, saying in as pleasant a voice as he could manage, "As you say, it was burning itself out. Do you bring news from Vitellius? Does he know what the idiot boy's been up to?"

"Caecina? Yes, I heard he'd also hit some difficulties."

Comparing the, in Valens' opinion, minor riot that had just been quelled to Caecina's failure to capture Placentia was too much for the commander.

"Difficulties?" he spluttered. "He's made fools of us all."

Such exertion caused a sudden rush of pain to his gut. "Crito!" he called. Remembering that Crito was no more, he changed this to, "Slave! My tonic."

A slave appeared with the bottle and dripped a small quantity of its contents into Valens' drink.

"Is that for your ailment?" asked Asiaticus.

"I am greatly improved since I started taking it," insisted Valens.

Asiaticus contemplated Valens' grey face and the tremor in his hands as he gripped the stem of his goblet.

"Can I see?" he asked the slave.

"Certainly, sir."

The slave handed over the small bottle. Asiaticus removed the cork and sniffed, his scar puckering on his forehead.

"Where did this come from?"

"Some wise woman in the town."

Asiaticus stood, taking the goblet from Valens' hands. "I'd send down some men to this wise woman of yours, Valens. There is nothing wrong with your stomach. You've been poisoned."

SEVENTY-ONE

"I'm sorry, Artemina, but it just doesn't seem likely," said Cassandra, passing her a honeyed almond cake. "I know Straton was your friend."

"He was!" said Mina, spluttering out crumbs. "He was one of the bestest friends I've ever had. Maybe bester than Sporus even."

Cassandra gave her an arched look.

"Because he never flounced," explained Mina. "You know Sporus, he's a walking flounce in waiting. Straton was solid. A solid guy. So it just doesn't make sense that he should have imagined a whole relationship with Philo."

"I'll credit that I never supposed Straton had the imagination or the brains to construct such a fallacy. I'd always assumed he was more act first, think about it never."

"Exactly! He was very detailed about things."

"Was he really? Or did you fill in the details for him?"

Mina brushed her hands together to get rid of the remaining crumbs. "I honestly don't know," she admitted. "I'm so confused about the whole thing."

Cassandra gave a humph and rested her hands in her lap. "I've worked with Philo for ten years. A few years back, I would go as far as to say that we were very close."

Mina's eyes sparkled with interest. She might have waggled an eyebrow.

"So I would say I know him well. I could certainly tell you in some detail what he thinks about various filing systems and papyri suppliers," she said with a smile. "I have never known him to look at men in that way. I've never heard any gossip that he does. And even if he did possess leanings in that direction, I really think he could do better than Straton of all people."

It was an argument Mina couldn't deny. I mean, look at Teretia, she was water nymph pretty.

"And I really think you agree with me," began Cassandra. "Because if you truly believed Straton and Philo were in some sort of crazy relationship, you wouldn't be talking about it with me. You'd be holed up with Sporus."

She was, as ever, infuriatingly right. Gossip, the juicier the better, was the basis of her friendship with Sporus. That she hadn't shared this all-time killer piece of gossip proved that deep down she didn't really believe it.

"I need another cake." She reached out for the plate. Cassandra slid it out of her reach.

"They're for Publius. Would you mind giving us space for a short while."

"Are you telling me to get lost?" grinned Mina, getting to her feet. "How very rude. But I shall comply. For who am to get in the way of true love?"

Walking round the table, she made a sudden grab for the cake and was out the door before Cassandra could object.

* * *

Munching on her cake, she wondered whether to visit Sporus. He was still a grey version of himself, moping for Otho and mourning Alex. He wasn't much fun at all. But then that was the palace all over recently.

At least, thought Mina, Cassandra was having a bit of fun. Maybe she and Publius would get married and there'd be a wedding feast to look forward to. Failing bookshop owner he might be, but nonetheless Mina had noted the expensive cut of Publius' tunics and his overly new sandals: he clearly wasn't destitute.

There was a tiny part of Mina that dared to recognise that when Cassandra left for marital bliss, she'd be missed. For goddess Vesta knew who she'd end up with as a roommate next!

Sporus' suite of rooms were located, by the empress' explicit orders, as far away as possible from her own and the emperor's rooms. Not that the walk had stopped Otho dropping in on Sporus whenever he fancied. Nor did it stop Mina visiting. Sporus had his bathroom complete with claw-footed bath tub, which she liked to take advantage of. In fact, she could do with a dip right now, to refresh herself and keep out of the way of Cassandra and Publius.

A yelled, "Fuckin' useless fuckwits the fuckin' lot of them," heralded the arrival of Felix. He barrelled round the corner with the gathering speed of a missile dropped from the top floor of the new palace onto the unsuspecting Praetorians beneath (a favourite slave pastime). Trotting ten paces behind the bristling red-beard and trying to keep up was his adopted son Ganymede.

Though avoiding Felix's eye, Mina gave a wave to Ganymede. The boy gave her a smile and waved back. Seeing the two of them put a thought into Mina's head. "Hey, Ganymede," she called after the boy. "You live on the Aventine, don't you?"

The boy stopped, turned round, and gave an enthusiastic nod that took in his whole body. "Yes, with my papa and my mama," he said with clear pride.

"Have you ever been in Publius' Book Emporium?"

"I can't read," replied Ganymede. "Not yet. But papa has been teaching me," he smiled.

"GANYMEDE?" A yell tinged with anxiety as Felix reappeared round the corner.

"Ah, there you are, lad. Thought I'd lost you for a moment then."

"Sorry papa. Mina wanted to know if I'd ever been to—?" he looked to Mina.

"Publius' Book Emporium," she replied, reluctant to get dragged into one of Felix's explosions.

"Wot he want to do that for? He can't read yet. Besides, we're in a fuckin'palace that has a fuckin' library in it and a fuckin' huge library at that. Why would he need to waste money in bookshops when we can pick 'em up for fuckin' free here?"

Mina, rightly surmising this was a rhetorical question, explained, "A friend of mine is the owner and as it is on the Aventine Hill, I was wondering if Ganymede knew of it."

"There aren't no bookshops on the Aventine," said Felix.

"Apart from Publius' Book Emporium," Mina found herself insisting.

Felix's eyebrow caterpillars went into battle across his nose. "No there ain't. There ain't any bookshops on the Aventine. Think those thick as pigs' intestines idiots that live on that foul cesspit of a dunghill can read? They're too busy drinkin', fightin', and touchin' up the prostitutes in broad daylight on the stinkin' streets to bother with their learning."

Then, seeing Mina's puzzled expression, Felix added, "I've lived in that fuckin' misery pit of a hill for two fuckin' decades and more. The Mamertine jail has better fuckin' facilities. There ain't no bookshop, there ain't any public lavvies. They just pull their putrid pricks out and piss out the windows. Don't matter to them who's passing by," Felix said with some feeling.

"Thank you, Felix. I might have been misinformed."

"I think the word you're looking for is lied to. Someone's been lying to you because there ain't no bookshop on the Aventine. Never has been. Never will be. Unless they demolish the lot of it and start all over again by repopulating it with actual human beings rather than hairy apes in tunics. Come along, Ganymede, we got work to do."

"Yes, papa."

And they set off again.

SEVENTY-TWO

"What news of the emperor?" asked Publius.

Having read Livy's account of the Sabine War and discussed and dissected it thoroughly, they were now relaxing with more general chit-chat over the plate of honeyed almond cakes. Publius was using a cupped hand to catch the crumbs, knowing how Cassandra liked to keep her side of the room tidy.

"Not much," she replied. "He writes to my mistress but tends to avoid any subject she might find distressing."

"Thoughtful of him," said Publius, similarly thoughtful as he bit into his cake. When his mouth was clear he asked, "How has he managed to cobble an army together? He can't have more than 5,000 men."

It was an innocently phrased question. However, it caused a prickling sensation to run up Cassandra's arms. She placed her plate slowly onto the table.

"That's the third time you've asked that question."

"What question?"

"How many men the emperor has."

"I didn't ask," smiled Publius, a few crumbs escaping from his mouth. "I speculated."

"No, you asked in a roundabout way. Like you did yesterday when you wondered about the catering arrangements for 4,000 men, then waited for me to correct you."

"Did I?" he smiled again. "What a memory you have! I wish I had such a brain. It would certainly help enormously remembering what books I sell each month. I'm not terribly good at record keeping and all that stuff." He gave her a hopeful look. "That's your strength. You make up for my weakness."

Further prickles. "You're changing the subject."

"Am I?"

"Yes, you are. You're changing the subject by flattering me. You do that a lot."

"Do I? Sorry if it bothers you. Now," he brushed his hands together to dispel the crumbs, "back to Livy. Did you want to move on to the next passage?"

"No," said Cassandra. "I want to discuss why you keep asking me about the number of men the emperor has at his disposal."

"I'm sorry, I have no idea what you are talking about," he smiled.

Another smile, thought Cassandra. He smiled a lot, didn't he? And not always at moments of joy, sometimes it was at moments that did not deserve a smile. Such as now. More prickles.

"Yes, you do, Publius."

Her eyes fell onto the leather bag that lay splayed open beside his chair. She could see a scroll in its interior. A broken seal that looked somewhat familiar.

"I'm sorry if I've upset you, Cassandra."

But she wasn't listening. Her eyes were firmly fixed on that seal and what it meant.

Publius followed her eye line, using his foot to fold the bag shut. Then he looked up, meeting Cassandra's eyes.

There was no smile now.

"Who are you?" she asked.

* * *

"I don't understand," said Mina, up to her neck in deliciously warm water. "He definitely said the Aventine, didn't he?"

Sporus, sat at the opposite end of the bath, shrugged. He rarely listened to anything anyone said unless it was about him.

"Why would he lie? Why would he make it all up?"

"Honestly, Mina, you are naïve," admonished Sporus. "Because he wanted to get under her dress, between her legs and thrust his way to a joyous spurt of happiness. What better way to seduce our bookish Cassie than by pretending to own a bookshop. I bet she gets wet dreaming of his musty old scrolls."

"But how could he possibly keep it up? At some point Cassandra would want to see the shop for herself," worried Mina.

"Perhaps he's counting on his bed performance being so legendary that she forgives any tales he's told her."

No, she wouldn't, thought Mina. Cassandra was scrupulously honest. Something any man would know on meeting her. She wouldn't tolerate any lie, no matter how well intentioned. Publius, the man who didn't own a bookshop on the Aventine Hill. The man whose great-grandfather hadn't been a lover of rhetoric. The man who didn't employ ten copyists. The man who'd spun a very thorough lie, even down to the names of those copyists: Onius, Balbus, Gaius, Gneus, Pyrrhus, Silvius, Rhemus, Telemachus, Fulvio, and Fronto. It was too good, too detailed to be merely an attempt at seduction.

And then she got it. She shot upwards splashing Sporus with water. "O gods! He doesn't need to keep up the lies!"

Sporus, wiping his eyes on a towel, enquired impatiently, "What?"

"Don't you see? Don't you see? She's the empress' private secretary! She's party to all kinds of secrets."

Sporus looked blank.

"He's a Vitellian spy!"

SEVENTY-THREE

Mina belted round the corner, pushing against the wall to steady herself and threw herself at the door. It flew open and revealed the scene.

At first Mina thought she'd burst in on Publius and Cassandra embroiled in an intimate moment. Cassandra was lying on her back on the bed with Publius lying on top of her. But then she saw Publius' forearm crushed across her friend's neck and Cassandra's legs kicking beneath him.

"You fiend!" she cried.

Publius turned his head, his arm still pressed against Cassandra's throat. "It's not what you think, Mina."

"Let her go, you filthy Vitellian spy!" she demanded, unhooking her whip from her belt.

"Mina, listen to me."

A strangulated cry from Cassandra was the signal for Mina to crack her weapon. It caught Publius on the arm. He gave a yell and released the other. Cassandra rolled from underneath him onto the floor. She knelt on all fours, coughing and spluttering, one hand on her reddened neck.

Publius rubbed at his bleeding arm, then held his hands up, palms facing Mina.

"Mina, listen to me. It is not what you think."

"Isn't it now? So you're not a filthy spy sent to squirrel secrets out of Cassandra?" she taunted. "Did she uncover your scheme? Is that why you were going to kill her?"

"I've no intention of killing anyone," said Publius. "Just put your weapon down so we can talk."

A calm instruction that set off a wave of merriment in Mina. "Not bloody likely! Zeus would have to strike off this hand with his lightning before I let go of my whip!"

* * *

Sporus had dallied in order to select the perfect footwear. While somewhat slower in running to the scene than Mina, he had nevertheless built up quite a speed. Unfortunately, the lack of grip on his fabulously flashy sandals meant that when he skidded into the room he found he couldn't stop. He careered straight into Mina.

The impact of a speeding eunuch, even the slightly built Sporus, was enough to knock Mina off her feet. Her hand let go of her whip. Rolling across the floor, it came to a stop right by Publius' toes.

A flailing Mina disentangled herself from Sporus. His floaty veil and shawl both seemed determined to attach themselves permanently to her face. She bounced to her feet to find Publius holding her whip.

"Now we can talk."

Mina disagreed. Taking off her helmet, she lobbed it straight at him. It got him in the stomach, doubling him over. With Publius incapacitated, heaving his stomach contents up on the floor, Cassandra crawled across towards him, two hairpins gripped in her hand.

"Argggh!" cried Publius, looking down to see the hairpins sticking out of his right foot.

Using his uninjured foot he kicked Cassandra in the face, knocking her over.

"You bastard!" screamed Mina.

"Will you bloody well listen to me now!" complained Publius. Sitting down on the bed, he pulled the pins out of his foot, teeth gritted.

Grabbing a nearby lamp stand, Mina cocked it over one shoulder like a spear. The action nearly toppled her backwards.

"Get up and fight me," she ordered, once she had gained an equilibrium.

Sporus had been sat on the floor examining a tear in his gown, which bothered him far more than the events unfolding in front of him. He now felt compelled to include himself in the drama. He took off his sandal and flung it at Publius' head.

Sadly, eunuchs are not known for their throwing abilities. The sandal fell short of its target. Instead landing on the recovering Cassandra's head.

Hand over mouth, Sporus expelled an, "Oops, sorry Cassie."

"Fight me! Fight me now. Or do you only get off on attacking defenceless girls?"

Mina swung the lamp stand round. It crashed into a wardrobe, caving in the door, and then knocked a over a vase, smashing it on the floor. Pointing to the debris, Mina warned him, "That's your head in exactly ten counts, spy."

"I am a spy, yes," admitted Publius, one leg crossed over the other as he rubbed at his sore foot.

"Ha!" said Mina.

"But I am not the Vitellian spy," he continued. "She is." He pointed at Cassandra.

All eyes turned to the correspondence clerk. She was sat on the floor, her eye swollen shut from Publius' kick.

"Rubbish," said Mina. One eye on Publius. One on Cassandra.

"Look in my bag. There's a scroll in there. You'll recognise the seal."

Unwilling to disarm herself of the lamp stand, Mina turned to Sporus. "Get it."

The eunuch sighed. "Get it, please. Manners don't cost an ass."

"Sporus!"

"Going, going."

He pulled out the scroll.

"Hand it to me," said Mina.

The eunuch folded his arms. "Who made you the boss? Why should you get the scroll?"

"Because you can't read."

It was a fair point so Sporus handed it to her.

Rolling it over Mina did indeed recognise the seal. "It's Epaphroditus' seal."

"Feel free to read it. I think it will clear matters up for you."

"Sporus, watch him." Handing over the lamp stand, the eunuch almost fell over from the weight of it.

Mina scanned its contents. It did indeed make matters clear. The missive from Epaphroditus congratulated his agent on finding the leak, advising him to keep close to try to uncover how much she knew. "For then," Epaphroditus wrote, "we shall know what she is passing on."

Mina looked at her roommate. "Cassandra?"

Cassandra looked up at her. "Do you know the story of that first Cassandra, Cassandra of Troy? No, of course you don't."

"She could see the future," said Mina stonily. "But she was destined always to be disbelieved."

"I see you remembered something from the imperial training school. But yes, this Cassandra can see the future too. And she sees that we all need to realign ourselves with the new regime."

"But Otho is emperor," protested Sporus.

"And here we come to Cassandra's tragic gift," she said. "Vitellius has 70,000 men at his disposal, who will easily crush Otho's puny force of gladiators and guards. He's doomed.

He always has been. But nobody wants to believe it. Not the mistress. Not Epaphroditus. None of you. I suppose it's because he's so charming, so witty, so nice. Though only if we overlook the fact he had the rightful emperor Galba murdered so he could take his place. That his selfish actions brought slaughter to the palace!"

"I lost friends that day too," said Mina in a tight voice.

"And me," added in Sporus. "And neither of us are traitors."

Cassandra shook her head. "Traitor to whom? Otho isn't coming back. You need to get on the winning side, because it won't be long before Vitellius is here in Rome and he and his wife will be seeking loyal attendants."

"And you're first in the queue, are you?" spat Mina.

Cassandra was unfazed by her hostility. "But of course," she said. "And you need to do this same. They'll be rooting out anyone considered too loyal to Otho. You need to get on the winning side now to secure your position."

"Never!" cried Sporus.

Mina shook her head in disbelief.

"Keep her here. I'll go get the guards," said Publius.

SEVENTY-FOUR

"She was such a good secretary," said Statilia. "I've never known anyone who could transcribe as quickly as her. Well, maybe Epaphroditus' little Indian boy. But aside from him."

"It's the good ones you've got to watch," said Calvia. "They're crafty. You can educate a slave too much. It gives them ideas."

"I still can't believe it. Cassandra! A traitor and a spy. It seems so unbelievable. She's worked for me all these years! I can't believe it. I just can't believe it."

"Imperial Mistress," prompted Publius, hands linked behind his back, head bowed respectfully.

"Yes, yes I know. I'm thinking."

"She has to be made an example of, Statilia my dear. A member of your own household betraying the emperor in such a low manner cannot be tolerated. She must be made an example of to inspire loyalty in the rest of the household."

Statilia bit at her lip.

"What were your orders?" she asked Publius.

"I was to uncover any Vitellian spies in the imperial household."

"And then?"

"My orders did not extend beyond that, Imperial Majesty. It is down to the emperor how he punishes his own household."

"Yes, but the emperor isn't here," complained Statilia.

Calvia touched her hand. "I know it's upsetting. It always is when one discovers the ones we trust are not worthy of it. But you simply must not show mercy. You cannot allow such treachery to go unpunished. She has to go in the arena."

Mina stepped forward. "Imperial Mistress, may I speak?"

"Go ahead, girl."

"The emperor has shown his clemency on more than one occasion, mistress."

"True, Marcus is a kind, generous man."

"Too kind, too generous," interjected Calvia.

Statilia bit her lip again. "I don't know. I just don't know."

"Statilia, it has to be done. Best to get it out of the way quickly, rather than let it fester. You don't need this matter hanging over you. Not when there are weightier matters like the emperor's safety to concern you."

"I don't. I don't need this at all," agreed Statilia. "But it is an internal matter for the household to deal with. Nobody out there knows about it, so why should we draw attention to her crime? Surely that can only encourage dissent. For if the people see that even the emperor's own slaves expect him to fall. Well, it hardly gives confidence, does it?"

"No, Imperial Mistress, it does not," said Mina.

"Tell that cross, red-bearded man that I want it done discreetly."

Publius nodded. "Yes, Imperial Mistress."

Mina followed him out into the corridor. "What does that mean? Discreetly?" she demanded, her throat tight, her voice shrill.

"After her interrogation it will come as a relief, I expect," said Publius evenly.

To her annoyance, Mina felt tears pricking at her eyes. "Did you ever like her? Even a little?"

Publius met her eyes. Gone was the earnest lover, the hapless project. These were hard eyes, cold eyes. There was no smile, no joy in him now.

"I had a job to do," he told her.

"And that's it?"

"Yes, that's it."

"MINA!"

The eunuch jumped on her. "Did you hear? Did you hear?" squeaked Sporus, twirling her round. "Caecina's been sent packing from Placentia. The emperor has scored an enormous victory! Isn't it marvellous!"

Mina placed the eunuch down and turned round.

Publius was nowhere to be seen.

SEVENTY-FIVE

Philo was sat on a stool in front of his boss. He kept his eyes firmly on the ground.

"I'm sorry to be the bearer of such terrible news," said Epaphroditus. "I know you and Cassandra were once close."

Epaphroditus bent his head down trying to catch Philo's eye, but his assistant evaded his apologetic gaze.

"There really was no doubt as to her guilt."

"No, I understand that," said Philo quietly.

"It's going to take a bit of time to digest it, I know. Why don't you take the night off? Go see what the gladiators are up to. It'll take your mind off it. I hear Brutus is going to fight three of the Praetorians."

"I have work to do, sir. I think I'd like to make a start on it," responded Philo.

Then he picked up his satchel, slung the strap over his head, and got to his feet.

"There are some letters that need to go with the messenger before sunset."

* * *

It had fully been Philo's intention to do some work. But he found himself walking straight past the HQ building and towards the exit gates of the fort. He needed to get out. To get some air. Some space away from the soldiers and the gladiators.

He walked through the fort gates past the sentries on duty. He followed the cobbled road outside until he could no longer hear the centurions' drilling yells. He stopped at the top of a hill and sat behind a mossy rock.

Traitors were executed. That was what happened. Philo had been a high-ranking official under Nero's particularly paranoid reign. He had seen many men arrested and executed. It was nothing new to him. But of course it was. Because the traitor in question was Cassandra.

Epaphroditus was correct in assessing Philo had once been close to Cassandra. They'd been friends. Good friends with much in common: a desire for order, a love of brand-new styli, and a passion for discovering the perfect filing system.

Over those years, Philo's feelings towards Cassandra had grown. He wouldn't have qualified it as love or even attraction. Just a desire to be near her, to spend time with her, to hear her views on the latest batch of papyri from Egypt, or to question the competence of the new assistant in the petitions office.

Then Straton had got in the way. He made it extremely and brutally clear to Philo how he felt about this friendship. Philo chose not to remember that episode. He'd pressed it deep down inside himself. He'd once attempted to talk about that day to Teretia. However, he'd only got to the point where Straton had pushed him through the door and he'd seen the manacles attached to the wall. Teretia had begged him to stop because she didn't think she could bear it.

That day with Straton had tainted his friendship with Cassandra. It had tainted Cassandra herself. He couldn't even look at her without recalling some of the horror of that day. So he didn't look at her. He didn't talk to her. He had, as he'd later confessed to Teretia, treated her quite abominably. He'd always hoped he could make that right. Apologise. Explain. Now he would never be able to. Cassandra was dead.

There was no doubt about her guilt. Philo had seen the evidence. He'd studied it carefully. The conclusion he'd come to had surprised him: it was stupid.

Cassandra had no access to imperial secrets. Nor had she attempted to uncover any to pass on. The essence of the notes she'd slipped between the scrolls in the Argentium bookshop to be collected by a slave of Vitellius' wife Galeria were mundane. They concerned the arrangements for the soon-to-be empress: the suites available for her to choose from; the staff that would be hers to command.

Fripperies, that was all. Knowing Cassandra, Philo knew exactly why she'd done it. She'd assessed that Otho was on the way out and she'd simply wanted to get things ready for the next inhabitant of the role of empress. It was admirable. It was sensible. It was treasonable. To predict the emperor's death or even to suggest it as a possibility was unthinkable.

Philo hugged his knees. He wished Teretia was with him. He missed her dreadfully. Every morning he awoke without her soft body beside him, he felt a physical pang that left him desolate and reminded him horribly of the years he'd lived before he met her. Years that now seemed to him dreadfully lonely. Which brought him straight back to thinking about Cassandra, and the tiny spark of light she'd provided him before Straton violently snuffed it out.

Staring up at the sky, tears began to form in his eyes and a gloom descended. That was when he heard it. A clip-clopping noise from the road beneath him. He wouldn't have paid it much notice if it hadn't been for the accompanying cheerful humming. It sounded to his ear oddly familiar.

He peered round his rock. On the road below, a woman was walking along with a small kitbag slung over her shoulder. She was somewhere in her middle years and well-dressed in a loose blue gown. But her most distinguishing feature was her hair. A blonde arch of curls piled high on her head with a veil attached to a bun at the nape of her neck.

Philo stepped forward. Hearing the motion, she turned her head. Her mouth formed an "O" then broke into a full smile.

"Philo, my darling boy!"

"Lysandria?"

SEVENTY-SIX

"But who is she?" asked Salvius.

Otho raised a hand to Epaphroditus.

"She's an imperial freedwoman of two superior talents," explained the secretary. "One is hairdressing. She was Agrippina's chief hairdresser for many years."

"And her other talent?"

"Is poisoning."

"Poisoning?" gasped Salvius in clear shock.

"Are you sure about that?" asked a sceptical Onomastus.

"Let's just say I know of several people who have procured her services."

"You?" asked the dwarf.

Epaphroditus ignored this question, saying, "I'm wondering if her presence in these parts might have something to do with the mysterious halt of Valens' legions."

"How so?" asked Otho.

"Didn't one report say Valens had fallen ill? I wouldn't be at all surprised if it's a tummy bug."

"You mean—?"

"Well, she's not nursing a sick friend in Baiae, which is where she's supposed to be," said Epaphroditus. "The question is, did she succeed in her task? Is Valens dead?"

A silence as they absorbed this. If Valens was dead, then there was only Caecina to face. And he was an idiot. Which meant their odds at winning this war had shot upwards like Actaeon's cock when he caught sight of the bathing Diana.

"Do you think she did?" Otho asked.

"Only one way to find out."

* * *

The palace's arch poisoner was at that very moment reproving her son.

"And you've got dirt under those fingernails. Look at them! When was the last time you had a manicure?"

"Mother, I've gone to war. You don't take manicurists to war!" Actually, they had done exactly that. And accompanying those manicurists were hairdressers, masseurs, pedicurists, and perfume squirters.

"Lucky I always travel prepared."

Lysandria reached up into her extraordinary hair and removed a pin. She used this to root out the filth from under Lysander's nails.

"Must you, mother?"

"I must, darling boy. Cleanliness is very important, Lysander. Haven't I always said so? I hope this isn't indicative of how you are living your life on the outside."

Lysander winced as Lysandria continued her task with a forceful diligence learnt whilst attacking that she-wolf Agrippina's hair with hot curling tongs.

"Mother, I've met a girl."

Lysandria looked up. "A girl? What girl? Do I know her?"

"I'm going to marry her. Instantly. Well, as soon as we get back home and if her father lets me. But even if he says no, I'll not give up on her. I'll be persistent. I won't give up on her, ever. Because we are meant to be together, we truly are."

"Who is this girl? And why haven't I heard of her until now?"

"She's *Verenia*," pronounced Lysander beautifully. "And she's wonderful."

"Darling, this girl …"

"Verenia."

"This girl, Verenia, how does she feel about these feelings of yours?" she asked, aware of her son's thwarted history with the opposite sex.

"She loves me, mother."

"And she said that did she, darling?"

"She cried because I left Rome. That's how much she loves me."

"She cried?"

"Her lovely eyes were brimming with tears."

It seemed too unkind to query whether there was a smoky fire burning nearby so Lysandria said carefully, "And she told you she loves you?"

"Well, not in those words exactly."

Confirming his mother's worst fears.

"She's wonderful. I can't wait for you to meet her."

A cough and an, "Er," announced Philo.

Lysandria's worried expression softened to one of glee. "My other boy! How is the *married* man? I want to hear all about it. How does Teretia fare in her pregnancy? Is she finding it hard yet? You tell her if she ever needs a pick-me-up, I'll be straight round with my tongs to beautify those golden locks of hers. Now sit and tell me everything."

"I'm afraid our catch-up will have to wait, Lysandria. Epaphroditus has requested to see you."

* * *

Philo led her to a sparsely furnished room. There were but two chairs and a desk, which Epaphroditus was sat behind.

"Here I am!" she announced cheerfully, sitting down on the spare chair. She leaned forward, putting her elbows on the edge of the desk. "Now tell me. What's all this about my Lysander and some girl?"

The direction of her gaze informed Epaphroditus that this was directed to Philo, who was stood to his right-hand side with a note tablet at the ready.

"Do you mean Verenia?"

"That was the name. Lysander declares he loves her and he says that she loves him. Now I know you will tell me the truth. Is it all in my poor boy's head again?" she asked, rubbing her hands together anxiously.

"Well, erm, she seems taken with him."

Lysandria brightened considerably. "Really? Is that so? Genuinely?"

"Teretia says she's been very sad since Lysander left. Though he writes to her each day, Verenia fears he is honey-coating his words so as not to distress her. She wanted to know what I'd said to Teretia so she could know the truth of it."

"Oh, that is encouraging. Thank you, Philo. I was so worried. You know what he's like. He will walk straight into heartbreak. I don't think I could bear to see him hurt again."

"Lysandria," broke in an irritated Epaphroditus, "what are you doing here?"

Confused, she replied, "You requested to see me, didn't you?" She looked again to Philo for confirmation.

"Not in this room. I mean this town. What are you doing in this town?"

"I'm going home."

"From?"

"From where I've been. What does that matter when my boy has finally found himself a decent girl! She is a decent girl, isn't she, Philo? Not a flighty type? She won't hurt him, will she? He's such a sensitive boy."

"Lysandria!"

She jumped in her chair, her hand going automatically up to her hair. "Venus' lover!" she exclaimed, holding the other hand over her heart.

"Your movements?" persisted Epaphroditus.

"What is this? Some kind of interrogation?" She gave a tinkly laugh.

"Yes, it is," said the secretary neutrally.

That caught her attention and she narrowed her eyes. "If it is so important to you, I have been nursing an old friend of mine in Bedriacum."

Epaphroditus laced his fingers together. "Yet you told your son you were in Baiae."

Lysandria looked at Philo, clearly assuming him to be the source of the information. He concentrated on his tablet, avoiding her enquiring gaze.

"He obviously wasn't listening properly. It's a dreadful fault of his."

"I think not," was Epaphroditus' calm response. "I think he heard you perfectly correctly."

"I've answered your question. Whether you believe me or not is irrelevant. It is a failing I have found in imperial freedmen, you all become paranoid. It cannot be healthy to be constantly suspicious. You mind that, Philo. Don't you get like him."

"Tell me about Valens."

"Valens, I have no idea who that is. Why would I when I haven't had anything to do with palace matters these last ten years?"

"He is a commander for Aulus Vitellius. Don't deny you've heard of him."

"Of course. I don't think anyone who worked at the palace could deny knowing Vitellius. He was a permanent fixture. When he fell asleep at banquets they'd just leave him there and give him a nudge when the next one started."

"Valens has been taken quite unexpectedly ill. He's been lying in his bed leaning towards death for the best part of a month now." Epaphroditus placed his own elbows on the table, leaning forward so his face was a few inches away from Lysandria's. "Who hired you to poison him?"

Lysandria had shaved off her eyebrows years back, as the fashion had dictated. The best she could do to express her shock was to flounce backwards into her chair with an, "Oh."

"Who hired you?" persisted Epaphroditus. "Because it's not come out of my budget."

"I have no idea what you are talking about," insisted Lysandria. "I have been nursing a very sick friend in Bedriacum. I know nothing of this Fabius Valens."

Epaphroditus leaned back in his chair, crossing his arms. "I don't believe I mentioned his name was Fabius."

Caught out, Lysandria fiddled with her shawl. "Lucky guess?" she attempted.

"Drop the act and tell me what I need to know."

"Or what?" she enquired.

Epaphroditus met her gaze. "Or I can make things very uncomfortable for you."

Beside him, Philo expelled a small noise.

"No need to worry," Lysandria assured Philo. "I have the measure of him. We've known each other always. Since we were children. Many, many, many years back we even had sexual intercourse."

"I barely remember it."

"Yes, that's what I thought at the time," commented Lysandria with a sweet smile.

Epaphroditus did not drop his gaze from her. "Who was it who insisted on the most awkward position so as not to mess up her hair?"

"So you do remember!" Lysandria clapped her hands together in glee.

"Let's try again, shall we?"

"With the sex? I'd rather not. I have a very jealous husband."

"Who nonetheless lets you potter around the countryside poisoning Roman officials."

Lysandria gave him a hard stare. "I've already told you that I know nothing about whatever it is you want to know about. So us sitting here like this really is a complete waste of your time. I'm sure you'd much rather be stuffing some young slave girl or ordering my lovely boy, Philo, about."

"We will sit here until you tell me what I need to know," said Epaphroditus. "I'm quite a patient man. I'm prepared to sit it out until that edifice atop your head wilts."

Lysandria gave a small squeal as her hand went back up to her hair.

"If you're finding this uncomfortable, it might be better if you leave, Philo."

Philo certainly was finding it uncomfortable. Epaphroditus was the best boss he'd ever had and he respected him enormously. But before he'd met Teretia, Lysander and Lysandria were the closest thing he had to family. Lysandria was the one who'd taken care of him after his mother died. She'd been a soft bosom to rest his head against when he'd been at his most despairing.

"No, sir, I'd like to stay. Lysandria, it's really quite important we find out all we can about Valens' army. It will help the emperor if you can tell us everything you can remember about the camp."

"Very well, for *you*, Philo," she sighed, throwing another hard glare at Epaphroditus. "Flip open a new tablet, Philo, because there's much I can tell you.

SEVENTY-SEVEN

Lysandria proved to be extremely informative on the tensions brewing in Valens' ranks: the mutiny, the bitter Batvarians, and a whole host of details that were extremely helpful. Including that Valens was very much alive and in her opinion likely to recover from his "illness" shortly.

"Excellent," was Otho's view of Philo's summary report.

"She'd make an excellent spy," commented Onomastus.

"You're assuming she's not?" queried Epaphroditus wryly.

"Did she say who she's working for?" asked Otho.

Philo made the pretence of flipping through his note tablet, as if he couldn't remember every word he'd transcribed. "No, Imperial Majesty. But I doubt it would be anyone detrimental to Caesar's cause."

"We'll never know, I guess," said Otho.

"Can't we torture her?" suggested Onomastus.

"We can't do that."

"Yes we can. You're emperor, you can do anything," insisted Onomastus.

Philo's face revealed his panic.

Epaphroditus said, "Be my guest, Imperial Majesty. Torture a free woman against the law. You might get your answer, you might not. Though it might be interesting to hear what her husband makes of it. I hear he's very influential with the guilds on the Caelian Hill and beyond. And he's rich, very rich, richer than Caesar. He has enough money to hire an army to avenge his wife."

"Alright, alright, it was just a suggestion. What've you got?" sulked Onomastus.

"Send her home. Then keep her under surveillance. She'll have to contact her boss at some point."

* * *

Watching from the doorway of their hut as Lysandria bid farewell to her son with a flurry of kisses, Epaphroditus asked Philo, "What do you make of it?"

The scribe sucked on the end of his stylus. "I don't think she's working on the emperor's, our emperor's, behalf."

"No, neither do I. If she were, then Valens would be dead. But he isn't. He's merely been slowed down on his progression."

Philo removed the stylus from his lips. "And Caecina's been speeding ahead," he said with a thoughtful expression.

Epaphroditus pulled his fingers through his hair. A suspicion forming in his mind. "Two armies," he began. "One deliberately slowed down via an agent we now know to be Lysandria. The other deliberately speeded up."

Epaphroditus and Philo's eyes met and they said in unison, "Salonina."

SEVENTY-EIGHT

Alright, thought Caecina. So the siege of Placentia had concluded with a less than satisfactory outcome. And then there'd been that embarrassing defeat at the hands of a band of gladiators. And he'd lost nearly all his auxiliaries to a series of lightning raids by the Othonians. But still, not all was lost, was it?

Salonina assured him not. Snuggling into him, she'd rallied his confidence.

"You have to think like the enemy, my darling. That's the key!"

Think like the enemy? Caecina had tried his very best to do so. What had he learnt about his opponents, the Othonians? They were determined. More determined than he'd expected, given they were hopelessly outnumbered. Valens had said they'd be dispirited, resigned to failure. Valens back in Germania had doubted they'd even bother to fight. Such was the certainty of victory. So much for Valens! To think Caecina had once admired that man, had bent to his superiority of years and experience. Well, not anymore! He'd show Valens. He'd show them all!

Think like the enemy, hey? The most recent humiliation reaped upon his men had been by the Othonians' sudden raids on his auxiliaries. They'd been trapped in unforgiving terrain and their numbers decimated. Caecina mentally slapped his forehead. That's what he'd do! He'd lay a trap for them instead. Ha! Let him see their shocked faces when they were attacked for a change.

Happy, Caecina hurried back to Salonina with his plan. She, always his most ardent supporter, naturally thought it was quite brilliant. Which cheered his battered confidence no end.

* * *

He chose the spot carefully. It was a few miles outside Cremona, an area named the Castores after the temple of Castor and Pollux that stood there. It was a pretty spot surrounded by woodland, gently sloping vineyards, and farmland split into plots by ditches and channels. Plenty of cover, in other words, for a carefully staged ambush.

This was a plan that necessitated clear organisation and secrecy. The former was accomplished with help from Salonina and his officers. The latter, Caecina frankly struggled with. Pleased as a dog who'd successfully raided the butcher for a bone and as excited as the same dog anticipating another successful mission, Caecina simply could not stop himself chattering away on this masterstroke of his.

This was his moment to prove himself as adept a commander as the great Julius Caesar. Had not Caesar taken on Pompey in his own civil war? And had he not totally triumphed through his daring and marvellous vision. Caecina too had that vision, that greatness of command. And today, he was finally getting the chance to prove it.

* * *

Inevitably, word of Caecina's daring plan quickly reached Otho's camp.

Celsus gazed down at the map and placed a thumb on a line. "Here is where he plans to ambush us."

"What's his plan? Do we know the details?"

"He is going to move a small group of his cavalry along the road. When they come across our forces they will retreat, leading our men back down the road. The woods either side are where he has hidden his auxiliaries and further cavalry. They will jump out and attack."

Otho blinked. "Haven't I heard of this tactic before?"

"Many times, Caesar," groaned Celsus. "It's as old as Cato the elder. No doubt they made you study it at school. I certainly did. Clearly Caecina's pedagogue was as miserable a military historian as mine."

"Thoughts, Epaphroditus?"

The secretary smiled. "My thoughts are that Celsus' thoughts will be far more valuable. Alas, my schooling was more practically minded. We didn't study the great battles of history. We were far too busy learning how to scribe neatly and add up lines of figures."

Celsus gave a grimace of a smile. "That'll be extremely useful for tallying up Caecina's dead, Imperial Majesty. This is our chance to wipe him out. We know Valens has to be on the move again."

"Now that Lysandria has ceased doctoring his after-dinner beverage," added Epaphroditus.

"News has to have reached him of Placentia, so he'll be moving fast to catch up. This is our best chance to finish this. I say we throw everything at him."

"Agreed!" said Otho brightly. "What's your plan?"

Celsus crossed his arms. "Be a shame to waste Caecina's plan."

"We're going to ambush him while he ambushes us?" queried a confused Salvius.

"Exactly," said Celsus. "My old teacher Herodias would be thrilled."

SEVENTY-NINE

Caecina's first surprise of the day was brought to him by his scouts.

"The Othonians are there."

"What?" he gasped. "But they can't be. We're going to get there first and hide the main bulk of our forces in the woods. Then the Othonians are going to march through. We'll send a smaller cavalry force out and they'll think, 'Oh, they've made a mistake. We can easily wipe out those fellows.' Then they'll follow the cavalry into the woods where they'll be cut to pieces. That is what is going to happen."

Salonina placed a calming hand on the agitated Caecina's thigh.

"Darling, calm yourself. You are spooking your horse."

Pulling himself together, Caecina patted his horse's mane gently. "Whoa boy, sorry boy."

Then to his scouts, "How many are there?"

"It appears to be four cohorts of Praetorians."

"See, that's not so bad, my darling," cooed Salonina.

A thwarted Caecina gave a humph. "Hardly worth the effort for so few men. I want to wipe out an Othonian legion at the very least!"

"But darling, think how it'll affect Otho if you destroy his personal guards."

Another humph. "You think it'll upset him?"

"I think, darling, that it could be a pivotal move. It could be exactly the disaster that breaks Otho."

"But Salonina, they know of our plan. Why else would they be there?"

"You don't know that. All you know is that they are at Castores. If they've come from Rome then they will naturally be passing this point, as we ourselves plan to do on our route. It's a coincidence, that's all."

* * *

So Caecina stuck to his plan, trotting his small cavalry unit along the road, past the wood where the main bulk of his army was hiding. As he rounded the corner, the upward sweep of the plains was clear. As were the expected Othonian forces on its top. The scouts had been correct in their estimate of numbers. There were 500 Praetorians lined up on the hill. Easily outnumbering his cavalry, they wouldn't be able to resist attacking. Especially when they saw that Caecina was present, so Salonina had said.

Caecina raised his sword in the air. "The enemy! Charge!"

The horses sped upwards towards the Othonians.

Caecina in the middle of the group and halfway up the hill suddenly realised that the Praetorians weren't moving. Why weren't they moving? They were meant to chase down the hill to meet them. Then Caecina would feign his retreat into the woods luring them into a total massacre.

If one is required to mount a defence of Caecina, it is that the speed at which his horse was moving really didn't give him a lot of time to think. Near enough to see the eyebrows of the first line of Othonian horsemen, he panicked. He couldn't really mount a retreat from battle if there'd never been a battle in the first place. That would look odd to say the least. So he needed a new plan and quickly.

Still ploughing towards the Othonians, he raised up his arm. This was the signal for his men to materialise in their thousands from the dense woodland with a, "Ha!"

In front of Caecina, the Othonian front line threw down their shields and began running away. Otho's cavalry turned their horses round and galloped away. It had worked! Seeing his superior numbers, they had panicked. Caecina grinned. "They're fleeing. They're fleeing! Men charge! Let's annihilate them!"

Caecina's jubilance lasted until he got to the higher ground. A good spot that allowed him a vision of the two legions lined up waiting for him.

He'd been tricked by his own trick!

Horrified, he tried to simultaneously whoa his horse to a stop and cry out a warning to his advancing cohort. He was not nearly quick enough.

The Praetorians were the first to charge. Their numbers and brutal tactics, practised for years on the innocent civilians of Rome, overwhelmed the small Vitellian cavalry force. Caecina was thrown from his horse into the squelching mud. Panic-stricken, he struggled to pull his leg from the quagmire. Using one hand, he heaved at his thigh and managed to pull the leg free.

Standing up, he gazed about, dazed by the chaos surrounding him. The noise was immense. Grunts, yells, the occasional scream, the clunk of sword on shield, bash, bash, thump.

Behind him, down the hill, his men appeared to be fighting off a band of gladiators. Their helmets flashed in the sun, blinding him for a moment. Soon, the gladiators were obscured from view by the mass of Othonian legionaries advancing on them.

They were overwhelmed. That was clear. Off in the distance, Caecina could see two Othonian cohorts as yet unused waiting for the signal to advance. Retreat. They had to retreat. Either that or surrender. Caecina's inner Julius Caesar quaked at such a thought. It was a tactical retreat. One Caesar would have approved of.

"RETREAT!!!!"

EIGHTY

The gates were thrown open and in marched the triumphant army to cheers. The gladiators marched down the centre of the road, their forearms raised, clutching their bloody daggers.

Otho stood outside his quarters, flanked by Epaphroditus and Onomastus, clapping his palms together, beaming from ear to ear.

"My men!" he called. "My gloriously brave men!"

The celebrations that night were loud and raucous, Otho had declared triple the wine ration for all, purchasing extra amphora personally from a nearby town. The emperor partook fully in the jollities. He entered into arm wrestling contests with the gladiators. Gambled with the Praetorians. Thrashed the legionaries at various elaborate drinking games.

Epaphroditus, in contrast, sat with Celsus in the emperor's own quarters. Their faces lit by the dancing flames of the oil lamps liberally placed about the room. Philo stood as usual to one side.

"So Caecina is alive?"

Celsus nodded. "The man's a bloody giant. You'd think someone would have spotted him. But no."

"How do his forces stand?"

"Defeated but not depleted," admitted Celsus. "I gave the order for Paulinus to destroy him. He did not. You'll have to ask him why because I cannot credit it."

"Valens is on the move," Epaphroditus told him. "And he's moving fast."

Celsus rubbed his hands across his face.

* * *

Asiaticus was not the greatest of companions to travel with. A fully recovered Valens found him infuriating. He had no interest in any of the leisure opportunities passed his way. He declined Valens' invitations to the theatre, to the games, and even to the brothel.

"Which you'd think he'd be up for," Valens complained to his tribune. "It's not as if any bitch is going to come to his bed willingly. Not with that face."

Valens almost began to miss Caecina. That handsome buck had always been up for a nocturnal adventure. He also bloody responded when you talked to him. In fact, Caecina was good company all in all.

This nostalgia lasted until news of Caecina's disaster at Castores reached them.

"What do you make of this?" demanded Valens, slapping the scroll on the table.

"If it is about Castores, I heard," replied Asiaticus.

"A defeat!" Valens squawked. "He's been defeated in battle by the forces of that bathroom buggerer Otho!"

"Yes, so I read."

"Well?" persisted Valens, one foot tapping on the floor.

Asiaticus stood. "I suggest you march your men double pace to catch up with him."

And that was that. No condemnation of the idiot boy's venture. Not even any disgust with the pointless loss of life. Asiaticus remained similarly non-judgemental during the entire march. Valens' attempts to pull him into an opinion, any kind of opinion on Caecina's actions resulted in failure.

Even when Valens informed him, "I have written a letter to Vitellius to make him aware of events." The heavy, unspoken accusation in his tone that Asiaticus had not.

The undamaged eye of the freedman didn't even blink. "Your correspondence to Vitellius is your own concern," he'd replied evenly. Before picking up a scroll and reading it, totally ignoring Valens' presence, to the commander's absolute fury.

But they were here now, ten miles from Caecina's camp. It was Valens' chance to tear strips off his colleague. To let Caecina know exactly what he thought of him. He'd rehearsed his invective all evening. Every insult, every parry. He had it word-perfect to throw full force into that handsome face.

Riding beside Asiaticus en route to the confrontation, the freedman said, "My master has instructed me to tell you that he considers this meeting to be one of reconciliation rather than of recrimination."

"Which means?"

"Which means there are to be no insults, no accusations, no airings of petty grievances. What we do here in this world is greater than anything you might wish to say to Caecina. My master was very clear on that."

In Valens' experience of Asiaticus' master, he was a jelly of a man, prepared to go along with any daft scheme rather than make the effort to resist. Wasn't that how this whole adventure started in the first place? This new determined Vitellius was not one he recognised. It left him with two possibilities: either he'd got the measure of the man entirely wrong or Asiaticus was the force behind this determination.

As it was, Valens' desires tied with those of Asiaticus: to unite the armies and defeat Otho. Therefore, he determined to play along with him. For now.

EIGHTY-ONE

Otho opened one eye, then the other. He appeared to be on the floor. An unrugged floor, which was most unusual for an emperor. Sitting up with a groan caused by a sharp pain to his hip, Otho discovered he was in a barrack hut. The lack of windows meant he was unable to ascertain whether it were day or night.

He appeared to be alone. Gods! He hoped he hadn't lost Onomastus in a dice game again. The dwarf always got quite cross about that. Even though Otho had never yet failed to raise the necessary funds to buy him back. Although, sometimes it did take him a few days. He had better go check.

He pulled himself to his feet, surprised to find there remained no sign of the night's activities. That was the great thing about soldiers. They weren't half tidy, thought Otho, noting the crisply folded blankets at the bottom of each bed.

He swung open the door and was blinded by sunlight. So it was day after all. Here were his attendants lined up outside waiting for him, though there was no sign of Onomastus. He swatted the attendants away as they tried to straighten his clothing and force refreshments upon him. Otho's attention was taken by the soldiers neatly lined up in front of the barrack huts for their daily roll call.

Otho leant against the door frame and listened as the centurions shouted out the names.

"Decian!"

"Yes, sir."

"Marcellus!"

"Yes, sir."

"Ennius!"

"Yes, sir."

"Paulus!" A pause. "Paulus!" Then another pause. "Paulus!"

Otho glanced about wondering where Praetorian Paulus had got to.

The centurion conversed with his clerk who noted something down on a tablet.

"Sextus!"

"Yes, sir."

"Proculus!" Silence. "Proculus!" And again. "Proculus!"

The centurion turned to the clerk again.

The puckered frown on Otho's head entrenched itself further as seven more names went unanswered. Where were they all? he wondered, as the missing kept increasing. The clerk had to flip over page after page in his tablet.

Roll call concluded, the soldiers were sent off on a drill. Otho watched them depart through the camp's gates. Seeing the clerk scurry past him, Otho yelled out a, "Stop!"

The clerk skidded on his heels. "Imperial Majesty."

"Your tablet. What's that written on your tablet?"

The clerk flipped it open to consult. "The roll call, Imperial Majesty. So the quartermasters can work out the men's pay."

"But the names, the names you wrote down?"

"The men no longer on the roll, Imperial Majesty."

"No longer on the roll?"

"Because they fell in battle, Imperial Majesty. We need to establish who has died so we can send the necessary compensation to their families."

"Died? Let me see."

The clerk handed over his tablet. Otho flipped through it. Pages and pages of names. All of them dead. Unbelieving, he looked at the clerk. "But we won. We won at Castores."

* * *

The wagon ground to a wobbling halt. The clerk dismounted from the rear by way of a leap. He offered a hand to the emperor, aiding his descent.

"I still don't understand why you wanted to come here, Imperial Majesty," said the clerk, who over the course of the journey Otho had learned was named Atto.

In true Otho fashion he'd also established that Atto was the second of five brothers all serving in the legions. That he also had an older sister who was married to a man Atto considered a borderline imbecile. And that at the end of his twenty-five years' service, Atto hoped to have a small farm with goats. Atto was fond of goats; he considered them more intelligent than sheep.

"I've come because I need to." Otho gazed around at his surroundings.

It was a pleasant spot with a path that curved through a wood and a green expanse that inclined upwards into rolling hill land, with dense vineyards to the east.

"So this is where the battle took place?"

It was a rhetorical question but Atto answered it. "Yes, Imperial Majesty. They hid their main force in the woods here. Caecina and his cavalry then advanced upwards towards where we were on the hill. Of course he couldn't see the main bulk of our forces, which we'd hidden the other side of the hill. Idiot boy."

However, Otho wasn't listening to Atto's keen analysis of Caecina. His eyes had fallen on a body that lay beside the road a few feet from them. Otho walked over and knelt beside it.

The soldier lay, one arm outstretched, his eyes open gazing upwards. His lower half soaked in blood.

"Who is he? Is he one of ours? Or one of theirs? Is there any way of telling?"

"I don't recognise him," said Atto.

"How do we know?"

"We know from the roll call, Imperial Majesty."

Otho stood up. "An administrative corpse. How very Roman," he said, and walked off the road onto the grass.

Atto followed him. He was close enough to see Otho's expression as he saw the vast number of bodies that lay in that field.

"This is war," the clerk told him.

The emperor didn't reply. A flash of sunlight had caught his attention and he went to find its source. It seemed callous to step over the fallen soldiers. Instead, he weaved in-between them.

Atto caught up and stood beside the emperor. At Otho's feet was a solid form. A body of pure muscle and strength.

"Brutus."

"He fought bravely," said Atto. "I was behind the gladiators. They ran full pelt for those German barbarians. No fear at all. They cleared a path through the Germans for us."

Otho stared at the blank silver helmet. The only gap in the metal work, the two tiny eyehole slits.

"I've never seen his face," he commented.

Then he bent down and gently removed the helmet . For the first time, he was face to face with the fearsome Brutus. The gladiator's mouth was frozen in a fighting grimace, revealing a sparse set of blackened teeth. His nose was flat and crooked. His eyes bulging and fierce. It was not a handsome face for sure. But it was a determined one.

"He was the bravest of them all. He must have taken down twenty Germans. He was felling them even as they thrust their swords into him."

Otho closed his eyes, his hands grasped around the silver helmet. He told Atto, "If this is victory, I don't think I want to see defeat."

EIGHTY-TWO

Asiaticus sat himself at the head of the table. Valens sat down on one side with a scowl.

"Where is he then?" demanded Valens.

"Patience."

After what seemed at least an hour of Valens fidgeting on his chair and threatening to go hunt down Otho without Caecina's help, there came a trumpet blast. In strode Caecina in the process of nonchalantly removing a glove.

He sat opposite Valens and placed his gloves carefully on the table.

"So you made it did you, Valens. Makes a change. My men and I seem to have been waiting forever for you."

Valens bristled instantly. "At least I've not lost two whole cohorts to a pack of gladiators!"

"Yes, I've been fighting, Valens. My men have been fighting and risking their lives while you've been lying in bed with a dicky tummy."

"Dicky tummy?" Valens stood, slamming his palms on the table. "I was poisoned by an Othonian spy."

Caecina smirked. "Spy? You let a spy into your camp? They tried to infiltrate ours but of course we spotted them instantly."

"Enough!" barked Asiaticus before Valens could burn any further. "Shake hands," he insisted. When neither of them made a move, "We have a common enemy in Otho. He must be laughing his head off at you two. Shake hands now or retreat back home. Your choice." He fixed first Valens, then Caecina with his one good eye.

* * *

Salonina rolled up the scroll, sealing it with a blob of wax. Handing it to the messenger she told him, "The usual arrangements please."

He nodded and departed.

So this was it, the end of her adventure. She'd done all she could, throwing a few final suspicions Caecina's way that morning. Entreating him to take care with Valens, for that man only had his own interests at heart. And to be sure that Caecina wrote to Vitellius first with his account of his actions, lest that man spew out his lies to the emperor.

But her work was done. It was down to the men with swords now. Her father had once told her that men with swords were the result of a lack of intelligence. If you had to resort to men with swords then you truly were out of ideas.

Time to go home. Farewell to army camps and tents and mud and soldiers. And farewell to her handsome young stud. Ah, Caecina. He'd been fun and energetic and young and malleable in all kinds of ways that Salonina liked. She'd miss him.

At that thought, in strode the empty-headed boy. "Ah, here you are! I wondered where you'd got to. We thought we'd have a drink and then study the map. I left it here, the map."

"I believe it's here. Yes, here it is," she said, handing it over as two men strode in.

The grey-haired man assessed Salonina, his hooded eyes hungry. Such a look would normally have distracted her. But it was not Valens who had her attention. Rather, his companion.

Asiaticus crossed his arms, a crinkle to the edges of his eyes indicating amusement. "Well, well, well," he said.

As they were standing in front of the only exit, she really did have only one option. She walked over and embraced him. "Hullo, my darling. It's been too long. How in the world are you?

"You two know each other?" asked a puzzled Caecina. "Salonina?"

"Salonina? Is that what you're calling yourself?"

"Soldiers!" yelled Valens.

Two legionaries appeared. "Take hold of that woman," Valens insisted.

Caecina's mouth opened and closed without sound.

"Oh really, darling," drawled Salonina. "Is there really any need?" She was looking to Asiaticus.

"I suppose not, Nymphidia. Stand down."

Valens looked put out.

Caecina's mouth fell open. "Nymphidia?"

* * *

"We may have lost the bitch who poisoned me but give me but an hour with this whore and I'll have all the answers you want."

"It would be a waste of time," dismissed Asiaticus. "This is no ordinary whore you can torture for your pleasure. This is Nymphidia Sabina. There is no degraded act she hasn't committed, or indeed instigated."

Caecina played no part in this conversation. He sat on a chair, arms hanging despondently down, eyes fixed on the floor. This was the first betrayal he'd ever experienced and it had hit him with the force of a slingshot.

Salonina, the woman he loved, the woman he'd bed-sparred with at least twice a day for the last two months, was not Salonina at all. She never had been.

"So what do you propose?" asked Valens, in a tone that suggested he'd dislike it, whatever it was.

"We take her with us to Rome," said Asiaticus. "She can cause no further mischief with our eyes on her. Besides which, Vitellius was always very fond of Nymphidia."

"But she's an Othonian spy," spat Valens.

"She was an Othonian spy," corrected Asiaticus. "A spy whose sudden silence will unsettle her master at this most crucial point in our venture. She's a spy no longer. She's a pleasant addition to our entourage. Don't you agree, Caecina?"

The boy playing at general looked up. "Whatever," he said, standing. "Whatever you think."

And he left them there in the tent.

EIGHTY-THREE

For such a small man, Onomastus knew how to make an entrance. He flung open the door to Epaphroditus' makeshift office with a crash, sauntered his little legs across the room, and deposited himself on a chair in front of the secretary. Resting his feet on the desk with a stretch that looked unlikely to hold in Epaphroditus' view.

Using a rolled-up scroll to push Onomastus' muddy boots off his desk, Epaphroditus asked, "What is it?"

"I have concerns for His Imperial Majesty," said the dwarf. "Serious concerns."

"Such as? No, Philo, I don't think we'll need this minuted."

His assistant folded shut his note tablet. "Shall I?" indicating his head towards the door.

Epaphroditus looked to Onomastus who said, "He can stay. Though can't you let him sit down for a change. It gives me a crick in my neck to look up at him like that."

"Onomastus requests you have a seat."

Philo sat himself down awkwardly on the edge of a stool beside Epaphroditus' desk.

"He's not himself. He's not himself at all. Since Castores he's spent all his time with the soldiers," said Onomastus.

"How is that different? Otho loves hanging out with soldiers. He's the only man I know who can out-drink a legionary. Maybe even a centurion."

"He's not partying with them. He's commiserating with them. He's listening to their tales about their fallen comrades. It's affecting him. He's sort of droopy."

Epaphroditus raised an eyebrow. "Droopy?"

"That's what I said. Droopy. Go see him. See the droopiness for yourself."

"Very well, I shall. But nothing you've said so far seems out of character for the emperor. He's always been a soft touch for a sad story. He just wants to help."

"Yeah, but how is he going to make this one right? He can't bring them back from the dead."

* * *

Epaphroditus found the emperor sat at a desk, a pen in his hand. "Are you actually writing a letter?"

Otho gave a wan smile. "To my brother. I know I usually leave all that stuff to Onomastus but today it seems appropriate." He placed down his pen.

"I was just chatting with Onomastus. He says you've been spending a lot of time with the men."

"Proculus died. He was one of my guard. I bought the farm next to his mother's for him to settle a land dispute." Otho rubbed his eyes. "I played dice with him on the way from Spain. He was a good dice player, fleeced me for 1,000 denaii! I wonder how his mother is? Lucullus is particularly cut up about it. They signed up together you know."

"I didn't."

"And Brutus? Did you hear? The mighty Brutus fell."

"I heard," said Epaphroditus.

"He was so close to Cyprian's record in the arena."

"Perhaps we could count the Vitellians he despatched in his totals," suggested Epaphroditus.

"And Antonius Honoratus. He was going to adopt a boy from the palace but Galba had him crucified. I can't help thinking that if Alex had lived, he wouldn't have put himself in the way of danger at Placentia."

"Caesar, this is war. Regrettably, people die. It is the nature of it."

Otho looked up. "And Claudia Aphrodite?"

To hear her name caught at Epaphroditus' heart.

"Is she a casualty of war too?"

"She…" he began, uncertain whether he would be able to continue with the words. "She was unfortunate. She was in the wrong place at the wrong time. I don't blame you for it."

A moment of silence. Otho responded, "I blame me."

It took the secretary by surprise. "You shouldn't," said Epaphroditus. "It is the nature of things. The nature of this world we live in."

"Is it really? Then I'm not sure I like the nature of this world. I'm not sure I'm cut out for it."

His voice was weary and Epaphroditus experienced some of the same concerns that Onomastus had voiced.

"Caesar!"

It was Celsus breaking the reflective mood. Epaphroditus got to his feet. Otho raised a finger to Celsus.

"Caesar, they've met. Valens and Caecina. They've patched up their differences and combined their armies."

"Oh," said Otho.

"There is no hurry to engage them, Imperial Majesty," said Celsus. "The Moesian legions are only two days' march away now. The longer we wait the greater the advantage there is to us."

"Right, let's forestall Valens and his puppet boy with a correspondence. I'll get Philo onto some suitably vague sentiments that'll have them hanging about for the next instalment," said Epaphroditus. "And let's send out Brutus and his pals to cause some mischief." Remembering, "No, not Brutus. The others, the ones that are left. Celsus, you—"

"No," said Otho. "No. We engage them now. No more waiting."

"But Caesar."

"We fight today."

Celsus and Epaphroditus exchanged looks. An action not lost on Otho who said, "I just want it over with."

EIGHTY-FOUR

"He won't wait for reinforcements?" queried Philo.

"No. He won't," said a terse Epaphroditus, recalling his and Celsus' hour of pleading. "He won't change his mind."

A "but" formed on Philo's lips. Yet tactful as ever he didn't say what Epaphroditus knew he was thinking.

"It'll be many hours before we have any news," he said. "So if you want to take a break, please do."

Philo, who'd never been terribly good at taking time off, gave Epaphroditus a nervous look. "What will you do, sir? Will you stay with the emperor?"

"No, His Imperial Majesty has requested some time alone."

The look that formed on Philo's face reflected the unusualness of this request.

"I think I'll go for a walk. It might kill some time."

* * *

Epaphroditus found himself a small hillock to sit on some miles from the camp. Perhaps he hoped to be able to see some of the battle from this vantage point. Instead, all he could see was a path curling into the distance, disappearing between green hills. There was nothing he could do to help the emperor now.

It was all down to the Praetorian Guard who'd never shown much prowess in anything, a handful of legionaries, and a band of gladiators who'd lost their star billing.

Maybe they'll do it, thought Epaphroditus. They were fiercely loyal to the emperor and prepared to fight down to bloody stumps for him. They'd held the far more experienced Germans off at Placentia and thrashed them at Castores. There was some hope, wasn't there?

* * *

Philo had returned to his quarters. Lysander was sat on the bed, a scroll unfurled on his lap.

"What is it?" he asked, noting the announcer's troubled expression.

"It's from Verenia."

Philo sat down on the bed beside him. "Oh," he said, fearing that Lysandria's greatest worry for her son had come to pass. "Is she, er, alright?"

Rolling up the scroll Lysander said, "She says that Teretia is looking fatter each day. She thinks it's because of all the dried bread she keeps eating."

"It's the only food that doesn't make her sick."

"Yes, that's what Verenia writes," replied Lysander distractedly.

"Does she have anything else to report?" he prompted, gearing himself up for an evening of sympathy, tears, and bolstering of Lysander's fragile ego.

"She writes that her father is on his way back to Rome. He should be back within the month, she says."

"But that's good news, surely," said Philo, confused by Lysander's despondency. "You'll be able to ask him for permission to marry Verenia." A horrible thought suddenly occurred to Philo. "You do still want to marry her, don't you?" he asked, fearing the ramifications in the family if Lysander should back out of his proposal.

"More than anything," said Lysander with, for Philo, reassuring grit. "I love her. She's wonderful. But her father? What's he going to say?"

So this was what was causing the announcer's dismal mood.

"He'll be pleased."

"Will he? Will he really? I have nothing to offer her. Or him. No business that will fit in nicely with his enterprises. No money to add to his fortune. I don't even have a home of my own to take Verenia off his hands. What good am I? I'm just a slave."

"Imperial freedman," corrected Philo with emphasis. "With an important job."

"Pah. I train fools to say words correctly. What sort of job is that? What possible merit could a merchant see in it?"

"You're close to the emperor. Don't underestimate that. Verenius certainly won't. He'll see you as the conduit to him successfully snapping up imperial trade licences."

Lysander was not to be cheered. "I'm close to this emperor. But how long has he got?"

For this, Philo had no answer. "There's a temple down the road. Let's go make some offerings for the emperor's victory and Verenius' goodwill."

Lysander huffed but he complied. And evidently he was keen both to aid the emperor and to gain Verenius' approval. For he filled his bag with plentiful offerings to the gods.

EIGHTY-FIVE

A solitary Caecina paced the ramparts of the fort. He'd left the battle-planning to Valens and his tribunes. He couldn't concentrate on all those flanks and manoeuvres. Even the legion numbers blurred before his eyes. He'd made his excuses that he needed an early night to be properly refreshed for victory. Instead, he'd come to this lonely spot to pace, tormented by his thoughts.

It was a new experience for him. He'd tended not to have many thoughts in the past. Caecina was a man of action. But he couldn't forget the image of Salonina— No, Nymphidia, for that's who she was. Nymphidia lying across his chest in the afterglow of their bed acrobatics, sweaty and sated, and how he'd poured out his heart to her.

He'd told her about his strict parents, his mother's friend whose sexuality had awoken something new and powerful within him, and onwards even to his seduction by Galba.

"He was such a proper man," Caecina had told Nymphidia one night. "He'd done all the right things, held all the right positions, made all the right contacts, the right friends, even married the right woman. Yet in his intimate tastes, he broke just about every right and proper thing. It didn't surprise me at all when he made himself emperor. My knowing him as I did. There was always something dark and powerful at the heart of him. I could tell that from the first time I slept with him. You can tell a lot about a person by their style of lovemaking."

And then he had kissed Salonina. Knowing at that moment that he knew the true her. The strong woman whose most secret desire was to be dominated, overpowered, led by a man.

Except he hadn't known her true self at all. Even in bed that had all been a lie.

As Asiaticus had told him, Nymphidia had been trained in espionage by her father, Callistus. He'd encouraged her to sleep with his rivals to whore out their secrets. She had played him. She had tricked him. Here Caecina's delicate ego, battered certainly by events, reasserted itself. How dare she? How dare she do this to him?

"Sir!"

Caecina paused in his pacing and looked down at the legionary. "What is it?" he yelled down impatiently.

"Sir, Valens asked me to get you. The Othonians are marching out from their camp. They intend to fight us today."

So this was it. The final reckoning. It seemed a moment fit for a great thought.

"Thank you, legionary. We shall meet them today and we shall be victorious. Tell the men that their commander says we will be victorious."

He congratulated himself on his words and for omitting his true feelings. Namely, that crushing Otho's forces was the perfect vengeance on the man who'd sent Salonina to trick him.

* * *

"So you're here," said Valens as Caecina drew up his stallion beside Valens' own horse. "The scouts have sent a full description of the Othonian forces." A sneer formed on Valens' lips. "I doubt this will take long."

EIGHTY-SIX

A grey cloud moved across the sky, speeding with tempestuous billows. It left behind a brief patch of blue until that too was overwhelmed into the darkness.

There was a metaphor in there somewhere, mused Epaphroditus, lying on his back and staring up at the changing skyscape. Epaphroditus was not a man to dwell. He'd made a conscious decision never to look back. He'd once commented to Aphrodite early on in their relationship that if he paid attention to all the unspeakable things that had happened to him, he wouldn't be able to get out of bed in the morning.

No, Epaphroditus was a man of the present. Only now the present wasn't somewhere he wanted to be. There was a battle taking place which he was impotent to influence and a gaping hole in his life which he was only now beginning to process.

There would be no shared glee over the first grandchild. No heated conversations on who to marry Faustina to. No pride in Pollus as he took his first steps on a public career denied to his freedman father. No family seaside holidays. No morning kisses. No late-night lovemaking. No anything, ever again.

There was nothing but a blackness in his future.

He rubbed the wetness from his eyes with the heels of his hands, feeling a bleakness and helplessness he hadn't experienced since he was a boy.

And then he heard it, hooves, thundering hooves. He sat up with a jolt and just managed to catch the disappearing form of a horse. A messenger! And coming from the direction of Cremona. Epaphroditus was on his feet, running back to camp. This had to be news from the battle.

* * *

He didn't bother with the niceties of an introduction, striding straight into the emperor's quarters. The first thing he noticed was Salvius' quivering bottom lip.

"I see," Otho was saying to the messenger.

Onomastus was sat on a stool, looking furious. "Valens' forces overran ours. We lost," said the dwarf.

Epaphroditus looked to the emperor. Otho's eyes were cast downwards. His hands gripped together in front of his stomach.

* * *

Returning from their temple visit, Philo and Lysander found themselves lost amongst the lines of Othonian soldiers. They stopped and sat beside the road, watching them march by. Some were marching in step. Others staggering, holding bloodied cloths to their injuries. On the wagons lay the more seriously injured.

"That doesn't look good," murmured Philo.

"We've lost, haven't we?"

Philo presumed so. A victorious force sang their way back to camp, clasping the booty they'd nobbled from the enemy. There was no coinage. No women. No slaves. No captured

captured Caecina and Valens to be seen. Just a tired, dusty, dejected, bloodied line of men plodding their way home.

"What happens now?" asked Lysander.

"I have no idea."

* * *

"It's a setback," said Epaphroditus. "That's all. We had our victories over Caecina. The wheel of fortune has turned to their advantage for this one battle."

Otho was flopped back onto his couch, his arms hanging loosely by his side.

"Imperial Majesty?" prompted Epaphroditus. "Caesar?" And when that elicited no response from the frozen emperor. "Marcus?"

Otho looked up. "Atto!" he said, and walked straight past Epaphroditus to the door.

Outside, the returning soldiers had been gathering. At the sight of their emperor, they cheered.

"Hail Caesar! Hail Caesar!"

Men with bloodied faces and violent gashes grinned and yelled. A centurion approached the dazed Otho.

"They got us today, Imperial Majesty. But by Jupiter's thunderbolt, we'll have them tomorrow. Won't we lads?"

A huge cheer broke out and a dozen more shouts of "Hail Caesar!"

"Tell me centurion. Atto? Where is Atto? Did he come back?"

"Atto? What cohort is he in?"

Though Otho had extracted much of Atto's life history, this was a piece of information he didn't have. "I don't know. I'm sorry."

"No matter, Imperial Majesty. I'll find him."

The centurion set off, leaving Otho with a bunch of excitable tribunes eager to recount their stories of heroism. The emperor nodded distractedly as they told of the fearsome battles that had taken place near Cremona.

"Those gladiators though! I swear they are born of the blood of Mars! They were unstoppable in their bloodlust!"

From out of the crowd, a single legionary was pushed forward.

"Atto!" cried Otho, brushing off the tribunes.

He pulled Atto into an embrace. "You survived."

When he was released, feeling all in all a little uncomfortable with the situation, particularly in front of his camp mates, Atto told the emperor, "Yes, Imperial Majesty, I did."

"That's good. That's very good."

Otho scanned the faces before him. Atto the would-be goat herder. The young, eager tribunes excited by their first taste of war. The gnarly faced centurions who'd made it through again. The gladiators slapping each other on the back. Then he turned on his heels and strode back into his quarters.

Looking at Salvius, Epaphroditus, and Onomastus he said, "This ends. This ends now."

EIGHTY-SEVEN

He should have been happy. He'd finally got his glorious victory, and not against some ill-trained barbarian horde. No, against proper soldiers as well equipped as his own. A victory to wipe out all those humiliating failures. For what did they matter after the battle of Cremona? He was within his rights to drink himself stupid. To promise insane and unachievable amounts of coinage for his troops. To ride into Rome atop his stallion as a legitimately conquering hero.

Except that Caecina did not feel like doing any of that. He'd even turned down Valens' offer of a night of whoring. A gesture made in genuine reconciliation, but even knowing this Caecina couldn't bring himself to accept. The thought of being surrounded by all that noise, all that cheer, was too much for him tonight.

Wandering round the camp, a solitary figure, Caecina attempted to uncover the reason for his despondency. He'd achieved everything he wanted, hadn't he? Military glory, an assured place by the emperor's side, and the chance of further enrichment. So what was it that was eating at his insides? What had left a hollow in his centre where there should have been nothing but joy?

He looked up from the trodden earth and saw it right in front of him. Her tent. His feet had walked him here. Here to his very own Medusa who had turned his heart to stone. He would never be able to love again. To feel again.

He would show her. He would show her what she had done to him. Show her the hollow shell of a man she'd created by her deceit and treachery!

Caecina had no doubt that when she saw how broken he was, she would repent. How could she not? When she begged his forgiveness he would show clemency like a good Roman. He would embrace her as a friend. And then he would ... Images of Salonina's body, her lithe, extraordinarily flexible body flitted into Caecina's hurt. There was no harm in one final wrestle was there? Just one to say farewell. To draw a line under affairs. Their affair. One last satisfying fuck.

His hand was on the tent flap when a man stepped out of the darkness.

"Not a good idea," said Asiaticus.

Caecina dropped his hand.

"It's no reflection on your character, Caecina Alienus," said Asiaticus. "It's a reflection on hers. She's a siren born to tempt men."

Caecina shot one longing look at her tent before giving a grudging nod and accepting Asiaticus' invitation to join him for a drink.

Inside the tent, Nymphidia swore quietly and pulled herself upwards from the provocative and alluring pose she had fashioned herself into.

EIGHTY-EIGHT

"What are you talking about, Marcus?" said Epaphroditus. "We lost one battle. We won the other two. Valens and Caecina had a good day today. We'll have a good one tomorrow."

"We have two legions due here in two days and the eastern legions are on the march," said Onomastus. "With their strength, we can match Vitellius' forces. They'll be fresh from not fighting. That could be the decider."

"No," said Otho. "I need to end this now. I need to take my own life."

"Uncle Marcus?" squeaked Salvius.

"Salvius, my boy." He put an arm around him.

"You've listened to too many tales of old Rome," scorned Epaphroditus, throwing his hands in the air. "Golden Rome when men routinely threw themselves on their swords at the first sign of trouble. And every single woman was a virtuous, unimpeachable virgin. Even the mothers and grandmothers.

"If there is one thing I have learned in nearly fifty years of imperial service, it's that when you face adversity you don't evade it, you don't run away from it. You get up tomorrow and you do it all over again until you succeed. There are men out there willing to die for you."

"I don't want them to!" exclaimed Otho. "Don't you see? I'm not worth it." He removed his laurel leaf garland and placed it on the table. "This is not worth a single more drop of blood."

"But Vitellius?" pressed Onomastus.

"He's not so bad," said Otho. "I remember him being rather fun. It'll be a sprightly court. One with music and parties. I did so love the parties."

"Fine, relinquish the emperorship. Let that fat slob rule. But there is no need to go all Cato the Younger," said Epaphroditus. "Get in a wagon and let's head somewhere sunny. We have enough guards here to make sure your route is a safe one."

"Excellent plan," agreed Onomastus. "You and me master. Not Lusitania though. Somewhere better. Somewhere the girls are lusciously dark and squishy to the touch."

Otho gave a shudder. "And the men? The men who died for me? Honoratus and Brutus and the thousands of others. Are they really to be repaid for that ultimate sacrifice by their emperor swanning about on some island into his degenerate old age?"

"They're dead. What do they care?" said Epaphroditus, his voice raised.

"You did your best for me. You all did. But you know. You know as Cato and Mark Antony did. There is only one way to end a civil war. You eliminate all competition. This way is the only way."

Epaphroditus felt his throat tighten, cutting off his words.

"No, Uncle Marcus," wept Salvius. "You can't. You just can't. We can win. We can still win. I don't want you to—"

Otho embraced his nephew. "I know you'll miss me but I am one man to be missed. What about all those men who are out there? They'll keep fighting if I live. I'll not make an army of the missed."

He kissed him on both cheeks and passed him to Onomastus. "Take him out, please."

The dwarf escorted the distraught youth out.

Epaphroditus was shaking his head. "You are being ridiculous, Marcus."

Otho met his gaze. "I'm not and you know I'm not."

"I'll not let you do this," said the secretary. "If you are so determined to be a martyr for Rome, then fake it. I faked my own death and I can highly recommend it as a tactic."

Otho shook his head.

"Alright, alright," said Epaphroditus, his mind churning. "I have information that may sway you from this insane course."

"Vitellius has been squashed by a rhino? Valens has declared himself emperor, bumped off Caecina, and sent the lovely Lysandria to dispose of the fat slug in Germania? No? Then I'm afraid there is nothing—"

"You have a daughter."

That paused Otho.

"Silvia. She's yours, Marcus."

Another pause. "Silvia? Your daughter Silvia? The one whose wedding I attended?"

"She's your daughter. I only found out recently. We didn't know, Dite and I. We weren't sure. It wasn't until we saw the two of you sitting together that we knew for sure, she was yours."

Otho offered up his main objection to this titbit of information: "But I've never slept with your wife. I mean, I know I've been guilty of some low acts in the past, but sleeping with another man's wife? Alright, actually I may have done that but not with your wife. Honestly. I swear I wouldn't do that to you. I know how much you love her. Besides, Claudia Aphrodite hated me. I can't see her lowering herself for the likes of me. Is this some kind of wheeze to stop me doing what I have to do?"

"It was a long time ago, back when she was a slave." Speaking the "s–word" was something that he generally avoided. "It was when Agrippina was at her worst, trying to part Nero from Acte's maternal bosom. She presented you with an older woman so that you wouldn't be jealous."

At the start of Epaphroditus' speech Otho had been relaxed and disbelieving. By the end, his mouth had formed an "O" shape.

"That was Aphrodite?" he asked.

Epaphroditus nodded.

Otho rubbed his palm across his face. "O gods! That's why she hated me, isn't it?"

"That and the amount of trouble you always got me into."

Otho looked up. "I am so, so sorry. If I'd known who she was… Why didn't you ever tell me? Hang on." He stopped. "You were there. You were there that day."

"I've had better days," admitted Epaphroditus. "It was a long time ago, Marcus. A different time. I've never held it against you. It was just difficult for Dite because of the pregnancy that followed."

"Silvia's mine?"

"Undoubtedly." Epaphroditus gave a tight smile.

Otho flopped onto a chair. After some moments of deep thought, he said, "I have a daughter?"

"Yes, you do, and a beautiful one at that."

"She is beautiful, isn't she?"

"I've always thought so."

"A daughter, hey? Who'd have thought it?" A grin began to form. "Thank you, old friend. Thank you for telling me this." He stood. "It's been quite something this life, hasn't it? And then just as it draws to its end, I find out I have a daughter." He gave a chortle. "Life never ceases to amaze me."

"Marcus?"

"Tiberius," he replied, grasping Epaphroditus' hands in his. "Look after this daughter of mine, and Salvius too. Make sure he's alright. He's a good lad."

Epaphroditus looked into Otho's eyes. They were the colour of a summer sky and just as warming. "You're not going to change your mind, are you?"

"No, I'm not. For once Marcus Salvius Otho is going to do the right thing."

Epaphroditus bit back his emotions. "If you need any help, I was quite useful to Nero."

"I'm quite capable. Besides we don't want to elicit gossip. To be present at the death of one emperor is unfortunate. To be present at the death of two starts to look suspicious."

Epaphroditus gave a wry smile. "Actually my total is four emperors." He laughed at Otho's shocked expression.

"Then this is goodbye, Imperial Majesty."

"Imperial Majesty? I suppose that's the last time I'll hear that. Ahh," he sighed. "It had a nice ring to it but—alas." He gave a half-guilty grin.

"Farewell then."

"Farewell, old friend."

They embraced one final time.

* * *

On Epaphroditus' exit, Otho sucked in a deep breath.

"Master."

"Ah, Onomastus. Salvius is…?"

"As you'd expect, master."

"We had quite a ride, didn't we?"

"Like a horseless chariot," grinned the dwarf.

"May the gods give you that luscious heathen you always desired."

"Leave me something in your will, master, and I'll buy her myself."

That certainly made Otho laugh.

Onomastus dropped his grin. "Master, I want to be here with you when… I don't want to leave you. I won't leave you."

Otho ruffled the dwarf's hair. "Leave me, please. Let it be the last thing you ever do for me."

"Master—"

"Please, Onomastus," said Otho. "Do this for me, chum."

Onomastus nodded.

Finally alone, Otho sat on his couch, put his head in his hands, and wept.

EIGHTY-NINE

He slept surprisingly well. Waking early with a sleepy, blurry awareness that there was something he needed to do that day. Spying the letter to Statilia Messalina on his desk, he recalled what it was, a stone of dread settling in his chest.

He put it out of his mind. Put off thinking about it entirely as he washed and breakfasted in solitude. It was a state he rather regretted insisting upon the previous evening, for he could have done with a cheerful discourse with Onomastus or Epaphroditus or Salvius or anyone. But there was just he, the emperor soon-not-to-be. The breakfast knife in his hand began to shake, so he placed it back down carefully on the table and walked over to the flaps of the tent.

Standing on the threshold, he sucked in the day. It was a blue spring morning with a bright sun that spread warmth onto Otho's bare arms. The grass was damp on his toes. He wriggled them, enjoying the sensation of the soft grass. It had been years since he'd stepped with bare feet on such lush sward.

He tried to recall the last occasion he'd been barefoot on the earth. Pulling out from his memories, a particular picnic with Poppaea on the slopes of a Cambrian mountain.

"Is this how the peasants eat?" she'd enquired, half-joking, half-annoyed at being dragged such a distance for a basic meal of bread and cheese.

"When they're not bothering goats," he'd replied with a lascivious smile, caressing her ankle.

"There's some goats over there if that's your mood."

"But they are all the way over there and you are right here." Kissing her toes one by one. As he got to the little one, she snatched her foot back.

"Catch me a goat and you can have me any way you want. Repeatedly. Endlessly. Until your cock drops right off."

Otho bounced to his feet. "Challenge accepted!"

And off he'd sped, barefoot, up the mountain. Three stubbed toes, one thistle incident, and several goat-inflicted bruises later, he'd returned with his goat to claim his prize.

That memory plastered a beam across his face. The dread in his breast dissolved and was replaced with a swelling, a bursting, a joy. It had been marvellous, hadn't it? All of it. Every last day of it. When he'd been banished to Lusitania, he and Onomastus had made an adventure of it. Being stuck there had been the making of Otho. Away from the court diversions, he'd been able to concentrate. To apply what turned out to be a keen intelligence and an undoubtable level of ability he'd never known he owned.

Even losing Poppaea, painful though it had been, had made him truly appreciate and cherish such memories as the goat-chasing incident.

He puffed out his chest, sucking in a lungful of air, watching the scene in front of him. Sentries marching to their new positions, slaves bustling back and forth with supplies, the gentle braying of the cavalry horses.

He didn't regret it. He didn't regret any of it. Not even this jaunt at being emperor. For there was nothing to regret, not if he ended it now. Salvius could return to Rome and work towards the post of aedile. Philo would be reunited with that little blonde wife of his. Lysander could try his luck with her cousin and perhaps, just perhaps, it would work out for him this time. Epaphroditus would be back with his children, including Silvia, the daughter Otho had never known he'd had. She was a bright girl, from what he remembered. She'd do well in life. Epaphroditus would make sure she did.

The senators could return to their posturings on moral conduct while fathering family after family with their slaves. And all these soldiers, these legionaries of Rome, they could lay down their weapons and go back to all that infernal marching, road building, and decimating of barbarians that they so excelled at.

It really was marvellous.

Otho closed the tent flaps with a smile. Then he walked to his desk and picked up the scroll to Statilia. He gave it a kiss before picking up the dagger that lay beside it. He'd had Onomastus sharpen it so he had no doubts it would do the job. Otho had no doubts at all, about anything. Sitting down on the couch he took the dagger, held it over his heart, and thrust.

NINETY

Onomastus had been sat outside the tent all night despite his master's entreaties to leave. Crouched down by a tent pole, he'd seen his master take his final glimpses of the world before retreating inside. Hearing the cry and then a thump, he'd pressed his fingernails into his palm. Desperate to rush to his master, he'd held himself back to give the emperor the death he'd wanted. Onomastus had stood there, just outside the flaps, until the choking gasps ceased. Only then did he go in.

He found his master slumped on a couch. One arm hung down, fingers touching the pool of blood forming on the floor beneath. His cornflower blue eyes which had never been less than sparky in life, now stared blankly at some point far from this world. Using his fingertips, Onomastus gently closed the lids.

He arranged the body on the couch: folding the arms across the chest, smoothing down the toga, straightening the runinously expensive toupee. Otho had always claimed it as man's greatest discovery; trumping fire, the wheel, and the effects of fermented grape juice on a man's ability to enjoy himself.

Bending down, he gently kissed the emperor's forehead.

"My master. My friend."

He sat down on the floor beside the couch and picked up the dagger. He held it in his lap for a few moments, smiling as he remembered the adventures he'd survived in Otho's company. Then when he felt the time was right, he pressed it against his flesh and pushed.

NINETY-ONE

Statilia was struggling to concentrate. She fidgeted on her cushion as the bestiarii stalked their prey in an unconvincingly reconstructed woodland glen—since when did leopards live in forests not unlike those of the Italian countryside? The leopard had taken up position in one of the faux trees, lying prostrate across a branch. The bestiarius walking beneath looked every which way but up. The crowd attempted to be helpful, yelling, "He's above you." But the bestiarii were fully immersed in their task and appeared not to hear.

"Someone's going to have to throw a stick at that leopard," yawned Calvia, "or else this day will never end."

These games were part of the Cerealia, a seven-day extravaganza in honour of Ceres, goddess of agriculture and grain. Statilia, nervous and jumpy, had insisted on attending every single ceremonial event. Partly to placate the goddess, for with Vitellius' troops ransacking the countryside they needed a good harvest, and partly to have something to keep her mind off events further north.

Otho had written to her every single day he'd been away. Statilia treasured his cheery words on the scenery, the losses at dice night, the gladiators who were putting on a good show in the evenings to keep the troops entertained. Not once did he mention anything relating to the fighting, the battles, or even a note on the other side, those abhorrent Vitellians.

Such it was to be a woman, continually kept to the side of important matters.

"Oh, for Ceres' sake! Throw a ruddy stick at it!" cursed Calvia, echoing the impatience of the crowd.

"I reckon I could get that leopard with a javelin from here," Mina whispered to one of the Praetorians.

The guard weighed up the distance, the trajectory, the obstacles in the way.

"No, you can't."

"Could so," insisted Mina, eyeing up the Praetorian's spear which he held in one hand.

The guard grasped his weapon tighter. "Not a chance. This is army equipment. I can't hand it over to anyone."

Calvia gave a yawn. "The crowd look like they are about to start throwing stuff."

Actually they'd already started. Some wags from the fifth level lobbing down their fruit snacks. A well-aimed apple smacked into the leopard's tree. The creature opened one eye, yawned, and closed it again, encapsulating the collective mood of the arena.

Mina bent down and whispered to the empress.

"And you think you can hit it?" asked Statilia.

"I should like to see that," commented Calvia. "I should like to see that very much."

"Give her your weapon," Statilia commanded.

Sadly for Mina, who'd wrestled the guard's spear away from him, she never got to prove she could spear a leopard from the imperial box at the games. At that moment, a blast of trumpets broke out.

Statilia froze in her seat. The leopard, spooked, leapt from his hiding place. Landing on top of the unfortunate bestiarii beneath.

Nobody paid much attention to the vicious mauling that followed. This was a shame. That was precisely why most of them attended the games in the first place. Rather, all eyes fell on the soldiers appearing through the top-level entrance.

"Empress."

Statilia turned.

"Flavius Sabinus?"

He bowed his head. "I have a message that needs to be read out to the people. To the city."

There was really only one man with the necessary gravitas, the necessary projection, the necessary talent to deliver the message. Lysander shuffled forward. To Statilia's eye he looked pale, red of eye. A small part of her quibbled that could be over anything, a girl who'd tossed him over, a terrible night's sleep. She tried to ignore Flavius' similarly tense expression.

"The scroll."

Lysander waved it away. "There's no need. I know it by heart."

A further trumpet blast silenced the restless crowd. Then Lysander took centre position at the front of the imperial box.

"Senators and populace of Rome, I bring news that the pretender to the imperial throne has been decisively broken in battle. Imperator Aulus Vitellius is en route to Rome. Until his arrival, Flavius Sabinus has taken command of the troops at his behest."

Statilia's hands went to her throat.

"All hail Imperator Aulus Vitellius Caesar!"

There followed a polite round of applause.

Statilia struggled to her feet, leaning on Mina. "I need to get out of here. Get me out of here!"

* * *

Statilia staggered down the corridors devoid of her usual attendants. She wanted to be, alone. Alone with her grief. Alone with Otho. Entering Otho's chamber, she was ready to throw herself onto his bed. To weep. To wail. To hug that pillow that had born his head into her bosom. Only there was already someone there. Someone who'd felt the exact same need.

Sat on the floor was a slumped figure in a green gown, skirts pooling around him.

"Sporus?"

He turned, his face a mess of make-up.

"It was always about her. Always."

Statilia sat beside him, following his gaze through the open door to the storage area beyond. Shelf after shelf of busts of varying sizes faced them. From one the size of a fist to a monstrous double life-sized image towering from floor to ceiling. They all depicted the exact same woman. An extremely beautiful woman with pouty lips, wide eyes, and flame-red hair painted onto every single bust.

"Poppaea," breathed Statilia, her own figure slumping. "He couldn't let her go. Not ever."

Sporus' shoulders began to shake. Statilia reached over and hugged him. Her own defences broke and she sobbed into Sporus' slight form.

And that was how Mina found them. The eunuch and the empress. Once arch enemies, now united in their grief and their love for the same man.

NINETY-TWO

"I suppose word will have reached Rome by now, sir."

Epaphroditus did not respond. His attention was caught by the sight of two soldiers passing by. One with his arm across the second's shoulders, supporting him as his comrade wept.

He should be used to such scenes now, he thought. It had been five days since Otho's death and news of legionaries taking their own lives in despair were still arriving. Then there'd been that gladiator who'd thrown himself onto the funeral pyre right in front of him. Not to mention the ongoing wailing all round.

For Epaphroditus, who'd experienced the deaths of five emperors, it was utterly extraordinary. Even Nero, who was beloved by the ordinary people, had not been mourned so fiercely. All of which pulled painfully at his heart.

"They would have fought on," he told Philo.

"But they wouldn't have won, sir," he assistant replied kindly. "Vitellius has the greater force. He was always going to win."

"I know," Epaphroditus admitted out loud for the first time since tackling Otho back in January.

Epaphroditus had endured a rough few nights. He'd barely slept as his active mind refused to let go of the "what if's".

He couldn't accept his failure. He was tormented. Why hadn't he changed Otho's mind on holding his forces back as Celsus had advised? Why hadn't he persuaded him to step aside the moment they'd heard of Vitellius' claim? How had he been unable to save his friend? He sympathised with those suicides: a world without Otho was a world sucked dry of improbable jollity.

Seeing his troubled expression, Philo said, "It's time to go, sir. Time to go home."

"Yes, it is."

"Sir!"

The crisp bark of a messenger broke into the sadness. "A message for you, sir."

The scroll was handed to Philo who broke the seal and quickly read its contents. Then he handed it to Epaphroditus. "You'd better read this, sir. It's from Gellianus."

Gellianus was the guard he'd charged with trailing Lysandria. In all the gloom, he'd completely forgotten the matter. A tiny bubble of intrigue grew in his breast.

"Alright, Lysandria, friend of old. Let's see who's been paying for your mischief making," he said to himself.

After reading he let the paper spring shut, sharing a look with Philo.

"I can't say I expected that."

"Me neither, sir."

NINETY-THREE

Since discovering his stepmother was in the habit of hiring assassins, Domitian had held onto his secret. He kept it tight inside him, letting it gnaw and worry. He'd kept a close eye on Caenis, which was not difficult since she spent most of her time at Flavius' home and seemed extremely desirous for Domitian's conversation. He'd suffered through her kind hectoring without a single sulk off. That was how seriously he was taking this matter.

He knew he would have to eventually confront her. This was exactly what he intended to do this day.

"Caenis?"

She placed down the tablet she'd been reading. "Hello there. Do come on in."

He shuffled in and sat down on a wicker chair opposite hers.

"I am glad our dismal spring appears to be over."

They were sat in a small garden courtyard that was filled with plants in bud. The day was warming on the skin and the sky a pleasant blue, neither of which cheered Domitian in his task.

"Hopefully it's here to stay. It'll give them a chance to clear out some of the mess caused by those dreadful floods on the Aventine Hill."

Domitian cleared his throat. "Did you hear about the emperor?"

"Yes, yes I did. It is all very sad. I don't think I can say Otho was a good man but he was definitely a fun one!" She gave a smile, which dropped as she told her stepson, "Your uncle has taken it badly. He's locked himself in his study. The last time I looked in he was knee-deep in correspondence. I think it's his way of keeping his mind busy. Whatever his faults, Flavius was very fond of Otho."

"Caenis," pressed Domitian. "Won't Vitellius seek revenge upon those loyal to Otho?"

"So that's what's worrying you," she said, placing down her drink. "My dear, there's no need to worry about Flavius. He's been city prefect for twelve years through three emperors. Vitellius will need capable men like Flavius. So please don't fret, Domitian, he's quite safe."

Domitian cleared his throat again. "I meant you," he said, shuffling his bottom on the chair.

Caenis frowned. "Me? But I have no affiliation with Otho. Unless you count attending a dinner or two."

She was so convincing that doubt set in. Had he got it all wrong? Had he read something into the Julia and Claudia letters that simply wasn't there? Was he about to make a complete fool of himself? Something that Caenis would no doubt report back to his father.

And that nearly stopped him. Nearly had him muttering an apology and departing with a flushed face. But then he recalled their conversation on the night of the banquet.

"I know," he said firmly. "I know you were working for Otho. For the palace."

Another frown combined with a confused look. "Domitian, my dear, I retired many years ago."

"I know," he persisted before she could set more doubts in his mind. "I saw your letters. I deciphered the code: FV stall end?"

Caenis narrowed her eyes.

"So you see, I do know. And yes, uncle will be fine because he works hard and people respect him but you've been running spies in Vitellius' camp. Won't he be cross about that? Won't he seek revenge? I think you should leave Rome before Vitellius gets here. You could go back to Judaea and I could come too and then we'd all be safe: Father, Titus, you, and I."

"Oh, Domitian," she sighed affectionately, leaning forward and giving his curly hair a ruffle.

Domitian moved his head out of her reach. "Caenis."

"You are so kind," she said. "And I appreciate your concern for me. Which is why I shall overlook you reading my personal letters."

Domitian's cheeks flushed.

"But really, I have never worked for Otho."

"But Caenis!"

"You should listen to your stepmother, boy."

Domitian spun round in his seat to see Epaphroditus and some Indian boy stood by the door. "It's amazing how easily one can avoid announcers and chamberlains when one owns a handful of Praetorians."

He strode in, followed by Philo.

"Please don't stand," he told Caenis as he sat down beside Domitian.

The anger in Epaphroditus' voice was audible to all. Domitian felt his glaring stare burning into him.

"She speaks the truth, boy. She has never worked for Otho."

Domitian looked back to Caenis. She was sitting very still, her hands gripping the arms of the chair.

"Have you?" Fixing her with angry eyes, he held up two fingers. "Two armies. Valens and Caecina. And two agents. Lysandria." He dropped one finger. "And Salonina," dropping the remaining finger. "They were to keep the armies apart. Not forever but just long enough. I'll admit that had me stumped for a time. Why didn't Lysandria kill Valens? We both know she's more than capable of murder."

Caenis didn't respond.

"The answer was quite simple," continued Epaphroditus in a voice potent with contained fury. "It wasn't necessary. I've been doing everything in my power to stop those two armies forming because we had absolutely no chance of beating them. So I asked myself: who wouldn't fear seven legions of Germans?" He leaned further forward, only a few inches away from Caenis. "A man who has access to a similar force. A man sitting in the East with four legions of his own."

It was Domitian who voiced it. "Father?"

It was as if he hadn't spoken. Epaphroditus' eyes did not leave Caenis.

"He must be mightily sure that he can attract more legions to his cause. No doubt that's what he's been busy doing while you have been buying him time to secure allegiances. And of course fostering dissent between Vitellius' two commanders. Tell me, who is it you have playing Salonina?"

Caenis did not reply.

"Someone I know? Or did you bring her back from the East with you? Ah, no matter."

He broke the connection, his eyes falling onto a plant pot.

"You must have been planning this for months," he said quietly to the plant pot. "You must have started this venture the moment you and your boyfriend heard about Nero's end." Looking back at Caenis, he said, "You started this when Marcus was still alive."

She released her hands from the arms of the chair. "I didn't know about Otho until I reached Rome," she said softly. "By then it was too late to change plans. Everything was already in place."

"You could have told me. You could have warned me," said Epaphroditus. "You owed me that at least."

She reached across to him. "I'm sorry that I couldn't."

Sitting beside him, Domitian was in prime position to see Epaphroditus flinch away from his former mentor.

"Caenis!" Flavius blustered his way into the scene. "There you are. And, good day, Epaphroditus, Philo," he said, clearly confused.

"Good day to you, Flavius," greeted Epaphroditus in as frosty a tone as he'd addressed Caenis.

"There are soldiers in my house," commented Flavius. "What is going on?"

Epaphroditus got to his feet. "You're under house arrest," he said firmly. "All of you."

Domitian felt his stomach flip over as his uncle's face fell in surprise.

"What? What in Jupiter's name for?" Flavius blustered.

Caenis stood and addressed Epaphroditus directly, "Arrest me if you think it worth your while. But Flavius knew nothing about this. Nor did Domitian."

Epaphroditus' gaze fell on Flavius. "I suggest you have a talk with Antonia Caenis. She can tell you what that brother of yours is up to."

The secretary's gaze fell downwards onto the seated and very unhappy Domitian. "He stays here," he said.

Epaphroditus stormed out followed by a stumbling Philo.

"Caenis?" asked a bewildered Flavius.

Antonia Caenis took hold of the trembling Domitian's hand and facing him, kissed him lightly on the forehead.

"That night of the banquet, I told you that your father had sent me to Rome to look after you. That you are extremely important. You must see it now. Your father is going to declare himself emperor shortly. But he is in the East. You are in Rome. That makes you the figurehead of his intentions. You are him. You are emperor. And you need to be strong."

Domitian swallowed hard, consumed as he was by two contrasting emotions: a private glee that his father trusted him to play this role and an unadulterated terror as to what that meant for him.

NINETY-FOUR

Vitellius yawned, a sight much like that of a roaring hippo. He waved the messenger away as if he were a circling fly. Then he slowly stood, heaving up his enormous bulk, six slaves on hand to assist with this momentous task.

On arrival in Germania, it had taken four slave boys to rouse Vitellius. But since his army had in the main departed, Vitellius had much less to do and had filled the extra time with some additional gorging.

When he was finally on his feet and suitably balanced, the slave boys returned to their positions.

Aulus Vitellius, now sole emperor of Rome and her empire, let out one almighty belch and then offered his very first imperial order.

"Load up the whores and eunuchs. We're going to Rome."

AUTHOR'S NOTE

Marcus Salvius Otho is an enigma. He was a man with a dubious past as one of Nero's inner circle. Alleged to have enjoyed a threesome with his wife Poppaea and Nero, Poppaea left him for Nero and Otho was made governor of Lusitania. It was an appointment that had tongues wagging that this was his reward for handing over his wife.

Yet he proved a surprisingly effective governor.

He was a man who some claim never really wanted to be emperor but who nonetheless fought against overwhelming odds to hold onto the title.

This supposedly effeminate, lazy creature of Nero's lays down his life to save further bloodshed, despite knowing that further reinforcements, which could swing the war his way, are only days away.

Even the cynical Tacitus cannot help but be moved by Otho's almost perfect, by Roman standards, death.

It is the great "what if" of 69 AD. What if Vitellius hadn't already declared himself in Germania? What if Otho had resisted fighting until his reinforcements arrived? It's the "what ifs" that make Otho's story so poignant and sad.

We will never know what kind of emperor Otho would have made given longer to reign but the manner of his death suggests that it might have been as surprising as his successful governorship of Lusitania. The wild child had matured.

The details of Otho's short reign are as recounted, including the first siege of Placentia where the German legions did indeed turn up drunk and without any actual siege equipment. The Praetorian storming of the banquet is also a real event. As are some of the gloriously abusive letters that flew back and forth between Vitellius and Otho (though not the toupee description).

On the subject of Valens' poisoning, we know that both sides attempted to place spies in each other's camps. Tacitus says they failed but maybe one did sneak in. Valens certainly fell ill very quickly and at a most inopportune moment!

However, I will admit to taking advantage of the scarce historical record on Nymphidia Sabina and Salonina. Both receive only a couple of lines in the written record, which allowed me to invent a tale around them. So for the record, there is absolutely no evidence that they were the same person.

Finally, a few thank yous. Thank you Stephen Francis Phenow for your assistance on battle matters. Super librarian Phoebe Harkins for your invaluable assistance in locating the exact texts I required when I had no idea I required them. And to Jamie and Rob at Totalus Rankium Podcast for your support.

L. J. Trafford

ABOUT THE AUTHOR

L. J. Trafford worked as a tour guide, after gaining a BA Hons in ancient history. This experience was a perfect introduction to writing, involving as it did the need for entertainment and a hefty amount of invention (it's how she got tips!). She now works in London doing something whizzy with databases.

Find out more about L. J. Trafford and the Four Emperors series at facebook.com/lj.trafford and follow her on Twitter @ TraffordLJ.

If you've enjoyed this book, please let others know by leaving a review on Amazon. Let's spread the word: the Four Emperors series is a five star read!

Praise for *Otho's Regret*

"There have been several novels about the events of AD 69, but none quite like this one. L. J. Trafford takes us behind the scenes at the palace, revealing a vivid world of scheming slaves and conniving courtiers, with the occasional hapless innocent caught up in the action. Fast-moving, irreverent, and often very funny, *Otho's Regret* is a wild gallop down the corridors of Roman power."

Ian Ross
bestselling author of the *Twilight of Empire series*

Praise for *Galba's Men*

"Roman fiction as I really like it—told from the gross underbelly of Imperial Court politics. Highly recommended."

Richard Blake
author of *Conspiracies of Rome* and *Game of Empires*

"A lively and entertaining read. Galba's court leaps off the page at you—sex, violence, self-interest, intrigue—seen through the eyes of the hierarchy of slaves and free men whose labours made it work."

Rosemary Rowe
author of the *Libertus Mysteries* series

Praise for *Palatine*

"The politics of the Palatine, during the last days of Nero and beyond, are beautifully played out in a tense atmosphere of ruthless ambition and distrust. The characters are very well drawn, with hardly a shred of our own western morality; they fit into the age very believably and yet aie recognisable to the modern reader. I found it to be a thoroughly enjoyable and riveting read, full of intrigue and depravity with a fast-paced plot. Great fun!"

Robert Fabbri
bestselling author of the *Vespasian series*

"What a great read *Palatine* is! I thoroughly enjoyed this fresh and engaging take on a well-known story: it's quick-witted, well observed, and packed with characters that stay in the mind long after the last page has been turned."

Ruth Downie
bestselling author of the *Medicus mystery series*

"*Palatine* is *Downton Abbey* with teeth, a racy, entertaining, largely slave's-eye view of Nero's final months in power combining historical fact, Suetonian mud-slinging, skulduggery both above and below stairs, a touch of romanticism, and more than a smidgen of period brutality. It's well written (page-turningly so), and Trafford has a good eye for character and a good ear for dialogue, as well as knowing her stuff historically. Excellent. I look forward to the next one in the series."

David Wishart
bestselling author of the *Marcus Corvinus Mystery series*